SHAW FESTIVAL
PRODUCTION RECORD
1962-2007

SHAW FESTIVAL
PRODUCTION RECORD
1962-2007

Fourth Edition

compiled and edited by
L.W. Conolly and Jean German

based on First and Second Editions
compiled and edited by
Dan H. Laurence

and the Third Edition compiled and edited by
Denis Johnston and Jean German

Shaw
FESTIVAL
The Academy of the Shaw Festival

mosaic press

Library and Archives Canada Cataloguing in Publication

Conolly, L.W. (Leonard W.)
        Shaw Festival Production Record, 1962-2007 4th edition,
compiled and edited by L.W. Conolly and Jean German.

Co-published by the Academy of the Shaw Festival.
Includes index.

ISBN 978-0-9699478-8-2 (Academy of the Shaw Festival)
ISBN 978-0-88962-886-1 (Mosaic Press)

1. Shaw Festival (Niagara-on-the-Lake, Ont.) – History.
2. Theatre – Ontario – Niagara-on-the-Lake – History. I. Conolly, Leonard W., 1941- .
II. German, Jean 1953- . III. Academy of the Shaw Festival. IV. Title.

PN2306.N5C66 2008   792'.09713'38   C2007-907151-1

Published by Mosaic Press, offices and warehouse at 1252 Speers Road, Units 1&2, Oakville, Ontario, L6L 5N9, Canada and Mosaic Press, PMB 145, 4500 Witmer Industrial Estates, Niagara Falls, NY 14305-1386, USA.

Mosaic Press in Canada   Mosaic Press in the USA:
1252 Speers Road, Units 1&2,   4500 Witmer Industrial Estates
Oakville, Ontario, L6L 5N9   PMB 145, Niagara Falls, NY 14305-1386
Phone / Fax: 905-825-2130   Phone: 1-800-387-8992
info@mosaic-press.com   info@mosaic-press.com
www.mosaic-press.com   www.mosaic-press.com

Co-published by Mosaic Press and the
Academy of the Shaw Festival
Box 774, Niagara-on-the-Lake,
Ontario, L0S 1J0, Phone: 905-468-2153
Fax: 905-468-7140

Cover designed by Scott McKowen, Punch & Judy Inc.

CONTENTS

INTRODUCTION and ACKNOWLEDGEMENTS

This is the fourth *Shaw Festival Production Record*. The first, compiled and edited by Dan H. Laurence, published in 1990 by the University of Guelph (repository of the Shaw Festival archives), covered the years 1962 to 1989. Mr Laurence published (also with the University of Guelph) an updated version in 1991 that extended the period covered by an additional season. The third *Record*, compiled and edited by Denis Johnston and Jean German, was co-published in 2000 by the Academy of the Shaw Festival and Mosaic Press. It covered the period 1962 to 1999.

The Shaw Festival Production Record 1962-2007 is heavily indebted to the earlier *Records*, reprinting the data they contain for the first 38 seasons of the Shaw Festival, with only minor revisions and corrections. It is fitting that the late Dan Laurence's initiative in establishing the *Production Record* should continue to be reflected in this new edition, both because of his commitment to the Shaw Festival (for which he served as Literary Adviser and Corresponding Scholar) and because of the enormous contribution he made to Shaw studies in so many spheres and for so many years. And while Denis Johnston is no longer with the Shaw Festival, his presence remains prominent in this new *Record* through his expert editorial guidance for the 1962-1999 *Record*, just one of the several important publishing ventures he oversaw during his time at The Shaw.

Jean German, Publications Co-ordinator at The Shaw, served with Denis Johnston as co-compiler and co-editor of the 1962-1999 *Record*, and has again proved invaluable in entering the new data (2000-2007) for the 1962-2007 *Record* and doing the layout for the book. It has been a great pleasure to work with her.

Since initially raising the question of updating the *Production Record* with Colleen Blake, Shaw Festival Executive Director, I have received nothing but encouragement and support from her, for which I am most grateful. Artistic Director Jackie Maxwell, Planning Director Jerry Doiron, Literary Manager Joanna Falck, Librarian Nancy Butler, and Public Relations Director Odette Yazbeck have been equally encouraging and supportive. Warm thanks are also due to Scott McKowen for providing the striking cover design and a selection of production photographs throughout the book. Howard Aster and his staff at Mosaic Press have been collegially professional throughout the production process. The permission of Shaw

Festival actors, past and present, to reproduce production photographs in which they appear is also gratefully acknowledged.

The addition of a further eight seasons of data – eighty-six productions and over 6,000 performances – has greatly enlarged the size of the *Production Record*, so much so that it has been necessary, with regret, to drop two of the four appendices that appeared in the 1962-1999 *Record*, one on the annual Shaw Seminars (which will henceforth be covered in a separate publication) and one on company members who have won various Shaw Festival awards. Appendices that relate directly to Festival productions (The Toronto Project, 1982-88, and the Directors Project) have been retained and, in the case of the ongoing Directors Project, updated, and a third appendix, a summary of productions listed by season and theatre, has been added.

In the period since the publication of the 1962-1999 *Record* the Shaw Festival has undergone some significant changes, changes that are reflected in this new *Record*. In 2000 the mandate of the Festival was altered to include not only the production of plays written *during* the lifetime of Bernard Shaw (1856-1950), but also plays (including new plays) written *about* or *set in* the period of Shaw's life. And when Christopher Newton retired in 2002 (after a celebrated twenty-two years as artistic director) his successor, Jackie Maxwell, signalled her intention of shaping the mandate "to provide creative friction by juxtaposing the old with the new" by regularly incorporating new work, particularly new Canadian plays, into the Festival's programming.

A publication such as the *Production Record* is not the place to discuss and analyze mandate, policy, and personnel changes, or the artistic and economic fluctuations of an organization as large and diverse as the Shaw Festival. And any such discussion must go well beyond the bare statistics presented in a record of productions. But it is hard to imagine a well-informed discussion of the Festival that does not need at some point to draw on and to interpret what is presented in these pages. The *Shaw Festival Production Record* is, to be sure, a handy and quick reference source, but it is also the essential documentary evidence of the life of a vibrant cultural force in Canada – whose impact reverberates far beyond its borders – and a tribute to the hundreds of people whose achievements over nearly fifty years of theatrical activity at The Shaw are here recorded.

Leonard Conolly
Corresponding Scholar, Shaw Festival
Professor of English, Trent University

KATE TROTTER, RIC WAUGH, CALLUM RENNIE, WILLIAM HUTT, AND MICHAEL BALL IN THE
DON JUAN IN HELL SCENE IN *MAN AND SUPERMAN*, 1989 (PHOTO BY DAVID COOPER).

SHAW FESTIVAL
ARTISTIC DIRECTORS

1963-1965	ANDREW ALLAN
1966	BARRY MORSE
1967-1977	PAXTON WHITEHEAD
1975	TONY VAN BRIDGE (Acting Artistic Director during Whitehead's sabbatical year)
1978	RICHARD KIRSCHNER
1979	LESLIE YEO (Acting Artistic Director)
1980-2002	CHRISTOPHER NEWTON
2003-Present	JACKIE MAXWELL

CAROLE SHELLEY, TONY VAN BRIDGE, IAN RICHARDSON, AND NORMAN WELSH IN THE *DON JUAN IN HELL* SCENE IN *MAN AND SUPERMAN*, 1977 (PHOTO BY ROBERT C. RAGSDALE).

1962

FIRST SEASON

June 29 to August 11 (8 performances)

"Salute to Shaw!"

DON JUAN IN HELL by Bernard Shaw
(from *Man and Superman*, Act 3)
Court House Theatre, June 29 to 30, July 13 to 14 (4 performances)

Don Juan	David Loveless
Doña Ana	Mavis Corser
The Statue	Eric Davis
The Devil	Maynard Burgess

Directed by Maynard Burgess
Set designed by Alice Crawley
Costumes designed by Louis G. Berai

Stage Manager	Calvin Rand
Assistant Stage Manager	Joan Fordham

CANDIDA by Bernard Shaw
Court House Theatre, July 27 to 28, August 10 to 11 (4 performances)

Prossy	Jean Malloy
Morell	David Michener
Lexy	Terry Cahill
Burgess	Edward Forham
Candida	Barbara Ransom
Marchbanks	Tim Devlin

Directed by Maynard Burgess
Set designed by Alice Crawley
Costumes designed by Louis G. Berai

Stage Manager	Calvin Rand
Assistant Stage Manager	Joan Fordham

1963

July 10 to 28 (15 performances)

YOU NEVER CAN TELL by Bernard Shaw
Court House Theatre, July 10 to 14 (5 performances)

Dolly Clandon	Mary Barton
Mr Valentine	Seán Mulcahy
Parlormaid	Maggie Smith
Philip Clandon	Roy Wordsworth
Mrs Lanfrey Clandon	Juliana Saxton
Gloria Clandon	Margaret Griffin
Fergus Crampton	James Edmond
Finch M'Comas	Alfred Gallagher
Waiter	Gerard Parkes
Jo	James Beggs
Walter Bohun, Q.C.	Ian Thorne

Directed by Andrew Allan
Designed by Martha Mann

Stage Manager	David M. Twiby
Assistant Stage Manager	Maggie Smith

HOW HE LIED TO HER HUSBAND by Bernard Shaw
Court House Theatre, July 17 to 21 (5 performances)

Henry	Michael Tabbitt
Aurora	Denise Fergusson
Teddy	James Edmond

Directed by Andrew Allanv
Designed by Martha Mann

THE MAN OF DESTINY by Bernard Shaw
(on the same bill as *How He Lied to Her Husband*)

Giuseppe	Guy Sanvido
Napoleon Bonaparte	Ian Thorne
Sub-Lieutenant	James Edmond
The Strange Lady	Margaret Griffin

Directed by Andrew Allan
Designed by Martha Mann

Stage Manager	David M. Twiby
Assistant Stage Manager	Maggie Smith

ANDROCLES AND THE LION by Bernard Shaw
Court House Theatre, July 24 to 28 (5 performances)

The Lion	James Beggs
Androcles	Maynard Burgess
Megaera	Barbara Spigel
The Centurion	Gerard Parkes
The Captain	Ian Thorne
Lavinia	Denise Fergusson
Lentulus	Roy Wordsworth
Metellus	Michael Tabbitt
Ferrovius	Percy Rodriguez
Spintho	Guy Sanvido
Ox-Driver	Lowell Patterson
Secutor	Alastair Summerfield
Retiarius	Ian Gent
Call Boy	Roger Picken
The Editor	Alfred Gallagher
Menagerie Keeper	Lowell Patterson
The Emperor	Andrew Allan
Trumpeter	Brian Yanik
Christians	Corinna Bruce, Bonnie Bowering, Jennifer Brunton, Sandy Clair, Heather Fyfe, Margo Fyfe, Barbara Harrison, Pam Hiscott, Jean Herzog, Ann Hustleby, Lyn Munroe, Robin Rand, Betty Robertson
Roman Soldiers	W.W. Blue, Roderick Brennan, Eddie Yates
Gladiators	Vincent Burt, Gary Middleditch

Directed by Seán Mulcahy
Designed by Martha Mann

Stage Manager	David M. Twilby
Assistant Stage Manager	Maggie Smith

1964

HEARTBREAK HOUSE by Bernard Shaw
Court House Theatre, June 23 to 28 (6 performances)

Ellie Dunn	Mary Benning
Nurse Guinness	Joyce Campion
Captain Shotover	Norman Welsh
Lady Utterword	Betty Leighton
Hesione Hushabye	Moya Fenwick
Mazzini Dunn	Alfred Gallagher
Hector Hushabye	Christopher Newton
Boss Mangan	Robert Hewitt
Randall Utterword	Michael Tabbitt
The Burglar	Donald Ewer

Directed by Andrew Allan
Designed by Lawrence Schafer
Lighting designed by Donald Acaster

Stage Manager	Christian Gurney
Assistant Stage Manager	Terry Tweed

VILLAGE WOOING by Bernard Shaw
Court House Theatre, June 30 to July 5 (6 performances)

"Z"	Linda Livingston
"A"	Christopher Newton
Deck Steward	W.W. Blue

Directed by Seán Mulcahy
Designed by Lawrence Schafer
Lighting designed by Donald Acaster

Stage Manager	Christian Gurney
Assistant Stage Manager	Terry Tweed

THE DARK LADY OF THE SONNETS by Bernard Shaw
(on the same bill as *Village Wooing*)

The Beefeater	Donald Ewer
William Shakespeare	Jack Medley
Queen Elizabeth I	Moya Fenwick
The Dark Lady	Linda Livingston

Directed by Seán Mulcahy
Designed by Lawrence Schafer
Lighting designed by Donald Acaster

Stage Manager   Christian Gurney
Assistant Stage Manager   Terry Tweed

JOHN BULL'S OTHER ISLAND by Bernard Shaw
Court House Theatre, July 7 to 19 (12 performances)

Tom Broadbent   Paul Craig
Hodson   Leo Phillips
Tim Haffigan   Michael Tabbitt
Larry Doyle   Seán Mulcahy
Peter Keegan   Gerard Parkes
Patsy Farrell   Lawrence Beattie
Nora Reilly   Mary Benning
Father Dempsey   Alfred Gallagher
Cornelius Doyle   Michael Snow
Aunt Judy   Joyce Campion
Matthew Haffigan   Leo Leyden
Barney Doran   John W. McMullan

Barney Doran's friends   W.W. Blue, Roger Picken, Michael
                                 Tabbitt, Terry Tweed, Mary Welsman

Directed by Andrew Allan
Associate director: Seán Mulcahy
Designed by Lawrence Schafer
Lighting designed by Donald Acaster

Stage Manager   Christian Gurney
Assistant Stage Manager   Terry Tweed

MARY BENNING AND
NORMAN WELSH IN
HEARTBREAK HOUSE,
1964 (PHOTO BY
ROBERT C. RAGSDALE).

1965

FOURTH SEASON

June 29 to August 8 (42 performances)

PYGMALION by Bernard Shaw
Court House Theatre, June 29 to August 8 (14 performances)

Clara Eynsford-Hill	Mary Barton
Mrs Eynsford-Hill	Joyce Campion
Independent Bystander	Randolph Rhodes
Freddy Eynsford-Hill	Howard Lever
Eliza Doolittle	Anne Butler
Colonel Pickering	Alfred Gallagher
Henry Higgins	Paul Craig
Sarcastic Bystander	Norman Harding
Mrs. Pearce	Betty Leighton
Alfred Doolittle	Gerard Parkes
Mrs Higgins	Juliana Saxton
The Parlormaid	Jean Stainer
People in Covent Garden	Elaine Freeman, W.W. Blue, Joan Huggins, Jane McEwan, Susan McEwan, Roger Picken

Directed by Andrew Allan
Designed by Lawrence Schafer
Lighting designed by Donald Acaster

Stage Manager	Peter Taylor
Assistant Stage Managers	Carol O. Jessop
	Laurence Siegel

THE SHADOW OF A GUNMAN by Seán O'Casey
Court House Theatre, July 13 to 25 (14 performances)

Donal Davoren	Seán Mulcahy
Seumas Shields	Gerard Parkes
Mr Maguire	Laurence Siegel
Mr Mulligan	John W. McMullan
Minnie Powell	Nuala FitzGerald
Tommy Owens	Michael Snow
Mrs Henderson	Marie Pringle
Mr Gallogher	Alfred Gallagher
Mrs Grigson	Joyce Campion
Adolphus Grigson	Lawrence Beattie
An Auxiliary (Black and Tan)	Paul Craig

Directed by Seán Mulcahy
Designed by Lawrence Schafer
Lighting designed by Donald Acaster

Stage Manager   Peter Taylor
Assistant Stage Managers   Carol O. Jessop
                                           Laurence Siegel

THE MILLIONAIRESS by Bernard Shaw
Court House Theatre, July 27 to August 8 (14 performances)

Julius Sagamore	Seán Mulcahy
Epifania Ognisanti di Parerga	Anne Butler
Alastair Fitzfassenden	Paul Craig
Patricia Smith	Mary Barton
Adrian Blenderbland	Alfred Gallagher
The Doctor	Roger Dauphin
The Sweatshop Man	Michael Snow
The Sweatshop Woman	Betty Leighton
The Hotel Manager	Howard Lever

Directed by Andrew Allan
Designed by Lawrence Schafer
Lighting designed by Donald Acaster

Stage Manager   Peter Taylor
Assistant Stage Managers   Carol O. Jessop
                                           Laurence Siegel

MICHAEL SNOW, BETTY
LEIGHTON, AND ANNE BUTLER
IN *THE MILLIONAIRESS*, 1965
(PHOTO BY ROBERT C. RAGSDALE).

1966

FIFTH SEASON

June 28 to August 28 (61 performances)

MAN AND SUPERMAN by Bernard Shaw
Court House Theatre, June 28 to July 16 (20 performances)

Roebuck Ramsden	Norman Welsh
Parlormaid	Janet Gladish
Octavius Robinson	Paxton Whitehead
John Tanner	Barry Morse
Ann Whitefield	Pat Galloway
Mrs Whitefield	Betty Leighton
Miss Ramsden	Molly Hancock
Violet Robinson	Susan Clark
Henry Straker	Tom Kneebone
Hector Malone	Paul Craig
Mendoza	Hugh Webster
Mr Malone	Leslie Yeo
Brigands and Soldiers	Michael Bain, Stephen Boal, Bill Bye, James Cull, Tim Hanson, Norman Harding, Grant Hawes, Roger Ivey, John Lubeck, Ellen Pierce, Tom Rosser

Directed by Barry Morse
Designed by Lawrence Schafer
Lighting designed by Donald Acaster

Stage Managers	Larry Warne
	Tom Legg
Assistant Stage Managers	Jennifer Stewart
	Janet Gladish

TOM KNEEBONE AND
BARRY MORSE IN *MAN AND
SUPERMAN*, 1966 (PHOTO
BY ROBERT C. RAGSDALE).

MISALLIANCE by Bernard Shaw
Court House Theatre, July 19 to August 6 (20 performances)

Johnny Tarleton	Paul Craig
Bentley Summerhays	Tom Kneebone
Hypatia Tarleton	Susan Clark
Mrs Tarleton	Betty Leighton
Lord Summerhays	Paxton Whitehead
John Tarleton, Sr	Leslie Yeo
Joseph Percival	Michael Bradshaw
Lina Szczepanowska	Zoe Caldwell
Julius Baker ("Gunner")	Howard Lever

Directed by Barry Morse
Designed by Lawrence Schafer
Lighting designed by Donald Acaster

Stage Managers	Larry Warne
	Tom Legg
Assistant Stage Managers	Jennifer Stewart
	Janet Gladish

THE APPLE CART by Bernard Shaw
Court House Theatre, August 9 to 28 (21 performances)

Pamphilius	Michael Bradshaw
Sempronius	Howard Lever
Boanerges	Henry Ramer
Magnus	Paxton Whitehead
The Princess Royal	Judy Holmes
Proteus	Patrick Boxill
Nicobar	Paul Craig
Crassus	Alfred Gallagher
Pliny	Sandy Webster
Balbus	Jon Granik
Amanda	Sheila Haney
Lysistrata	Margaret MacLeod
Orinthia	Zoe Caldwell
Queen Jemima	Betty Leighton
Mr Vanhattan	Percy Rodriguez*

succeeded by Franz Russell

Directed by Edward Gilbert
Designed by Lawrence Schafer
Lighting designed by Donald Acaster

Stage Managers	Larry Warne
	Tom Legg
Assistant Stage Managers	Jennifer Stewart
	Janet Gladish

1967

SIXTH SEASON

June 21 to September 10 (89 performances)

ARMS AND THE MAN by Bernard Shaw
Court House Theatre, June 21 to July 15 (29 performances)

Catherine Petkoff	Betty Leighton
Raina Petkoff	Martha Henry
Louka	Suzanne Grossmann
Captain Bluntschli	Douglas Rain
Russian Officer	Detlef Berthelsen
Nicola	Heath Lamberts
Major Petkoff	Sandy Webster
Major Sergius Saranoff	Paxton Whitehead

Directed by Edward Gilbert
Sets designed by Maurice Strike
Costumes designed by Hilary Corbett
Lighting designed by Christopher Root

Stage Manager	Gerry Eldred
Assistant Stage Manager	Jean Bergmann

THE CIRCLE by W. Somerset Maugham
Court House Theatre, July 19 to August 12 (29 performances)

Arnold Champion-Cheney	Steven Sutherland
A Butler	Norman Harding
Mrs Shenstone	Margaret MacLeod
Elizabeth	Susan Ringwood
Edward Luton	Paul Collins
Clive Champion-Cheney	Hiram Sherman
Lady Catherine	
Champion-Cheney	Kate Reid
Lord Porteous	Leslie Yeo
A "Tweenie"	Pamela Brook

Directed by Paxton Whitehead
Sets designed by Maurice Strike
Costumes designed by Hilary Corbett
Lighting designed by Christopher Root

Stage Manager	Gerry Eldred
Assistant Stage Manager	Jean Bergmann

MAJOR BARBARA by Bernard Shaw
Joint production with Manitoba Theatre Centre, Winnipeg.
Court House Theatre, August 16 to September 10 (31 performances)

Lady Britomart	Renée Asherson
Stephen Undershaft	Thomas Clark
Morrison	Ian Downie
Sarah Undershaft	Margot Gillies
Barbara Undershaft	Irena Mayeska
Adolphus Cusins	Paxton Whitehead
Charles Lomax	Steven Sutherland
Andrew Undershaft	Larry Gates
Rummy Mitchens	Jennifer Phipps
Snobby Price	Eric House
Jenny Hill	Deborah Kipp
Peter Shirley	Patrick Boxill
Bill Walker	Roy Cooper
Mrs Baines	Margaret MacLeod
Bilton	James Cull

Directed by Edward Gilbert
Designed by Maurice Strike
Lighting designed by Christopher Root

Stage Manager	Gerry Eldred
Assistant Stage Manager	Jean Bergmann

Post-season Tour
MAJOR BARBARA

Théâtre Port-Royal, Montreal
September 16 to 23 (8 performances)

Manitoba Theatre Centre, Winnipeg
October 3 to 21 (22 performances)

Assistant Stage Managers
Jean Bergmann, Clarke Rogers

MARTHA HENRY IN *ARMS AND THE MAN*,
1967 (PHOTO BY ROBERT C. RAGSDALE).

1968

SEVENTH SEASON

June 27 to September 1 (65 performances)

THE CHEMMY CIRCLE by Georges Feydeau
translated from *La Main passe* by Suzanne Grossmann

Court House Theatre, August 8 to September 1 (26 performances)

Chanal	John Horton
Fédot	James Valentine
Hubertin	Jack Creley
Coustouillu	Paxton Whitehead
Planteloup	Patrick Boxill
Belgence	Kenneth Dight
Etienne	Kenneth Wickes
Auguste	Gary McKeehan
LaPige	James Cull
Germal	Norman Harding
Francine Chanal	Frances Hyland
Sophie Fédot	Patricia Gage
Cecille	Sandy Nicholls
Madeleine	Margot Sweeney

Directed by Paxton Whitehead
Sets designed by Joseph Cselenyi
Costumes designed by Hilary Corbett
Lighting designed by Donald Acaster

Stage Manager	Michael Tabbitt
Assistant Stage Managers	Cathy McKeehan
	Clarke Rogers
	Nancy Sheffner

THE IMPORTANCE OF BEING OSCAR
based on the Life and Works of Oscar Wilde

Court House Theatre, July 30 to August 4 (6 performances)

Performed by Micheál MacLiammóir

Designed and directed by Hilton Edwards

Stage Manager	Brian Tobin

HEARTBREAK HOUSE by Bernard Shaw
Court House Theatre, June 27 to July 28 (33 performances)

Nurse Guinness	Eleanor Beecroft
Ellie Dunn	Diana Leblanc
Captain Shotover	Tony van Bridge
Lady Utterword	Frances Hyland
Hesione Hushabye	Jessica Tandy
Mazzini Dunn	Patrick Boxill
Hector Hushabye	Paxton Whitehead
Boss Mangan	Bill Fraser
Randall Utterword	James Valentine
The Burglar	Kenneth Wickes

Directed by Val Gielgud
Sets designed by Maurice Strike
Costumes designed by Hilary Corbett
Lighting designed by Donald Acaster

Stage Manager	Michael Tabbitt
Assistant Stage Managers	Cathy McKeehan
	Clarke Rogers
	Nancy Sheffner

PAXTON WHITEHEAD, JESSICA TANDY, DIANA LEBLANC, PATRICK BOXILL, TONY VAN BRIDGE, AND FRANCES HYLAND IN *HEARTBREAK HOUSE*, 1968 (PHOTO BY ROBERT C. RAGSDALE).

1969

June 21 to August 31 (81 performances)

THE DOCTOR'S DILEMMA by Bernard Shaw
Court House Theatre
previews June 21 to 22, opening June 23 to July 20 (36 performances)

The Young Man	Malcolm Armstrong
Emmy	Gertrude Bradley
Sir Colenso Ridgeon	Robert Flemyng
Leo Schutzmacher	Sam Moses
Sir Patrick Cullen	James Edmond
Cutler Walpole	Kenneth Dight
Sir Ralph Bloomfield Bonington	David Hutcheson
Blenkinsop	Patrick Boxill
Jennifer Dubedat	Helen Finn
Louis Dubedat	Paxton Whitehead
Minnie Tinwell	Sylvia Feigel

Directed by Dillon Evans
Sets designed by James Tilton
Costumes designed by Hilary Corbett
Lighting designed by Donald Acaster

Stage Manager	Cathy McKeehan
Assistant Stage Manager	Dwight Griffin

BACK TO METHUSELAH
Part I: IN THE BEGINNING by Bernard Shaw
Court House Theatre, preview July 22, opening July 23 to August 3 (15 performances)

Adam	Jonathan White
Eve	Frances Hyland
The Serpent	Barbara Chilcott
Cain	Roland Hewgill

Conceived and directed by Marigold Charlesworth
Designed by Les Lawrence
Music composed and directed by Eugene Martynec
Original song composed and played
    by the Kensington Market
Environmental lighting and special effects by Catharsis,
    in collaboration with Donald Acaster

14

FIVE VARIATIONS FOR CORNO DI BASSETTO:
A MUSICAL ENTERTAINMENT
(on the same bill as *Back to Methuselah, Part I*, above)

Arranged, from Shaw's music criticism, by Louis Applebaum and
Ronald Hambleton.

Corno di Bassetto	John Horton
Compère	Patrick Boxill
Musicians	Mary Simmons (soprano)
	Reginald Godden (piano)
	Gerard Kantarjian (violin)
	Alvin Berky (cello)
	Jay Morton (clarinet)

Staged by Patrick Boxill

THE GUARDSMAN by Ferenc Molnár
Court House Theatre, preview August 6, opening August 7 to 31 (30 performances)

The Actress: Ilona	Lila Kedrova
The Actor: Nandor	Paxton Whitehead
The Critic: Bela	Carl Don
The "Mother"	Hanna Sarvasova
The Maid: Liesl	Susan King
The Creditor: Rosenzweig	Tibor Fehereghazi
The Usherette: Mrs Nagy	Molly Rutledge
The Cook	Margot Sweeney

Directed by Stephen Porter
Sets designed by Maurice Strike
Costumes designed by Tiina Lipp
Lighting designed by Donald Acaster

Stage Manager	Cathy McKeehan
Assistant Stage Manager	Dwight Griffin

Post-season Tour
THE GUARDSMAN
National Arts Centre, Ottawa, September 2 to 7 (7 performances)
For the tour Trudi Renés appeared as Mrs Nagy.

1970

Pre-season Tour

CANDIDA by Bernard Shaw
Grand Theatre, Kingston, May 28 to 30 (4 performances)
National Arts Centre, Ottawa, June 3 to 13 (12 performances)
Cast as listed below

NINTH SEASON

June 20 to September 6 (89 performances)

CANDIDA by Bernard Shaw
Court House Theatre
previews June 20 to 21, opening June 22 to July 26 (39 performances)

Prossy	Jennifer Phipps
Morell	Tony van Bridge
Lexy	Leslie Carlson
Burgess	Stanley Holloway
Candida	Frances Hyland
Marchbanks	Chris Sarandon*

succeeded in final week by Donald Warfield

Directed by Harris Yulin
Sets designed by Maurice Strike
Costumes designed by Hilary Corbett
Lighting designed by Gil Wechsler

Stage Managers	Bernard Harvard (tour)
	William Warnke
Assistant Stage Manager	David E. Barlow

Five additional performances were cancelled when Frances Hyland developed laryngitis. For these performances, July 17 to 19, a substitute program was created, consisting of portions of Tony van Bridge's *G.K.C.* and songs and recitations from Stanley Holloway's music-hall repertoire.

G.K.C.: THE WIT AND WISDOM OF GILBERT KEITH CHESTERTON
St Mark's Church, July 31 to August 2 (3 performances)

Compiled, arranged, and performed by Tony van Bridge
Direction assistance by Frances Hyland
Designed by Jane Boland

Stage Manager	David E. Barlow
Assistant Stage Manager	Linda Smith

16

LES CARLSON, FRANCES HYLAND, TONY VAN BRIDGE, JENNIFER PHIPPS, STANLEY HOLLOWAY,
AND CHRIS SARANDON IN *CANDIDA*, 1970 (PHOTO BY ROBERT C. RAGSDALE).

FORTY YEARS ON by Alan Bennett
Court House Theatre
previews August 1 to 2, opening August 3 to September 6 (42 performances)

Headmaster	Robert Harris
Franklin	Alan Scarfe
Tempest	Paxton Whitehead
Matron	Jennifer Phipps
Miss Nisbitt	Amelia Hall
Organist	Peter Orme
The Boys of Albion House	Peter Bennett, David Eden, Roy Hopper, Glen Kotyk, Stephen Lane, Richard Lawrence, Ian MacLaren, Evan McCowan, John Nicholl, Peter Pilgrim, Tim Pilgrim, Nicholas Pope, Christopher Szczucinski, Michael Thompson, Thomas Weld, Reid Willis, Alexander Willows

Directed by Paxton Whitehead
Sets designed by Maurice Strike
Costumes designed by Tiina Lipp and Reg Samuel
Lighting designed by Gil Wechsler
Musical direction by Peter Orme

Stage Manager	William Warnke
Assistant Stage Manager	David E. Barlow

17

1971

Pre-season Tours

THE PHILANDERER by Bernard Shaw

Grand Theatre, Kingston, May 12 to 15 (5 performances)
Clarke Theatre, Montreal, May 20 to 23 (5 performances)
National Arts Centre, Ottawa, May 24 to June 5 (20 performances)
Arts Center, Rochester, NY, June 9 to 10 (2 performances)

> Cast as listed below, except:
> Patricia Gage played Julia Craven in Ottawa and Montreal,
> Louise Marleau in Kingston and Rochester.

SUMMER DAYS by Romain Weingarten
translated by Suzanne Grossmann

National Arts Centre, Ottawa, May 31 to June 12 (16 performances)

TENTH SEASON

June 12 to September 5 (99 performances)

THE PHILANDERER by Bernard Shaw

Court House Theatre
previews June 12 to 13, opening June 14 to July 17 (36 performances)

Leonard Charteris	Paxton Whitehead
Grace Tranfield	Patricia Collins
Julia Craven	Louise Marleau
Joseph Cuthbertson	Norman Welsh
Colonel Craven	Patrick Boxill
Dr Paramore	James Valentine
Sylvia Craven	Diana Barrington
Page (alternating on tour)	Glen Kotyk, Robert Freeman, Jerrold Karch, Roddy Olafson, Christopher Toye

Directed by Tony van Bridge
Sets designed by Maurice Strike
Costumes designed by Tiina Lipp
Lighting designed by Donald Acaster

Stage Manager	Ron Nipper
Assistant Stage Manager	Glenda Ferrall

SUMMER DAYS by Romain Weingarten
translated by Suzanne Grossmann

Court House Theatre
preview June 21, opening June 22 to July 18 (10 performances)

Simon	Derek McGrath
Semi-Succotash	Eric House
Lorette	Nancy Beatty
Lord Garlic	Jack Creley

Directed by Michael Bawtree
Designed by Brian Jackson
Music by Poldi Shaetzman
Lighting designed by Donald Acaster

Stage Manager	Bill Millerd
Assistant Stage Manager	Derek McGrath

PAXTON WHITEHEAD WITH NORMAN WELSH, DIANA BARRINGTON, PATRICK BOXILL, JAMES VALENTINE, PATRICIA COLLINS, AND LOUISE MARLEAU IN *THE PHILANDERER*, 1971 (PHOTO BY ROBERT C. RAGSDALE).

1971

TONIGHT AT 8:30 by Noel Coward
Court House Theatre
previews July 24 to 25, opening July 26 to September 4 (28 performances)

WE WERE DANCING

Ippaga	Derek McGrath
George Davies	James Valentine
Eva Blake	Susan Hogan
Louise Charteris	Carole Shelley
Karl Sandys	Paxton Whitehead
Hubert Charteris	Hiram Sherman
Clara Bethel	Barbara Hamilton
Major Blake	Michael Hogan

FAMILY ALBUM

Jasper Featherways	Hiram Sherman
Jane Featherways	Carole Shelley
Lavinia Featherways	Barbara Hamilton
Richard Featherways	Derek McGrath
Harriet Winter	Nancy Beatty
Charles Winter	Michael Hogan
Emily Valance	Susan Hogan
Edward Valance	Paxton Whitehead
Burrows	Patrick Boxill

SHADOW PLAY

Lena	Nancy Beatty
Victoria Gayforth	Carole Shelley
Martha Cunningham	Barbara Hamilton
Simon Gayforth	Paxton Whitehead
Hodge	Derek McGrath
Sibyl Heston	Susan Hogan
Michael Doyle	Michael Hogan
A Young Man	James Valentine
George Cunningham	Hiram Sherman
At the piano	Peter Orme, Lynne Honsberger

Directed by Eric House
Sets designed by Maurice Strike
Costumes designed by Hilary Corbett
Lighting designed by Donald Acaster
Music arranged and directed by Peter Orme

Stage Manager	Bill Millerd
Assistant Stage Manager	Glenda Ferrall

20

WAR, WOMEN AND OTHER TRIVIA
Court House Theatre
previews July 22 to 23, opening July 29 to September 3 (25 performances)

A SOCIAL SUCCESS by Max Beerbohm

Tommy Dixon	James Valentine
Duchess of Huntington	Barbara Hamilton
Earl of Amersham	Hiram Sherman
Henry Robbins	Eric House
Countess of Amersham	Susan Hogan
Hawkins	Derek McGrath

Directed by Patrick Boxill
Designed by Maurice Strike
Lighting designed by Donald Acaster

O'FLAHERTY, V.C. by Bernard Shaw

O'Flaherty	Michael Hogan
Sir Pearce	Patrick Boxill
Mrs O'Flaherty	Barbara Hamilton
Teresa	Susan Hogan

Directed by Patrick Boxill
Set designed by Maurice Strike
Costumes designed by Hilary Corbett
Lighting designed by Donald Acaster

PRESS CUTTINGS by Bernard Shaw

General Mitchener	James Valentine
Orderly	Eric House
Balsquith	Patrick Boxill
Mrs Farrell	Nancy Beatty
Mrs Banger	Barbara Hamilton
Lady Corinthia	Carole Shelley

Directed by Paxton Whitehead
Set designed by Maurice Strike
Costumes designed by Hilary Corbett
Lighting designed by Donald Acaster

Stage Manager	Ron Nipper
Assistant Stage Manager	Glenda Ferrall

1972

Pre-season Tour

MISALLIANCE by Bernard Shaw
National Arts Centre, Ottawa, May 22 to June 3 (16 performances)
Nazareth Arts Center, Rochester, NY, June 6 to 7 (2 performances)
Grand Theatre, Kingston, June 8 to 10 (4 performances)
Théâtre Maisonneuve, Montreal, June 13 to 18 (5 performances)
Eisenhower Theatre, Washington, DC, June 26 to July 8 (16 performances)

ELEVENTH SEASON

June 10 to September 10 (101 performances)

GETTING MARRIED by Bernard Shaw
Court House Theatre
previews July 14 to 15, opening July 16 to September 2 (29 performances)

Mrs Bridgenorth	Betty Leighton
Collins	Owen Foran
General Bridgenorth	Ronald Drake
Lesbia Grantham	Susan Chapple
Reginald Bridgenorth	James Valentine
Leo Bridgenorth	'Wenna Shaw
Alfred Bridgenorth,	
Bishop of Chelsea	Noel Howlett
St John Hotchkiss	Heath Lamberts
Cecil Sykes	Michael Hogan
Edith Bridgenorth	Susan Hogan
Reverend Oliver Cromwell	
Soames	Tom Kneebone
The Beadle	Pat Roberto
Mrs George Collins	Moya Fenwick

Directed by Paxton Whitehead
Set designed by Maurice Strike
Costumes designed by Judy Peyton-Ward
Lighting designed by Al Anderson

Stage Manager	Ron Nipper
Assistant Stage Manager	Lani Reynolds

THE ROYAL FAMILY by George S. Kaufman and Edna Ferber
Court House Theatre
previews June 10 to 11, opening June 12 to July 9 (35 performances)

Della	Cosette Lee
Jo	Larry Reynolds
Hallboys	Peter Kufluk, Alexander Willows
McDermott	Jonathan White
Herbert Dean	Shepperd Strudwick
Kitty Dean	Patricia Gage
Gwen	Susan Hogan
Perry Stewart	Michael Hogan
Fanny Cavendish	Ruth Nelson
Oscar Wolfe	Paul Kligman
Julie Cavendish	Charmion King
Anthony Cavendish	Jim McQueen
Gilbert Marshall	Jonah Royston
Miss Peake	Betty Thompson
Chauffeur	Tom Strawford
Gunga	MacCowan Thomas
Aubrey Cavendish Stewart	Bradley Southam

Directed by Donald Davis
Sets designed by Tom Doherty
Costumes designed by Hilary Corbett
Lighting designed by Donald Acaster

Stage Manager	Catherine McKeehan
Assistant Stage Manager	Russell Peacock

MISALLIANCE by Bernard Shaw
Court House Theatre
preview July 18, opening July 19 to September 10 (37 performances)

Johnny Tarleton	Malcolm Armstrong
Bentley Summerhays	Tom Kneebone*
Hypatia Tarleton	'Wenna Shaw
Mrs Tarleton	Betty Leighton
Lord Summerhays	Noel Howlett
John Tarleton, Sr	Ronald Drake
Joseph Percival	James Valentine
Lina Szczepanowska	Angela Wood
Julius Baker ("Gunner")	Heath Lamberts

succeeded by Robin Marshall in September

Directed by Paxton Whitehead
Set designed by Maurice Strike
Costumes designed by Hilary Corbett
Lighting designed by Lynne Hyde

Stage Manager	Ron Nipper
Assistant Stage Manager	Lani Reynolds

1973

Pre-season Tour

THE PHILANDERER by Bernard Shaw

Eisenhower Theatre, Washington, D.C., January 2 to 13 (15 performances)

Leonard Charteris	Paxton Whitehead
Grace Tranfield	Charlotte Blunt
Julia Craven	Patricia Gage
Joseph Cuthbertson	Sandy Webster
Colonel Craven	Patrick Boxill
Dr Paramore	James Valentine
Sylvia Craven	'Wenna Shaw
Page	Christopher Gladstone

Directed by Tony van Bridge
Sets designed by Maurice Strike
Costumes designed by Tiina Lipp
Lighting designed by Donald Acaster

Stage Manager	Ron Nipper
Assistant Stage Manager	Ron Francis

TWELFTH SEASON

June 12 to September 23 (119 performances)

YOU NEVER CAN TELL by Bernard Shaw

Inaugural production in the Festival Theatre
previews June 12 to 19, opening June 20 to August 5
additional performances September 6 to 23 (62 performances)

Special performance on June 28 in the presence of
Her Majesty the Queen and His Royal Highness The Duke of Edinburgh.

Dolly Clandon	'Wenna Shaw
Mr Valentine	Paxton Whitehead
Parlormaid	Melody Horbulyk
Philip Clandon	Peter Blais
Mrs Clandon	Mary Savidge
Gloria Clandon	Patricia Gage
Fergus Crampton	Norman Welsh*
Finch M'Comas	Patrick Boxill
Waiters	Stanley Holloway**
	Howard Hughes
Walter Bohun, Q.C.	James Valentine***

succeeded by Richard Farrell on September 6

**succeeded by Richard Murdoch on September 6
***succeeded by Laurie Freeman on September 6

Directed by Edward Gilbert
Sets designed by Maurice Strike
Costumes designed by Hilary Corbett
Lighting designed by Donald Acaster

Stage Manager	Ron Nipper
Assistant Stage Manager	David Bunyan
	Nancy Boake (tour)

NORMAN WELSH AND PAXTON WHITEHEAD IN *YOU NEVER CAN TELL*, 1973 (PHOTO BY ROBERT C. RAGSDALE).

THE BRASS BUTTERFLY by William Golding
Festival Theatre
preview June 19, opening June 21 to August 25 (27 performances)

Mamillius	Stephen Markle
Captain of the Guard	John Swindells
Postumus	August Schellenberg
Emperor	Lockwood West
Phanocles	James Valentine
Euphrosyne	Melody Horbulyk
A Sergeant	Chris Kelk
Attendants	Carol Crawford, Hollis McLaren, Milton Branton, Simon Briand, Klaus Gorges, Howard Hughes

Directed by Joseph Shaw
Set designed by Brian Jackson
Costumes designed by John Fenney
Lighting designed by Donald Acaster

Stage Manager	Ron Nipper
Assistant Stage Manager	David Bunyan

FANNY'S FIRST PLAY by Bernard Shaw
Festival Theatre
preview August 8, opening August 9 to September 8 (29 performances)

The Audience:

A Footman	Maynard Burgess
Count O'Dowda	Maury Cooper
Cecil Savoyard	Paxton Whitehead
Fanny O'Dowda	Blair Brown

The Critics:

Mr Trotter	Patrick Boxill
Mr Vaughan	John Swindells
Mr Gunn	Chris Kelk
Mr Flawner Bannal	Howard Hughes

The Players:

Billy Burjoyce	Peter Kufluk
Robin Gilbey	Alan Nunn
Mrs Gilbey	Marjorie Le Strange
Juggins	James Valentine
Dora Delaney	'Wenna Shaw
Mrs Knox	Mary Savidge
Mr Knox	Gerard Parkes
Margaret Knox	Domini Blythe
Bobby Gilbey	Stephen Markle
M. Duvallet	August Schellenberg

Directed by Brian Murray
Sets designed by Maurice Strike

26

Costumes designed by Hilary Corbett
Lighting designed by Donald Acaster

Stage Manager	Ron Nipper
Assistant Stage Manager	David Bunyan

GBS IN LOVE
Court House Theatre, August 6 (1 performance)

A dramatic narrative devised and performed by Dan H. Laurence, from the correspondence of Bernard Shaw and Alice Lockett, presented in conjunction with the Shaw Seminar.

SISTERS OF MERCY:
A MUSICAL JOURNEY INTO THE WORDS OF LEONARD COHEN
Court House Theatre
previews June 30 to July 4, opening July 5 to August 5 (42 performances)

Sisters of Mercy was an independent production, sponsored by the Shaw Festival in collaboration with its producer Martin J. Machat.

Players:	Nicolas Surovy	Musicians:	Zizi Mueller
	Emily Bindiger		Dean Kelso
	Gale Garnett		
	Pamela Paluzzi		
	Rosemary Radcliffe		
	Michael Calkins		

Conceived and directed by Gene Lesser
Musical director: Zizi Mueller
Set designed by Robert U. Taylor
Costumes designed by Carrie F. Robbins
Lighting designed by Donald Acaster

Stage Manager	Ginny Freedman
Assistant Stage Manager	Ray Frederick

Post-season Tour

YOU NEVER CAN TELL
National Arts Centre, Ottawa, September 27 to October 13 (20 performances)
Manitoba Theatre Centre, Winnipeg, October 19 to November 10 (27 performances)
Music Hall Center for the Performing Arts, Detroit, November 12 to 17 (8 performances)
Shubert Theatre, New Haven, November 19 to 24 (8 performances)
Mendelssohn Theatre, Ann Arbor, December 6 to 9 (6 performances)

For the tour Janet Doherty and Margaret Lamb (uncredited) appeared as the Parlormaid. Sheila Haney appeared as Mrs Clandon in Winnipeg.

1974

Pre-season Tour

THE DEVIL'S DISCIPLE by Bernard Shaw
Neptune Theatre, Halifax, April 4 to 20 (18 performances)
Nova Scotia Teachers' College, Truro, April 22 (1 performance)
Consolidated Memorial H.S., Yarmouth, April 23 (1 performance)
Confederation Theatre, Charlottetown, April 25 to 26 (2 performances)
Arts and Sculpture Centre, St John's, April 30 to May 1 (3 performances)
Theatre New Brunswick, Fredericton, May 3 to 6 (4 performances)
Centennial Secondary School, Belleville, May 9 (2 performances)
Grand Theatre, Kingston, May 10 to 11 (2 performances)

> For the tour Jeanette Romeril appeared as Mrs William Dudgeon, Joan Orenstein as Mrs Titus Dudgeon. A number of the extras on the tour were replaced for the Niagara-on-the-Lake season.

THIRTEENTH SEASON

May 13 to October 5 (218 performances)

ROSMERSHOLM by Henrik Ibsen
Court House Theatre, opening July 9 to July 27 (22 performances)

Rebekka West	Elizabeth Shepherd
Mrs. Helseth	Betty Thompson
Dr Kroll	Kenneth Dight
John Rosmer	Neil Vipond
Ulrik Brendel	Gillie Fenwick
Peter Mortensgaard	Tom Celli

Directed by Tony van Bridge
Designed by Tiina Lipp
Lighting designed by Al Anderson

Stage Manager	Gully Stanford
Assistant Stage Manager	Laurie Freeman

Five performances, including two previews and the originally scheduled opening on July 2, were cancelled due to the illness of Neil Vipond.

CHARLEY'S AUNT by Brandon Thomas
Festival Theatre
previews May 23 to June 1 (matinee)
opening June 1 (evening) to July 28, September 3 to October 5 (61 performances)

Jack Chesney	James Valentine
Brassett	Kenneth Wickes
Charley Wykeham	John Horton
Lord Fancourt Babberley	Paxton Whitehead
Kitty Verdun	Hollis McLaren
Amy Spettigue	Janet Doherty
Colonel Sir Francis Chesney	Norman Welsh
Stephen Spettigue	Patrick Boxill
Donna Lucia d'Alvadorez	Lorraine Foreman
Ela Delahay	Mary Long

Directed by Paxton Whitehead
Sets designed by Maurice Strike
Costumes designed by Hilary Corbett
Lighting designed by Donald Acaster

Stage Manager	Ron Nipper
Assistant Stage Manager	Nancy Boake

THE ADMIRABLE BASHVILLE by Bernard Shaw
Court House Theatre
previews July 30 to 31, opening August 1 to August 25 (28 performances)

Edgar, Lord Fanshaw (Lord Worthington)	Kenneth Dight
Elizabeth, Lady Fanshaw (Adelaide Gisborne)	Irene Hogan
The Hon. Eustace Fanshaw (Lucian)	Rafe MacPherson
The Hon. Cecily Fanshaw (Lydia)	Dorothy-Ann Haug
Cedric FitzSimmons Esq. (Mellish)	Don Le Gros
Edward FitzSimmons Esq. (Bashville)	James Valentine
Alistair FitzSimmons Esq. (Cashel Byron)	Terence Kelly
Members of Lady Fanshaw's Household:	
The Housekeeper (Musical Accompanist)	John Buckingham
The Butler (Cetewayo)	Wayne Robson
The Parlormaid (A Policeman)	Faye Davis
The Groom (Paradise)	Paul-Emile Frappier

Directed by Stephen Katz
Set designed by Mary Kerr
Costumes designed by Hilary Corbett
Lighting designed by Al Anderson

Stage Manager	Gully Stanford
Assistant Stage Manager	Laurie Freeman

1974

THE DEVIL'S DISCIPLE by Bernard Shaw

Festival Theatre, student matinees May 13 to 18, 23, 24, previews May 28 to 30
opening May 31 to August 11 (70 performances)

Mrs Timothy Dudgeon	Eleanor Beecroft
Essie	Karen Austin
Christopher Dudgeon	Heath Lamberts
Reverend Anthony Anderson	Norman Welsh
Judith Anderson	Domini Blythe
Lawyer Hawkins	Patrick Boxill
Mrs William Dudgeon	Joyce Hayward
William Dudgeon	Vincent Cole
Mrs Titus Dudgeon	Alice Crawley
Titus Dudgeon	Kenneth Wickes
Richard Dudgeon	Alan Scarfe
Sergeant	Stuart Kent
Major Swindon	James Valentine*
General Burgoyne	Tony van Bridge
Reverend Mr Brudenell	Drew Russell
Soldiers, Officers, Townspeople, etc.	Christopher Britton, Leon Fermanian, Gillian Hannant, John Meyers, Maynard Burgess, Laird Evans, Evan Hughes, Jack Katzman, Bing Raven, John Sweeney, Thomas Strawford

succeeded by Paxton Whitehead on July 27

Directed by Brian Murray
Designed by Robert Doyle
Lighting designed by Lynne Hyde

Stage Manager	Ron Nipper
Assistant Stage Manager	Nancy Boake

TOO TRUE TO BE GOOD by Bernard Shaw

Festival Theatre
previews July 31, August 3 to 4, opening August 5 to September 1 (37 performances)

The Patient (Mops)	Domini Blythe
The Day Nurse	Maggi Payne
The Mother	Elisabeth Orion
The Doctor	Thomas Strawford
The Night Nurse (Sweetie)	Elizabeth Shepherd
The Burglar (Aubrey)	John Horton
Colonel Tallboys	Tony van Bridge
Private Meek	Heath Lamberts
Sergeant Fielding	Stuart Kent
The Elder	Gillie Fenwick
The Writer	Howard Mawson

Directed by Douglas Seale
Sets designed by Maurice Strike

Costumes designed by Hilary Corbett
Lighting designed by Donald Acaster

Stage Manager   Ron Nipper
Assistant Stage Manager   Nancy Boake

Post-season Tours

TOO TRUE TO BE GOOD

Loeb Drama Center, Harvard University, September 24 to 29 (8 performances)

For the tour, Jackie Burroughs appeared as The Patient,
Marilyn Flynn as The Day Nurse, Betty Leighton as The Mother,
and Frank Pollard as The Doctor.

Stage Manager   David Bunyan
Assistant Stage Manager   Laurie Freeman

CHARLEY'S AUNT

Loeb Drama Center, Harvard University, September 17 to 22 (8 performances)
National Arts Centre, Ottawa, October 7 to 26 (24 performances)
Zellerbach Theatre, Philadelphia, November 5 to 17 (16 performances)

For the tour, Rafe MacPherson appeared as Charley Wykeham,
Robert Goodier as Colonel Sir Francis Chesney, and James Edmond
as Stephen Spettigue.

Stage Manager   David Bunyan
Assistant Stage Manager   Laurie Freeman

TONY VAN BRIDGE IN *TOO TRUE TO BE GOOD*, 1974 (PHOTO BY ROBERT C. RAGSDALE).

1975

FOURTEENTH SEASON
May 6 to October 5 (222 performances)

PYGMALION by Bernard Shaw
Festival Theatre
student matinees May 6 to 16
previews May 9 to 27, opening May 28 to September 21 (79 performances)

Miss Eynsford Hill	Jane Usher
Mrs Eynsford Hill	Joan Boyd
Bystander	Stuart Kent
Freddy Eynsford Hill	Edward Henry
Eliza Doolittle	Elizabeth Shepherd
Colonel Pickering	Edward Atienza
Henry Higgins	Powys Thomas
Sarcastic Bystander	Robin Marshall
Taximan	François-Régis Klanfer
Mrs Pearce	Irene Hogan
Alfred Doolittle*	Tony van Bridge
Mrs Higgins	Christine Bennett
Parlormaid	Pam Rogers
Market people	William Samples, Betty Thompson, Karen Wiens
Opera-goers	Maynard Burgess, Wendi Hallett, Joyce Hayward

performed by Stuart Kent on August 22, 24, and 30

Directed by Eric Till
Sets designed by Maurice Strike
Costumes designed by Hilary Corbett
Lighting designed by Don Acaster

Stage Manager	David Bunyan
Assistant Stage Manager	Laurie Freeman

LEAVEN OF MALICE by Robertson Davies
Festival Theatre
previews May 21 to 27, opening May 28 to August 1 (35 performances)

Gloster Ridley	Powys Thomas
Dean Jevon Knapp	James Valentine
Professor Walter Vambrace	François-Régis Klanfer
Pearl Veronica Vambrace	Charlotte Odele
Mrs Bridgetower	Christine Bennett

32

Humphrey Cobbler	Maurice Good
Edith Little	Irene Hogan
Solomon Bridgetower	Heath Lamberts
Dutchy Yarrow	Pam Rogers
Norman Yarrow	Don Allison
Tessie Forgie	Anna Sandor
Swinthin Shillito	Patrick Boxill
George Morphew	Jack Katzman
Kitten Morphew	Jane Usher
Beville Higgin	Robin Marshall
Molly Cobbler	Joyce Gordon
Secretary	Joyce Hayward
Hallowe'en guests	Miles Cohen, Leon Fermanian, Wendi Hallett, Joyce Hayward, William Samples, Karen Wiens

Directed by Tony van Bridge
Sets designed by Maurice Strike
Costumes designed by Hilary Corbett
Lighting designed by Donald Acaster

Stage Manager	David Bunyan
Assistant Stage Manager	Laurie Freeman

THE FIRST NIGHT OF PYGMALION by Richard Huggett
Court House Theatre
previews July 4 to 6, opening July 8 to August 17 (45 performances)

Narrators	Daphne Gibson, Kenneth Dight
Mrs Patrick Campbell	Moya Fenwick
Bernard Shaw	Gillie Fenwick
Sir Herbert Beerbohm Tree	Gerard Parkes

Directed by Tony van Bridge
Designed by David R. Dague
Lighting designed by Al Anderson

Stage Manager	Renée Schouten

G.K.C.: THE WIT AND WISDOM OF GILBERT KEITH CHESTERTON
Court House Theatre, August 22 to August 31 (6 performances)

Devised, arranged, and performed by Tony van Bridge
Set designed by David R. Dague
Lighting designed by Al Anderson

Stage Manager	Renée Schouten

1975

CAESAR AND CLEOPATRA by Bernard Shaw
Festival Theatre
previews July 3 to 6, opening July 7 to October 5 (57 performances)

Julius Caesar	Edward Atienza
Cleopatra	Domini Blythe
Nubian	Philip Akin
Ftatateeta	Mary Savidge
Pothinus	Heath Lamberts
Theodotus	Patrick Boxill
Achillas	Jan Muszynski
Ptolemy XIV	Paul Wardle
Rufio	Maurice Good
Britannus	James Valentine
Lucius Septimius	Don Allison
Wounded Soldier	Terry Judd
Centurion	Stuart Kent
Apollodorus	Edward Henry
Sentinel	Robin Marshall
1st Porter	Leon Fermanian
Boatman	William Samples
Professor of Music	Leon Fermanian
Iras	Charlotte Odele
Charmian	Jane Usher
Major Domo	Philip Akin
Belzanor	Terry Judd
Persian	Leon Fermanian

Cleopatra's women,
   Ptolemy's court ladies — Wendi Hallett, Joyce Hayward, Pam Rogers, Anna Sandor, Betty Thompson, Karen Wiens

Officials, priests, Roman soldiers, Egyptian soldiers, etc. — Keith Anderson, Maynard Burgess, Miles Cohen, Evan Hughes, Jack Katzman, Merton Malmo, Kevin McKendrick, Tom Strawford, Cloyce Weaver

Directed by Douglas Seale
Designed by Leslie Hurry
Lighting designed by Donald Acaster

Stage Manager	David Bunyan
Assistant Stage Manager	Laurie Freeman

34

Post-season Tours

CAESAR AND CLEOPATRA

National Arts Centre, Ottawa, October 6 to 25 (24 performances)
Zellerbach Theatre, Philadelphia, October 27 to November 8 (16 performances)

For the tour, Gillie Fenwick appeared as Pothinus, Robin Marshall as Theodotus, Donna Quenan and Anna Sandor as court ladies. The non-speaking roles were cut.

Stage Manager	Ronald Francis
Assistant Stage Manager	Laurie Freeman

THE DEVIL'S DISCIPLE

Zellerbach Theatre, Philadelphia, September 29 to October 11 (16 performances)
National Theatre, Washington, D.C., October 13 to 25 (16 performances)
Royal Alexandra Theatre, Toronto, October 27 to November 1 (8 performances)

Mrs Timothy Dudgeon	Sheila Haney
Essie	Pam Rogers
Christopher Dudgeon	Heath Lamberts
Reverend Anthony Anderson	Neil Vipond
Judith Anderson	Elizabeth Shepherd
Lawyer Hawkins	Patrick Boxill
Mrs William Dudgeon	Joan Boyd
William Dudgeon	Patrick Sinclair
Mrs Titus Dudgeon	Faye Davis
Titus Dudgeon	Kenneth Wickes
Richard Dudgeon	Paul Hecht
Sergeant	Graeme Campbell
Major Swindon	Kenneth Dight
General Burgoyne	Paxton Whitehead
Reverend Mr Brudenell	Rafe Macpherson
Soldiers and Officers	Members of the Fort Henry Guard of Kingston, Ontario: G.A. Brock, G.S. Campbell, B.D. Evernden, R.E. Gaudet, P.A. Hamon, P.R. King, D.C. Koval, J.I. MacDonald, B.A. Saunders, J.C. Umpherson

Directed by Paxton Whitehead and Tony van Bridge
Sets designed by Maurice Strike
Costumes designed by Hilary Corbett
Lighting designed by Donald Acaster

Stage Manager	Katherine Robertson
Assistant Stage Manager	Peter Roberts

1976

FIFTEENTH SEASON

April 27 to September 26 (223 performances)

ARMS AND THE MAN by Bernard Shaw

Festival Theatre, school matinees April 27 to May 21 (16 performances)
Court House Theatre, previews June 17 to 19, opening June 20 to September 4
(60 performances)

Two casts were employed, one from *Mrs Warren's Profession*, the other from *The Admirable Crichton*, "to facilitate continuous playing of *Arms and The Man* through the season at the Court House Theatre, and to establish a unified company playing both [theatres]."

Cast A:		
	Catherine Petkoff	Kate Reid
	Raina Petkoff	Roberta Maxwell
	Louka	Susan Hogan
	Captain Bluntschli	John Cutts
	Russian Officer	Greg Morley
	Nicola	Peter Mews
	Major Petkoff	Patrick Boxill
	Major Sergius Saranoff	Paxton Whitehead
Cast B:		
	Catherine Petkoff	Sydney Sturgess*
	Raina Petkoff	Alexandra Bastedo
	Louka	Pamela Brook
	Captain Bluntschli	Michael Ball
	Russian Officer	Greg Morley
	Nicola	Paul-Emile Frappier
	Major Petkoff	Leslie Yeo
	Major Sergius Saranoff	Paxton Whitehead

succeeded by Betty Leighton on August 6

Directed by Paxton Whitehead
Designed by Maurice Strike
Lighting designed by Robert Bryan

Stage Manager	Laurie Freeman
Assistant Stage Managers	Catherine Russell
	Michael Shamata

THE ADMIRABLE CRICHTON by J.M. Barrie

Festival Theatre, previews May 26 to 29 (matinee)
opening May 29 (evening) August 1 (43 performances)

Crichton	Michael Ball
The Honourable Ernest	
Woolley	Christopher Gaze
Lady Agatha Lasenby	Lynne Griffin
Lady Catherine Lasenby	Candace O'Connor

36

ROBERTA MAXWELL
AND PAXTON
WHITEHEAD IN
ARMS AND THE MAN,
1976 (PHOTO BY
ROBERT C. RAGSDALE).

Lady Mary Lasenby	Alexandra Bastedo
Reverend John Treherne	Paul-Emile Frappier
Earl of Loam	Wensley Pithey
Lord Brocklehurst	Christopher Britton
Mrs Perkins	Maggi Payne
Monsieur Fleury	Jack Katzman
Mr Rolleston	Cloyce Weaver
Mr Tompsett	Thomas Strawford
Miss Fisher	Angela Winter
Miss Simmons	Wendi Hallett
Mlle Jeanne	Virginia Reh
John	Ted Phythian
Gladys	Theresa Goode
Tweeney	Pamela Brook
Stable Boy	Chris Keppy
A Kitchen Maid	Faye Davis
A Page Boy	Andrew Noell
A Naval Officer	Cloyce Weaver
A Seaman from the yacht "Bluebell"	Chris Keppy
A Naval Rating	Ted Phythian
Countess of Brocklehurst	Sydney Sturgess

Directed by Barry Morse
Designed by Maurice Strike
Lighting designed by Robert Bryan

Stage Manager	Ron Nipper
Assistant Stage Manager	Michael Shamata

MRS WARREN'S PROFESSION by Bernard Shaw

Festival Theatre

previews May 15 to 28, opening May 30 to September 12 (60 performances)

Vivie Warren	Roberta Maxwell
Praed	Patrick Boxill
Kitty Warren	Kate Reid
Sir George Crofts	Barry Morse*
Frank Gardner	Christopher Gaze
Reverend Samuel Gardner	Peter Mews

succeeded by Wensley Pithey

Directed by Leslie Yeo
Sets designed by Robert Winkler
Costumes designed by Hilary Corbett
Lighting designed by Robert Bryan

Stage Manager	Laurie Freeman
Assistant Stage Manager	Catherine Russell

THE APPLE CART by Bernard Shaw

Festival Theatre

previews August 4 to 7, opening August 8 to September 26 (44 performances)

Pamphilius	Christopher Britton
Sempronius	Christopher Gaze
Boanerges	Leslie Yeo
King Magnus	Paxton Whitehead
Princess Royal	Virginia Reh
Proteus	Patrick Boxill
Nicobar	Sam Moses
Crassus	John Cutts
Pliny	Peter Mews
Balbus	Michael Ball
Amanda	Faye Davis
Lysistrata	Kate Reid
Orinthia	Roberta Maxwell
Queen Jemima	Betty Gable
Mr Vanhattan	Paul-Emile Frappier

Directed by Noel Willman
Designed by Maurice Strike
Lighting designed by Donald Acaster

Stage Manager	Laurie Freeman
Assistant Stage Managers	Catherine Russell
	Michael Shamata

1977

SIXTEENTH SEASON
May 13 to October 2 (226 performances)

MAN AND SUPERMAN by Bernard Shaw
Festival Theatre
previews May 13 to 24, opening May 26 to October 1 (69 performances)

The DON JUAN IN HELL scene was added to Act III at a matinee on July 17, for fourteen performances, through September 25.

The performance of August 3 was dedicated to Her Majesty Queen Elizabeth II, on the occasion of her Silver Jubilee.

Roebuck Ramsden / The Statue	Norman Welsh*
Maid	Jody Evans
Octavius Robinson	Michael Ball
John Tanner / Don Juan	Ian Richardson
Mrs Whitefield	Ann Casson
Ann Whitefield / Doña Ana	Carole Shelley
Miss Ramsden	Maggie Askey
Violet Robinson	Lynne Griffin
Henry Straker	Heath Lamberts
Hector Malone, Jr	Grant Roll
Mendoza / The Devil	Tony van Bridge
Anarchist	Tom Strawford
Sulky Social Democrat	Robin Marshall
Rowdy Social Democrat	James Cotroneo
Duval	Yves Mercier
Brigands	Marvin Ishmael, Robert Keppy, Robert Tanos
Spanish Officer	Marvin Ishmael
Spanish Soldiers	Scott Dickson, Robert Tanos
Hector Malone, Sr	Gillie Fenwick**

succeeded by Gillie Fenwick on September 9
**succeeded by Peter Mews on September 9*

Directed by Tony van Bridge
Designed by Brian H. Jackson
Lighting designed by John Stammers
Music arranged and recorded by Dennis Patrick

Stage Manager	Laurie Freeman
Assistant Stage Manager	Michael Shamata

THARK by Ben Travers
Festival Theatre
previews May 20 to 25, opening May 27 to October 9 (51 performances)

Hook	Patrick Boxill*
Warner	Maureen Press
Cherry Buck	Carole Shelley
Lionel Frush	Christopher Gaze
Mrs Frush	Maggie Askey
Sir Hector Benbow,	
Bart, M.F.H.	Tony van Bridge
Ronald Gamble	Paxton Whitehead
Lady Benbow	Ann Casson
Kitty Stratton	Lynne Griffin
Jones	Gillie Fenwick
Whittle	Heath Lamberts

Patrick Boxill died suddenly on October 5. The October 6 performance was cancelled in respect for his passing. For the final five performances on October 7 to 9 the role of Hook was played by Heath Lamberts and that of Whittle by Michael Franks.

Directed by Michael Meacham
Sets designed by Maurice Strike
Costumes designed by Hilary Corbett
Lighting designed by John Stammers

Stage Manager	Laurie Freeman
Assistant Stage Manager	Michael Shamata

THE MILLIONAIRESS by Bernard Shaw
Festival Theatre
previews July 7 to 10, opening July 12 to October 9 (37 performances)

Julius Sagamore	Christopher Gaze
Epifania Ognisanti di Parerga	Carole Shelley
Alastair Fitzfassenden	Michael Ball
Patricia Smith	Judy Leigh-Johnson
Adrian Blenderbland	Norman Welsh
The Doctor	Ian Richardson
The Man	Gillie Fenwick
His Wife	Ann Casson
The Hotel Manager	Grant Roll

Directed by Michael Meacham
Sets and lighting designed by John Jenson
Costumes designed by Hilary Corbett

Stage Manager	Laurie Freeman
Assistant Stage Manager	Michael Shamata

IAN RICHARDSON AND CAROLE SHELLEY IN *MAN AND SUPERMAN*, 1977 (PHOTO BY ROBERT C. RAGSDALE).

WIDOWERS' HOUSES by Bernard Shaw
Court House Theatre
previews June 8 to 10, opening June 11 to September 3 (31 performances)

Dr Harry Trench	Neil Munro
Cokane	Patrick Boxill
A Waiter	Bruce Kyle
Sartorius	Ronald Bishop
Blanche	Kristin Griffith
A Porter	Scot Whitham
Lickcheese	Owen Foran
Annie	Maureen Press

Directed by Paxton Whitehead
Sets designed by Maurice Strike
Costumes designed by Hilary Corbett
Lighting designed by Robert Thomson

Stage Manager	Catherine Russell
Assistant Stage Manager	Sandra Robinson

41

1977

GREAT CATHERINE by Bernard Shaw

Court House Theatre
previews June 24 to July 13 (matinee), opening July 13 (evening) to September 4
(38 performances)

Varinka	Maureen Press
Prince Patiomkin	Ronald Bishop
Cossack Sergeant	Owen Foran
Captain Edstaston	Paxton Whitehead
Naryshkin	Patrick Boxill
The Empress Catherine II	Dana Ivey
Princess Dashkoff	Mary Souchotte
Claire	Denise Alain Baillargeon
Tretiak	Scot Whitham
Maltsev	Greg Morley
Tanya	Sandi Simpson

Directed by Heath Lamberts
Sets designed by Maurice Strike
Costumes designed by Maxine Graham
Lighting designed be Robert Thomson

Stage Manager	Catherine Russell
Assistant Stage Manager	Sandra Robinson

PAXTON WHITEHEAD AND TONY VAN BRIDGE IN *THARK*, 1977 (PHOTO BY ROBERT C. RAGSDALE).

1978

Pre-season Tour

THARK

National Arts Centre, Ottawa, April 10 to 29 (24 performances)
Théâtre Maisonneuve, Montreal, May 2 to 7 (8 performances)

Cast as on page 40.
Heath Lamberts played Hook and Barrie Baldaro played Whittle.

Stage Manager	Katherine Robertson
Assistant Stage Manager	Ken A. Smith

SEVENTEENTH SEASON

May 11 to October 1 (247 performances)

MAJOR BARBARA by Bernard Shaw

Festival Theatre
previews May 11 to 23, opening May 25 to September 30 (74 performances)

Lady Britomart Undershaft	Betty Leighton
Stephen Undershaft	Hayward Morse
Morrison	Tom Strawford
Sarah Undershaft	Janet Barkhouse
Barbara Undershaft	Janet Amos
Adolphus Cusins	Tom Kneebone
Charles Lomax	Briain Petchey
Andrew Undershaft	Douglas Campbell
Rummy Mitchens	Kate Reid*
Snobby Price	James Rankin
Jenny Hill	Mary Haney
Peter Shirley	Eric House
Bill Walker	Peter Messaline
Mrs Baines	Amelia Hall
Bilton	Tom Strawford

succeeded by Kate McDonald at the end of June

Directed by Michael Meacham
Sets designed by Murray Laufer
Costumes designed by Marie Day
Lighting designed by Nick Cernovitch

Stage Manager	Ron Nipper
Assistant Stage Manager	Sandra Robinson

1978

JOHN GABRIEL BORKMAN by Henrik Ibsen
Festival Theatre
previews May 18 to 24, opening May 26 to July 23 (42 performances)

Gunhild Borkman	Frances Hyland
Marlene	Miriam Newhouse
Ella Rentheim	Kate Reid*
Fanny Wilton	Diana Barrington
Erhart Borkman	Hayward Morse
John Gabriel Borkman	Douglas Campbell
Frida Foldal	Mary Haney
Vilhelm Foldal	Tom Kneebone

succeeded by Betty Leighton at the end of June

Directed by George McCowan
Sets designed by Michael Eagan
Costumes designed by Hilary Corbett
Lighting designed by Nick Cernovitch

Stage Manager	Michael Shamata
Assistant Stage Manager	Sandra Robinson

HEARTBREAK HOUSE by Bernard Shaw
Festival Theatre
previews July 27 to August 2, opening August 4 to October 1 (43 performances)

Ellie Dunn	Susan André
Nurse Guinness	Amelia Hall
Captain Shotover	Douglas Campbell
Lady Utterword	Frances Hyland
Hesione Hushabye	Pat Galloway
Mazzini Dunn	Eric House
Hector Hushabye	Paul Harding
Boss Mangan	Leslie Yeo
Randall Utterword	Briain Petchey
The Burglar	Tom Kneebone

Directed by Noel Willman
Sets designed by Val Strazovec
Costumes designed by Horst Dantz
Lighting designed by Nick Cernovitch

Stage Manager	Michael Shamata
Assistant Stage Manager	Sandra Robinson

LADY AUDLEY'S SECRET: A MUSICAL MELODRAMA
by Mary Elizabeth Braddon
adapted by Douglas Seale
music by George Goehring
lyrics by John Kuntz

Court House Theatre
previews June 9 to 15, opening June 16 to September 3 (88 performances)

Phoebe	Beth Anne Cole
Luke Marks	Barrie Baldaro
Lady Audley	Marie Baron
Sir Michael Audley	Gillie Fenwick
Bridget the Housemaid	Susan Anderson
Smithers the Butler	Robert Rozen
Alicia	Angela Fusco
Captain Robert Audley	Bill Cole
George Talboys	Donald Saunders
Rustics	Norman Brown, William Moyer, Avery Saltzman

Directed by Douglas Seale
Musical direction by William Skolnik
 (succeeded by Leonard Atherton)
Choreography by Sheila McCarthy
Designed by Maxine Graham
Lighting designed by Robert Thomson

Stage Manager	Catherine Russell
Assistant Stage Manager	Dianne Woodrow

Post-season Tour

HEARTBREAK HOUSE
National Arts Centre, Ottawa, October 9 to 28 (24 performances)

For the tour, Lynne Griffin appeared as Ellie Dunn, Tony van Bridge
as Captain Shotover, Patrick Christopher as Hector Hushabye,
Rowland Hewgill as Boss Mangan, and Kenneth Wickes as The Burglar.

Assistant Stage Manager	Chris Pearce

1979

YOU NEVER CAN TELL by Bernard Shaw
Festival Theatre
previews May 22 to 27, opening May 30 to September 27 (55 performances)

Dolly Clandon	Mary Haney
Valentine	James Valentine
Parlormaid	Elizabeth Mabee
Philip Clandon	Christopher Gaze
Mrs Lanfrey Clandon	Mary Savidge
Gloria Clandon	Merrilyn Gann
Fergus Crampton	Gillie Fenwick
Finch M'Comas	Sandy Webster
Waiter	Leslie Yeo
Jo	Jon Comerford
Cook	Garry Hunt
Bohun	Jack Roberts

Directed by Tony van Bridge
Designed by Maxine Graham
Lighting designed by Nick Cernovitch

Stage Manager	Ron Nipper
Assistant Stage Manager	Deborah Osborne

BLITHE SPIRIT by Noel Coward
Court House Theatre
previews June 23 to 27 (matinee), opening June 27 (evening) to September 16
(51 performances)

Edith	Judy Leigh-Johnson
Ruth	Moira Wylie
Charles	Joseph Shaw*
Dr Bradman	Jack Medley**
Mrs Bradman	Jill Frappier
Madame Arcati	Betty Leighton
Elvira	Jackie Burroughs

succeeded by Jack Medley
**succeeded by Michael Franks*

Directed by Leslie Yeo
Designed by Phillip Silver
Lighting designed by Robert Thomson

Stage Manager	Sid Kozak
Assistant Stage Managers	Christina Trunn
	Dianne Woodrow

DEAR LIAR by Jerome Kilty

Festival Theatre, previews May 24 to 29, opening May 31 to June 23, August 12
Court House Theatre, July 1 to August 12 (24 performances)
(including two "Bonus Night" performances at the Court House Theatre,
doubling with "Sneak Previews" of *Village Wooing*)

Mrs Patrick Campbell	Pat Galloway
Bernard Shaw	Colin Fox

Directed by Douglas Campbell
Set designed by Maurice Strike
Costumes designed by Hilary Corbett
Lighting designed by Nick Cernovitch for Festival Theatre
Lighting designed by Robert Thomson for
   Court House Theatre

Stage Manager	Sid Kozak
Assistant Stage Manager	Dianne Woodrow

MARY SAVIDGE AND SANDY WEBSTER IN *YOU NEVER CAN TELL*, 1979 (PHOTO BY ROBERT C. RAGSDALE).

1979

THE CORN IS GREEN by Emlyn Williams
Festival Theatre
previews May 23 to 30, opening June 1 to September 29 (54 performances)

John Goronwy Jones	Eric House
Miss Ronberry	Judy Leigh-Johnson
Idwal Morris	Peggy Coffey
Sarah Pugh	Betty Gable
Old Tom	Michael Franks
The Squire	Tony van Bridge
Mrs Watty	Betty Leighton
Bessie Watty	Mary Haney
Miss Moffat	Mary Savidge
Robbart Robbatch	Christopher Barry
Morgan Evans	Peter Hutt
Glyn Thomas	Geraint Wyn Davies
John Owen	David Nairn
Will Hughes	Kelly Fiddick
Villagers	Heidi Thompson, Jon Comerford, David Eden, Elizabeth Mabee

Directed by Leslie Yeo
Set designed by Maurice Strike
Costumes designed by Hilary Corbett
Lighting designed by Nick Cernovitch

Stage Manager	Sandra Robinson
Assistant Stage Manager	Deborah Osborne

CAPTAIN BRASSBOUND'S CONVERSION by Bernard Shaw
Festival Theatre
previews July 11 (matinee and evening), opening July 12 to September 30
(38 performances)

Lady Cicely Waynflete	Pat Galloway
Sir Howard Hallam	Tony van Bridge
Captain Brassbound	Peter Jobin
Rankin	Gillie Fenwick
Drinkwater	Eric House
Redbrook	Christopher Gaze
Johnson	Jack Roberts
Marzo	Don Keppy
Sidi el Assif	Vikén Vartanian
The Cadi	Sandy Webster
Osman	Peter Hutt
Hassan	Garry Hunt
Krooboys	Christopher Barry, David Nairn
American Bluejacket	Garry Hunt
Captain Hamlin Kearney, U.S.N.	James Valentine
Chaplain to the Saratoga	Sandy Webster

First Officer	Peter Hutt
Captain Brassbound's Crew	Christopher Barry, Jon Comerford, David Eden, Kelly Fiddick, David Nairn, Geraint Wyn Davies
Muley	Peggy Coffey
Arabs, American Officers, and Marines	Christopher Crumb, Levi de Jonge, Gary MacLeod, Larry Mannell, Kirk McMahon, Graeme S. Thomson
Arab followers of Sidi el Assif	David Ballet, Robert Cleaver
Arab followers of Cadi of Kintafi	Christopher Crumb, Levi de Jonge, Ron MacIntyre, Gary McLeod, Larry Mannell, Kirk McMahon, Pierre Oliver, Graeme S. Thomson

Directed by Douglas Campbell
Sets designed by Michael Eagan
Costumes designed by Astrid Janson
Lighting designed by Robert Thomson

Stage Manager	Sandra Robinson
Assistant Stage Manager	Deborah Osborne

MY ASTONISHING SELF:
an entertainment devised by Michael Voysey from the writings of GBS
Court House Theatre
previews June 23 to 26, opening June 28 to September 14 (24 performances)

Bernard Shaw	Donal Donnelly

Set designed by Phillip Silver
Lighting designed by Robert Thomson

Stage Manager	Christina Trunn

Three performances were "Bonus Nights," doubling with *Village Wooing*.

VILLAGE WOOING by Bernard Shaw
Court House Theatre, July 12 to September 1 (29 Lunchtime performances)
(preceded by two "sneak previews" following performances of *Dear Liar*)

"A"	Jack Medley
"Z"	Merrilyn Gann

Directed by Scott Swan
Designed by Phillip Silver
Lighting designed by Robert Thomson

Stage Manager	Christina Trunn

1979

Special Events

June 24:   John Cairney as Robert Burns. Festival Theatre

August 26:   Irving Layton, poet, reading excerpts from his
                  anthology of love poems, *Droppings from Heaven*.
                  Court House Theatre

September 9:   Tony van Bridge in *G.K.C.: The Wit and Wisdom
                  of Gilbert Keith Chesterton*. Festival Theatre

Post-season Tour

BLITHE SPIRIT (41 performances)
(one performance in each city, except as noted):

Hamilton Place, Hamilton, September 18 to 19 (3 performances)
Corning Glass Center, Corning, NY, September 20
Nazareth Arts Center, Rochester, NY, September 21 to 22 (2 performances)
Waterman Theatre, State University College, Oswego, NY, September 25
Grand Theatre, Kingston, September 27 to 29 (5 performances)
Nuttsville Hall, St Lawrence College, Cornwall, September 30
Civic Auditorium, Brockville, October 1
War Memorial Hall, University of Guelph, Guelph, October 2
West Ferris Secondary School, North Bay, October 3
White Pines Auditorium, Sault St Marie, October 4
Elliot Lake Secondary School, Elliot Lake, October 6
Parry Sound High School, Parry Sound, October 7
Bernard Childs Auditorium, Deep River, October 9
Centennial Secondary School, Belleville, October 10
Waterloo Arts Centre, Kitchener, October 11
Alumni Hall, University of Western Ontario, London, October 12
Thames Arts Centre, Chatham, October 13
Collegiate Institute East, Cobourg, October 14
Théâtre Maisonneuve, Montreal, October 16 to 21 (8 performances)
Shaw Festival Theatre, Niagara-on-the-Lake, October 24 to 28 (8 performances)

              For these productions:

              Stage Manager   Sid Kozak
              Assistant Stage Manager   Dianne Woodrow

1980

NINETEENTH SEASON
May 6 to October 5 (470 performances)

MISALLIANCE by Bernard Shaw
Festival Theatre
previews from May 6, opening May 28 to October 5 (68 performances)

Johnny Tarleton	Peter Hutt
Bentley Summerhays	James Rankin
Hypatia Tarleton	Deborah Kipp
Mrs Tarleton	Marion Gilsenan
Lord Summerhays	David Dodimead
John Tarleton, Sr	Sandy Webster
Joseph Percival	Geraint Wyn Davies
Lina Szczepanowska	Carole Shelley
Julius Baker ("Gunner")	Andrew Gillies

Directed by Christopher Newton
Designed by Cameron Porteous
Lighting designed by Jeffrey Dallas

Stage Manager	Don Thomas
Assistant Stage Manager	John Tiggeloven

CAROLE SHELLEY AND SANDY WEBSTER (LEFT) IN *MISALLIANCE*, 1980 (PHOTO BY DAVID COOPER).

1980

THE CHERRY ORCHARD by Anton Chekhov
Festival Theatre
previews from May 7, opening May 29 to August 10 (36 performances)

Mme Ranevsky	Carole Shelley
Anya	Martha Burns
Varya	Deborah Kipp
Gayev	David Dodimead
Lopakhin	Terence Kelly
Trofimov	Heath Lamberts
Simeonov-Pischik	Sandy Webster
Charlotte Ivanovna	Irene Hogan
Epikhodov	Andrew Gillies
Dunyasha	Mary Haney
Firs	Gillie Fenwick
Yasha	Jim Mezon
A Passer-by	Ronn Sarosiak
Stationmaster	Ronn Sarosiak
Postal Clerk	James Rankin
Servants	Maurice Godin, James Rankin, Ronn Sarosiak
Party-goers	Marion Gilsenan, Maurice Godin, Ronn Sarosiak

Directed by Radu Penciulescu
Designed by Astrid Janson
Lighting designed by Jeffrey Dallas

Stage Manager	Sandra Robinson
Assistant Stage Manager	John Tiggeloven

THE PHILANDERER by Bernard Shaw
Court House Theatre
preview June 24, opening June 26 to October 5 (64 performances)

Leonard Charteris	Christopher Newton
Grace Tranfield	Susan Wright
Julia Craven	Dana Ivey
Joseph Cuthbertson	David Renton
Colonel Daniel Craven	Jack Medley
Dr Percival Paramore	Michael Fawkes
Sylvia Craven	Francine Volker
Page	Jeremy Henson

Directed by Paul Reynolds
Designed by Guido Tondino
Lighting designed by Jeffrey Dallas

Stage Manager	Catherine Russell
Assistant Stage Manager	Susan Monis

A FLEA IN HER EAR by Georges Feydeau
Festival Theatre
previews from May 20, opening May 30 to October 5 (59 performances)

Camille Chandebise	Christopher Newton*
Antoinette Plucheux	Mary Haney
Etienne Plucheux	Gillie Fenwick
Dr Finache	Jack Medley
Lucienne Homenides de Histangua	Dana Ivey
Raymonde Chandebise	Susan Wright
Victor Emmanuel Chandebise	Heath Lamberts
Romain Tournel	Jim Mezon
Carlos Homenides de Histangua	Michael Fawkes
Eugénie	Martha Burns**
Augustin Feraillon	Terence Kelly
Olympe	Irene Hogan
Baptistin	Barney O'Sullivan
Herr Schwarz	David Renton
Poche	Heath Lamberts
Guests	Maurice Godin, Robin Harvey, Jeremy Henson, Jean McNeil, Ronn Sarosiak

replaced twice weekly from August 5 by Jeremy Henson
**replaced at one performance by Jean McNeil*

Directed by Derek Goldby
Designed by Cameron Porteous
Lighting designed by Jeffrey Dallas

Stage Managers	Catherine Russell
	Sandra Robinson (after August 27)
Assistant Stage Manager	Susan Monis

OVERRULED by Bernard Shaw
Court House Theatre
preview July 15, opening July 17 to August 31 (33 Lunchtime performances)

Mrs Juno	Susan Cox
Mr Lunn	Hayward Morse*
Waiter	Maurice Godin
Mr Juno	Leon Pownall
Mrs Lunn	Nora McLellan

succeeded by Brian Tree on August 6

Directed by Paul Reynolds
Designed by Guido Tondino
Lighting designed by Jeffrey Dallas

Stage Managers	Sandra Robinson
	Dianne Woodrow

1980

PUTTIN' ON THE RITZ: *the music and lyrics of Irving Berlin*
Royal George Theatre
preview June 24, opening June 25 to October 5 (101 performances)

Barbara Barsky*
Sheila McCarthy
Marek Norman**
Claude Tessier***

succeeded by Linda Third on July 14
**succeeded by Terry Harford on July 21*
***succeeded by Calvin McRae on July 21*

Directed by Don Shipley
Designed by Ken McDonald
Lighting designed by Jeffrey Dallas
Choreography by Judith Marcuse
Musical direction by Joan Beckow
Assistant Musical Director: Christopher Donison
Musicians: Christopher Donison (piano),
Richard Griffo (saxophone and clarinet)

Stage Manager   Winston Morgan

A RESPECTABLE WEDDING by Bertolt Brecht
translated by Jean Benedetti

Court House Theatre
preview June 25, opening June 27 to October 5 (50 performances)

Mother	Susan Cox
Young Man	Geraint Wyn Davies
Wife	Diane Douglass
Friend	Peter Hutt
Husband	Al Kozlik
Bride	Nora McLellan
Father	Leon Pownall
Sister	Francine Volker
Groom	Joe Ziegler

Directed by Derek Goldby
Designed by Guido Tondino
Lighting designed by Jeffrey Dallas

Stage Manager   Dianne Woodrow
Assistant Stage Manager   Carolyn Mackenzie

CANUCK by John Bruce Cowan
Court House Theatre
preview August 13, opening August 14 to October 3 (15 performances)

Terence Ormsby-Grey	James Rankin
Paul Ecclestone	Joe Ziegler
Ruth Ormsby-Grey	Mary Haney
Christine the maid	Robin Harvey
Richard Grey	Barney O'Sullivan
Geoffrey Ormsby-Grey	John Gardiner
Megan Ormsby-Grey	Martha Burns
Beverley Reginald Alward	Geraint Wyn Davies
Clare Ormsby-Grey	Marion Gilsenan

Directed by Christopher Newton
Designed by Guido Tondino
Lighting designed by Jeffrey Dallas

Stage Manager	Dianne Woodrow
Assistant Stage Manager	Carolyn Mackenzie

THE GRAND HUNT by Gyula Hernády
adapted by Suzanne Grossmann

Festival Theatre
preview August 14, opening August 15 to October 4 (15 performances)

Istvan Rakovszky	Gillie Fenwick
Gustav Gratz	Sandy Webster
Colonel Antal Lehar	Al Kozlik
Lieutenant Stefan Elias	Andrew Gillies
Captain Gabor Primasz	Terence Kelly
Count Paul Erdody	Roland Hewgill
The Butler (Lieutenant	
Sandor Boross)	Peter Hutt
Woman	Carole Shelley
Man	Jan Triska
Guards	Ronn Sarosiak,
	Maurice Godin
Lieutenant Geza Ruppert	Jim Mezon
George Schrei	Karel Behavy
Eva Aldoboi	Ilona Schota

Directed by John Hirsch
Designed by Cameron Porteous
Lighting designed by Jeffrey Dallas

Stage Manager	Don Thomas
Assistant Stage Manager	John Tiggeloven

1980

GUNGA HEATH: compiled and performed by Heath Lamberts
Royal George Theatre, opening August 13 to October 5 (26 performances)

> Directorial assistance from Paul Reynolds
> Designed by Cameron Porteous
> Lighting designed by Jeffrey Dallas

Stage Manager   Allan Meuse

MIRRORS, MASQUES AND TRANSFORMATIONS
(a dance production)

Festival Theatre, September 5 to 7 (3 performances)

Company	Peggy Smith Baker, Sacha Bélin, David Brown, Pattie Caplette, John Kaminski, James Kudelka, Judith Marcuse, Claudia Moore
Woman whose day it is	Sheila McCarthy
Musicians	Don Englert, David Keeble, Robert Occhipinti, Rick Skol
Composers	David Jaggs, Terry Crack, Michael Baker, Gary Marcuse, Judith Marcuse, David Keeble, Rick Skol

> Conceived and choreographed by Judith Marcuse
> Designed by Cameron Porteous and Judith Marcuse
> Lighting designed by Jeffrey Dallas

Stage Manager   Mark Hammond

Post-season Tour

THE GRAND HUNT
National Arts Centre, Ottawa, October 6 to 25 (23 performances)
Seattle Repertory Theatre, Seattle, Washington, November 26 to December 21
(31 performances)

> For the tour Jack Medley appeared as Gustav Gratz.

1981

TWENTIETH SEASON
May 7 to October 4 (462 performances)

THE SUICIDE by Nikolai Erdman
Festival Theatre
previews from May 21, opening May 28 to August 2 (28 performances)

Semyon Semyonovich Podsekalnikov	Andrew Gillies
Maria Lukianivna (Masha)	Robin Craig
Serafima Ilyinichna	Irene Hogan
Alexander Petrovich Kalabushkin	Michael Ball
Margarita Ivanovna	Araby Lockhart
Aristarkh Dominikovich Grand-Skubnik	Leon Pownall
Cleopatra Maximovna	Marion Gilsenan
Igor, a mailman	Stephen Ouimette
Nikifor Pugachev	Michael Fawkes
Victor Victorivich	Al Kozlik
Raisa Filipovna	Wendy Thatcher
Alexander's nephew	Bill Gibbs
Kostya, a waiter	Christopher Newton
A Seamstress	Dianne Sokoluk
A Priest	Joseph Ziegler
An Old Woman	Rita Tuckett
Faceless Proletariat	Paul Eves
Guests and Mourners	Peter Krantz, Duncan McIntosh, Elizabeth Christmas

Directed by Stephen Katz
Designed by Cameron Porteous
Lighting designed by Nick Cernovitch

Stage Manager	Dianne Woodrow
Assistant Stage Manager	Martha Campbell

1981

SAINT JOAN by Bernard Shaw
Festival Theatre
previews from May 7, opening May 27 to October 4 (69 performances)

Robert de Baudricourt	William Webster
The Steward	Al Kozlik
Joan	Nora McLellan
Bertrand de Poulengy	Stephen Ouimette
Archbishop of Rheims	Jack Medley
Duc de la Trémouille	Richard Farrell
Page to Charles VII	Dan Lett
Gilles de Rais	James Rankin
Captain La Hire	John Lefebvre
The Dauphin, Charles VII	Heath Lamberts
Duchesse de la Trémouille	Dianne Sokoluk
Dunois	Peter Dvorsky
Page to Dunois	Duncan McIntosh
Earl of Warwick	Robert Benson
John de Stogumber	Barry MacGregor
Peter Cauchon	David Hemblen
Page to Warwick	Paul Eves
Sergeant at Arms	Andrew Lewarne
The Inquisitor	Herbert Foster*
Brother Martin	Tom McCamus
D'Estivet	Stephen Ouimette
De Courcelles	William Webster
Executioner	Keith James
English Soldier	Richard Farrell
English Gentleman	John Lefebvre
Duc de Vendome	Peter Krantz
Ladies in Waiting	Elizabeth Christmas, Dianne Sokoluk
Page / Monk	Andrew Lewarne

succeeded by Allen Doremus on September 10

Directed by Christopher Newton
Designed by Cameron Porteous
Lighting designed by Jeffrey Dallas
Music by Allan Rae

Stage Manager	Ron Nipper
Assistant Stage Manager	Carolyn Mackenzie

TONS OF MONEY by Will Evans and Valentine
Festival Theatre
previews from May 9, opening May 29 to October 4 (80 performances)

Sprules	Barry MacGregor
Simpson	Fiona McMurran
Benita Mullett	Araby Lockhart
Louise Allington	Robin Craig

Aubrey Allington	Heath Lamberts
Giles	Charles Palmer
James Chesterman	Jack Medley
Jean Everard	Wendy Thatcher
Henery	Andrew Gillies
George Mitland	Peter Dvorsky

Directed by Derek Goldby
Designed by Guido Tondino
Lighting designed by Nick Cernovitch

Stage Manager	Donald K. Thomas
Assistant Stage Manager	Susan Monis

CAMILLE by Robert David MacDonald

Festival Theatre
previews from August 11, opening August 14 to October 3 (23 performances)

Monsieur Mephisto	Andrew Gillies
Gaston Rival	David Schurmann
Vassili	Christopher Newton
Grand Duke	Al Kozlik
Prudence Duvernoy	Irene Hogan
Olympe	Marion Gilsenan
Atalante	Fiona McMurran
Doctor Korev	Michael Fawkes
Violetta Valery	Robin Craig
Alfredo Germont	William Webster
Marguerite Gautier	Jocelyn Cunningham
Armand Duval	Peter Krantz
Marie Duplessis (Camille)	Goldie Semple
Cupidon	Duncan McIntosh
Alexandre Dumas	Joseph Ziegler
Claude de Mauxcroizay	Stephen Ouimette
Baron de Varville	Michael Ball
M. Duval	Leon Pownall
Giorgio Germont	Al Kozlik
Vicomte	Paul Eves
Cora Pearl	Dianne Sokoluk
Blanche d'Antigny	Elizabeth Christmas
Paul Murat	Brad Berg

Directed by Christopher Newton
Assisted by Paul Reynolds
Designed by Cameron Porteous
Lighting designed by Jeffrey Dallas

Stage Manager	Don Thomas
Assistant Stage Manager	Susan Monis

1981

ROSE MARIE
music by Rudolf Friml and Herbert Stothart
book and lyrics by Otto Harbach and Oscar Hammerstein II
adapted by Paula Sperdakos

Royal George Theatre
previews from June 26, opening July 8 to October 4 (120 performances)

Rose Marie	Beth Anne Cole
Jim Kenyon	Michael James
Sergeant "Bulldog" Malone	Rod Campbell
Edward Hawley	Barry Stilwell
Wanda	Theresa Tove
"Lady" Jane	Carol Forte
Black Eagle	Lawrence Phillips
Emile LaFlamme	Peter Zednik

Directed by Paula Sperdakos
Designed by Guido Tondino
Lighting designed by Donald Finlayson
Choreography by Robert Ainslie
Musical direction by Noreen Waibel

Stage Manager	Winston Morgan
Assistant Stage Manager	Martha Campbell

IN GOOD KING CHARLES'S GOLDEN DAYS by Bernard Shaw
Court House Theatre
previews from July 4, opening July 9 to September 20 (52 performances)

Mrs Basham	Irene Hogan
Maid (Sally)	Jean McNeil
Isaac Newton	Joseph Ziegler
George Fox	Michael Ball
King Charles II ("Mr Rowley")	Michael Fawkes
Nell Gwyn	Goldie Semple
Barbara Villiers, Duchess	
of Cleveland	Marion Gilsenan
Louise de Kéroualle	Jocelyn Cunningham
James, Duke of York	David Schurmann
Godfrey Kneller	Peter Donaldson
Catherine de Braganza	Jane Casson

Directed by Paul Bettis
Designed by Peter Wingate
Lighting designed by Jeffrey Dallas

Stage Manager	Ken Smith
Assistant Stage Manager	Terry Ingram

THE MAGISTRATE by Arthur W. Pinero
Court House Theatre
previews from July 5, opening July 10 to September 19 (49 performances)

Beatie Tomlinson	Camille Mitchell
Cis Farringdon	James Rankin
Wyke	David Hemblen
Popham	Jean McNeil
Agatha Posket	Jane Casson
Mr Posket	Robert Benson
Mr Bullamy	Allen Doremus
Charlotte Verrinder	Nora McLellan
Isidore	Andrew Lewarne
Achille Blond	Herbert Foster*
Colonel Lukyn	Richard Farrell
Captain Horace Vale	Keith James
Inspector Messiter	John Lefebvre
Constable Harris	Dan Lett
Sergeant Lugg	William Webster**
Mr Wormington	Larry Aubrey

*succeeded by Tom McCamus from September 9
**succeeded by Jay Macdonald from July 28

Directed by Derek Goldby
Designed by Peter Wingate
Lighting designed by Jeffrey Dallas

Stage Manager	Ron Nipper
Assistant Stage Manager	Carolyn Mackenzie

THE MAN OF DESTINY by Bernard Shaw
Royal George Theatre
previews from July 14, opening July 16 to September 6 (41 Lunchtime performances)

Napoleon	Tom McCamus
Giuseppe Grandi	Leon Pownall
The Lieutenant	Peter Donaldson
The Lady	Camille Mitchell

Directed by Paul Reynolds
Designed by Cameron Porteous
Lighting designed by Donald Finlayson

Stage Manager	Dianne Woodrow
Assistant Stage Manager	Martha Campbell

Special Event

Festival Theatre, August 27 to 29 (3 performances)

Les Ballets Jazz, Artistic director: Genevieve Salbaing

ANDREW GILLIES, TOM MCCAMUS, GOLDIE SEMPLE, DAN LETT, SUSAN COX, AND IRENE HOGAN IN *CAMILLE*, 1982 (PHOTO BY DAVID COOPER).

Post-season

BILLY BISHOP GOES TO WAR by John Gray and Eric Peterson
Festival Theatre, October 6 to 10 (6 performances)

A production of Vancouver East Cultural Centre

all portrayed by Cedric Smith

> Narrator and Pianist: Ross Douglas
> Directed by John Gray
> Designed by David Gropman
> Lighting designed by Bill Williams

1982

TWENTY-FIRST SEASON

May 5 to September 26 (496 performances)

CAMILLE by Robert David MacDonald
Festival Theatre
previews from May 21, opening May 27 to August 1 (34 performances)

Marie Duplessis (Camille)	Goldie Semple
Marguerite Gauthier	Shelley Thompson
Violetta Valery	Robin Craig
Alexandre Dumas	Joseph Ziegler
Armand Duval	Peter Krantz
Alfredo Germont	Herb Foster
M. Duval	Robert Benson
Giorgio Germont	Al Kozlik
Prudence Duvernoy	Irene Hogan
Olympe	Susan Cox
Atalante Causarescu	Nicola Cavendish
Dr Korev	Michael Fawkes
Baron de Varville	Michael Ball
Grand Duke	Al Kozlik
Vassili	Christopher Newton
Gaston Rival	David Schurmann
Cupidon	Duncan McIntosh
Monsieur Mephisto	Andrew Gillies
Claude de Mauxcroizay	Dan Lett
Cora Pearl	Nancy Kerr
Blanche d'Antigny	Lois Lorimer
Le Vicomte	Tom McCamus
Paul Murat	Andrew Lewarne

Directed by Christopher Newton
Assistant director: Paul Reynolds
Designed by Cameron Porteous
Lighting designed by Jeffrey Dallas

Stage Manager	Don Thomas
Assistant Stage Manager	Terry Ingram

PYGMALION by Bernard Shaw

Festival Theatre
previews from May 5, opening May 26 to September 26 (65 performances)

G.B.S.	Herb Foster
Clara Eynsford Hill	Shelley Thompson
Mrs Eynsford Hill	Nancy Kerr
Sarcastic Bystander	Al Kozlik
Freddy Eynsford Hill	Duncan McIntosh
Eliza Doolittle	Nicola Cavendish
Colonel Pickering	Richard Farrell
Henry Higgins	Barry MacGregor
Alfred Doolittle	Sandy Webster
Mrs Higgins	Frances Hyland
Footman	Andrew Lewarne
The Ambassador's Wife	Nancy Kerr
The Ambassador	Al Kozlik

Directed by Denise Coffey
Designed by Cameron Porteous
Lighting designed by Jeffrey Dallas

Stage Manager	Don Thomas
Assistant Stage Manager	Carolyn Mackenzie

SEE HOW THEY RUN   by Philip King

Festival Theatre
previews from May 12, opening May 28 to September 26 (67 performances)

Ida, a maid	Nora McLellan
Miss Skillon	Jennifer Phipps
Reverend Lionel Toop	Barry MacGregor
Penelope Toop	Robin Craig
Corporal Clive Winton	David Schurmann
The Intruder	Al Kozlik
Bishop of Lax	Richard Farrell
Reverend Arthur Humphrey	Heath Lamberts
Sergeant Towers	Michael Fawkes

Directed by Adrian Brine
Designed by Peter Wingate
Lighting designed by Robert Thomson

Stage Manager	Ron Nipper
Assistant Stage Manager	Martha Campbell

THE DESERT SONG
music by Sigmund Romberg
book and lyrics by Otto Harbach, Oscar Hammerstein II, and Frank Mandel
adapted by Christopher Newton

Royal George Theatre
previews from May 19, opening May 28 to September 26 (148 performances)

Ali ben Ali / General Birabeau / Old Man	Charles Kerr
Sid / Corporal La Vergne	Paul Gatchell
Hassi / Captain Paul Fontaine	Rod Campbell
Mindar / Corporal Beaupré / Guard	Stephen Simms
Red Shadow / Pierre Birabeau	Terry Harford
Bennie	Gerald Isaac
Azuri / Henrietta	Alicia Jeffery
Susan	Jo-Anne Kirwan Clark
Edith / Old Woman	Pamela Kinsman
Margot Bonvalet	Beth Anne Cole

Directed by Christopher Newton
Co-directed and choreographed by Robert Ainslie
Designed by Mary Kerr
Lighting designed by Graeme S. Thomson
Musical directors: Roger Perkins and Christopher Donison

Stage Manager	Alan Wallis
Assistant Stage Manager	Carole Macomber

TOO TRUE TO BE GOOD by Bernard Shaw
Court House Theatre
previews from June 26, opening July 2 to September 18 (55 performances)

The Microbe	Tom McCamus
Miss Mopply	Goldie Semple
Mrs Mopply	Irene Hogan
Doctor	Keith Knight
Susan Simpkins	Wendy Thatcher Leicester
Aubrey Bagot	Andrew Gillies
Colonel Tallboys	Robert Benson
Private Meek	Geoffrey Bowes
Sergeant Fielding	David Hemblen

Directed by Paul Bettis
Designed by Jim Plaxton
Lighting designed by Jeffrey Dallas

Stage Manager	Ken Smith
Assistant Stage Manager	Terry Ingram

THE SINGULAR LIFE OF ALBERT NOBBS: adapted for the stage by Simone Benmussa, from "Albert Nobbs" by George Moore

Court House Theatre
previews from June 29, opening July 1 to September 19 (55 performances)

Voice of George Moore	Richard Farrell
Voice of Alec	Dan Lett
Albert Nobbs	Nora McLellan
Mrs Baker	Jennifer Phipps
Hubert Page	Mary Vingoe
Helen Dawes	Camille Mitchell
Kitty MacCan	Jean McNeil
Maids	Ellen R. McMeekin
	Ann Turnbull

Directed by Christopher Newton
Designed by Cameron Porteous
Lighting designed by Jeffrey Dallas

Stage Manager	Ron Nipper
Assistant Stage Manager	Martha Campbell

THE MUSIC-CURE by Bernard Shaw

Royal George Theatre
previews from June 29, opening July 2 to September 5 (46 Lunchtime performances)

Strega Thundridge	Susan Cox
Lord Reginald Fitzambey	Geraint Wyn Davies
Dr Dawkins	Keith Knight

Directed by Paul Reynolds
Designed by Mary Kerr
Lighting designed by Graeme S. Thomson
Musical direction by David Fleury

Stage Manager	Don Thomas
Assistant Stage Manager	Carolyn Mackenzie

CYRANO DE BERGERAC by Edmond Rostand
translated and adapted by Anthony Burgess

Festival Theatre
previews from August 10, opening August 14 to September 25 (26 performances)

Cyrano	Heath Lamberts
Roxanne	Marti Maraden
Christian de Neuvillette	Geoffrey Bowes
Comte de Guiche	David Hemblen
Le Bret	Joseph Ziegler
Ragueneau	Robert Benson
De Valvert	David Schurmann
Lise	Irene Hogan
Mother Marguérite	Frances Hyland
Duenna	Nancy Kerr

Brissaille	Michael Fawkes
Bellrose	Christopher Newton
Cuigy	Andrew Gillies
Jodelet	Tom McCamus
Montfleury	Keith Knight
Sister Marthe	Nicola Cavendish
Sister Claire	Susan Cox
Grey d'Artagnan	Matt Kerr
A Citizen	Sandy Webster
1st Marquis	Geraint Wyn Davies
2nd Marquis	Ken McAuliffe
Foodseller	Wendy Thatcher Leicester
Amorous Musketeer	Andrew Lewarne
An Actor	Stuart Hughes
A Précieuse	Lois Lorimer
Pickpocket	Dan Lett
Liguière	Stanley Coles
Boy	Duncan McIntosh
Cadets	Jean Daigle, James Humphries, Robert Scott, Peter Krantz
Cooks, Poets, Soldiers, Nuns, Précieuses, Actors, and Apprentices	The Company

Directed by Derek Goldby
Designed by Cameron Porteous
Lighting designed by Robert Thomson
Fights directed by Patrick Crean

Stage Manager	Ken Smith
Assistant Stage Manager	Terry Ingram

67

1982

Special Event
Festival Theatre, August 26 to September 5 (6 performances)
Les Ballets Jazz de Montréal

Post-season Tour
THE DESERT SONG
Ross Hall, Guelph, September 29
Georgian College Theatre, Barrie, September 30
West Ferris Secondary School, North Bay, October 1
Elliot Lake Secondary School, Elliot Lake, October 2
Sheridan Auditorium, Sudbury, October 4
Haileybury School of Mines, Haileybury, October 5
District High School, Kapuskasing, October 6
École Theriault, Timmins, October 7
Whizte Pines Auditorium, Sault Ste Marie, October 9
Prince Edward Collegiate Institute, Picton, October 12
Centennial Secondary School, Belleville, October 13
Perth & District Collegiate Institute, Perth, October 14
Grand Theatre, Kingston, October 15 to16 (2 performances)
Goderich & District Collegiate Institute, Goderich, October 17
Victoria Playhouse, Petrolia, October 19
Chatham Cultural Centre, Chatham, October 20
Talbot College, London, October 21 to 22 (2 performances)
Blyth Memorial Hall, Blyth, October 23 to 24 (2 performances) matinees
Saidye Bronfman Centre, Montreal, October 28 to November 21 (25 performances)

For the tour the roles performed by Stephen Simms and Pamela Kinsman were
deleted, reducing the touring cast to eight. Bill Copeland succeeded to the roles
played at the Royal George Theatre by Charles Kerr. Simms and Kinsman were
restored to the production for the Montreal engagement.

1983

TWENTY-SECOND SEASON
May 4 to October 2 (526 performances)

ROOKERY NOOK by Ben Travers
Festival Theatre
previews from May 18, opening May 27 to July 31 (44 performances)

Gertrude Twine	Nicola Cavendish
Mrs Leverett	Irene Hogan
Harold Twine	Jack Medley
Clive Fitzwatters	Jim Mezon
Augustus Popkiss	Heath Lamberts
Rhoda Marley	Camille Mitchell
Putz	Michael Ball
Admiral Juddy	Sandy Webster
Poppy Dickey	Mary Ellen Maguire
Clara Popkiss	Lois Lorimer
Mrs Possett	Rita Tuckett
Conrad	Caesar Polischuk

Directed by Derek Goldby
Designed by Peter Wingate
Lighting designed by Robert Thomson

Stage Manager	Dianne Woodrow
Assistant Stage Manager	Janet Kennedy

PRIVATE LIVES by Noel Coward
Festival Theatre
previews from August 7, opening August 12 to October 2 (35 performances)

Sybil Chase	Nicola Cavendish
Elyot Chase	Christopher Newton
Victor Prynne	Jim Mezon
Amanda Prynne	Fiona Reid
Louise, a maid	Lois Lorimer

Directed by Denise Coffey
Designed by Mary Kerr
Lighting designed by Jeffrey Dallas

Stage Manager	Ken A. Smith
Assistant Stage Manager	Janet Kennedy

1983

CYRANO DE BERGERAC by Edmond Rostand
translated and adapted by Anthony Burgess

Festival Theatre
previews from May 4, opening May 26 to October 2 (65 performances)

Cyrano	Heath Lamberts
Roxanne	Marti Maraden
Christian de Neuvillette	Geoffrey Bowes
Comte de Guiche	David Hemblen
Le Bret	Rodger Barton
Ragueneau	Robert Benson
De Valvert	Peter Krantz
Lise / Mother Marguerite	Irene Hogan
Duenna	Diane Douglass
Brissaille	Hugo Dann
Bellrose	Christopher Newton
Cuigy	Jack Medley
Jodelet	Tom McCamus
Montfleury	Keith Knight
Sister Marthe	Nicola Cavendish
Sister Claire	Camille Mitchell
Grey d'Artagnan	Christopher Thomas
A Citizen / Bertrandou	John Gilbert
1st Marquis	Peter Keleghan
2nd Marquis	Ken McAuliffe
Foodseller	Mary Ellen Maguire
Amorous Musketeer	Andrew Lewarne
An Actor	Stuart Hughes
A Précieuse	Lois Lorimer
Pickpocket	Dan Lett
Liguière / Richelieu	Al Kozlik
Boy	Duncan McIntosh
Nun / Précieuse	Tracy Bell
Ragamuffin	Leonard Chow
Cadets	Carl Marotte, Richard Rebiere, Peter Krantz, Andrew Lewarne, Tom McCamus, Christopher Thomas, Peter Keleghan
Doorkeeper	Craig Walker
Cooks, Poets, Soldiers, Nuns, Précieuses, Actors, and Apprentices	The Company

Directed by Derek Goldby
Designed by Cameron Porteous
Lighting designed by Robert Thomson
Fights directed by Patrick Crean

Fight Captain: Peter Krantz
Mime: Harro Maskow
Original music by Roger Perkins

Stage Manager	Ken A. Smith
Assistant Stage Manager	Terry Ingram

CAESAR AND CLEOPATRA by Bernard Shaw

Festival Theatre
previews from May 11, opening May 25 to October 1 (62 performances)

Caesar	Douglas Rain
Cleopatra	Marti Maraden
Nubian Slave / Courtier	David Collins
Ftatateeta	Diane Douglass
Charmian	Susan Stackhouse
Iras	Brigit Wilson
Harpist / Courtier	Tracy Bell
Rufio	David Hemblen
Centurion	Christopher Thomas
Roman Soldier / Porter	Richard Rebiere
Roman Soldier	Peter Keleghan
Roman Soldier / Court Official	Dan Lett
Roman Soldier	Carl Marotte
Roman Soldier	Craig Walker
Sentinel	Stuart Hughes
Courtier / Votary	Leonard Chow
Pothinus	Robert Benson
Ptolemy / Courtier	Duncan McIntosh
Theodotus	Al Kozlik
Achillas	David Schurmann
Britannus	Herb Foster
Lucius Septimius	Rodger Barton
Apollodorus	Geoffrey Bowes
Courtier / First Porter	Ken McAuliffe
Boatman / Courtier	Keith Knight
Musician / Porter	Andrew Lewarne
Major Domo	John Gilbert
Bel Affris	Peter Krantz
The Persian	Tom McCamus
Belzanor	Hugo Dann

Directed by Christopher Newton
Designed by Cameron Porteous
Lighting designed by Jeffrey Dallas
Fight staged by Peter Krantz

Stage Manager	Ron Nipper
Assistant Stage Manager	Carolyn Mackenzie

71

TOM JONES: an operetta by Sir Edward German
libretto by Robert Courtneidge and A.M. Thompson,
from the novel by Henry Fielding
lyrics by Charles H. Taylor and Basil Hood
libretto and lyrics adapted by Christopher Newton and Sky Gilbert

Royal George Theatre
previews from May 18, opening May 27 to October 2 (152 performances)

Molly / Mrs Waters	Jo-Anne Kirwan Clark
Mr Allworthy / Soldier / Gregory / Partridge	Rod Campbell
Dr Thwackum / Sedan Servant /Major Fitzpatrick	John MacMaster
Blifil / Soldier / Jake / Turnkey /Sedan Servant	Stephen Simms
Miss Western / Landlady / Lady Bellaston	Nancy Kerr
Squire Western	Allen Stewart-Coates
Honour / Mrs Fitzpatrick	Linda Eyman-Johnson
Tom Jones	Bruce Clayton
Sophia Western	Valerie Galvin
Keyboards	Roger Perkins, Christopher Donison

Directed by Christopher Newton
Co-directed and choreographed by Robert Ainslie
Designed by Peter Wingate
Lighting designed by Jeffrey Dallas
Musical direction by Roger Perkins
Fight staged by Patrick Crean

Stage Manager	Alan Wallis
Assistant Stage Manager	Carole Macomber

THE SIMPLETON OF THE UNEXPECTED ISLES by Bernard Shaw
Court House Theatre
previews from June 25, opening June 30 to September 18 (52 performances)

Hugo Hyering (Emigration Officer)	David Schurmann
Wilks	Douglas Rain
Young Woman (Mrs Hyering)	Nora McLellan
Pra, a priest	Herb Foster
Prola, a priestess	Frances Hyland
Lady Farwaters	Joyce Campion
Sir Charles Farwaters	Richard Farrell
Reverend Phosphor Hammingtap	Tom Wood
Maya	Brigit Wilson
Vashti	Susan Stackhouse

Kanchin	James Millan
Janga	David Collins
The Angel	Douglas Rain

Directed by Denise Coffey
Designed by Cameron Porteous
Lighting designed by Bill Williams

| Stage Manager | Ron Nipper |
| Assistant Stage Manager | Carolyn Mackenzie |

CANDIDA by Bernard Shaw
Court House Theatre
previews from June 26, opening July 1 to September 18 (59 performances)

Proserpine Garnett	Nora McLellan
Reverend James Mavor Morell	Michael Ball
Reverend Alexander Mill	Jim Mezon
Mr Burgess	Sandy Webster
Candida Morell	Goldie Semple
Eugene Marchbanks	Geraint Wyn Davies

Directed by Bill Glassco
Designed by Astrid Janson
Lighting designed by Bill Williams

| Stage Manager | Dianne Woodrow |
| Assistant Stage Manager | Janet Kennedy |

A joint production with Bastion Theatre, Victoria, B.C.

O'FLAHERTY, V.C. by Bernard Shaw
Royal George Theatre
previews from June 28, opening July 1 to September 18 (49 Lunchtime performances)

O'Flaherty, V.C.	Dan Lett
Mrs O'Flaherty	Joyce Campion
Sir Pearce	Richard Farrell
Teresa	Mary Ellen Maguire

Directed by Paul Reynolds
Designed by Peter Wingate
Lighting designed by Jeffrey Dallas

| Stage Manager | Terry Ingram |

1983

THE VORTEX by Noel Coward
Court House Theatre, opening August 21 to September 2 (5 performances)

Preston	Brigit Wilson
Helen Saville	Goldie Semple
Pauncefort Quentin	Herb Foster
Clara Hibbert	Camille Mitchell
Florence Lanchester	Frances Hyland
Tom Veryan	Peter Krantz
Nicky Lanchester	Geraint Wyn Davies
David Lanchester	Robert Benson
Bunty Mainwaring	Susan Stackhouse
Bruce Fairlight	Tom McCamus

Directed by David Hemblen
Designed by Diz Marsh
Lighting designed by Jeffrey Dallas (uncredited)
Assistant Director and Choreographer Duncan McIntosh

Stage Manager	Dianne Woodrow
Assistant Stage Manager	Christopher Brown

Special Events

July 11 — Patrick Crean in THE SUN NEVER SETS
Court House Theatre

a one-man show based on the works of Rudyard Kipling, directed by Powys Thomas.

July 21 and 23 — GBS IN LOVE, a dramatic narrative
First performance in the Royal George Theatre.
Second performance in the Court House Theatre.

devised and performed by Dan H. Laurence, from the correspondence of Bernard Shaw and Alice Lockett.

Musical Mondays, Court House Theatre

July 18 — Accordes (quintet)
July 25 — Marc Widner
August 8 — Tim Brady Ensemble
August 15 — Claude Ranger Sextet

Post-season Tours

TOM JONES (21 performances)
Ross Hall, Guelph, October 5
Georgian College Theatre, Barrie, October 6 to 7
Capitol Theatre, North Bay, October 8

74

White Pines Auditorium, Sault Ste Marie, October 9
Ecole Theriault, Timmins, October 11
Northern College Auditorium, Kirkland Lake, October 12
F.W. Sheridan Auditorium, Sudbury, October 13
Bernard Childs Auditorium, Deep River, October 14
Perth District Collegiate Institute, Perth, October 15
Grand Theatre, Kingston, October 16 to 17
Centennial Auditorium, Belleville, October 19
Orillia Opera House, Orillia, October 20
Port Perry Town Hall, Port Perry, October 21
Oakville Centre, Oakville, October 22 to 23
Centre for the Arts, Waterloo, October 25
Victoria Playhouse, Petrolia, October 26
Althouse College, University of Western Ontario, London, October 27
Chatham Cultural Centre, Chatham, October 28

For the tour Sandy Winsby succeeded John MacMaster, Richard Farrell
succeeded Allen Stewart-Coates.

CANDIDA
Bastion Theatre, Victoria, B.C., October 6 to 29 (23 performances)

HERB FOSTER, DOUGLAS RAIN, AND MARTI MARADEN IN *CAESAR AND CLEOPATRA*, 1983 (PHOTO BY DAVID COOPER).

1984

TWENTY-THIRD SEASON

May 2 to October 14 (546 performances)

THE DEVIL'S DISCIPLE by Bernard Shaw
Festival Theatre
previews from May 9, opening May 23 to October 7 (64 performances)

Mrs Dudgeon	Jennifer Phipps
Essie	Brenda Robins
Christopher Dudgeon	Peter Krantz
Reverend Anthony Anderson	Michael Ball
Judith Anderson	Camille Mitchell
Mrs Titus Dudgeon	Susan Stackhouse
Mrs William Dudgeon	Joyce Campion
William Dudgeon	Richard Farrell
Titus Dudgeon	John Gilbert
Lawyer Hawkins	Al Kozlik
Richard Dudgeon	Jim Mezon
Officer	Ken McAuliffe
Soldiers	Hume Baugh, Stephen Black, David Blacker, Jim Jones
Sergeant	Geraint Wyn Davies
Officer	John MacKenzie
Major Swindon	David Schurmann
General Burgoyne	David Hemblen
Officers	Richard Farrell, John Gilbert
Townspeople	Joyce Campion, Richard Farrell, Lorena Gale, John Gilbert, Alison Lawrence, Lois Lorimer, Susan Stackhouse
Reverend Brudenell	Allan Gray

Directed by Larry Lillo
Designed by Cameron Porteous
Lighting designed by Robert Thomson

Stage Manager	Ron Nipper
Assistant Stage Manager	Janet Kennedy

76

CÉLIMARE or FRIENDS OF A FEATHER by Eugène Labiche
adapted by Allan Stratton

Festival Theatre
previews from August 12, opening August 17 to October 14 (50 performances)

Decorators	Hume Baugh, John MacKenzie
Adeline	Alison Lawrence
Pitois	Norman Browning
M. Colombot	Michael Ball
Paul Célimare	Tom Wood
Vernouillet	Richard Farrell
M. Bocardon	Barry MacGregor
Madame Colombot	Irene Hogan
Emma Colombot	Brenda Robins
Madame Bocardon	Dorothy Thistle*

* This was a company jest, as Madame Bocardon is a non-appearing character. "Dorothy Thistle" was the pseudonym adopted by Nancy Kerr in the same season for her role as Minnie Roberts in *Roberta*.

Directed by Wendy Toye
Designed by Cameron Porteous
Lighting designed by Robert Thomson
Original music by Roger Perkins
Lyrics by Allan Stratton

Stage Manager	Ken A. Smith
Assistant Stage Manager	Martha Campbell

THE VORTEX by Noel Coward
Court House Theatre
previews from June 30, opening July 6 to September 23 (50 performances)

Preston	Jackie Samuda
Helen Saville	Goldie Semple
Pauncefort Quentin	David Schurmann
Clara Hibbert	Wendy Thatcher
Florence Lanchester	Frances Hyland
Tom Veryan	Peter Krantz
Nicky Lanchester	Geraint Wyn Davies
David Lanchester	John Gilbert
Bunty Mainwaring	Susan Stackhouse
Bruce Fairlight	Allan Gray

Directed by David Hemblen
Designed by Diz Marsh
Lighting designed by Jeffrey Dallas
Assistant Director and Choreographer: Duncan McIntosh

Stage Manager	Ron Nipper
Assistant Stage Manager	Janet Kennedy

1984

THE SKIN OF OUR TEETH by Thornton Wilder
Festival Theatre
previews from May 15, opening May 24 to October 6 (62 performances)

Announcer / Broadcaster	Ron White
Miss F. Muse / Miss Runner Up	Rosalind Goldsmith
Hester / Miss M. Muse	Joyce Campion
Miss T. Muse / Ivy	Lorena Gale
Mr Fitzpatrick	Norman Browning
Sabina	Nora McLellan
Mrs Maggie Antrobus	Jennifer Phipps
Frederick Dinosaur / Drum Major	Leonard Chow
Dolly Mammoth / Drum Major	Ric Sarabia
Telegraph Boy / Conventioneer	Stuart Hughes
Henry Antrobus	Dan Lett
Gladys Antrobus	Fiona Reid
Mr George Antrobus	Robert Benson
Mr Tremayne / Moses / Conventioneer	Hugo Dann
Fred Bailey / Professor / Conventioneer	Al Kozlik
Doctor / Conventioneer	Tom McCamus
Homer / Conventioneer	David Mucci
Esmeralda, a Fortune Teller	Irene Hogan
Conventioneers	Hume Baugh, Stephen Black, David Blacker, Jim Jones, Ken McAuliffe
Chair Pusher	John MacKenzie

Directed by Christopher Newton
Designed by Michael Levine
Lighting designed by Jeffrey Dallas

Stage Manager	Dianne Woodrow
Assistant Stage Manager	Carole Macomber

ROBERTA
music by Jerome Kern
book and lyrics by Otto Harbach
adapted by Duncan McIntosh and Christopher Newton

Royal George Theatre
previews from May 16, opening May 25 to October 7 (163 performances)

John Kent	Nicolas Colicos
Stephanie	Colleen Winton
Lord Henry Delves	Rod Campbell
Ladislaw	Mario Di Iorio
Luilla La Verne	Michelyn Emelle
Anna	Linda Gambell

Mrs Teale	Nancy Kerr
Sophie Teale	Jo-Anne Kirwan Clark
Huckleberry Haines	Stephen Simms
Scharwenka	Athena Voyatzis
Minnie Roberts	Dorothy Thistle (Nancy Kerr)

Directed and choreographed by Duncan McIntosh
Co-directed by Christopher Newton
Designed by Peter Wingate
Lighting designed by Jim Plaxton
Musical direction by Roger Perkins
Associate Musical Director / Arranger:
    Christopher Donison

Stage Manager	Alan Wallis
Assistant Stage Manager	S. Tigger Journard

THE LOST LETTER by Ion Caragiale
adapted by Christopher Newton and Sky Gilbert

Court House Theatre
preview August 16, opening August 17 to August 29 (6 performances)

Stephan Tipatescu	Ron White
Ghitsa Pristanda	Keith Knight
Zaharia Trahanache	Robert Benson
Zoe Trahanache	Fiona Reid
Iordache Branzovenescu	Rodger Barton
Tache Farfuridi	Al Kozlik
Servant to Tipatescu	Christopher Thomas
A Drunken Citizen	Tom McCamus
Nae Catsavencu	Hugo Dann
Father Prepici	David Hemblen
Ionescu	Stuart Hughes
Popescu	Peter Krantz
Maids	Morag Sinkins, Susan Stackhouse
Agamemnon Dandanache	David Schurmann
Citizens	Steve Adams, Stephen Black, Hans Böggild, Leonard Chow, Richard Fellbaum, Jim Jones, Dan Lett, Ken McAuliffe, Jackie Samuda, Craig Walker

Directed by Christopher Newton
Designed by Diz Marsh
Lighting designed by Jeffrey Dallas

Stage Manager	Dianne Woodrow
Assistant Stage Manager	Carole Macomber

CHRISTOPHER NEWTON AND FIONA REID IN *PRIVATE LIVES*, 1984 (PHOTO BY DAVID COOPER).

PRIVATE LIVES by Noel Coward
Festival Theatre
previews from May 2, opening May 25 to August 5 (55 performances)

Sybil Chase	Camille Mitchell
Elyot Chase	Christopher Newton
Victor Prynne	Jim Mezon
Amanda Prynne	Fiona Reid
Louise, a maid	Lois Lorimer

Directed by Denise Coffey
Designed by Mary Kerr
Lighting designed by Jeffrey Dallas

Stage Manager	Ken A. Smith
Assistant Stage Manager	Martha Campbell

ANDROCLES AND THE LION by Bernard Shaw
Court House Theatre
previews from June 28, opening July 5 to September 23 (57 performances)

Lion	Ric Sarabia
Androcles	Tom McCamus
Megaera	Valerie Boyle
Centurion	Dan Lett
Lavinia	Goldie Semple
Captain	Ron White

80

Ferrovius	Robert Benson
Spintho	Ric Sarabia
Lentulus	Duncan McIntosh
Metellus	Rodger Barton
Servants	Christopher Thomas, Craig Walker
Christians	Valerie Boyle, Kim Dunn, Richard Fellbaum, Rosalind Goldsmith, Stuart Hughes, Morag Sinkins
Roman Soldiers	Steve Adams, Hans Böggild, Keith Knight, David Mucci, Christopher Thomas
Lurker	Siew Hung Chow
Beggar	Hugo Dann
Ox Driver	Hans Böggild
Editor	Kim Dunn
Call Boy	Stuart Hughes
Retiarius	David Mucci
Secutor	Christopher Thomas
Emperor	Hugo Dann
Menagerie Keeper	Keith Knight
Gladiators	Steve Adams, Hans Böggild
Etruscan	Duncan McIntosh
Roman Ladies	Valerie Boyle, Rosalind Goldsmith, Morag Sinkins

Directed by Denise Coffey
Designed by Cameron Porteous
Lighting designed by Jeffrey Dallas

Stage Manager	Dianne Woodrow
Assistant Stage Manager	Carole Macomber

TORONTO DANCE THEATRE
Royal George Theatre, July 4 to 15 (10 Lunchtime performances)

EMMA, QUEEN OF SONG
Royal George Theatre, July 18 to 22 (5 Lunchtime performances)

Mary Lou Fallis, with Carl Morey (piano)

Directed by Duncan McIntosh
Designed by Diz Marsh
Lighting designed by Brenda Powell

THE SUN NEVER SETS
Patrick Crean in a one-man show based on the works of Rudyard Kipling
Royal George Theatre, July 25 to 29 (5 Lunchtime performances)

Directed by Powys Thomas
Lighting designed by Brenda Powell

1984

SHAW PLAYLETS
HOW HE LIED TO HER HUSBAND by Bernard Shaw
Royal George Theatre, August 10 to 19 (8 Lunchtime performances)

Her Lover	Geraint Wyn Davies
Her Husband	Allan Gray
Herself	Wendy Thatcher

THE FASCINATING FOUNDLING by Bernard Shaw
Royal George Theatre, August 10 to 19 (8 Lunchtime performances)

Horace Brabazon	Geraint Wyn Davies
Lord Chancellor	Allan Gray
Anastasia Vulliamy	Wendy Thatcher
Mercer	Kim Dunn

Directed by Paul Reynolds
Designed by Peter Wingate
Lighting designed by Brenda Powell
Fight staged by Cat Heaven

Stage Manager	Terry Ingram

THEATRE BEYOND WORDS (Mime Company)
Royal George Theatre, August 22 to September 2 (10 Lunchtime performances)

1984 by George Orwell
Court House Theatre, Festival Theatre, Royal George Theatre, Academy Warehouse, Streets and parks of Niagara-on-the-Lake, September 18 (1 performance)

At 7:30 pm on September 18th, the Shaw Festival Acting Ensemble and Company took over the town of Niagara-on-the-Lake to re-create George Orwell's *1984* simultaneously in all three of its theatres, its warehouse, and a variety of locations in the town itself, barricading the central streets.

The workshop extravaganza employed the services of nine producers, twenty-one directors, six photographers, thirty-two writers, ten stage managers, ten computer operators, eleven video technicians, 123 actors, and forty-seven "Passport Control" personnel to channel the audience members (dressed in "Prole" overalls) through the complicated performance.

In all, more than 300 members of the company participated, including crew, administrators, and front-of-house services, box-office, production, and communications staff.

Principal roles:

Rally speaker	Robert Benson
Mrs Parsons	Valerie Boyle
Martin	Norman Browning
Musical actor	Rod Campbell
Mrs Smith	Joyce Campion
Charrington	Richard Farrell
Tillotson	John Gilbert
Julia	Rosalind Goldsmith
Winston Smith	Allan Gray

Musical Actor	Stuart Hughes
Mr Parsons	Keith Knight
Goldstein	Al Kozlik
Wilsher	Dan Lett
O'Brien	Barry MacGregor
Bumstead	Tom McCamus
Syme	Duncan McIntosh
Katherine	Nora McLellan
Big Brother	Murray Morrison
Washerwoman	Jennifer Phipps
Sandy Haired Woman	Brenda Robins
Parsons' Daughter	Jessica Severin
Parsons' Son	Matthew Severin
Ampleforth	Craig Walker
Foreign Spy	Ron White
Exercise Mistress	Colleen Winton
Syme	Tom Wood
Musical Actor	Geraint Wyn Davies

Artistic Co-ordinator: Johanna Mercer
Technical Co-ordinator: Terry Ingram
Designers: Charlotte Dean, Alana Guinn

Directors of Major Scenes: David Hemblen, Keith Knight, Duncan McIntosh, Johanna Mercer, Camille Mitchell, Christopher Newton, Jennifer Phipps, David Schurmann, Geraint Wyn Davies

Special Events

St Mark's Church, Sunday Chamber Music Matinees

July 8	Hidy-Ozolins-Tsutsumi Trio
July 22	A Baroque Birthday Celebration: Bach, Handel, Scarlatti
July 29	McMaster String Quartet: Music from Paris Soloists: Marta Hidy (violin) and Valerie Tyron (piano)
August 3	G.B.S.: The Music Critic (McMaster Quartet) Narrator: Barry MacGregor

Post-season Tours

ROBERTA (19 performances)
Ross Hall, Guelph, October 10
Gryphon Theatre Foundation, Barrie, October 11
Rainbow Theatre, Parry Sound, October 12
Capitol Theatre, North Bay, October 13
McKenzie High School, Deep River, October 15
Perth District Collegiate Institute, Perth, October 16
Centennial Secondary School, Belleville, October17
Oakville Auditorium, Oakville, October 19 to 20
Chatham Cultural Centre, Chatham, October 24
University of Waterloo, Waterloo, October 25
Victoria Playhouse, Petrolia, October 26
Meaford Thornbury Secondary School, Georgian Bay, October 27
Orillia Opera House, Orillia, October 28
Ecole Thériault, Timmins, October 30
Kapuskasing Civic Centre, Kapuskasing, November 1
Atikokan High School, Atikokan, November 3
Queen Elizabeth High School, Sioux Lookout, November 4
Dryden High School, Dryden, November 5

CÉLIMARE

National Arts Centre, Ottawa, October 25 to November 10 (20 performances)
Grand Theatre, London, November 12 to December 1 (24 performances)

For the tour Camille Mitchell appeared as Emma Colombot.

Célimare was taped before a specially-invited audience on October 19 for presentation on CBC-TV, with its original cast, on February 14, 1985, under the title *Friends of a Feather*.

For this production:

Stage Manager	Ken A. Smith
Assistant Stage Manager	Martha Campbell

CYRANO DE BERGERAC

Festival Theatre, December 21 to 23 (4 performances)
Royal Alexandra Theatre, Toronto, December 31 to February 9, 1985
(40 performances)

Cyrano	Heath Lamberts
Roxanne	Marti Maraden
Christian de Neuvillette	Geraint Wyn Davies
Comte de Guiche	David Hemblen
Ragueneau	Robert Benson
Le Bret	Rodger Barton
A Child	Sean Collins

Cavalier / Cadet / Musketeer	Shaun Austin-Olsen
Précieuse / Nun	Joyce Campion
Actor / Cadet	Nicolas Colicos
Duenna / Nun	Susan Cox
2nd Marquis / Pikeman	Hugo Dann
Drunken Citizen / Spanish Soldier	Kim Dunn
Citizen / Cook / Bertrandou	Richard Farrell
Brissaille / Spanish Soldier	Michael Fawkes
Cuigy / Musketeer Soldier	Andrew Gillies
Précieuse / Sister Claire	Marion Gilsenan
A Child	John Guenther
Précieuse / Lise / Nun	Irene Hogan
Mother Marguérite	Frances Hyland
Montfleury / Cook / Monk / Spanish Soldier	Keith Knight
Pickpocket / Lackey / Poet / Soldier	Al Kozlik
1st Marquis / Pikeman	Dan Lett
Amorous Musketeer / Spanish Soldier	Andrew Lewarne
Cadet / Liguière	Barry MacGregor
Red Officer / Poet / Lackey / Spanish Soldier	John MacKenzie
Boy / Page / Cook / Drummer	Duncan McIntosh
Bellerose / Poet	Jack Medley
De Valvert / Cadet	Jim Mezon
Doorkeeper / Citizen / Spanish Soldier	David Mucci
Jodlet / Poet / Spanish Soldier	Ric Sarabia
Précieuse / Sister Marthe / Actress	Goldie Semple
Foodseller / Cook / Nun	Wendy Thatcher
Red Officer / Cadet	Christopher Thomas
D'Artagnan / Cadet	Brian Tree
Actor / Cook / Page / Spanish Soldier	Craig Walker
Alternate for Cyrano	Andrew Gillies

Directed by Derek Goldby, with David Hemblen
Designed by Cameron Porteous
Lighting designed by Robert Thomson
Fights directed by Patrick Crean
Original music by Roger Perkins

Stage Manager	Ken A. Smith
Assistant Stage Managers	Terry Ingram
	Christopher Brown

1985

TWENTY-FOURTH SEASON
May 1 to October 13 (542 performances)

THE WOMEN by Clare Boothe Luce
Court House Theatre
previews from June 28, opening July 4 to September 22 (51 performances)

Mrs Miriam Aarons	Margaret Bard
Hairdresser / Miss Shapiro / Helene / A Dowager	Jillian Cook
Mrs Edith Potter	Robin Craig
Little Mary Haines	Kate Cullen
Miss Crystal Allen	Michelle Fisk
Olga / A Sales Girl / Miss Watts	Rosalind Goldsmith
Flora (Countess De Lage)	Irene Hogan
Mrs Morehead	Frances Hyland
Euphie / Miss Fordyce / Maggie / Lucy / Sadie	Nancy Kerr
Hairdresser / A Sales Girl / Exercise Instructress	Lois Lorimer
Mrs Mary Haines	Nora McLellan
Jane / A Nurse / Cigarette Girl	Chick Reid
Miss Nancy Blake	Victoria Snow
Mrs Peggy Potter	Susan Stackhouse
Pedicurist / Princess Tamara / Miss Trimmerback / A Debutante	Ann Turnbull
Mrs Sylvia Fowler	Susan Wright

Directed by Duncan McIntosh
Designed by Michael Levine
Lighting designed by Patsy Lang

Stage Manager	Dianne Woodrow
Assistant Stage Manager	Carole Macomber

THE MADWOMAN OF CHAILLOT by Jean Giraudoux
adapted by Maurice Valency

Festival Theatre
previews from May 14, opening May 23 to August 4 (47 performances)

The Waiter / A President	Andrew Gillies
Irma	Donna Goodhand
Claude / Adolphe Bertaut	Jim Jones
The Prospector	Al Kozlik
The Shoelace Peddler / A Press Agent	Michael Besworth
The Little Man	Brad Dalcourt
Paulette	Goldie Semple
The Street Juggler / A Press Agent	Ric Sarabia
The Deaf Mute	Tom McCamus
The Flower Girl	Tracey Ferencz
The Rag Picker	Tom Wood
The President / Adolphe Bertaut	Rodger Barton
The Doorman / A Prospector	Joe-Norman Shaw
Therese	Fiona Reid
The Professor	Hugo Dann
The Baron / A President / Adolphe Bertaut	David Schurmann
The Street Singer / A Press Agent	Duncan McIntosh
The Broker / A President / Adolphe Bertaut	Allan Gray
Ginette	Barbara Worthy
Dr Jadin / The Sewer Man	Jack Medley
Countess Aurelia, the Madwoman of Chaillot	Irene Hogan
Pierre	Peter Krantz
The Policeman / A Prospector	Ken McAuliffe
The Sergeant	Norman Browning
Madame Constance, the Madwoman of Passy	Frances Hyland
Mlle Gabrielle, the Madwoman of St Sulpice	Marion Gilsenan
Madame Josephine, the Madwoman of La Concorde	Nancy Kerr

Directed by Wendy Toye
Designed by Cameron Porteous
Lighting designed by Sholem Dolgoy

Stage Manager	Dianne Woodrow
Assistant Stage Manager	Carole Macomber

1985

HEARTBREAK HOUSE by Bernard Shaw
Festival Theatre
previews from May 8, opening May 22 to October 5 (63 performances)

Ellie Dunn	Marti Maraden
Nurse Guinness	Jennifer Phipps
Captain Shotover	Douglas Rain
Lady Utterword	Fiona Reid
Hesione Hushabye	Goldie Semple
Mazzini Dunn	Allan Gray
Hector Hushabye	Norman Browning
Boss Mangan	Robert Benson
Randall Utterword	Peter Krantz
Burglar	Andrew Gillies
Gardener's Boys	Jim Jones, Ric Sarabia

Directed by Christopher Newton
Designed by Michael Levine
Lighting designed by Jeffrey Dallas

Stage Manager   Ken A. Smith
Assistant Stage Manager   Carolyn Mackenzie

NAUGHTY MARIETTA
music by Victor Herbert
book and lyrics by Rida Johnson Young
adapted by Christopher Newton

Royal George Theatre
previews from May 15, opening May 24 to October 5 (134 performances)

Uncle / Governor Grandet	Rod Campbell
Lizette / Flower Girl / Maid	Faye Cohen
Manuelo / Florenz / Rudolfo	Gregory Cross
Adah / Gypsy	Susan Gudgeon
Nanette / Flower Girl	Gail Hakala
Marietta / Flower Girl	Jo-Anne Kirwan Clark
Captain Richard Warrington	David Playfair
Silas	Stephen Simms
Etienne	Alec Tebbutt
Lieutenant Harry Blake	Scott Weber
Marionette Operators	Susan Gudgeon, Gail Hakala, Scott Weber

Directed by Christopher Newton
Designed by Peter Wingate
Lighting designed by Robert Thomson
Choreographed by Duncan McIntosh
Musical direction by Roger Perkins

Stage Manager   Alan Wallis
Assistant Stage Manager   Martha Campbell

JOHN BULL'S OTHER ISLAND   by Bernard Shaw
Court House Theatre
previews from June 30, opening July 5 to September 22 (51 performances)

Hodson	John Gilbert
Tom Broadbent	Barry MacGregor
Tim Haffigan	Dan Lett
Larry Doyle	Jim Mezon
Peter Keegan	Herb Foster
Patsy Farrell	Stuart Hughes
Nora	Martha Burns
Corney Doyle	Sandy Webster
Father Dempsey	Richard Farrell
Aunt Judy	Joyce Campion
Matthew Haffigan	Dan Lett
Barney Doran	Wes Tritter
Youths of the Village	Hume Baugh, L. James Beales

Directed by Denise Coffey
Designed by Diz Marsh
Lighting designed by Jeffrey Dallas

Stage Manager	Ron Nipper
Assistant Stage Manager	Janet Kennedy

MURDER ON THE NILE   by Agatha Christie
Royal George Theatre
previews from August 11, opening August 16 to October 6 (39 performances)

The Steward	Hugo Dann
Abdul, a beadseller	Ric Sarabia
Kareem, a beadseller	Jim Jones
Miss ffoliot ffoulkes	Nancy Kerr
Christina Grant	Lois Lorimer
Smith	Tom McCamus
Louise	Victoria Snow
Dr Bessner	Al Kozlik
Kay Mostyn	Michelle Fisk
Simon Mostyn	Richard Hardacre
Canon Pennefather	Rodger Barton
Jacqueline de Severac	Marti Maraden
Babi, a crew member	Ric Sarabia
Ali, a crew member	Jim Jones
McNaught	Hugo Dann

Directed by Margaret Bard
Designed by Peter Wingate
Lighting designed by Brenda Powell

Stage Manager	Carolyn Mackenzie
Assistant Stage Manager	Alan Wallis

1985

TROPICAL MADNESS NO. 2:
METAPHYSICS OF A TWO-HEADED CALF by Stanislaw Witkiewicz
translated by Daniel and Eleanor Gerould

Court House Theatre
preview August 13, opening August 15 to August 22 (6 performances)

Lady Leocadia Clay	Joyce Campion
Patricianello	Hume Baugh
Professor Mikulini	Herb Foster
Prince Ludwig Parvis	Dan Lett
King of Aparura	Wes Tritter
Sir Robert Clay	Richard Farrell
Sailor	James Beales
Natives	Kate Cullen, Tracey Ferencz
Princess Mirabella	Martha Burns
Jack Rivers	Barry MacGregor
Hooded Figure	Stuart Hughes
Old Hag	Ann Turnbull

Directed by Steven Schipper
Designed by Diz Marsh
Lighting designed by Patsy Lang
Original piano music composed and
performed by Stephen Raiman

Stage Manager	Ron Nipper
Assistant Stage Manager	Janet Kennedy

ONE FOR THE POT by Ray Cooney and Tony Hilton
Festival Theatre
previews from May 1, opening May 24 to October 13 (84 performances)

Amy Hardcastle	Marion Gilsenan
Cynthia Hardcastle	Donna Goodhand
Jugg	David Schurmann
Jonathan Hardcastle	Jack Medley
Jennifer	Barbara Worthy
Stanley	Tom McCamus*
Clifton Weaver	Peter Hutt
Arnold Piper	Richard Farrell
Charlie Barnet	Barry MacGregor
Hickory Wood	Heath Lamberts
Winnie	Joyce Campion
Guests	Brad Dalcourt, Tracey Ferencz,
	Ken McAuliffe, Joe-Norman Shaw,
	Wes Tritter

succeeded by Hume Baugh on June 4

Directed by Chris Johnston
Designed by Debra Hanson
Lighting designed by Jeffrey Dallas

Stage Manager   Ron Nipper
Assistant Stage Manager   Janet Kennedy

One for the Pot was taped from October 27 to November 1 in the Festival Theatre, including a live performance on October 31, for presentation on CBC-TV on April 6, 1986.

THE INCA OF PERUSALEM by Bernard Shaw
Royal George Theatre
previews from July 3, opening July 5, July 3 to 7, 24 to 28, August 21 to 25
(15 Lunchtime performances)

The Archdeacon	Allan Gray
Ermyntrude	Marti Maraden
The Bellman	L. James Beales
The Manager	John Gilbert
The Princess	Jennifer Phipps
The Waiter	Allan Gray
The Inca of Perusalem	Robert Benson

Directed by Paul Reynolds
Designed by Peter Wingate
Lighting designed by Brenda Powell

Stage Manager   Carolyn Mackenzie

MRS BACH
Royal George Theatre, July 10 to 21 (10 Lunchtime performances)

Mary Lou Fallis

Directed by Duncan McIntosh
Designed by Sue LePage
Lighting designed by Brenda Powell

DANNY GROSSMAN DANCE COMPANY
Royal George Theatre, August 28 to September 1 (5 Lunchtime performances)

CAVALCADE by Noel Coward

Festival Theatre

previews from August 11, opening August 16 to October 6 (37 performances)

Jane Marryot	Fiona Reid
Robert Marryot	Andrew Gillies
Ellen Bridges	Goldie Semple
Alfred Bridges	David Schurmann
Marion Christie	Barbara Worthy
Newsboy	Joe-Norman Shaw
Lieutenant Edgar Tyrell	Paul Gatchell
Tom Jolly	Stephen Simms
Uncle George	Tom Wood
Douglas Finn	Ken McAuliffe
Uncle Jack	Roger Perkins
Pearly King	Scott Weber
Duchess of Churt	Marion Gilsenan
Tim Bateman	Michael Besworth
Uncle Bob	Rod Campbell
Major Domo	Gregory Cross
Flo Grainger	Robin Craig
Cook	Irene Hogan
Uncle Dick	Robert Benson
George Grainger	Allan Gray
Joe Marryot	Peter Krantz
Annie	Rosalind Goldsmith
Stage Manager	Norman Browning
Darcy	Jillian Cook
Lord Martlet	Brad Dalcourt
Uncle Jim	Alec Tebbutt
Edward Marryot	Peter Hutt
Young Joe Marryot	Trevor MacDonald
Young Edith Harris	Jessica Severin
Young Edward Marryot	Mike Shara
Margaret Harris	Susan Wright
Fanny Bridges	Faye Cohen
Salvation Army Singer	Susan Gudgeon
Netta Lake	Gail Hakala
Daisy Devon	Chick Reid
Princess Mirabelle	Jo-Anne Kirwan Clark
Rose Darling	Nora McLellan
Edith Harris	Donna Goodhand
Connie Crayshaw	Susan Stackhouse
Mrs Snapper	Jennifer Phipps
Lord Esher	Jack Medley
Young Fanny Bridges	Emily West
Uncle Reg	Christopher Donison
The Dog	Rhonda Honeybeare

(Members of the ensemble played the other approximately 200 parts.)

A SCENE FROM *CAVALCADE*, 1985 (PHOTO BY DAVID COOPER).

Musicians were identified in the programme only by the names of characters in the play. Identification of performers is given within brackets:

Dick Soveral (Robert Benson), euphonium; Laura Marsden (Jo-Anne Kirwan Clark), trombone; Bob Grandet (Rod Campbell), trumpet; Norman Snapper (Roger Perkins), piano/banjo/bass drum; Harry Domo (Gregory Cross), tuba/triangle; Felicity Snapper (Jennifer Phipps), double bass; Reg Franks (Christopher Donison), piano/saxophone/snare drum; Tom Jolly (Stephen Simms), cornet; Bob Marryot (Andrew Gillies), percussion; Jim Chamberlain (Alec Tebbutt), violin/percussion; Netta Lake (Gail Hakala), piano. Susan Gudgeon was the vocalist and played tambourine in the Salvation Army Band.

Directed by Christopher Newton and Duncan McIntosh
Designed by Cameron Porteous
Lighting designed by Jeffrey Dallas
Musical direction, arrangements, and orchestrations
by Christopher Donison

Stage Manager	Dianne Woodrow
Assistant Stage Managers	Martha Campbell
	Carole Macomber

Post-season Tour

HEARTBREAK HOUSE

National Arts Centre, Ottawa, October 10 to 26 (20 performances)

For the tour Nancy Kerr appeared as Nurse Guinness and Wendy Thatcher appeared as Lady Utterword.

1986

TWENTY-FIFTH SEASON

May 1 to October 12 (547 performances)

ARMS AND THE MAN by Bernard Shaw

Festival Theatre
previews from May 7, opening May 28 to October 5 (68 performances)

Raina Petkoff	Donna Goodhand
Catherine Petkoff	Jennifer Phipps
Louka	Nora McLellan
Captain Bluntschli	Andrew Gillies
Plechanoff	Michael Besworth
Soldier	Richard Waugh
Nicola	Al Kozlik
Major Paul Petkoff	Sandy Webster
Major Sergius Saranoff	Jim Mezon

Directed by Leon Major
Designed by Michael Levine with Charlotte Dean
Lighting designed by Jeffrey Dallas

Stage Manager	Laurie Champagne
Assistant Stage Manager	Debra McKay

BANANA RIDGE by Ben Travers

Festival Theatre
previews from May 1, opening May 30 to October 4 (57 performances)

Eleanor Pound	Mary Haney
Mason	Al Kozlik
Susan Long	Wendy Thatcher
Digby Pound	Barry MacGregor
Willoughby Pink	Herb Foster
Julius Jones	Ted Dykstra
Cora Pound	Helen Taylor
Basil Bingley	Tom McCamus
Jean Pink	Marti Maraden
Wun	Douglas Chamberlain*
Boy	David Matheson
Staples	Stephen Hair
Sir Ramsey Tripp	Jack Medley

*succeeded by Keith Knight on July 26

Directed by Ian Judge
Designed by Peter Wingate
Lighting designed by Steven Hawkins

Stage Manager	Carole Macomber
Assistant Stage Manager	Jennifer White

94

ANDREW GILLIES AND DONNA GOODHAND IN *ARMS AND THE MAN*, 1986 (PHOTO BY DAVID COOPER).

TONIGHT WE IMPROVISE by Luigi Pirandello
Court House Theatre
preview August 12, opening August 14 to August 21 (6 performances)

Sampognetta	Michael Ball
Ricco Verri	Norman Browning
Nightclub Singer	Jillian Cook
Pometti	George Dawson
Totina	Kelly Denomme
The Gentleman	James Edmond
The Other Gentleman	Richard Farrell
Customer	John Gilbert
Dr Hinkfuss	Allan Gray
Ignazia	Irene Hogan
Nardi	Michael Howell
Mangini	Geordie Johnson
Customer	Jim Jones
Dorina	Corrine Koslo
Pomarici	John Moffat
Serelli	Ric Sarabia
Nene	Deborah Taylor
Customer	Wes Tritter
Mommina	Kate Trotter
Customer	Ted Wallace
The Lady	Barbara Worthy

Directed by Christopher Newton with Marti Maraden
Set, costumes, and lighting designed by Patsy Lang

Stage Manager	Laurie Champagne
Assistant Stage Manager	Debra McKay

GIRL CRAZY
words and music by George and Ira Gershwin
libretto by John McGowan and Guy Bolton

Royal George Theatre
previews from May 7, opening May 30 to October 5 (104 performances)

Sam Mason / Cowboy / Mexican Policeman	Rod Campbell
Molly Moorhead	Jo-Anne Kirwan Clark
Pianist	Christopher Donison
Johnny Churchill	Paul Gatchell
Rose Hippe	Gail Hakala
Zoli Gabor	Stan Lesk
Charity de Nations	Lorelyn Morgan
Manuel / Deputy / Bellboy / Cowboy	Paul Mulloy
Pianist	Roger Perkins
Doc Parkhurst / Cowboy	Stephen Simms
Harold "Snake Eyes" Jessup / Cowboy	Alec Tebbutt
"Frisco" Kate Fothergill-Gabor	Mary Trainor

Directed by Duncan McIntosh and Christopher Newton
Designed by Christina Poddubiuk
Lighting designed by Allan Stichbury
Musical direction by Roger Perkins
Associate musical director: Christopher Donison

Stage Manager	Alan Wallis
Assistant Stage Manager	Randy Thiessen

BLACK COFFEE by Agatha Christie
Royal George Theatre
previews from May 22, opening May 29 to October 5 (94 performances)

Doctor Graham	Guy Bannerman
Miss Caroline Amory	Joyce Campion
Richard Amory	Ted Dykstra
Sir Claud Amory	Stephen Hair
Lucia Amory	Lois Lorimer
Hercule Poirot	Barry MacGregor
Captain Arthur Hastings, O.B.E.	Jack Medley
Edward Raynor	John O'Krancy
Tredwell / Johnson (A Constable)	Ian Prinsloo
Inspector Japp	Harry Stevens
Barbara Amory	Ann Turnbull
Doctor Carelli	Kent Staines

Directed by Frances Hyland
Designed by Christina Poddubiuk
Lighting designed by Patsy Lang

Stage Manager   Ron Nipper
Assistant Stage Manager   Victoria Vasileski

ON THE ROCKS by Bernard Shaw
Court House Theatre
previews from July 3, opening July 10 to September 21 (49 performances)

Sir Arthur Chavender	Michael Ball
Sir Dexter Rightside	Norman Browning
Miss Hilda Hanways	Jillian Cook
Sir Broadfoot Basham	George Dawson
Miss Flavia Chavender	Kelly Denomme
Mr Hipney Domesday	James Edmond
Duke of Domesday	Richard Farrell
Admiral Sir Bemrose Hotspot	John Gilbert
Sir Japhna Pandranath	Allan Gray
Lady Chavender	Irene Hogan
Mr Blee	Michael Howell
Mr David Chavender	Jim Jones
Viscount Barking	Lindsay Merrithew
Mayor Humphries	Wes Tritter
Mr Glenmorrison	Ted Wallace
The Woman	Christine Willes
Alderman Aloysia Brollikins	Barbara Worthy

Directed by Christopher Newton
Designed by Pam Johnson
Lighting designed by Patsy Lang

Stage Manager   Laurie Champagne
Assistant Stage Manager   Jennifer White

MICHAEL BALL,
GEORGE DAWSON,
AND JOHN GILBERT
IN *ON THE ROCKS*,
1986 (PHOTO BY
DAVID COOPER).

1986

CAVALCADE by Noel Coward
Festival Theatre
previews from May 14, opening May 29 to October 12 (86 performances)

Alfred Bridges	Michael Ball
Uncle Dick	Robert Benson
Tim Bateman	Michael Besworth
Stage Manager	Norman Browning
Uncle Bob	Rod Campbell
Laura Marsden (Mirabelle)	Jo-Anne Kirwan Clark
Darcy	Jillian Cook
Ronnie James	George Dawson
Uncle Reg	Christopher Donison
Annie	Tracey Ferencz
Henry Charteris (Tyrell)	Paul Gatchell
Robert Marryot	Andrew Gillies
Edith Harris	Donna Goodhand
George Grainger	Allan Gray
Netta Lake	Gail Hakala
Margaret Harris	Mary Haney
Cook	Irene Hogan
Douglas Finn	Jim Jones
Flo Grainger	Nancy Kerr
Major Domo	Stan Lesk
Young Joe	Trevor MacDonald
Jane Marryot	Nora McLellan
Joe Marryot	Lindsay Merrithew
Salvation Army Singer	Lorelyn Morgan
Pearly King	Paul Mulloy
Uncle Jack	Roger Perkins
Mrs Snapper	Jennifer Phipps
Daisy Devon	Chick Reid
Young Edith	Jessica Severin
Young Edward	Mike Shara
Micky Banks (Tom Jolly)	Stephen Simms
Connie Crawshay	Susan Stackhouse
Uncle Jim	Alec Tebbutt
Ellen Bridges	Wendy Thatcher
Fanny Bridges	Mary Trainor
Lord Martlet	Wes Tritter
Edward Marryot	Ted Wallace
Private Ball	Richard Waugh
Uncle George	Sandy Webster
Young Fanny	Emily West
Rose Darling (Ada)	Christine Willes
Gladys	Barbara Worthy

The musicians (uncredited in the programme) were the same as in the 1985 production except for the following changes or additions:

Stan Lesk replaced Gregory Cross on tuba/triangle
Lorelyn Morgan replaced Susan Gudgeon in the Salvation Army Band
Tracey Ferencz played clarinet
Robert Benson second violin
Jillian Cook bells in the Mirabelle orchestra

Directed by Christopher Newton and Duncan McIntosh
Designed by Cameron Porteous
Lighting designed by Jeffrey Dallas
Musical direction by Christopher Donison

Stage Manager	Dianne Woodrow
Assistant Stage Managers	Janet Kennedy
	Randy Thiessen

HOLIDAY by Philip Barry

Court House Theatre
previews from July 4, opening July 11 to September 21 (54 performances)

Julia Seton	Deborah Taylor
Henry	Ric Sarabia
Charles	David Matheson
Johnny Case	John Moffat
Linda Seton	Kate Trotter
Ned Seton	Tom McCamus
Edward Seton	Douglas Chamberlain*
Seton Cram	Keith Knight
Laura Cram	Marti Maraden
Nick Potter	Geordie Johnson
Susan Potter	Corrine Koslo
Delia	Helen Taylor

succeeded by John Gilbert

Directed by Duncan McIntosh
Designed by John Pennoyer
Lighting designed by Robert Thomson

Stage Manager	Carole Macomber
Assistant Stage Manager	Jennifer White

BACK TO METHUSELAH by Bernard Shaw

Festival Theatre

previews from August 5, opening August 15 to September 14 (12 performances)

Presented in two parts: afternoon and evening

Part I

IN THE BEGINNING

Adam	John O'Krancy
Eve	Ann Turnbull
The Serpent	Frances Hyland,
	Joyce Campion (voice only)
Cain	Robert Benson

THE GOSPEL OF THE BROTHERS BARNABAS

Franklyn Barnabas	Herb Foster
Conrad Barnabas	Tom Wood
The Parlormaid	Nora McLellan
Reverend William Haslam	Jim Mezon
Cynthia ("Savvy") Barnabas	Susan Stackhouse
Joyce Burge	Barry MacGregor
Lubin	Sandy Webster

THE THING HAPPENS

Burge-Lubin	Robert Benson
Barnabas	Tom Wood
Telephone Operator Voice	Lois Lorimer
Confucius	Sandy Webster
Negress (Minister of Health)	Michelyn Emelle
The Archbishop of York	Jim Mezon
Mrs Lutestring	Nora McLellan

Part II

THE TRAGEDY OF AN ELDERLY GENTLEMAN

Elderly Gentleman (Joseph Popham Bolge Bluebin Barlow, O.M.)	Herb Foster
Fusima	Michelyn Emelle
Zozim	John O'Krancy
Zoo	Susan Stackhouse
General Aufsteig	Tom Wood
The Oracle	Frances Hyland
Ambrose Bluebin (Prime Minister)	Robert Benson
Mrs Badger Bluebin	Nancy Kerr
Ethel Bluebin	Lois Lorimer

AS FAR AS THOUGHT CAN REACH

Strephon	Michael Besworth
Chloe	Tracey Ferencz
He-Ancient	Jack Medley
Acis	Kent Staines
She-Ancient	Joyce Campion
Amaryllis	Ann Turnbull
Ecrasia	Leonard Chow
Arjillax	Guy Bannerman
Martellus	Jim Mezon
Pygmalion	Andrew Gillies
Ozymandias	Duncan McIntosh
Cleopatra-Semiramis	Chick Reid
Ghost of Adam	John O'Krancy
Ghost of Eve	Ann Turnbull
Ghost of Cain	Robert Benson
Ghost of the Serpent	Joyce Campion
Ghost of Lilith	Frances Hyland

Directed by Denise Coffey
Designed by Cameron Porteous
Lighting designed by Jeffrey Dallas
Original music and sound design by Roger Perkins

Stage Manager	Ron Nipper
Assistant Stage Manager	Victoria Vasileski

101

1986

PASSION, POISON, AND PETRIFACTION by Bernard Shaw
Royal George Theatre
previews from July 9, opening July 11 to August 3 (17 Lunchtime performances)

George Fitztollemache	Guy Bannerman
Adolphus Bastable	Ted Dykstra
Lady Magnesia Fitztollemache	Donna Goodhand
The Doctor	Stephen Hair
Police Constable	Keith Knight
The Landlady	Jennifer Phipps
Phyllis	Wendy Thatcher

Heavenly Choir:
Robert Benson, Michael Besworth, Norman Browning, Rod Campbell,
Leonard Chow, Jo-Anne Kirwan Clark, Jillian Cook, Kelly Denomme,
Richard Farrell, Tracey Ferencz, John Gilbert, Andrew Gillies, Allan
Gray, Gail Hakala, Irene Hogan, Michael Howell, Geordie Johnson,
Jim Jones, Lois Lorimer, Tom McCamus, Nora McLellan, Lindsay
Merrithew, Jim Mezon, John Moffat, Lorelyn Morgan, Paul Mulloy,
John O'Krancy, Ian Prinsloo, Stephen Simms, Susan Stackhouse, Kent
Staines, Deborah Taylor, Helen Taylor, Alec Tebbutt, Mary Trainor, Wes
Tritter, Ann Turnbull, Ted Wallace, Richard Waugh, Christine Willes,
Barbara Worthy

Directed by Paul Reynolds
Set designed by Margaret Coderre-Williams
Costumes designed by Terry Nicholls
Lighting designed by Jeffrey Dallas

Stage Manager	Alan Wallis
Assistant Stage Manager	Debra McKay

Special Events

Festival Theatre, June 15, 22, 29, July 6
Classical Cabaret, with members of the musical ensemble

Niagara Historical Society Museum, July 3 to September 28
The Pictorial Stage: A Design Retrospective

Festival Theatre, July 7
A Tribute to the Artistry in Rhythm of Stan Kenton

Festival Theatre, July 20
Silver Anniversary Gala

Performances by members of the Shaw Festival,
the Stratford Festival, the Canadian Opera Company,
the National Ballet of Canada, and the Toronto
Symphony Orchestra.

THE BLACK GIRL IN SEARCH OF GOD by Bernard Shaw
A Staged Reading adapted for the stage by Dan H. Laurence

Royal George Theatre, September 9

The Black Girl	Michelyn Emelle
Narrator	Dan H. Laurence
Missionary / First Lady of the Caravan	Susan Stackhouse
Lord of Hosts / First Gentleman	Robert Benson
Nailer / Second Gentleman / Old Gentleman (Voltaire)	Alan Wallis
Ecclesiastes / Third Gentleman	Ian Prinsloo
Micah / Roman Soldier	Kent Staines
The Myop / The Image Maker	Steve Wilhite
Conjurer / Mr Croker / Irishman	Christopher Newton
Second Lady of the Caravan	Joyce Campion
Arab / Fisherman	Rod Campbell

Directed by Duncan McIntosh

STARTING HERE, STARTING NOW
music by David Shire
lyrics by Richard Maltby, Jr

Royal George Theatre, September 16

Nora McLellan
Rod Campbell
Gail Hakala

Directed by Duncan McIntosh
Choreography by Mary Trainor
Musical direction by Roger Perkins

For the benefit of the Craniofacial Family Society and the Royal George
Restoration Fund.

Post-season

Festival Theatre, December 4 to January 25, 1987

Theatre Beyond Words

FIVE GOOD REASONS TO LAUGH (14 performances)

THE POTATO PEOPLE (7 performances)

1987

Pre-season Tours

ONE FOR THE POT by Ray Cooney and Tony Hilton
Festival Theatre, January 2 to 4 (4 performances)
National Arts Centre, Ottawa, January 7 to 24 (21 performances)

Amy Hardcastle	Fiona McMurran
Cynthia Hardcastle	Donna Goodhand
Jugg	David Schurmann
Jonathan Hardcastle	Jack Medley
Jennifer	Ellen-Ray Hennessy
Stanley	George Dawson
Clifton Weaver	Peter Krantz
Arnold Piper	Richard Farrell
Charlie Barnet	Norman Browning
Hickory Wood	Andrew Gillies
Winnie	Barbara Worthy
Guests	Paul Mulloy, Richard Waugh, Gail Hakala

Directed by Ian Judge
Designed by Debra Hanson
Lighting designed by Jeffrey Dallas

Stage Manager	Ron Nipper
Assistant Stage Manager	Janet Kennedy
	Victoria Vasileski

THE WOMEN by Clare Boothe Luce
Festival Theatre, February 13 to 15 (4 performances)
Royal Alexandra Theatre, Toronto, February 20 to April 4 (51 performances)

Mrs Sylvia Fowler	Susan Cox
Miss Nancy Blake	Marti Maraden
Mrs Edith Potter	Robin Craig
Mrs Peggy Day	Susan Stackhouse
Jane / Nurse / Cigarette Girl	Chick Reid
Mrs Mary Haines	Lally Cadeau
Flora (Countess de Lage)	Irene Hogan
Hairdresser / Saleswoman / Instructress / Society Girl	Lois Lorimer
Hairdresser / Miss Shapiro / Helene / Dowager	Jillian Cook
Olga / Princess Tamara / Miss Trimmerback / Debutante	Ann Turnbull
Pedicurist / Saleswoman / Miss Watts / Society Girl	Deborah Taylor

Euphie / Miss Fordyce /
    Maggie / Lucy / Sadie   Nancy Kerr
Mrs Miriam Aarons   Wendy Thatcher
Little Mary Haines   Jackie Mahon
Mrs Morehead   Frances Hyland
Miss Crystal Allen   Camille Mitchell

Directed by Duncan McIntosh
Designed by Michael Levine
Lighting designed by Patsy Lang

Stage Manager   Dianne Woodrow
Assistant Stage Manager   Carole Macomber

TWENTY-SIXTH SEASON
April 29 to October 18 (599 performances)

MAJOR BARBARA by Bernard Shaw
Festival Theatre
previews from May 6, opening May 27 to October 11 (73 performances)

Lady Britomart Undershaft   Frances Hyland
Stephen Undershaft   Steven Sutcliffe
Morrison   Al Kozlik
Barbara Undershaft   Martha Burns
Sarah Undershaft   Barbara Worthy
Adolphus Cusins   Jim Mezon
Charles Lomax   Michael Howell
Andrew Undershaft   Douglas Rain
Rummy Mitchens   Irene Hogan
Snobby Price   Ted Dykstra
Peter Shirley   Herb Foster
Jenny Hill   Helen Taylor
Bill Walker   Jon Bryden
Mrs Baines   Jennifer Phipps
Salvation Army Worker   Grant Carmichael
Bilton   Al Kozlik

Directed by Christopher Newton
Designed by Cameron Porteous
Lighting designed by Jeffrey Dallas
Musical arrangement by Roger Perkins
Sound designed by Walter Lawrence

Stage Manager   Dianne Woodrow
Assistant Stage Manager   Carolyn Mackenzie

HAY FEVER by Noel Coward

Festival Theatre

previews from April 29, opening May 29 to October 18 (91 performances)

Sorel Bliss	Helen Taylor
Simon Bliss	Richard Binsley
Clara	Jill Frappier
Judith Bliss	Jennifer Phipps
David Bliss	Robert Benson
Sandy Tyrell	Roy Lewis
Myra Arundel	Marti Maraden
Richard Greatham	Norman Browning
Jackie Coryton	Barbara Worthy

Directed by Denise Coffey
Designed by John Pennoyer
Lighting designed by Sholem Dolgoy
Sound designed by Walter Lawrence

Stage Manager	Janet Kennedy
Assistant Stage Manager	Jennifer White

ANYTHING GOES

music and lyrics by Cole Porter
book by Guy Bolton and P.G. Wodehouse
revised by Howard Lindsay and Russell Crouse

Royal George Theatre

previews from May 6, opening May 30 to October 10 (106 performances)

Whitney / Captain / Bishop / Pornographer	Ross Driedger
Reporter / Steward / Drunk	Paul Mulloy
Sir Evelyn Oakleigh	Rod Campbell
Mrs Harcourt	Nancy Kerr
Hope	Elizabeth Beeler
Chastity	Deann DeGruijter
Reno Sweeny	Nora McLellan
Bonnie / Virtue	Gail Hakala
Billy Crocker	Kerry Dorey
Moonface	William L. Vickers
Pianists	Roger Perkins, Christopher Donison

Directed by Sky Gilbert
Designed by Christina Poddubiuk
Lighting designed by Patsy Lang
Musical direction by Roger Perkins
Choreography by Valerie Moore

Stage Manager	Ron Nipper
Assistant Stage Manager	Randy Thiessen

MARATHON 33 by June Havoc
Festival Theatre
previews from May 13, opening May 28 to July 29 (39 performances)

Mr Dankle	Michael Ball
The Mick*	Elizabeth Beeler
Mr Forbes	Rod Campbell
Helen Bazoo	Joyce Campion
Rae Wilson	Robin Craig
A Trainer / A Spectator	Steven Cumyn
Schnozz Wilson	George Dawson
Al Marcioni	Kerry Dorey
A Legionnaire / A Spectator /	
A Musician	Ross Driedger
A Cook / A Spectator	Deann DeGruijter
Robin Murphy	Tracey Ferencz
Mr James, the Floor Judge	Andrew Gillies
A Dancer / A Spectator	Gail Hakala
Evie Adamanski	Frances Hyland
Blanket Girl / A Spectator	Gabrielle Jones
Melba Marvel	Nancy Kerr
Patsy	Dan Lett
Scotty Schwartz	Tom McCamus
A Spectator / The Minister	Lance McDayter
June	Camille Mitchell
Blanket Boy	Paul Mulloy
A Legionnaire / A Spectator	Roger Perkins
Lusty Hutchinson	Ian Prinsloo
Flo Marcioni	Chick Reid
Rita Marimba	Brigitte Robinson
Bozo Bazoo	David Schurmann
Pearl Schwartz	Susan Stackhouse
"Sugar Hips" Johnson	Wendy Thatcher
A Trainer / A Spectator	Richard Thorne
A Workman / A Dancer /	
A Spectator	William Vickers
Abe O'Brien	Richard Waugh
A Workman / A Spectator	Peter Windrem

Musicians: Al Bird (coronet), Ric Giorgi (bass sax/string bass/violin),
Ernie Porthouse (drums), Rex Rathgeber (trombone), Jim Weber
(clarinet/C melody sax), Willi Wilson (banjo, guitar).

performed by Deann DeGruijter June 4 to 30

Directed by Duncan McIntosh
Designed by Michael Levine
Lighting designed by Sholem Dolgoy
Musical direction / original music by Christopher Donison
Sound designed by Walter Lawrence

Stage Manager	Carole Macomber
Assistant Stage Managers	Debra McKay
	Randy Thiessen

1987

NOT IN THE BOOK by Arthur Watkyn
Royal George Theatre
previews from May 19, opening May 28 to October 11 (103 performances)

Sylvia Bennett	Jill Frappier
Michael Bennett	Duncan Ollerenshaw
Timothy Gregg	Richard Binsley
Inspector Malcolm	Norman Browning
Andrew Bennett	Jack Medley*
Pedro Juarez	Barry MacGregor**
Colonel Barstow	Robert Benson
Doctor Locke	Colin Miller

succeeded by Barry MacGregor on June 26
**succeeded by Peter Millard on June 26*

Directed by Maja Ardal
Designed by Pam Johnson
Lighting designed by Kevin Fraser
Sound designed by Walter Lawrence

Stage Manager	Alan Wallis
Assistant Stage Manager	Victoria Vasileski

FANNY'S FIRST PLAY by Bernard Shaw
Court House Theatre
previews from July 2, opening July 9 to September 27 (57 performances)

A Footman	Ian Prinsloo
Mr Savoyard	Guy Bannerman
Count O'Dowda	Michael Ball
Miss Fanny O'Dowda	Tracey Ferencz
Mr Raymond Trickowood	George Dawson
Mr Jamie Winebibber	C. Holte Davidson
Miss Eugena Hammer	Brigitte Robinson
Mr Flawner Bannal	Dan Lett
Mrs Maria Gilbey	Joyce Campion
Mr Robin Gilbey	John Gilbert
Mr Rudolph Juggins	David Schurmann
Miss Dora Delaney	Wendy Thatcher
Mrs Amelia Knox	Robin Craig
Mr Joseph Knox	Richard Farrell
Monsieur Duvallet	Dwight Koss
Mr Bobby Gilbey	Richard Waugh

Directed by Duncan McIntosh
Set designed by Jeffrey Dallas, executed by Pam Johnson
Costumes designed by Debra Hanson
Lighting designed by Patsy Lang
Sound designed by Walter Lawrence

Stage Manager	Carole Macomber
Assistant Stage Manager	Debra McKay

NIGHT OF JANUARY 16TH by Ayn Rand
Court House Theatre
previews from July 3, opening July 10 to September 27 (55 performances)

Bailiff	Patric Masurkevitch
Judge Heath	Al Kozlik
District Attorney Flint	Sandy Webster
Defense Attorney Stevens	Peter Hutt
Court Clerk	Steven Sutcliffe
Doctor Kirkland	John Gilbert
John Hutchins	Dennis Thatcher
Karen Andre	Tanja Jacobs
Homer Van Fleet	C. Holte Davidson
Officer Sweeney	Paul Larocque
Magda Svenson	Irene Hogan
Nancy Lee Faulkner	Martha Burns
John Graham Whitfield	Richard Farrell
James Chandler	Grant Carmichael
Seigurd Jungquist	Michael Howell
Larry "Guts" Regan	Jon Bryden
Reporters	Grant Carmichael, C. Holte Davidson, Michael Howell, Paul Larocque

Directed by Allen MacInnis
Designed by Pam Johnson
Lighting designed by Patsy Lang
Sound designed by Walter Lawrence

Stage Manager	Laurie Champagne
Assistant Stage Manager	Carolyn Mackenzie

AUGUSTUS DOES HIS BIT by Bernard Shaw
Royal George Theatre
previews from July 8, opening July 10 to August 30 (28 Lunchtime performances)

Lord Augustus Highcastle	Barry MacGregor
Horatio Floyd Beamish	Douglas Rain
The Lady	Tanja Jacobs

Directed by Paul Reynolds
Designed by Tanit Mendes
Lighting designed by Jennifer Bergeron
Sound designed by Walter Lawrence

Stage Manager	Janet Kennedy
Assistant Stage Manager	Victoria Vasileski

1987

PETER PAN by J.M. Barrie
Festival Theatre
previews from August 7, opening August 14 to October 11 (39 performances)

Mrs Darling	Nora McLellan
Mr Darling	Christopher Newton
Wendy Darling	Marti Maraden
John Darling	Andrew Gillies
Michael Darling	Ted Dykstra
Nana	Peter Windrem
Liza	Chick Reid
Peter Pan	Tom McCamus
Tinker Bell	Gail Hakala
Ostrich	Gabrielle Jones
Tootles	Michael Ball
Slightly	Jim Mezon
Curly	Guy Bannerman
First Twin	George Dawson
Second Twin	Rod Campbell
Nibs	William Vickers
Captain James Hook	Christopher Newton
Gentleman Starkey	David Schurmann
Smee	Herb Foster
Cecco	Kerry Dorey
Bill Jukes	Lance McDayter
Skylights	Roger Perkins
Robert Mullins	Dan Lett
Black Gilmour	Roy Lewis
The Crocodile	Deann DeGruijter, Gabrielle Jones
Tiger Lily	Nora McLellan
Great Big Little Panther	Ian Prinsloo
Lone Wolf	Paul Mulloy
The Picaninny Tribe	Steven Cumyn, Richard Waugh, Peter Windrem, Elizabeth Beeler, Deann DeGruijter, Gabrielle Jones
The Mermaids	Elizabeth Beeler, Gail Hakala, Gabrielle Jones
The Never Bird	Chick Reid
Canary Robb	Paul Mulloy
George Scourie	Ian Prinsloo
Chay Turley	Peter Windrem
Cookson	Steven Cumyn
Noodler	Richard Waugh
Whibbles	Ross Driedger
Jane	Erin Marian

110

Directed by Ian Judge
Designed by Cameron Porteous
Lighting designed by Robert Thomson
Sound designed by Walter Lawrence
Original music composed by Christopher Donison
Flight direction by Joe McGeough; Flying by Foy
Fights choreographed by F. Braun McAsh

Stage Manager   Dianne Woodrow
Assistant Stage Managers   Randy Thiessen
                                 Jennifer White

MARTI MARADEN WITH THE LOST BOYS IN *PETER PAN*, 1987 (PHOTO BY DAVID COOPER).

1987

HOT HOUSE PLAYS FROM THE 1890s
Court House Theatre
previews from August 11, opening August 14 to August 30 (8 performances)

PLAYING WITH FIRE by August Strindberg

The Son	Jon Bryden
The Daughter-in-Law	Wendy Thatcher
The Mother	Joyce Campion
The Father	Sandy Webster
The Cousin	Susan Stackhouse
The Friend	Peter Hutt

Directed by Frances Hyland
Designed by Terry Nicholls
Lighting designed by Jennifer Bergeron
Sound designed by Hollis Dykens

SALOMÉ by Oscar Wilde

Tigellinus	Grant Carmichael
Herodias	Robin Craig
Theologist	C. Holte Davidson
Cappadocian	Richard Farrell
Slave	Tracey Ferencz
Theologist	John Gilbert
Second Soldier	Michael Howell
Iokanaan	Dwight Koss
Theologist	Al Kozlik
First Soldier	Paul Larocque
Herod	Barry MacGregor
Young Syrian	Patric Masurkevitch
Narcissistic Twin	Duncan McIntosh
Theologist	Colin Miller
Salomé	Camille Mitchell
Narcissistic Twin	Duncan Ollerenshaw
Page of Herodias	Steven Sutcliffe
Theologist	Dennis Thatcher
Executioner	Richard Thorne

Directed by Sky Gilbert
Designed by Pam Johnson
Lighting designed by Jennifer Bergeron
Sound designed by Hollis Dykens

Stage Manager	Alan Wallis
Assistant Stage Manager	Victoria Vasileski

112

Special Events

Festival Theatre, August 10

The King of Swing Lives On: A Tribute to Benny Goodman.

> Peter Appleyard and The All-Star Swing Band, with special guests
> Butch Miles, Bucky Pizzarelli, Slam Stewart, and Abe Most on clarinet.

Post-season Tour

HAY FEVER

National Arts Centre, Ottawa, November 18 to December 5 (19 performances)

Festival Theatre, Niagara-on-the-Lake, December 9 to 12 (6 performances)

> For the tour Robin Craig appeared as Myra Arundell and Nancy Kerr
> appeared as Clara.

HELEN TAYLOR, JENNIFER PHIPPS, AND RICHARD BINSLEY IN *HAY FEVER*, 1987 (PHOTO BY DAVID COOPER).

1988

Pre-season Tour

YOU NEVER CAN TELL by Bernard Shaw
Festival Theatre, Niagara-on-the-Lake, January 17 – 22 (5 performances)
Manitoba Theatre Centre, Winnipeg, January 27 – February 20 (29 performances)
Olympic Arts Festival, Calgary, February 23 – 27 (7 performances)
Theatre Calgary, Calgary, March 1 – 20 (24 performances)

> Camille Mitchell played Gloria Clandon, Frances Hyland played Mrs Clandon, Jim Mezon played Bohun, and Gail Hakala and George Dawson appeared as the Parlormaid and Third Waiter.

TWENTY-SEVENTH SEASON
April 14 to October 16 (633 performances)

YOU NEVER CAN TELL by Bernard Shaw
Festival Theatre
previews from April 14, opening May 25 to October 15 (79 performances)

Dolly	Helen Taylor
Mr Valentine	Andrew Gillies
Parlormaid	Jane Wheeler
Philip	Steven Sutcliffe
Mrs Clandon	Barbara Gordon
Gloria	Mary Haney
Mr Crampton	Sandy Webster
M'Comas	Robert Benson
The Waiter	Douglas Rain
Bohun	Craig Davidson
The Cook	Patric Masurkevitch
Jo (A Waiter)	Lance McDayter
Waiter	Mark Burgess

Directed by Christopher Newton
Designed by Cameron Porteous
Lighting designed by Robert Thomson
Original music composed by Christopher Donison

Stage Manager	Brian Meister
Assistant Stage Managers	Carole Macomber
	Kathleen P. Smith

ANDREW GILLIES AND SANDY WEBSTER IN *YOU NEVER CAN TELL*, 1988 (PHOTO BY DAVID COOPER).

THE DARK LADY OF THE SONNETS by Bernard Shaw
Royal George Theatre
previews from July 6, opening July 8 to August 28 (29 Lunchtime performances)

The Beefeater	John Gilbert
Queen Elizabeth	Barbara Gordon
Shakespear	Peter Krantz
The Dark Lady	Sarah Orenstein

Directed by Paul Reynolds
Set designed by Christine Plunkett
Costumes designed by Julia Tribe
Lighting designed by Kevin Lamotte

Stage Manager	Janet Kennedy
Assistant Stage Manager	Brian Meister

PETER PAN by J.M. Barrie
Festival Theatre
previews from May 5, opening May 27 to October 16 (84 performances)

Mrs Darling	Robin Craig*
Mr Darling	Christopher Newton
Wendy Darling	Marti Maraden
John Darling	Andrew Gillies
Michael Darling	Ted Dykstra
Nana	Peter Windrem**
Liza	Chick Reid
Peter Pan	Tom McCamus
Tinker Bell	Gail Hakala
Ostrich	Gabrielle Jones
Tootles	Robert Benson
Slightly	Peter Millard
Curly	Guy Bannerman
First Twin	George Dawson
Second Twin	Rod Campbell
Nibs	William Vickers
Captain James Hook	Christopher Newton
Gentleman Starkey	David Schurmann
Smee	Al Kozlik
Cecco	Richard Binsley
Bill Jukes	Lance McDayter
Skylights	Doug Adler
Robert Mullins	Dan Lett
Cookson	Shawn Wright
Noodler	Todd Stewart
The Crocodile	Deann DeGruijter, Susan Johnston
Tiger Lily	Robin Craig***
Great Big Little Panther	Duncan Ollerenshaw
Lone Wolf	Paul Mulloy
Indians	June Crowley, Deann DeGruijter, Susan Johnston, Karen Wood, Dean Cooney, Ian Simpson, Peter Windrem
The Mermaids	June Crowley, Gail Hakala, Gabrielle Jones
The Never Bird	Chick Reid
Jane	Erin Marian

succeeded by Nora McLellan on May 22
**succeeded by Dean Cooney on September 9*
***succeeded by Nora McLellan on May 24*

Karen Wood performed the roles of Mrs Darling and Tiger Lily
on August 23, September 13, 25, 27 and October 4

Original production directed by Ian Judge
Restaged by Christopher Newton and Duncan McIntosh
Original music composed by Christopher Donison
Designed by Cameron Porteous
Lighting designed by Robert Thomson
Fights choreographed by F. Braun McAsh
Sound designed by Walter Lawrence
Flight directed by Joe McGeough; Flying by Foy

Stage Manager	Laurie Champagne
Assistant Stage Managers	Randy Thiessen
	Jennifer White

HIT THE DECK

music by Vincent Youmans
book by Herbert Fields
lyrics by Leo Robin, Clifford Grey, and Irving Caesar

Royal George Theatre
previews from May 11, opening May 28 to October 16 (118 performances)

Junior / Tough	Doug Adler
Chief Petty Officer / Robert	Bob Ainslie
Bilge Smith	Rod Campbell
Looloo	Beth Anne Cole
Dinty / Bunny / Tough / Iceman	Dean Cooney
Mary / Consuela	June Crowley
Lavinia	Deann DeGruijter
Evey / Rita	Gail Hakala
Toddy Gale	Susan Johnston
Lieutenant Alan Clark	Paul Mulloy
Donkey / Tough / Policeman	Ian Simpson
Eustace / Mat / Tough / Police Officer	Todd Stewart
Charlotte Payne	Karen Wood
Bat (Battling Smith) / Tough	Shawn Wright

Orchestra: Roger Perkins (Conductor/piano), Christopher Donison (Emulator II), Martin Arnold (clarinet/alto sax), Valerie Cowie (trumpet), John Loretan (trombone), Neal Evans (bass), Paul Houle (percussion).

Directed by Allen MacInnis
Designed by Patrick Clark
Lighting designed by Lesley Wilkinson
Choreography by Bob Ainslie
Musical direction by Roger Perkins

Stage Manager	Ron Nipper
Assistant Stage Manager	Randy Thiessen

1988

DANGEROUS CORNER by J.B. Priestley
Royal George Theatre
previews from April 27, opening May 27 to October 15 (118 performances)

Freda Caplan	Wendy Noel
Maud Mockridge	Nancy Kerr
Betty Whitehouse	Tracey Ferencz
Olwen Peel	Sharry Flett
Charles Trevor Stanton	Keith Knight
Gordon Whitehouse	Richard Waugh
Robert Caplan	Peter Hutt

Directed by Tony van Bridge
Designed by Peter Wingate
Lighting designed by Sholem Dolgoy
Sound designed by Walter Lawrence

Stage Manager	Janet Kennedy
Assistant Stage Manager	Victoria Vasileski

GENEVA by Bernard Shaw
Court House Theatre
previews from June 30, opening July 7 to September 24 (58 performances)

Begonia Brown	Wendy Thatcher
The Jew	Richard Partington
A Newcomer	Jon Bryden
The Widow	Irene Hogan
A Journalist	David Bloom
The Bishop	Dennis Thatcher
Commissar Posky	Guy Bannerman
Secretary of the League of Nations	George Dawson
Sir Orpheus Midlander	Herb Foster
The Judge	Peter Krantz
The Betrothed	Blair Williams
Bardo Bombardone	Michael Ball
Ernest Battler	Al Kozlik
The Deaconess	Susan Stackhouse
General Flanco de Fortinbras	Ian D. Clark

Directed by Christopher Newton
Designed by Diz Marsh
Lighting designed by Louise Guinand
Sound designed by Walter Lawrence

Stage Manager	Carole Macomber
Assistant Stage Manager	Jennifer White

PETER HUTT, WENDY NOEL, AND SHARRY FLETT IN *DANGEROUS CORNER*, 1988 (PHOTO BY DAVID COOPER).

HE WHO GETS SLAPPED by Leonid Andreyev
Court House Theatre
previews from August 9, opening August 12 to August 26 (7 performances)

Consuela	Helen Taylor
Count Mancini	Herb Foster
He	Michael Ball
Briquet	Al Kozlik
Zinida	Wendy Thatcher
Alfred Bezano	Lance McDayter
A Gentleman	Craig Davidson
Baron Regnard	John Gilbert
Jimmy Jackson	George Dawson
Tili	Steven Sutcliffe
Poli	Guy Bannerman
Thomas	Peter Krantz
Angelica	Barbara Worthy
Three Jockeys:	
Henri	Blair Williams
Grab	David Bloom
Alphonse	Mark Burgess
Waiter	Dan H. Laurence
Wardrobe Mistress	Lorna Wilson
Circus Girl	Jane Wheeler
Orchestra Conductor	Richard Partington

Directed by Marti Maraden
Designed by Tanit Mendes
Lighting designed by Kevin Lamotte

Stage Manager	Carole Macomber
Assistant Stage Manager	Kathleen P. Smith

119

THE VOYSEY INHERITANCE by Harley Granville Barker

Court House Theatre

previews from July 1, opening July 8 to September 25 (63 performances)

Mr Voysey	Douglas Rain
Peacey	John Gilbert
Edward Voysey	Joseph Ziegler
Major Booth Voysey	Ian D. Clark
George Booth	Sandy Webster
Denis Tregoning	Steven Sutcliffe
The Reverend Evan Colpus	Dennis Thatcher
Ethel Voysey	Helen Taylor
Alice Maitland	Susan Stackhouse
Honor Voysey	Mary Haney
Beatrice	Barbara Worthy
Mrs Voysey	Irene Hogan
Mary	Jane Wheeler
Phoebe	Lorna Wilson
Emily	Sarah Orenstein
Trenchard Voysey	Craig Davidson
Hugh Voysey	Jon Bryden
Christopher Voysey	Mark Burgess

Directed by Neil Munro
Designed by Cameron Porteous
Lighting designed by Louise Guinand
Sound designed by Walter Lawrence

Stage Manager	Carolyn Mackenzie
Assistant Stage Manager	Kathleen P. Smith

120

WAR AND PEACE by Leo Tolstoy
adapted by Alfred Neumann, Erwin Piscator, and Guntram Pruefer
translated by Robert David MacDonald

Festival Theatre

previews from May 13, opening May 26 to July 28 (36 performances)

Narrator	Gabrielle Jones
Pierre, Count Besukhov	Peter Hutt
Anatol Kuragin	Dan Lett
Lieutenant Fedya Dolokhov	Richard Waugh
Natasha, Comtesse Rostova	Tracey Ferencz
The Countess Rostova (mother)	Jennifer Phipps
Nicolai, Count Rostov	Richard Binsley
Andrei, Prince Bolkonski	Peter Millard
Nicholas, Prince Bolkonski (father)	David Schurmann
Maria, Princess Bolskonskaya	Sharry Flett
Elizavyeta, Princess Bolskonskaya	Chick Reid
Sergei Kusmich	Keith Knight
Alpatich	Sven van de Ven
Karatayev	William Vickers
Tsar Alexander I	Patric Masurkevitch
Michail Ilyarionovich Kutusov	Robert Haley
Napoleon I	Ted Dykstra
Marshal Soult	Declan Hill
A French Officer	Adrian Griffin
A Drunken Soldier	Duncan Ollerenshaw
A French Officer	Jeff Miller
A Lady in Waiting	Stephanie Kerr
A Midwife	Wendy Noel
A Boy	Peter Windrem

Serfs, maids, footmen, and members of Russian society
played by members of the Ensemble.

Directed by Duncan McIntosh
Designed by John Ferguson
Lighting designed by Sholem Dolgoy
Sound designed by Walter Lawrence

Stage Manager	Charlotte Green
Assistant Stage Managers	Carolyn Mackenzie
	Victoria Vasileski

ONCE IN A LIFETIME by Moss Hart and George S. Kaufman
Festival Theatre
previews from August 5, opening August 12 to October 16 (41 performances)

Susan Walker	Karen Bernstein
Mr Meterstein	Richard Binsley
Jerry Hyland	Ted Dykstra
Coat Check Girl	Tracey Ferencz
Helen Hobart	Sharry Flett
Second Electrician	Adrian Griffin
The Bishop	Robert Haley
Truckman	Declan Hill
Florabel Leigh	Gabrielle Jones
George's Secretary	Nancy Kerr
Miss Fontaine's Maid	Stephanie Kerr
Mr Flick	Keith Knight
George Lewis	Dan Lett
Leading Man	Patric Masurkevitch
Lawrence Vail	Tom McCamus
May Daniels	Nora McLellan
Rudolph Kammerling	Peter Millard
First Lighting Man	Jeff Miller
Miss Leighton	Wendy Noel
Miss Leigh's Chauffeur	Duncan Ollerenshaw
Mrs Walker	Jennifer Phipps
Miss Chasen	Chick Reid
Mr Moulton	David Schurmann
Phyllis Fontaine	Sherry Smith
The Porter	Richard Thorne
Herman Glogauer	Tony van Bridge
Mr Sullivan	Sven van de Ven
Mr Fulton	William Vickers
Mr Weisskopf	Richard Waugh
The Bellboy	Peter Windrem*

Schlepkin Brothers, Dancing Vaudevillians, fans, studio employees, waiters, and movie stars played by members of the Ensemble.

succeeded by Adrian Griffin on September 3

Directed by Duncan McIntosh
Musical direction by Christopher Donison
Designed by Mary Kerr
Lighting designed by Robert Thomson
Sound designed by Walter Lawrence

Stage Manager	Charlotte Green
Assistant Stage Manager	Victoria Vasileski

Special Events

Musical Mondays

Royal George Theatre

July 4	Aldeburgh Connection Presents Upstairs/Downstairs
July 18	Kurt Weill and Friends (Royal George Quintet and Shaw Festival Acting Ensemble)
July 25	Marek Jablonsky plays Chopin
August 1	Aldeburgh Connection Presents Noblesse Oblige: Music of Sir Hubert Parry and Lord Berners
August 22	A Palm Court Evening

On the Terrace

Festival Theatre	July 10 and 24, August 7 and 21 Roger Perkins (music director) and members of the Acting Ensemble.

GBS IN LOVE

Royal George Theatre, July 22, August 5 and 19

A Dramatic Narrative, based on the correspondence of Bernard Shaw and Alice Lockett, devised and performed by Dan H. Laurence.

> Lighting designed by Colin Hughes
> Benefit for the Shaw Festival Library Fund

The Stan Kenton Reunion

Festival Theatre, September 19

1989

TWENTY-EIGHTH SEASON
April 26 to October 29 (647 performances)

GOOD NEWS
music by Ray Henderson
book by Laurence Schwab and B.G. DeSylva
lyrics by B.G. DeSylva and Lew Brown

Royal George Theatre
previews from May 17, opening May 27 to October 15 (120 performances)

Windy	Brian Hill
Slats	David Hogan
Millie	Karen Wood
Flo	Charlotte Moore
Babe O'Day	Deann DeGruijter
"Beef" Saunders	Richard March
"Pooch" Kearney	Bob Ainslie
Bill Johnson	Alex Fallis
Tom Marlowe	Shawn Wright
Patricia Bingham	Gail Hakala
Sylvester	Doug Adler
Constance Lane	Michelle Todd
Bobby Randall	Richard Binsley
Charles Kenyon	Peter Millard

Orchestra: Christopher Donison (Conductor/piano), Jim Weber (clarinet, alto/tenor saxophone), William Mackay (drums), William Murphy (violin), Neal Evans (bass), Valerie Cowie (trumpet).

Directed by Allen MacInnis
Choreography by Bob Ainslie
Musical direction and orchestration
  by Christopher Donison
Designed by Leslie Frankish
Lighting designed by Lesley Wilkinson
Sound designed by Walter Lawrence

Stage Manager	Ron Nipper
Assistant Stage Manager	Jennifer White-Johnston

124

MAN AND SUPERMAN by Bernard Shaw
Festival Theatre
previews from April 26, opening May 24 to October 15 (79 performances)

Roebuck Ramsden	William Hutt
Octavius Robinson	Peter Krantz
Parlormaid	Monica Dufault
John Tanner	Michael Ball
Ann Whitefield	Kate Trotter
Mrs Whitefield	Jennifer Phipps
Miss Ramsden	Marion Gilsenan
Violet Robinson	Julie Stewart
Henry Straker	William Vickers
Hector Malone	Patric Masurkevitch
Mr Malone	Al Kozlik
Mendoza	Barry MacGregor
The Anarchist	Robert Haley
The English Socialist	Peter Windrem
The German Socialist	Dean Cooney
Duval	Tom Wood
The Sulky Social Democrat	Richard Waugh
The Rowdy Social Democrat	Blair Williams
Goatherd	Callum Rennie
A Spanish Officer	Dean Cooney
Singer	Gail Hakala
Pianist	Christopher Donison

The *Don Juan in Hell* scene was added to Act III at a preview on June 29, opening on July 6 and closing on August 31 (13 performances)

Don Juan Tenorio	Michael Ball
Doña Ana de Ulloa	Kate Trotter
Commander of Calatrava (The Statue)	William Hutt
The Devil	Barry MacGregor
Satanic Guests	Dean Cooney, Robert Haley, Callum Rennie, Ric Waugh, Blair Williams, Peter Windrem, Tom Wood

Directed by Christopher Newton
Designed by Eduard Kochergin
Music composed by Christopher Donison
Lighting designed by Robert Thomson
Sound designed by Walter Lawrence

Stage Manager	Laurie Champagne
Assistant Stage Manager	Charlotte Green

1989

ONCE IN A LIFETIME by Moss Hart and George S. Kaufman
Festival Theatre
previews from May 11, opening May 26 to July 23 (36 performances)

George Lewis	Dan Lett
May Daniels	Nora McLellan*
Jerry Hyland	Jim Mezon**
The Porter	Shawn Wright
Helen Hobart	Wendy Thatcher
Susan Walker	Karen Wood
The Bellboy	Peter Windrem
Coat Check Girl	Michelle Todd
Miss Fontaine's Maid	Jane Wheeler
Phyllis Fontaine	Sherry Smith
Miss Leigh's Chauffeur	Ronnie Burkett
Florabel Leigh	Deann DeGruijter
Mrs Walker	Jennifer Phipps
Movie Star / George's Secretary	Nancy Kerr
Mr Weisskopf	Peter Krantz
Mr Meterstein	Richard Binsley
Miss Chasen	Mary Haney
A Waiter	David Hogan
Ernest, the Headwaiter	Sven van de Ven
A Policeman	Alex Fallis
Herman Glogauer	Robert Haley
Miss Leighton	Charlotte Moore***
Lawrence Vail	William Vickers
Mr Moulton	Richard March
Mr Fulton	Bob Ainslie
Rudolph Kammerling	Peter Millard
Second Electrician	Adrian Griffin
Mr Flick	Ian D. Clark
The Bishop	Al Kozlik
Leading Man	Patric Masurkevitch
A Biographer	Doug Adler
A Reporter	Brian Hill

Schlepkin Brothers, Dancing Vaudevillians, fans, studio employees, waiters, and movie stars played by members of the Ensemble.

*succeeded by Charlotte Moore on May 31
**replaced by Richard Binsley from June 22 to July 12,
  the role of Meterstein being eliminated
***succeeded by Mary Haney on May 31

Directed by Duncan McIntosh
Musical direction by Christopher Donison
Designed by Mary Kerr
Lighting designed by Robert Thomson
Sound designed by Walter Lawrence

Stage Manager	Janet Kennedy
Assistant Stage Managers	Kim Barsanti
	Victoria Vasileski

126

BERKELEY SQUARE by John L. Balderston
Festival Theatre
previews from May 4, opening May 25 to October 14 (81 performances)

Tom Pettigrew	Dan Lett
Maid	Jane Wheeler
Kate Pettigrew	Sharry Flett
The Lady Anne Pettigrew	Susan Wright
Mr Throstle	George Dawson
Helen Pettigrew	Mary Haney
The Ambassador	Herb Foster
Mrs Barwick	Nancy Kerr
Peter Standish	Peter Hutt
Marjorie Frant	Nora McLellan*
Major Clinton	Ian D. Clark
Miss Barrymore	Paula Grove
The Duchess of Devonshire	Robin Craig**
Lord Stanley	Jack Medley
HRH The Duke of Cumberland	Sven van de Ven

*succeeded by Paula Grove on May 31
**succeeded by Marti Maraden on October 10

Directed by Neil Munro
Designed by Cameron Porteous
Lighting designed by Sholem Dolgoy
Sound designed by Walter Lawrence

Stage Manager	Carolyn Mackenzie
Assistant Stage Manager	Martha Campbell

AN INSPECTOR CALLS by J.B. Priestley
Royal George Theatre
previews from May 2, opening May 26 to October 14, held over to October 29
(126 performances)

Arthur Birling	Barry MacGregor
Gerald Croft	Richard Waugh
Sheila Birling	Susan Stackhouse*
Sybil Birling	Marion Gilsenan
Edna	Monica Dufault
Eric Birling	Blair Williams
Inspector Goole	Tony van Bridge

*succeeded by Tracey Ferencz on September 26

Directed by Tony van Bridge
Designed by Tanit Mendes
Lighting designed by Kevin Lamotte
Sound designed by Walter Lawrence

Stage Manager	Randy Thiessen
Assistant Stage Manager	Carolina Avaria

July 21 performance cancelled at end of Act II due to
the sudden illness of Marion Gilsenan.

NYMPH ERRANT
music and lyrics by Cole Porter
libretto by Romney Brent, from the novel by James Laver

Court House Theatre
previews from August 8, opening August 11 to 31 (9 performances)

Hercule / Giuseppe / Mr Jones / Concubine	Doug Adler
Dr Sanford / Constantine	Bob Ainslie
Vacationer / Mlle Doto Fuoto / Haidee / Folies Girl	Debra Benjamin
Alexei / Signor Castelnuova / Tourist / Concubine	Richard Binsley
Vacationer / Pierre Fort / Brother Karamazov / Pappas / Concubine	Mark Burgess
Waiter / Mr Huntington / Ali	Ronnie Burkett
Madeleine / Signora Castelnuova / Tourist	Deann DeGruijter
Reverend Pither / Customer / Graf von Anhaldt-Serbst / Tourist	Alex Fallis
Bertha / Vacationer / Bessie / Princess Volkonsky / Folies Girl	Susan Johnston
Edith Sanford / Cocotte / Contessa Buffalini / Tourist / Folies Girl	Gail Hakala
Vacationer / Brother Karamazov / Ben	Brian Hill
Porter / Vacationer / Café Waiter / Prince Volkonsky / Tourist / Adam	David Hogan
Aunt Ermyntrude / Mme Arthur / Mrs Bamberg	Nancy Kerr
Andre de Croissant / Manfredo / Concubine	Richard March
Count Hohenaldeborn-Mantelini / Concubine	Peter Millard
Evangeline	Charlotte Moore
Winnie / Joyce / Vacationer / Mrs Cohen	Elizabeth Richardson
Miss Pratt / Clara / Lady Nora Smeed	Michelle Todd
Henrietta / Tourist / Greek Woman / Folies Girl	Karen Wood
Pedro / Mr Hawkins / Kassim	Shawn Wright

Orchestra: Christopher Donison (piano), Valerie Cowie (trumpet), Neal Evans (bass), William MacKay (percussion), William Murphy (violin), Jim Weber (clarinet, bass clarinet, alto sax).

Directed by Allen MacInnis
Designed by Christine Plunkett
Lighting designed by Kevin Lamotte
Musical direction by Christopher Donison

Orchestration by Neal Evans
Choreography by Bob Ainslie
Sound designed by Walter Lawrence

Stage Manager	Jennifer White-Johnston
Assistant Stage Manager	Kim Barsanti

TRELAWNY OF THE 'WELLS' by Arthur W. Pinero

Festival Theatre

previews from August 4, opening August 11 to October 15 (47 performances)

Hall-keeper of the Pantheon	Jack Medley
Mrs Mossop	Irene Hogan
Sarah, a maid	Mary Haney
Mr Ablett	Al Kozlik
Tom Wrench	Tom Wood
Imogen Parrott	Wendy Thatcher
James Telfer	Robert Benson
Ferdinand Gadd	Robert Haley
Augustus Colpoys	William Vickers
Mrs Telfer (Violet Sylvester)	Joyce Campion
Avonia Bunn	Barbara Worthy
Rose Trelawny	Julie Stewart
Arthur Gower	Peter Krantz
Trafalgar Gower	Jennifer Phipps
Sir William Gower	William Hutt
Captain Frederick de Foenix	Peter Hutt
Clara de Foenix	Jane Wheeler
Charles Gibbons, a footman	Peter Windrem
Michael O'Dwyer	Dan Lett
Mr Mortimer	Patric Masurkevitch
Mr Denzil	Michael Ball
Miss Brewster	Mary Haney
Mr Hunston	Dean Cooney
Walking Gentleman	Ian D. Clark
General Utility	Callum Rennie
Second Comedienne	Jane Wheeler

Directed by Christopher Newton
Designed by Cameron Porteous
Lighting designed by Robert Thomson
Sound designed by Walter Lawrence
Fight choreographed by Richard Waugh

Stage Manager	Charlotte Green
Assistant Stage Manager	Victoria Vasileski

GETTING MARRIED by Bernard Shaw

Court House Theatre

previews from July 2, opening July 7 to September 24 (63 performances)

Alice Bridgenorth	Robin Craig
William Collins	Sandy Webster
General Bridgenorth ("Boxer")	Graham Harley
Lesbia Grantham	Sharry Flett
Reginald Bridgenorth	Douglas Rain
Leo (Mrs Reginald)	Gabrielle Rose
The Right Reverend Alfred	
Bridgenorth (The Bishop)	Herb Foster
St John Hotchkiss	Simon Bradbury
Cecil Sykes	Steven Sutcliffe
Edith Bridgenorth	Paula Grove
Reverend Oliver Cromwell	
Soames (Father Anthony)	George Dawson
The Beadle	Jack Medley *(to July 23)*
	Sven van de Ven *(from July 26)*
Mrs George Collins	Susan Wright

Directed by Marti Maraden
Designed by Christina Poddubiuk
Lighting designed by Robert Thomson
Sound designed by Walter Lawrence

Stage Manager	Carolyn Mackenzie
Assistant Stage Manager	Martha Campbell

PEER GYNT by Henrik Ibsen

translated by John Lingard

Court House Theatre

previews from July 4, opening July 8 to September 24 (36 performances)

Peer Gynt	Jim Mezon
Aase	Joan Orenstein
Woman with a Cornsack /	
Mads Moen's mother	Irene Hogan
Aslak / Ballon / Huhu / Ship's	
Cook / the Buttonmoulder	Robert Benson
Ingrid / a Seter Girl /	
Statue of Mamnon	Susan Stackhouse
Mads Moen's father / Troll	
King / Von Eberkopf /	
Begriffenfeldt / Ship's Captain	Sandy Webster
Mads Moen / Schafmann /	
Ship's Boy	Adrian Griffin
Solveig's mother / Woman	
in Green's sister / Kari	Joyce Campion

Solveig's father / Troll Prime
   Minister / Trumpeterstraale /
   Thin Character   Graham Harley
Solveig   Gabrielle Rose
Helga / Ugly Boy   Sherry Smith
A Seter Girl / Woman in Green   Elizabeth Richardson
A Seter Girl / Anitra   Wendy Thatcher
Mr Cotton / Hussain /
   Strange Passenger   Simon Bradbury
Thief / Schlingenberg / Watch   Mark Burgess
Receiver / Fellah / Bosun   Steven Sutcliffe

Villagers, trolls, desert people, madhouse inmates, and voices
in the air played by members of the Ensemble.

Directed by Duncan McIntosh
Designed by Phillip Clarkson
Lighting designed by Kevin Lamotte
Sound designed by Walter Lawrence

Stage Manager   Janet Kennedy
Assistant Stage Managers   Carolina Avaria
                         Randy Thiessen

SHAKES VERSUS SHAV and THE GLIMPSE OF REALITY
by Bernard Shaw

Royal George Theatre
previews from July 5, opening July 7 to September 3 (37 Lunchtime performances)

A production of the Shaw Festival Puppet Workshop,
created and performed by Ronnie Burkett.
Hostess: Mrs Patrick Campbell

SHAKES VERSUS SHAV

Characters: Shakes, Shav, Rob Roy, Macbeth, Captain Shotover,
Ellie Dunn. Voices of Shotover and Ellie Dunn by Douglas Rain.

THE GLIMPSE OF REALITY

Characters: Giulia (performed by Mrs Patrick Campbell),
Ferruccio, Squarcio, Sandro.

Directed by Paul Reynolds
Designed by Ronnie Burkett
Lighting designed by Ereca Hassell
Sound designed by Walter Lawrence

Stage Manager   Ron Nipper
Assistant Stage Manager   Kim Barsanti

1989

Special Events

Monday Concerts

St Marks Church, June 5 The BBC Singers

Festival Theatre, June 19 Manteca

Royal George Theatre
July 3	A Country House Weekend (Aldeburgh Connection)
July 17	Music from Sharon (Lawrence Cherney, oboe; Wendy Humphreys, soprano and harp; Michael Bloss, piano)
July 31	Moonlight Melodrama (William Tritt, piano; Christopher Newton, narrator)
August 14	The Lonely Heart: The songs of Tchai kovsky, with readings from his letters and diaries (Aldeburgh Connection; Christopher Newton, narrator)

Festival Theatre
August 21	Swingdance (The Frankie Phelan Five)
September 11	George Shearing Duo (with Neil Swainson)

BERNARD SHAW: ON STAGE
International Shaw Conference. August 23 to 26

co-sponsored by the Academy of the Shaw Festival and the University of Guelph, at Guelph and Niagara-on-the-Lake.

> Principal Participants: Jean-Claude Amalric (France), Alan Andrews, Douglas Campbell, Ann Casson, Leonard Conolly, Vincent Dowling (Ireland), Bernard F. Dukore (USA), Shafik Fayad (Kuwait), Andrew Gillies, Leon Hugo (South Africa), Dan Laurence (USA), Barry MacGregor, Masahiko Masumoto (Japan), Rhoda Nathan (USA), Christopher Newton, Anna Obraztsova (USSR), Marina Ochakovskaya (Estonia), Cameron Porteous, Toby Robertson (UK), Erik Wahlund (Sweden), Irving Wardle (UK), Tom Wood.

Post-season Tour

AN INSPECTOR CALLS
Annenberg Theatre Center, Philadelphia, November 1 to 4 (7 performances)

BERKELEY SQUARE
National Arts Centre, Ottawa, October 18 to November 4 (20 performances)

1990

TWENTY-NINTH SEASON
April 25 to November 4 (690 performances)

MISALLIANCE by Bernard Shaw
Festival Theatre
previews from April 25, opening May 23 to October 14 (91 performances)

The Maid	Michelle Cecile Martin
The Gardener	Bart Anderson
Jock	Murray Oliver
Bill Burt	Neil Barclay
Bentley Summerhays	Duncan Ollerenshaw
Johnny Tarleton	Mark Burgess
Hypatia Tarleton	Helen Taylor
Mrs Tarleton	Jennifer Phipps
Lord Summerhays	Richard Farrell
Mr Tarleton	Barry MacGregor
Joey Percival	Peter Krantz
Lina Szczepanowska	Sharry Flett
Gunner (Julius Baker)	Simon Bradbury

Directed by Christopher Newton
Designed by Leslie Frankish
Lighting designed by Robert Thomson
Sound designed by Walter Lawrence

Stage Manager	Ron Nipper
Assistant Stage Manager	Carolina Avaria

SHARRY FLETT AND
BARRY MACGREGOR
IN *MISALLIANCE*,
1990 (PHOTO BY
DAVID COOPER).

133

NIGHT MUST FALL by Emlyn Williams
Royal George Theatre
previews from May 1, opening May 25 to October 21, held over to November 4
(143 performances)

Lord Chief Justice	Graham Harley
Mrs Bramson	Jennifer Phipps
Olivia Grayne	Sharry Flett
Nurse Libby	Michelle Cecile Martin
Hubert Laurie	Ian D. Clark
Mrs Terence	Lorna Wilson
Dora Parkoe	Helen Taylor*
Inspector Belsize	Richard Farrell
Danny	Peter Krantz

succeeded by Deborah Lambie on October 25

Directed by Randy Maertz
Designed by John Dinning
Lighting designed by Kevin Lamotte
Sound designed by Walter Lawrence

Stage Manager	Carolyn Mackenzie
Assistant Stage Manager	Carolina Avaria

WHEN WE ARE MARRIED by J.B. Priestley
Royal George Theatre
previews from May 9, opening May 26 to October 13 (106 performances)

Alderman Joseph Helliwell	Jack Medley
Maria Helliwell	Joyce Campion
Councillor Albert Parker	Graham Harley
Annie Parker	Barbara Worthy
Herbert Soppitt	George Dawson
Clara Soppitt	Irene Hogan
Ruby Birtle	Sherry Smith
Gerald Forbes	Richard Waugh
Mrs Northrop	Lorna Wilson
Nancy Holmes	Ann Baggley
Fred Dyson	Peter Hutt
Henry Ormonroyd	Tony van Bridge
Lottie Grady	Mary Haney
Reverend Clement Mercer	Sven van de Ven

Directed by Tony van Bridge
Designed by John Dinning
Costumes designed by Carolyn Smith
Lighting designed by Kevin Lamotte
Original music composed by Christopher Donison
Sound designed by Walter Lawrence

Stage Manager	Charlotte Green
Assistant Stage Managers	Debbie Boult
	Randy Thiessen

TRELAWNY OF THE 'WELLS' by Arthur W. Pinero

Festival Theatre

previews from May 4, opening May 25 to July 22 (43 performances)

Sarah	Sherry Smith
Mrs Mossop	Irene Hogan
Mr Ablett	Sven van de Ven
Tom Wrench	William Vickers
Imogen Parrott	Mary Haney
James Telfer	George Dawson
Ferdinand Gadd	Barry MacGregor
Augustus Colpoys	Simon Bradbury
Mrs Telfer	Marion Gilsenan
Avonia Bunn	Barbara Worthy
Rose Trelawny	Julie Stewart
Arthur Gower	Duncan Ollerenshaw
Sir William Gower	William Hutt
Miss Trafalgar Gower	Joyce Campion
Clara de Foenix	Karen Wood
Captain Frederick de Foenix	Peter Hutt
Charles Gibbons	Richard Waugh
Michael O'Dwyer	Robert Haley
Hall-Keeper of the Pantheon	Jack Medley

Members of the Company at the Pantheon:

Mr Mortimer	Mark Burgess
Mr Denzil	Sven van de Ven
Miss Brewster	Deborah Lambie
Mr Hunston	Bart Anderson

Directed by Christopher Newton
Designed by Cameron Porteous
Lighting designed by Robert Thomson
Sound designed by Walter Lawrence

Stage Manager	Charlotte Green
Assistant Stage Managers	Debbie Boult
	Randy Thiessen

VILLAGE WOOING by Bernard Shaw

Royal George Theatre

previews from July 4, opening July 6 to September 30 (53 Lunchtime performances)

A	Michael Ball
Z	Wendy Thatcher
Deck Steward	Murray Oliver

Directed by Paul Lampert
Designed by Yvonne Sauriol
Lighting designed by Ereca Hassell

Stage Manager	Carolyn Mackenzie
Assistant Stage Manager	Jennifer White-Johnston

NYMPH ERRANT
music and lyrics by Cole Porter
book by Romney Brent, from a novel by James Laver

Court House Theatre
previews from June 12, opening July 6 to September 23 (70 performances)

Pedro Bernanos / Prince Ivan / Kassim	Bob Ainslie
Waiter / Mr Huntington / Ali	Robert Benson
Dr Sanford / Constantine	Hugo Dann
Madeleine St Maure / Signora	
Castelnuova / Tourist	Deann DeGruijter
The Reverend Malcolm Pither / French	
Man / Graf Von Anhaldt-Serbat	Robert Haley
Brother Karamazoff / Ben Winthrop	Brian Hill
Train Porter / Paris Waiter / Brother	
Karamazoff / Tourist /	
Adam the Gardener	David Hogan
Bertha / Bessie / Princess Ivan /	
Folies Girl	Susan Johnston
Winnie / Joyce Arbuthnot-Palmer /	
La Contessa Bufalini	Gabrielle Jones
Miss Washington / Mlle Doto Fuoto /	
Haidee Robinson / Folies Girl	Rosalind Keene
Aunt Ermyntrude / Mme Arthur /	
Mrs Bamberg	Nancy Kerr
Miss Pratt / Clara / Mrs Cohen	Jo-Anne Kirwan Clark
Andre de Croissant / Manfredo the	
Major-Domo / Tourist / Concubine	Richard March
Count Ferdinand / Concubine	Peter Millard
Evangeline	Charlotte Moore
Hercule / Giuseppe / Mr Jones /	
Tourist / Concubine	Stephen Simms
Alexei Stukin / Signor Castelnuova /	
Concubine	Steven Sutcliffe
Edith Sanford / Cocotte / Lady Norah	
Smeed / Tourist / Folies Girl	Bernadette Taylor
Henrietta Bamberg / Tourist /	
Feliza / Folies Girl	Karen Wood
Pierre Fort / Mr Hawkins /	
Mr Pappas / Concubine	William Vickers

Orchestra: Christopher Donison (Conductor/piano), Valerie Cowie (trumpet), Neal Evans (bass), William MacKay (percussion), William Murphy (violin), Jim Weber (clarinet, bass clarinet, alto saxophone).

Directed by Allen MacInnis
Choreography by Bob Ainslie
Musical direction by Christopher Donison
Orchestration by Neal Evans and Christopher Donison

Designed by Christine Plunkett
Lighting designed by Kevin Lamotte

| Stage Manager | Randy Thiessen |
| Assistant Stage Manager | Jennifer White-Johnston |

THE WALTZ OF THE TOREADORS by Jean Anouilh
translated by Lucienne Hill

Festival Theatre
previews from May 16, opening May 24 to October 12 (69 performances)

Léon, General St Pé	William Hutt
Emily, his wife	Marion Gilsenan
Gaston, his secretary	Blair Williams
Sidonia	Tracey Ferencz
Estelle	Deborah Lambie
Dr Bonfant	Allan Gray
Eugénie	Janet Snetsinger
Mlle de Ste Euverte	Diana Leblanc
Mme Dupont-Fredaine	Joan Orenstein
Father Ambrose	Sandy Webster
Pamela	Julie Stewart

Directed by David Giles
Settings designed by Kenneth Mellor
Costumes designed by Cameron Porteous
Lighting designed by Louise Guinand
Music composed by Christopher Donison
Sound designed by Walter Lawrence

| Stage Manager | Laurie Champagne |
| Assistant Stage Manager | Martha Campbell |

MRS WARREN'S PROFESSION by Bernard Shaw
Court House Theatre
previews from June 29, opening July 5 to September 23 (61 performances)

Praed	Allan Gray
Vivie Warren	Tracey Ferencz
Mrs Warren	Joan Orenstein
Sir George Crofts	Sandy Webster
Frank Gardner	Blair Williams
The Reverend Samuel Gardner	David Schurmann

Directed by Glynis Leyshon
Designed by Cameron Porteous
Lighting designed by Robert Thomson

| Stage Manager | Laurie Champagne |
| Assistant Stage Manager | Martha Campbell |

PRESENT LAUGHTER by Noel Coward

Festival Theatre

previews from August 3, opening August 10 to October 14 (47 performances)

Daphne Stillington	Ann Baggley
Miss Erikson	Wendy Thatcher
Fred	Peter Millard
Monica Reed	Nicola Cavendish
Gary Essendine	Christopher Newton
Liz Essendine*	Fiona Reid
Roland Maule	Steven Sutcliffe
Hugo Lyppiatt	Michael Ball
Morris Dixon	Peter Hutt
Joanne Lyppiatt	Deann DeGruijter
Lady Saltburn	Nancy Kerr

performed by Julie Stewart on October 10, 11 and 14

Directed by Bob Baker
Designed by Phillip Clarkson
Lighting designed by Robert Thomson
Sound designed by Walter Lawrence

Stage Manager	Charlotte Green
Assistant Stage Manager	Debbie Boult

UBU REX by Alfred Jarry

translated by David Copelin

Court House Theatre

previews from August 3, opening August 10 to 17 (7 performances)

Boleslas / Noble-Judge- Financier 5 / Russian / Partisan 1	Bart Anderson
Conspirator / Clerk / The Whole Polish Army / Jan Sigusmund	Neil Barclay
King Wenceslas / The Whole Russian Army / Peasant 2	Robert Benson
Captain Sexcrement	Simon Bradbury
Cootie	Mark Burgess
Soldier 3 / Queen Rosamund / Pa Ubu 5th Head	Hugo Dann
Ladislas / Noble-Judge-Financier 4 / Pa Ubu 2nd Head	Brian Hill
Soldier 1 / Peasant 1 / General Laskie	David Hogan
Noble-Judge-Financier 2 / Stanislas Leczinski / Partisan 2	Susan Johnston

Conspirator / Rensky / Mathias	Gabrielle Jones
Crotch	Jo-Anne Kirwan Clark
Soldier 2 / Counsellor /	
Guard / Pa Ubu 4th Head	Deborah Lambie
Ship's Master	Dan H. Laurence
Ma Ubu	Diana Leblanc
Pa Ubu	Barry MacGregor
Noble-Judge-Financier 1 /	
Czar Alexis	Charlotte Moore
Pile	Duncan Ollerenshaw
Noble-Judge-Financier 3 /	
Pa Ubu 3rd Head /	
Michael Federovitch	Janet Snetsinger
Buggerlas	Julie Stewart

Directed by Allen MacInnis
Designed by Yvonne Sauriol
Lighting designed by Ereca Hassell

Stage Manager	Ron Nipper
Assistant Stage Manager	Michelle Lagassé

Special Events

Monday Concerts

Royal George Theatre

June 25	The Great Lakes Brass
July 9	Glamourous Night: Music of Novello and Coward (Aldeburgh Connection)
July 16	William Tritt in Recital: The Virtuoso Piano
August 27	Upper Canada Saxophone Quartet

Festival Theatre

August 13	National Youth Orchestra
August 20	Swing Band Dance (The Frankie Phelan Five)

Benefit for the Acting Ensemble's Boxill-Doherty Fund.

Post-Season Tour

NIGHT MUST FALL

Annenberg Theatre Center, Philadelphia, November 6 to 11 (8 performances)

1991

THIRTIETH SEASON
April 19 to November 10 (659 Performances)

PRESS CUTTINGS by Bernard Shaw
Royal George Theatre
previews from July 6, opening July 13 to September 15 (43 Lunchtime performances)

General Mitchener	Richard Farrell
An Orderly	Blair Williams
Prime Minister Balsquith	Jack Medley
Mrs Farrell	Pat Armstrong
Mrs Rosa Carmina Banger	Joan Orenstein
Lady Corinthia Fanshawe	Marion Gilsenan

Directed by Glynis Leyshon
Designed by Sean Breaugh
Lighting designed by Matthew Flawn

Stage Manager	Randy Thiessen
Assistant Stage Manager	Michelle Lagassé

THE MILLIONAIRESS by Bernard Shaw
Court House Theatre
previews from June 30, opening July 11 to September 22 (53 performances)

Julius Sagamore	Blair Williams
Epifania Ognisanti Di	
Parerga Fitzfassenden	Nicola Cavendish
Alastair Fitzfassenden	David Christoffel
Patricia Smith	Sarah Orenstein
Adrian Blenderbland	Herb Foster
The Egyptian Doctor	George Dawson
Joe, the Elderly Man	Tony van Bridge
The Elderly Woman	Irene Hogan
Hotel Manager	Simon Bradbury

Directed by Christopher Newton
Designed by Cameron Porteous
Lighting designed by Robert Thomson

Stage Manager	Ron Nipper
Assistant Stage Manager	Carolina Avaria

LULU by Frank Wedekind
adapted by Peter Barnes

Festival Theatre

previews from May 8, opening May 23 to September 18 (47 performances)

Hunidei	David Adams
Crazy Girl / Statue	Kathryn Akin
Bob / Lead Guitar	Robin Avery
Henriette / Courtesan	Lorretta Bailey
Schon	Michael Ball
Rodrigo Quast	Neil Barclay
Dr Goll	Robert Benson
Schwarz	Derek Boyes
Heilman	Grant Cowan
Kungu Poti	Mark Cassius Ferguson
Countess Geschwitz	Sharry Flett
Dr Hilti	David Hogan
Mageleone	Maggie Huculak
Bianetta / Crazy Girl	Jane Johanson
Courtesan	Nancy Kerr
Ferdinand	Lee MacDougall
Casti-Piani	Richard McMillan
Puntschu	Peter Millard
Hugenburg / Keyboard / Statue	Greg Morris
Bass Guitar / The Observer / Statue	Tony Munch
Alwa	Robert Persichini
Policeman / Percussion	Ted Price
Escherich	Stephen Simms
Ludmilla	Karen Skidmore
Prince Escerny	Steven Sutcliffe
Kadidja / Crazy Girl	Bernadette Taylor
Lulu	Helen Taylor
Schigolch	William Vickers
Jack / Statue	Peter Wilds
Crazy Girl / Statue	Viviana Zarrillo

Directed by Christopher Newton
Designed by Leslie Frankish
Lighting designed by Robert Thomson
Music composed by Christopher Donison
Choreography by Caroline Smith

Stage Manager	Charlotte Green
Assistant Stage Manager	Jennifer Johnston

THE DOCTOR'S DILEMMA by Bernard Shaw

Festival Theatre

previews from April 19, opening May 22 to October 13 (101 performances)

Redpenny	Robert Persichini
Emmy	Pat Armstrong
Sir Colenso Ridgeon	Michael Ball
Leo Schutzmacher	Jack Medley
Sir Patrick Cullen	Richard Farrell
Mr Cutler Walpole	Barry MacGregor
Sir Ralph Bloomfield Bonington	Robert Benson
Dr Blenkinsop	William Vickers
Jennifer Dubedat	Maggie Huculak
Louis Dubedat	Steven Sutcliffe
Minnie Tinwell	Helen Taylor
The Newspaper Man	Greg Morris
Mr Danby	Stephen Flett

Directed by Paul Lampert
Designed by Leslie Frankish
Lighting designed by Kevin Lamotte

Stage Manager	Laurie Champagne
Assistant Stage Manager	Michelle Lagassé

A CONNECTICUT YANKEE

music by Richard Rodgers

lyrics by Lorenz Hart, book by Herbert Fields

Royal George Theatre

previews from April 25, opening May 24 to October 25 (126 performances)

Lieutenant Martin Barrett, USN	Richard McMillan
Lieutenant Kenneth Kay, USN	Neil Barclay
Judge Thurston Merrill	Grant Cowan
Admiral Arthur K. Arthur, USN	Peter Millard
Ensign Gerald Lake, USN	David Hogan
Captain Laurence Lake, USN	David Adams
Ensign Sagamore, USN	Stephen Simms
Lieutenant Tristan, USN	Lee MacDougall
A Waiter	Mark Cassius Ferguson
Lieutenant Fay Merrill, WAVE	Karen Skidmore

WAVEs:

Eve	Kathryn Akin
Gwen	Jane Johanson
Angie	Bernadette Taylor
Millie	Viviana Zarrillo
Alice Courtleigh	Lorretta Bailey

In Camelot

Sir Kay, the Seneschal	Neil Barclay
Martin	Richard McMillan

Vassal	Mark Cassius Ferguson
The Demoiselle Alisande La Courtelloise (Sandy)	Lorretta Bailey
Arthur, King of Britain	Peter Millard
Merlin	Grant Cowan
Queen Guinevere	Jane Johanson
Sir Launcelot of the Lake	David Adams
Sir Galahad, his Son	David Hogan
Sir Tristan	Lee MacDougall
Sir Sagamore	Stephen Simms
Angela, handmaiden to Queen Morgan La Fay	Bernadette Taylor
Queen Morgan La Fay	Karen Skidmore
Mistress Evelyn La Rondelle	Kathryn Akin
Millicent, Lady of the Court	Viviana Zarrillo

Directed by Tom Diamond
Designed by Phillip Clarkson
Lighting designed by Ereca Hassell
Musical direction and arrangements by
Christopher Donison
Choreography by Caroline Smith

Stage Manager	Randy Thiessen
Assistant Stage Managers	Jennifer Johnston
	Michelle Lagassé

STEVEN SUTCLIFFE AND MAGGIE HUCULAK IN *THE DOCTOR'S DILEMMA*, 1991 (PHOTO BY DAVID COOPER).

143

1991

HEDDA GABLER by Henrik Ibsen
adapted by Judith Thompson

Court House Theatre
previews from July 30, opening August 8 to September 22 (33 performances)

Manservant	Matthew Henry
Manservants	Robin Avery, Peter Wilds
Hedda Gabler	Fiona Reid
Eilert Lovborg	Jim Mezon
Aunt Juliana	Joan Orenstein
Berthe	Ann Holloway
George Tesman	Derek Boyes
Mrs Elvsted	Sharry Flett
Judge Brack	Roger Rowland

Directed by Judith Thompson
Designed by Cameron Porteous
Lighting designed by Ereca Hassell
Original Music composed by Bill Thompson
in consultation with Yuval R. Fichman

Stage Manager	Charlotte Green
Assistant Stage Manager	Jennifer Johnston

A CUCKOO IN THE NEST by Ben Travers
Festival Theatre
previews from April 27, opening May 25 to October 13 (84 performances)

Rawlins, a London Maid	Deborah Lambie
Mrs Bone	Marion Gilsenan
Major George Bone	Barry MacGregor
Barbara Wykeham	Mary Haney
Gladys	Sherry Smith
Alfred	Stephen Flett
Marguerite Hickett	Wendy Thatcher
Peter Wykeham	Simon Bradbury
Noony	Jack Medley
Voice of Mr Pillbutton	Christopher Newton
Mrs Spoker	Irene Hogan
Reverend Cathcart	
Sloley-Hones	Tony van Bridge
Chauffeur	Guy Bannerman
Claude Hickett, M.P.	George Dawson
Marguerite's Dog	Lady Sarah / Candy

Directed by Larry Dann
Designed by Patrick Clark
Lighting designed by Robert Thomson

Stage Manager	Ron Nipper
Assistant Stage Manager	Carolina Avaria

144

HENRY IV by Luigi Pirandello
translated by Robert Rietty and John Wardle

Court House Theatre
previews from June 28, opening July 12 to September 21 (38 performances)

Manservant	Robin Avery
Manservant	Peter Wilds
Landolf (Lolo)	Peter Krantz
Harold (Franco)	Tony Munch
Ordulf (Momo)	Matthew Heney
Bertold (Fino)	John Ormerod
Giovanni, the butler	Ted Price
Marquis Carlo Di Nolli	Ric Waugh
Baron Tito Belcredi	Herb Foster
Dr Dionisio Genoni	Roger Rowland
Marchesa Matilde Spina	Jennifer Phipps
Frida, her daughter	Elizabeth Brown
Henry IV	David Schurmann

Directed by Paul Lampert
Designed by Cameron Porteous
Lighting designed by Kevin Lamotte
Fight Choreographer Ric Waugh

Stage Manager	Carolyn Mackenzie
Assistant Stage Manager	Kevin Thomas

DAVID SCHURMANN, HERB FOSTER, JENNIFER PHIPPS, AND ROGER ROWLAND IN *HENRY IV*, 1991
(PHOTO BY DAVID COOPER).

HELEN TAYLOR IN *LULU*, 1991 (PHOTO BY DAVID COOPER).

THIS HAPPY BREED by Noel Coward
Royal George Theatre
previews from May 1, opening May 25 to November 10 (134 performances)

Mrs Flint	Jennifer Phipps
Ethel Gibbons	Wendy Thatcher
Sylvia Gibbons	Mary Haney
Frank Gibbons	David Schurmann
Bob Mitchell	Guy Bannerman
Reg Gibbons	John Ormerod
Queenie Gibbons	Elizabeth Brown
Vi Gibbons	Deborah Lambie
Sam Leadbitter	Ric Waugh
Phyllis Blake	Sherry Smith*
Edie	Monica Dufault
Billy Mitchell	Peter Krantz

succeeded by Lorretta Bailey on October 16

Directed by Susan Cox
Designed by Charlotte Dean
Lighting designed by Ereca Hassell

Stage Manager	Carolyn Mackenzie
Assistant Stage Managers	Debbie Boult
	Kevin Thomas

Post-Season Tour

THE DOCTOR'S DILEMMA
National Arts Centre, Ottawa, October 17 to November 2 (20 performances)

For the tour Nicola Cavendish appeared as Emmy, Sarah Orenstein appeared as Minnie Tinwell, and the Assistant Stage Manager was Jennifer Johnston.

1992

THIRTY-FIRST SEASON

April 21 to November 1 (683 Performances)

ON THE TOWN
music by Leonard Bernstein
book and lyrics by Betty Comden and Adolph Green
based on an idea by Jerome Robbins

Royal George Theatre
previews from May 6, opening May 30 to October 11 (132 performances)

The Sailors

Ozzie	W.J. Matheson
Chip	Roger Honeywell
Gabey	Brian Hill

The Girls

Hildy Esterhazy	Bridget O'Sullivan
Claire de Loone	Karen Skidmore
Ivy Smith	Veronica Tennant

The New Yorkers

The Master of Ceremonies	Lee MacDougall
Flossie	Jane Johanson
Pinkie	Frances Chiappetta
S. Uperman	Cassel Miles
Professor Waldo Figment	Jeffrey Prentice
The Dream Gabey	Mario Marcil
Madame Maude P. Dilly	Adele Clark / Janet Martin
Judge Pitkin W. Bridgework	David Adams
Lucy Schmeeler	Sherri McFarlane

Directed by Susan Cox
Designed by Peter Dillman
Lighting designed by Kevin Lamotte
Musical direction and arrangements
  by Christopher Donison
Choreography by Claudia Moore

Stage Manager	Charlotte Green
Assistant Stage Manager	Meredith Macdonald

HOLLY DENNISON, MICHAEL BALL, ANDREW GILLIES, DEBORAH LAMBIE, SEANA MCKENNA, PETER WILDS,
AND JENNIFER PHIPPS IN *PYGMALION*, 1992 (PHOTO BY DAVID COOPER).

PYGMALION by Bernard Shaw

Festival Theatre
previews from April 21, opening May 27 to November 1 (117 performances)

Clara Eynsford Hill	Deborah Lambie
Mrs Eynsford Hill	Holly Dennison
Bystander from Selsey / The Ambassador	Jack Medley
Freddy Eynsford Hill	Peter Wilds
Eliza Doolittle	Seana McKenna
Colonel Pickering	Michael Ball
Henry Higgins	Andrew Gillies
Sarcastic Bystander / Nepommuck	Neil Barclay
Bystander / Maid / Parlormaid / The Ambassador's Wife	Tracey Ferencz
Bystander / Footman / Taximan	Richard Kenyon
Mrs Pearce	Joan Orenstein
Alfred Doolittle	Barry MacGregor
Mrs Higgins	Jennifer Phipps

Directed by Christopher Newton
Designed by Leslie Frankish
Lighting designed by Robert Thomson

Stage Manager	Laurie Champagne
Assistant Stage Managers	Allan Teichman
	Randy Thiessen

148

COUNSELLOR-AT-LAW by Elmer Rice

Festival Theatre

previews from May 16, opening May 29 to October 11 (63 performances)

Bessie Green	Elizabeth Brown
Henry Susskind	W.J. Matheson
Sarah Becker	Jennifer Phipps
Mrs Moretti	Janet Martin
Mr Moretti	Mario Marcil
A Postman / Mr Crayfield	David Adams
Zedorah Chapman	Bridget O'Sullivan
Goldie Rindskopf	Karen Skidmore
Charles McFadden	Michael Ball
John P. Tedesco	Peter Hutt
A Bootblack / Errand Boy	Jeffrey Prentice
Regina Gordon	Mary Haney
Herbert Howard Weinberg	Brian Hill
Arthur Sandler	Roger Honeywell
Lillian Larue	Sherri McFarlane
Roy Darwin	David Christoffel
Western Union Messenger /	
Johann Breitstein	Lee MacDougall
George Simon	Jim Mezon
Cora Simon	Sarah Orenstein
Mrs Gardi	Frances Chiappetta
Tedesco's Client	Jane Johanson
Lena Simon	Joan Orenstein
Peter J. Malone	Roger Rowland
David Simon	George Dawson
Harry Becker	Blair Williams
Richard Dwight, Jr	Jonathan Veeneman
Dorothy Dwight	Amy Sanders
Francis Clark Baird	Craig Davidson

Directed by Neil Munro

Designed by Cameron Porteous

Lighting designed by Kevin Lamotte

Stage Manager	Carolyn Mackenzie
Assistant Stage Manager	Carolina Avaria

CHARLEY'S AUNT by Brandon Thomas

Festival Theatre
previews from June 9, opening July 11 to November 1 (90 performances)

Jack Chesney	Neil Barclay
Brasset	Christopher Newton
Charley Wykeham	Simon Bradbury
Lord Fancourt Babberley	Steven Sutcliffe
Kitty Verdun	Deborah Lambie
Amy Spettigue	Seana McKenna
Colonel Sir Francis Chesney	David Schurmann
Stephen Spettigue	Barry MacGregor
Donna Lucia D'Alvadorez	Fiona Reid
Ela Delahay	Ann Baggley

Directed by Susan Cox
Designed by Cameron Porteous
Lighting designed by Robert Thomson

Stage Manager	Randy Thiessen
Assistant Stage Manager	Allan Teichman

WIDOWERS' HOUSES by Bernard Shaw

Court House Theatre
previews from June 28, opening July 9 to September 27 (52 performances)

Waiter	Paul Lampert
Dr Harry Trench	Blair Williams
Mr William de Burgh Cokane	Craig Davidson
Sartorious	Roger Rowland
Miss Blanche Sartorious	Elizabeth Brown
Parlormaid	Sarah Orenstein
Mr Lickcheese	George Dawson

Directed by Jim Mezon
Designed by Yvonne Sauriol
Lighting designed by Graeme S. Thomson
Costumes designed by Sean Breaugh

Stage Manager	Carolyn Mackenzie
Assistant Stage Manager	Debbie Boult

DRUMS IN THE NIGHT by Bertolt Brecht
Court House Theatre
previews from June 30, opening July 10 to September 27 (39 performances)

Karl Balicke	Robert Benson
Amalie Balicke	Wendy Thatcher
Anna Balicke	Susan Coyne
Friedrich Murk	Robert Persichini
A Maid	Henriette Ivanans
Herr Babusch	Guy Bannerman
Andreas Kragler	Peter Millard
Manke, waiter at the Piccadilly	Peter Krantz
Marie, a prostitute	Henriette Ivanans
Man at the Piccadilly	Tony Munch
Valkyrie Man	Robert Benson
Valkyrie Man	Tony van Bridge
Glubb	Robert Benson
Drunk Man	Robert Persichini
Bulltrotter	Tony van Bridge
Manke, waiter at Glubb's	Peter Krantz
Augusta, a prostitute	Wendy Thatcher
Worker / Newspaperman	Tony Munch

Directed by Paul Lampert
Designed by Yvonne Sauriol
Lighting designed by Kevin Lamotte
Music composed by Rob Bryanton

Stage Manager	Ron Nipper
Assistant Stage Manager	Michelle Lagassé

OVERRULED by Bernard Shaw
Royal George Theatre
previews from July 1, opening July 10 to September 13 (43 Lunchtime performances)

Mrs Juno	Mary Haney
Mr Lunn	David Christoffel
Mr Juno	Peter Hutt
Mrs Lunn	Catherine Bruhier

Directed by Roy Surette
Designed by Monika Heredi
Lighting designed by Bonnie Beecher

Stage Manager	Charlotte Green
Assistant Stage Manager	Meredith Macdonald

1992

POINT VALAINE by Noel Coward
Court House Theatre
previews from July 28, opening August 8 to September 27 (39 performances)

Mrs Tillet	Irene Hogan
Major Tillet	Tony van Bridge
Elise Birling	Ann Baggley
Mrs Birling	Wendy Thatcher
Mortimer Quinn	David Schurmann
Stefan	Robert Persichini
Lola	Catherine Bruhier
Ted Burchell	Tony Munch
George Fox	Steven Sutcliffe
Linda Valaine	Fiona Reid
Mrs Hall-Fenton	Susan Cox
Gladys Hall-Fenton	Susan Coyne
Sylvia Hall-Fenton	Henriette Ivanans
Hilda James	Susan Stackhouse
Martin Welford	Simon Bradbury

Directed by Christopher Newton
Designed by Yvonne Sauriol
Lighting designed by Robert Thomson

Stage Manager	Randy Thiessen
Assistant Stage Manager	Season Osborne

TEN MINUTE ALIBI by Anthony Armstrong
Royal George Theatre
previews from May 12, opening May 28 to November 1 (108 performances)

Hunter	Guy Bannerman
Philip Sevilla	Andrew Gillies
Betty Findon	Tracey Ferencz
Colin Derwent	Peter Krantz
Sir Miles Standing	Robert Benson
Inspector Pember	Jack Medley
Sergeant Brace	Peter Millard
A.P. Body	Peter Wilds

Directed by Paul Lampert
Designed by Peter Hartwell
Lighting designed by Elizabeth Asselstine

Stage Manager	Ron Nipper
Assistant Stage Manager	Michelle Lagassé

1993

THIRTY-SECOND SEASON
April 21 to October 31 (706 Performances)

SAINT JOAN by Bernard Shaw
Festival Theatre
previews from April 21, opening May 26 to October 31 (114 performances)

Robert de Baudricourt	Guy Bannerman
Steward	Al Kozlik
Joan	Mary Haney
Bertrand de Poulengey	Cavan Young
La Trémouille	Tony van Bridge
Archbishop of Rheims	Anthony Bekenn
Gilles de Rais (Bluebeard)	Neil Barclay
Captain La Hire	Roger Honeywell
Dauphin (later Charles VII)	Simon Bradbury
Vendome	Sven van de Ven
Head Waiter	Andy Skelly
French Steward	Chris Mackie
Dunois	Peter Hutt
Dunois' Aide	Ian Vandeburgt
Richard, Earl of Warwick	George Dawson
Chaplain John de Stogumber	Richard Farrell
Warwick's Aide	Gordon Rand
Peter Cauchon, Bishop	
of Beauvais	Michael Ball
The Inquisitor	Barry MacGregor
Canon D'Estivet	John Ormerod
Canon de Courcelles	Peter Wilds
Brother Martin Ladvenu	Steven Sutcliffe
The Executioner	Dick Murphy
English Soldier	Troy Skog
Modern Gentleman	Jack Medley

Directed by Neil Munro
Designed by Cameron Porteous
Lighting designed by Robert Thomson

Stage Manager	Carolyn Mackenzie
Assistant Stage Manager	Michelle Lagassé

GENTLEMEN PREFER BLONDES
music by Jules Styne
lyrics by Leo Robin
book by Anita Loos and Joseph Fields
adapted from the novel by Anita Loos

Royal George Theatre
previews from April 28, opening May 28 to October 10 (122 performances)

Sir Francis Beekman	David Adams
Lorelei Lee	Rosemary Doyle
Robert Lemanteur /	
Esmond, Sr	Terry Harford
Gloria Stark	Jane Johanson
Lady Beekman	Gabrielle Jones
Josephus Gage	Lee MacDougall
Fifi	Sherri McFarlane
Gus Esmond, Jr	Paul McQuillan
Atkins	Cassel Miles
Coles	Jeffrey Prentice
Henry Spofford	Ian Simpson
Mrs Ella Spofford	Karen Skidmore
Dorothy Shaw	Jan Alexandra Smith
Louis Lemanteur	Geoffrey Whynot
Zizi	Viviana Zarrillo

Directed by Susan Cox
Musical direction and arrangements
    by Christopher Donison
Designed by William Schmuck
Lighting designed by Kevin Lamotte
Choregraphy by Claudia Moore
Assisted by Cassel Miles

Stage Manager	Charlotte Green
Assistant Stage Managers	Meredith Macdonald
	Todd Bricker

THE MARRYING OF ANN LEETE by Harley Granville Barker
Court House Theatre
previews from August 4, opening August 12 to September 25 (30 performances)

Ann Leete	Ann Baggley
Lord John Carp	David Schurmann
George Leete	Steven Sutcliffe
Sarah, Lady Cottesham	Seana McKenna
Daniel Tatton	Duncan Ollerenshaw
Carnaby Leete	Christopher Newton
John Abud	Roger Honeywell

Dr Remnant	Anthony Bekenn
Mrs Opie	Diane D'Aquila
Dimmuck	Al Kozlik
Mr Tetgeen	Sandy Webster
Lord Arthur Carp	Jim Mezon
Mr Smallpiece	Chris Mackie
Sir George Leete	Tony van Bridge
Mr Crowe	Sven van de Ven
Dolly	Elizabeth Brown
Lady Leete	Jennifer Phipps
Mr Tozer	Paul Lampert
Mr Prestige	Donald Carrier
Mrs Prestige	Sarah Orenstein

Directed by Neil Munro
Designed by Yvonne Sauriol
Lighting designed by Robert Thomson

Stage Manager	Randy Thiessen
Assistant Stage Manager	Ellen Flowers

AND THEN THERE WERE NONE by Agatha Christie
Royal George Theatre
previews from May 12, opening May 27 to October 31, held over to November 21
(138 performances)

Rogers	Peter Millard
Mrs Rogers	Susan Stackhouse*
Fred Narracott	Troy Skog*
Vera Claythorne	Tracey Ferencz
Philip Lombard	Peter Hutt*
Anthony Marston	Andy Skelly
William Blore	Norman Browning
General MacKenzie	Roger Rowland
Miss Emily Brent	Wendy Thatcher
Sir Lawrence Wargrave	Michael Ball*
Dr Armstrong	William Vickers*

*for the holdover, these cast changes were made

Mrs Rogers	Deborah Lambie
Fred Narracott	Dick Murphy
Philip Lombard	David Schurmann
Sir Lawrence Wargrave	Robert Benson
Dr Armstrong	Guy Bannerman

Directed by Jim Mezon
Designed by Cameron Porteous
Lighting designed by Elizabeth Asselstine

Stage Manager	Ron Nipper
Assistant Stage Manager	Allan Teichman

BLITHE SPIRIT by Noel Coward
Festival Theatre
previews from June 16, opening July 10 to October 31 (80 performances)

Edith	Deborah Lambie
Ruth Condomine	Diane D'Aquila
Charles Condomine	David Schurmann
Mrs Bradman	Mary Haney
Dr Bradman	Richard Farrell
Madame Arcati	Jennifer Phipps
Elvira	Sarah Orenstein

Directed by Susan Cox
Designed by Leslie Frankish
Lighting designed by Robert Thomson

Stage Manager	Carolyn Mackenzie
Assistant Stage Manager	Michelle Lagassé

CANDIDA by Bernard Shaw
Court House Theatre
previews from June 23, opening July 8 to September 26 (57 performances)

The Reverend James Mavor Morell	Jim Mezon
Miss Proserpine Garnett	Elizabeth Brown
The Reverend Lexy Mill	Donald Carrier
Mr Burgess	Sandy Webster
Candida Morell	Seana McKenna
Eugene Marchbanks	Duncan Ollerenshaw

Directed by Christopher Newton
Designed by Yvonne Sauriol
Costumes designed by Cameron Porteous
Lighting designed by Kevin Lamotte

Stage Manager	Randy Thiessen
Assistant Stage Manager	Ellen Flowers

THE MAN OF DESTINY by Bernard Shaw
Royal George Theatre
previews from June 30, opening July 9 to September 26 (52 Lunchtime performances)

Giuseppe	Robert Benson
Napoleon Bonaparte	Stuart Hughes
The Lady	Deborah Lambie
The Lieutenant	Peter Wilds

Directed by Miles Potter
Designed by Kenneth Shaw
Lighting designed by Aisling Sampson

Stage Manager	Charlotte Green
Assistant Stage Manager	Season Osborne

THE UNMENTIONABLES by Carl Sternheim

translated and adapted by Paul Lampert and Kate Sullivan

Court House Theatre

previews from June 27, opening July 9 to September 26 (40 performances)

Theodore Mask	Norman Browning
Louise Mask	Tracey Ferencz
Gertrude Wink	Wendy Thatcher
Frank Scarron	Peter Millard
Benjamin Mandelstam	William Vickers
A Stranger	Roger Rowland

Directed by Paul Lampert
Designed by Yvonne Sauriol
Lighting designed by Ereca Hassell

Stage Manager	Ron Nipper
Assistant Stage Manager	Allan Teichman

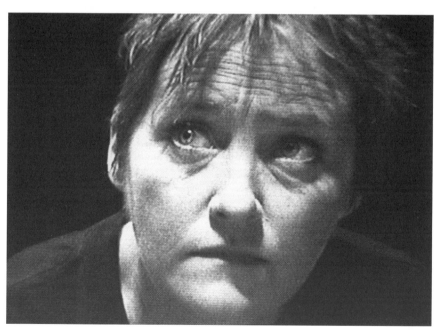

MARY HANEY IN *SAINT JOAN*, 1993 (PHOTO BY DAVID COOPER).

1993

THE SILVER KING by Henry Arthur Jones
Festival Theatre
previews from May 15, opening May 29 to October 10 (73 performances)

Role	Actor
Cripps / Man at the Station	David Adams
Mr Parkyn / Higher Servant	Guy Bannerman
Inspector Samuel Baxter	Neil Barclay
Eliah Coombe / Traveller	Robert Benson
Henry Corkett / Traveller	Simon Bradbury
Geoffrey Ware / Street Vendor	George Dawson
Girl on the Streets / Maid	Rosemary Doyle
Nelly Denver	Sharry Flett
Railway Inspector / Policeman / Higher Servant	Terry Harford
Wilfred Denver	Stuart Hughes
First Class Passenger / Maid	Jane Johanson
Mrs Gammage / Lady at the Station	Gabrielle Jones
Frank Selwyn / Street Gang Boss	Lee MacDougall
Captain Herbert Skinner, aka "Spider"	Barry MacGregor
Susy / Maid	Sherri McFarlane
Teddy / Lamplighter	Paul McQuillan
Daniel Jaikes	Jack Medley
Braggins / Street Gang / Porter	Cassel Miles
Tubbs / Driver / Pottle	Dick Murphy
Bilcher	John Ormerod
Leaker / Porter / Footman / Street Gang	Jeffrey Prentice
Street Gang / Porter / Footman	Gordon Rand
Mr Brownson / Street Gang / Footman	Ian Simpson
Tabitha / Lady at the Station	Karen Skidmore
Olive / Lady at the Station	Jan Alexandra Smith
Cissy Denver	Sherry Smith
Newsboy / Street Gang / Footman	Ian Vandeburgt
Bob Larkin	Geoffrey Whynot
Mr Binks / Street Gang	Cavan Young

Directed by Christopher Newton
Designed by Leslie Frankish
Lighting designed by Kevin Lamotte
Music composed by Christopher Donison

Stage Manager	Laurie Champagne
Assistant Stage Managers	Meredith Macdonald
	Season Osborne

158

1994

THIRTY-THIRD SEASON
April 20 to October 16 (729 Performances)

LADY, BE GOOD!
words and music by George and Ira Gershwin
book by Guy Bolton and Fred Thompson

Royal George Theatre
previews from May 7, opening May 28 to October 16, held over to November 13
(146 performances)

Watty Watkins	Richard Binsley
Dick Trevor	Paul Gatchell
Daisy Parke	Gail Hakala
Estrada	Terry Harford
Jean (French Waiter)	David Hogan
Susie Trevor	Patty Jamieson
Zoe	Jane Johanson
Parke	Sam Mancuso
Chloe	Sherri McFarlane
Flo	Kiri-Lyn Muir *(until July 10)*
	Frances Chiappetta *(from July 13)*
Jeffries	William Orlowski
Jack Robinson	Ian Simpson
Josephine Vanderwater	Karen Skidmore
Shirley Vernon	Jan Alexandra Smith
Bertie Bassett	Todd Waite

Directed by Glynis Leyshon
Musical direction and arrangements
    by Christopher Donison
Designed by William Schmuck
Lighting designed by Graeme S. Thomson
Choreography by Carol Anderson
Tap Choreography by William Orlowski

Stage Manager	Carolyn Mackenzie
Assistant Stage Managers	Todd Bricker
	Season Osborne

1994

THE FRONT PAGE by Ben Hecht and Charles MacArthur
Festival Theatre
previews from May 12, opening May 27 to October 16, held over to November 6
(79 performances)

Endicott (Post)	Guy Bannerman
Schwartz (Daily News)	Andrew Gillies
Murphy (Journal)	Norman Browning
Wilson (American)	David Schurmann
McCue (City Press)	Al Kozlik
Kruger (Journal of Commerce)	Neil Barclay
Bensinger (Tribune)	Peter Millard
Mrs Myrtle Schlosser	Jillian Cook
Woodenshoes Eichorn	Robert Benson
Diamond Louis	Peter Hutt
Hildy Johnson	
(Herald Examiner)	Stuart Hughes
Jennie	Irene Hogan
Mollie Malloy	Mary Haney
Sheriff Hartman	Richard Farrell
Peggy Grant	Alison Woolridge
Mrs Grant	Wendy Thatcher
The Mayor	Sandy Webster
Mr Pincus	Dick Murphy
Earl Williams*	William Vickers
Walter Burns	Michael Ball
Tony**	Matt Handy
Carl, a Deputy	Gordon Rand
Frank, a Deputy	Robert Clarke
Policemen	Ian Vandeburgt, Matt Handy

*performed by Matt Handy, May 25 to June 11
**performed by Ian Vandeburgt, May 25 to June 11

Directed by Neil Munro
Designed by Cameron Porteous
Lighting designed by Kevin Lamotte

Stage Manager	Laurie Champagne
Assistant Stage Manager	Meredith Macdonald

ARMS AND THE MAN by Bernard Shaw
Festival Theatre
previews from April 20, opening May 25 to October 16, held over to November 4
(111 performances)

Raina Petkoff	Elizabeth Brown*
Catherine Petkoff	Wendy Thatcher
Louka	Sarah Orenstein

Captain Bluntschli	Simon Bradbury
Major Plechanoff	
(A Russian Officer)	Donald Carrier
Bulgarian Soldiers	Matt Handy, Weston McMillan
Nicola	William Webster**
Major Paul Petkoff	Norman Browning
Major Sergius Saranoff	Andrew Gillies

*succeeded by Tracey Ferencz on October 20
**succeeded by Jim Mezon on October 20

Directed by Jim Mezon
Designed by Eduard Kochergin
Lighting designed by Robert Thomson

Stage Manager	Charlotte Green
Assistant Stage Manager	Michelle Lagassé

SHERLOCK HOLMES by William Gillette
Festival Theatre
previews from June 18 opening July 7 to October 15 (67 performances)

Madge Larrabee	Jan Alexandra Smith
John Forman	Peter Millard
Terese	Sherri McFarlane
James Larrabee	Peter Hutt
Mrs Faulkner	Irene Hogan
Sid Prince	Stuart Hughes
Alice Faulkner	Ann Baggley
Sherlock Holmes	Jim Mezon
Professor Moriarty	Michael Ball
John, a Clerk	Ian Simpson
Alfred Bassick	Sandy Webster
Billy	Bruce Davies
Dr Watson	Robert Benson
Lightfoot McTague	Dick Murphy
Jim Craigin	Al Kozlik
Thomas Leary	William Vickers
Percy Baskerville	Christopher Royal
Parsons	Richard Binsley
Count Von Stalburg	Sam Mancuso
Sir Edward Leighton	Richard Farrell

Directed by Christopher Newton
Designed by Leslie Frankish
Lighting designed by Kevin Lamotte

Stage Manager	Carolyn Mackenzie
Assistant Stage Managers	Meredith Macdonald
	Season Osborne

1994

BUSMAN'S HONEYMOON
by Dorothy L. Sayers and M. St Clare Byrne

Royal George Theatre
previews from April 21, opening May 26 to October 15, held over to November 13
(134 performances)

Mr Puffett	Tony van Bridge
Mr Bunter	Anthony Bekenn
Mrs Ruddle	Jennifer Phipps
Harriet (Lady Peter Wimsey)	Sharry Flett
Lord Peter Wimsey	David Schurmann
Miss Twitterton	Mary Haney
Frank Crutchley	Greg Spottiswood
Reverend Simon Goodacre	Jack Medley
Mr MacBride	Neil Barclay
Constable Sellon	Gordon Rand
Superintendent Kirk	Guy Bannerman
George	Robert Clarke
Bill	Ian Vandeburgt

Directed by Christopher Newton
Designed by Leslie Frankish
Costumes designed by Yvonne Sauriol
Lighting designed by Elizabeth Asselstine
Music composed by Christopher Donison

Stage Manager	Ron Nipper
Assistant Stage Manager	Ellen Flowers

TOO TRUE TO BE GOOD by Bernard Shaw
Court House Theatre
previews from June 18, opening July 8 to September 25 (52 performances)

The Microbe	George Dawson
The Patient (Miss Mopply)	Sarah Orenstein
The Elderly Lady (Mrs Mopply)	Diane D'Aquila
The Doctor	Roger Rowland
The Nurse ('Sweetie')	Elizabeth Brown
The Burglar ('Popsy')	Donald Carrier
Colonel Tallboys, VC, DSO	William Webster
Private Meek	Simon Bradbury
Sergeant Fielding	Weston McMillan
The Elder	George Dawson

Directed by Paul Lampert
Designed by Peter Hartwell
Lighting designed by Robert Thomson

Stage Manager	Charlotte Green
Assistant Stage Managers	Michelle Lagassé, Debra McKay

162

IVONA, PRINCESS OF BURGUNDIA by Witold Gombrowicz
Court House Theatre
previews from July 30, opening August 11 to September 24 (29 performances)

King Ignatius	Allan Gray
Queen Margaret	Goldie Semple
Prince Philip	Roger Honeywell
Lord Chamberlain	Paul Lampert
Simon	Patric Masurkevitch
Cyprian	Paul Gatchell
Isobel	Tracey Ferencz
Ivona	Jane Johanson
Innocent	David Hogan
Checkers	Terry Harford
First Lady of the Court	Frances Chiappetta
Second Lady of the Court	Gail Hakala
Third Lady of the Court	Patty Jamieson
Dandy / Chancellor	William Orlowski
First Aunt	Joyce Campion
Second Aunt	Karen Skidmore
Beggar	Todd Waite

Directed by Tadeusz Bradecki
Designed by Leslie Frankish
Lighting designed by Robert Thomson

Stage Manager	Randy Thiessen
Assistant Stage Manager	Allan Teichman

ROCOCO by Harley Granville Barker
Royal George Theatre
previews from June 25, opening July 9 to September 25 (47 Lunchtime performances)

Reverend Simon Underwood	Roger Rowland
Mrs Mary Underwood	Joyce Campion
Miss Carinthia Underwood	Diane D'Aquila
Mortimer Uglow	George Dawson
Reginald Uglow	Roger Honeywell
Mrs Reginald Uglow	Tracey Ferencz

Directed by Neil Munro
Designed by Tania Etienne
Lighting designed by Scott Henderson

Stage Manager	Randy Thiessen
Assistant Stage Manager	Allan Teichman

1994

EDEN END by J.B. Priestley
Court House Theatre
previews from June 22, opening July 9 to September 25 (54 performances)

Wilfred Kirby	Patric Masurkevitch
Sarah	Jennifer Phipps
Lilian Kirby	Sharry Flett
Dr Kirby	Tony van Bridge
Stella Kirby	Goldie Semple
Geoffrey Farrant	Anthony Bekenn
Charles Appleby	Allan Gray

Directed by Susan Cox
Designed by Peter Hartwell
Lighting designed by Graeme S. Thomson

Stage Manager	Ron Nipper
Assistant Stage Manager	Ellen Flowers

ANNAJANSKA, THE BOLSHEVIK EMPRESS by Bernard Shaw
Royal George Theatre
previews from August 3, opening August 11 to 28 (10 Lunchtime performances)

General Strammfest	Jack Medley
Lieutenant Schneidekind	Greg Spottiswood
The Grand Duchess	
Annajanska	Ann Baggley
First Soldier	Bruce Davies
Second Soldier	Christopher Royal

Directed by Sally Han
Designed by Tania Etienne
Lighting designed by Scott Henderson

Stage Manager	Laurie Champagne
Assistant Stage Manager	Todd Bricker

Post-Season Tour

ARMS AND THE MAN
Power Center for the Performing Arts, Ann Arbor, Michigan,
November 15 to 20 (5 performances)

THE FRONT PAGE
Power Center for the Performing Arts, Ann Arbor, Michigan,
November 15 to 20 (3 performances)

1995

THE PETRIFIED FOREST by Robert Sherwood
Festival Theatre
previews from May 7, opening May 26 to October 29 (79 performances)

First Lineman	Greg Spottiswood
Second Lineman	Richard Farrell
Boze Herzlinger	Roger Honeywell
Gramp Maple	Al Kozlik
Jason Maple	Guy Bannerman
Paula	Jane Johanson
Gabby Maple	Tracey Ferencz
Alan Squier	Peter Millard
Herb	Oliver Becker
Joseph	Nigel Shawn Williams
Mrs Chisholm	Brigitte Robinson
Mr Chisholm	George Dawson
Ruby	William Vickers
Jackie	Douglas E. Hughes
Duke Mantee	Jim Mezon
Pyles	Martin Villafana
Legion Commander	Lorne Pardy
Legionnaire	Robert Clarke
Sheriff	Dick Murphy
First Deputy	Mike Shara
Second Deputy	Christopher Royal
National Guardsmen	Shaun Phillips, Richard Farrell

Directed by Neil Munro
Designed by Leslie Frankish
Lighting designed by Kevin Lamotte

Stage Manager	Laurie Champagne
Assistant Stage Manager	Allan Teichman

1995

YOU NEVER CAN TELL by Bernard Shaw

Festival Theatre

previews from April 19, opening May 24 to October 29 (99 performances)

Dolly	Jan Alexandra Smith
Valentine	Richard Binsley
Philip	Gordon Rand
The Parlormaid	Jillian Cook
Mrs Lanfrey Clandon	Nora McLellan
Gloria	Helen Taylor
Fergus Crampton	Michael Ball
The Waiter (William)	Jack Medley
Finch M'Comas	Allan Gray
The Cook	Neil Barclay*
Jo, a Waiter	Matt Handy
A Waiter	Bruce Davies
Bohun	Norman Browning

succeeded by Robert Clarke on October 3

Directed by Christopher Newton
Designed by William Schmuck
Lighting designed by Kevin Lamotte

Stage Manager	Charlotte Green
Assistant Stage Manager	Ellen Flowers

CAVALCADE by Noel Coward

Festival Theatre

previews from June 14, opening July 8 to October 28 (91 performances)

Jane Marryot	Fiona Reid
Robert Marryot	Andrew Gillies
Edward Marryot	Roger Honeywell
Young Edward	Luke Woodyard
Joe Marryot	Ben Carlson
Young Joe	David Welsh
Margaret Harris	Mary Haney
Edith Harris	Tracey Ferencz
Young Edith	Maggie Blake
Ellen Bridges	Wendy Thatcher
Alfred Bridges	David Schurmann
Fanny Bridges	Lisa Waines
Young Fanny	Jenna Baldwin
Ronnie James	George Dawson
Mrs Snapper	Jennifer Phipps
Cook	Irene Hogan
Annie	Stephanie Belding

Gladys	Sherri McFarlane
Flo Grainger	Evelyne Anderson
George Grainger	Tony van Bridge
Laura Marsden (Mirabelle)	Sharry Flett
Henry Charteris (Tyrell)	Stephen Simms
Rose Darling (Ada)	Karen Wood
Mikey Banks (Tom Jolly)	Todd Waite
Connie Crawshay	Jane Johanson
Daisy Devon	Brigitte Robinson
Netta Lake	Gail Hakala
Stage Manager of *Mirabelle*	Peter Millard
Douglas Finn	Oliver Becker
Tim Bateman	Shaun Phillips
Clarence	Brian Brockenshire
Lord Martlet (Chubby)	Robert Clarke
Duchess of Churt	Nuala FitzGerald
Grand Duke Serge	Al Kozlik
Lord Esher	Dick Murphy
Major Domo	Guy Bannerman
Able Seaman Ball	Mike Shara
Pearly King	Terry Harford
Salvation Army singer	Karen Skidmore
Newsboy	Brian Marler
Policeman	Douglas E. Hughes
Uncle Dick	Robert Benson
Uncle George	William Vickers
Uncle Jack	Roger Perkins
Uncle Reg	Christopher Donison
Uncle Jim	Christopher Royal

Directed by Christopher Newton and Duncan McIntosh
Designed by Cameron Porteous
Lighting designed by Robert Thomson
  after the original design by Jeffrey Dallas
Musical direction and arrangements
  by Christopher Donison

Stage Manager	Laurie Champagne
Assistant Stage Managers	Meredith Macdonald
	Allan Teichman

THE PHILANDERER by Bernard Shaw
Court House Theatre
previews from June 18, opening July 6 to September 24 (59 performances)

Grace Tranfield	Sarah Orenstein
Leonard Charteris	Simon Bradbury
Julia Craven	Kelli Fox
Mr Joseph Cuthbertson	Sandy Webster
Colonel Daniel Craven	Roger Rowland
Dr Paramore	Peter Hutt
Sylvia Craven	Shauna Black
The Page / Spedding	Dil Kainth

Directed by Jim Mezon
Designed by Leslie Frankish
Lighting designed by Kevin Lamotte

Stage Manager	Ron Nipper
Assistant Stage Manager	Michelle Lagassé

AN IDEAL HUSBAND by Oscar Wilde
Court House Theatre
previews from June 24, opening July 7 to September 24 (42 performances)

Sir Robert Chiltern	Norman Browning
Lady Chiltern	Helen Taylor
Mrs Marchmont	Alison Woolridge
Countess of Basildon	Jillian Cook
Vicomte de Nanjac	Neil Barclay
Mason	Gordon Rand
Earl of Caversham	Michael Ball
Miss Mabel Chiltern	Ann Baggley
Lady Markby	Nora McLellan
Mrs Cheveley	Jan Alexandra Smith
Viscount Goring	Allan Gray
Mr Montford	Richard Binsley
Phipps	Jack Medley
James	Matt Handy
Harold	Bruce Davies

Directed by Duncan McIntosh
Designed by William Schmuck
Lighting designed by Elizabeth Asselstine

Stage Manager	Charlotte Green
Assistant Stage Manager	Ellen Flowers

WASTE by Harley Granville Barker
Court House Theatre
previews from July 27, opening August 11 to September 23 (24 performances)

Walter Kent	Ben Carlson
Countess Mortimer	Irene Hogan
Lady Julia Farrant	Wendy Thatcher
Miss Frances Trebell	Mary Haney
Miss Lucy Davenport	Stephanie Belding
Mrs Amy O'Connell	Fiona Reid
George Farrant	Andrew Gillies
Russell Blackborough	Peter Hutt
Footman	Brian Marler
Henry Trebell	David Schurmann
Bertha	Lisa Waines
Dr Gilbert Wedgecroft	William Webster
Lord Charles Cantilupe	Robert Benson
Cyril Horsham	Roger Rowland
Vivian Saumarez	Anthony Bekenn
Justin O'Connell	Paul Lampert

Directed by Neil Munro
Designed by Peter Hartwell
Lighting designed by Robert Thomson

Stage Manager	Bruce MacDonald
Assistant Stage Manager	Todd Bricker

THE VOICE OF THE TURTLE by John van Druten
Royal George Theatre
previews from April 12, opening May 27 to October 28 (130 performances)

Sally Middleton	Ann Baggley
Olive Lashbrooke	Alison Woolridge
Bill Page	Greg Spottiswood

Directed by Paul Lampert
Designed by Peter Hartwell
Lighting designed by Robert Thomson

Stage Manager	Carolyn Mackenzie
Assistant Stage Manager	Judy Farthing

1995

LADIES IN RETIREMENT by Edward Percy and Reginald Denham
Royal George Theatre
previews from May 2, opening May 25 to October 29 (112 performances)

Lucy Gilham	Shauna Black
Ellen Creed	Jennifer Phipps
Leonora Fiske	Nuala Fitzgerald
Albert Feather	Simon Bradbury
Louisa Creed	Sharry Flett
Emily Creed	Evelyne Anderson
Sister Theresa	Kelli Fox

Directed by David Oiye
Designed by Christina Poddubiuk
Lighting designed by Elizabeth Asselstine

Stage Manager	Ron Nipper
Assistant Stage Manager	Meredith Macdonald

THE ZOO by Arthur Sullivan and Bolton Rowe
Royal George Theatre
previews from May 10, opening May 26 to October 29 (92 Lunchtime performances)

Mr Grinder, a retired grocer	Terry Harford
Laetitia Grinder, his daughter	Karen Wood
Aesculapius Carboy	Stephen Simms
Eliza Smith	Karen Skidmore
Thomas Brown	Todd Waite
Members of the British Public	Gail Hakala, Sherri McFarlane, Brian Brockenshire

Directed by Glynis Leyshon
Designed by William Schmuck
Lighting designed by Elizabeth Asselstine
Music direction, arrangements, and
  additional lyrics by Christopher Donison
Choreography by Jane Johanson

Stage Manager	Bruce MacDonald
Assistant Stage Manager	Todd Bricker

THE SIX OF CALAIS by Bernard Shaw
Royal George Theatre
previews from August 2, opening August 11 to September 3
(11 Lunchtime performances)

British Captain *Eustache de St Pierre*	Anthony Bekenn

First British Officer	
Narrator	Richard Farrell
Young British Corporal	
John of Gaunt	Dil Kainth
Canadian Captain	
Edward III	Paul Lampert
German Soldier	Brian Marler
French Woman	
Queen Philippa	Sarah Orenstein
Third British Officer	
Narrator	Tony van Bridge
American Corporal	
Piers de Rosty	Martin Villafana
Older British Officer	
A Court Lady	Sandy Webster
Second British Officer	
Narrator	William Webster
Canadian Corporal	
The Black Prince	Nigel Shawn Williams

Directed by David Oiye
Designed by Kelly Wolf
Lighting designed by Christopher L. Dennis

| Stage Manager | Carolyn Mackenzie |
| Assistant Stage Manager | Judy Farthing |

A SCENE FROM *THE ZOO*, 1995 (PHOTO BY DAVID COOPER).

1996

Pre-Season Production

ONE FOR THE POT by Ray Cooney and Tony Hilton
Royal Alexandra Theatre, Toronto, March 2 to April 13 (51 performances)
A Mirvish Productions remount of The Shaw's 1985 and 1987 productions

Amy Hardcastle	Corrine Koslo
Cynthia Hardcastle	Helen Taylor
Jugg	David Schurmann
Jonathan Hardcastle	Roger Rowland
Clifton Weaver	Peter Millard
Arnold Piper	Robert Benson
Charlie Barnet	Simon Bradbury
Hickory Wood	Heath Lamberts
Winnie	Mary Haney
Jennifer Bowater-Smith	Jan Alexandra Smith
Stanley Bowater-Smith	Anthony Bekenn
Guest of Party	Robert Clarke
Guest of Party	Jillian Cook
Guest of Party	Matt Handy

Directed by Christopher Newton
Designed by Cameron Porteous
Lighting designed by Kevin Lamotte

Stage Managers	Bruce MacDonald *(until March 10)*
	Henry Bertrand *(from March 10)*
Assistant Stage Managers	Ellen Flowers
	Meredith Macdonald

THIRTY-FIFTH SEASON
April 12 to October 27 (768 Performances)

THE DEVIL'S DISCIPLE by Bernard Shaw
Festival Theatre
previews from May 1, opening May 22 to October 27 (88 performances)

Drummer	Todd Witham
British Soldier	Terry Harford
British Soldier	Graham Rowat
British Soldier	Kenneth Delaney
Essie	Maggie Blake
Mrs Timothy Dudgeon	Nora McLellan
Christy Dudgeon	Neil Barclay
The Reverend Anthony	
Anderson	Peter Hutt

Judith Anderson	Sarah Orenstein
Lawyer Hawkins	Richard Farrell
William Dudgeon	Richard Binsley
Mrs William Dudgeon	Karen Skidmore
Titus Dudgeon	William Vickers
Mrs Titus Dudgeon	Stephanie Belding
Richard Dudgeon	Gordon Rand
British Sergeant	Todd Waite
British Officer	Richard Binsley
Major Swindon	William Webster
General John Burgoyne	Andrew Gillies
Mr Brudenell	Oliver Becker
Townswomen	Gail Hakala, Nora McLellan, Jenny L. Wright

Directed by Glynis Leyshon
Designed by Peter Hartwell
Lighting designed by Robert Thomson

Stage Manager	Laurie Champagne
Assistant Stage Manager	Michelle Lagassé

GORDON RAND AND SARAH ORENSTEIN IN *THE DEVIL'S DISCIPLE*, 1996 (PHOTO BY DAVID COOPER).

1996

THE CONJUROR by Patrick Watson and David Ben
Royal George Theatre
previews from June 15, opening July 11 to September 14
(30 Lunchtime performances)

The Conjuror	David Ben
Conjuror's Assistant	Suleyman Fattah

Directed by Patrick Watson
Designed by Kelly Wolf
Lighting designed by Scott Henderson

Stage Manager	Laurie Champagne
Assistant Stage Manager	Michelle Lagassé

RASHOMON by Fay and Michael Kanin
based on stories by Ryunosuke Akutagawa

Festival Theatre
previews from May 9, opening May 24 to October 27 (74 performances)

The Priest	Greg Spottiswood
The Woodcutter	Roger Honeywell
The Wigmaker	Guy Bannerman
The Deputy	Dil Kainth
The Bandit	Jim Mezon
The Husband	Nigel Shawn Williams
The Wife	Laurie Paton
The Mother	Brenda Kamino
The Medium	Robert Benson

Directed by Neil Munro
Designed by Leslie Frankish
Lighting designed by Kevin Lamotte
Music composed by Christopher Donison
Fights directed by John Nelles

Stage Manager	Charlotte Green
Assistant Stage Manager	Allan Teichman

MARSH HAY by Merrill Denison
Court House Theatre
previews from August 9, opening August 23 to September 28 (22 performances)

Tessie Serang	Shauna Black
Sarilin Serang	Elizabeth Inksetter
Jo Serang	Jared Brown
Lena Serang	Corrine Koslo
Pete Serang	Brian Marler
John Serang	Michael Ball

Andrew Barnood	Allan Gray
Mrs Clantch	Jillian Cook
Tad Nosse	George Dawson
William Thompson	Richard Farrell
Walt Roche	Mike Shara
Tom Roche	Malcolm Scott

Directed by Neil Munro
Designed by Peter Hartwell
Lighting designed by Robert Thomson

Stage Manager	Bruce MacDonald
Assistant Stage Manager	Ellen Flowers

MR CINDERS

music by Vivian Ellis and Richard Myers
libretto and lyrics by Clifford Grey and Greatrex Newman
additional lyrics by Leo Robin and Vivian Ellis

Royal George Theatre
previews from April 12, opening May 23 to October 26 (126 performances)

Cynthia Boyce / Maid	Jane Johanson
Billy Whymper /	
Mr Henry Kemp	Terry Harford
Becky Bartlett / Maid	Jenny L. Wright
Charles Wylde / Smith	William Orlowski
Enid Brinkley / Lucy /	
Donna Lucia	Karen Skidmore
Guy Beardsley Lancaster	Todd Waite
Phyllis Patterson	Sherri McFarlane
Bunny Hayes / P.C. Merks	Graham Rowat
Lumley Beardsley Lancaster	Neil Barclay
Sir George Lancaster	William Vickers
Lady Lancaster	Nora McLellan
Jim Lancaster	Richard Binsley
Jill Kemp	Karen Wood
Minerva Kemp	Gail Hakala

Directed by Christopher Newton
Orchestration and Musical Direction
by Christopher Donison
Designed by William Schmuck
Lighting designed by Ereca Hassell
Choreography by William Orlowski

Stage Manager	Carolyn Mackenzie
Assistant Stage Managers	Judy Farthing
	Jennifer McKenna

1996

HOBSON'S CHOICE by Harold Brighouse
Festival Theatre
previews from June 19, opening July 12 to October 26 (86 performances)

Delivery Boy	Todd Witham
Alice Hobson	Alison Woolridge
Victoria Hobson	Shauna Black
Maggie Hobson	Corrine Koslo
Albert Prosser	Mike Shara
Henry Horatio Hobson	Michael Ball
Mrs Hepworth	Jillian Cook
Timothy (Tubby) Wadlow	Sandy Webster
Willie Mossop	Simon Bradbury
Jim Heeler*	Norman Browning
Ada Figgins	Elizabeth Inksetter
Freddy Beenstock	Brian Marler
Dr MacFarlane	Allan Gray

performed by Christopher Newton, August 3 to September 15

Directed by Christopher Newton
Designed by William Schmuck
Lighting designed by Kevin Lamotte

Stage Manager	Bruce MacDonald
Assistant Stage Manager	Ellen Flowers

THE HOLLOW by Agatha Christie
Royal George Theatre
previews from May 10, opening May 25 to October 27, held over to November 24
(158 performances)

Henrietta Angkatell	Jan Alexandra Smith*
Sir Henry Angkatell, K.C.B.	Tony van Bridge
Lady Angkatell	Jennifer Phipps
Midge Harvey	Isolde O Neill
Gudgeon	Jack Medley
Edward Angkatell	Peter Millard
Doris	Brigitte Robinson
Gerda Cristow	Sharry Flett
Dr John Cristow	Douglas E. Hughes
Veronica Craye	Tracey Ferencz
Inspector Colquhoun	David Schurmann**
Detective Sergeant Penny	Robert Clarke

* *succeeded by Stephanie Belding on October 29*
** *succeeded by Andrew Gillies on October 29*

Directed by Paul Lampert
Designed by Cameron Porteous
Lighting designed by Scott Henderson

Stage Manager	Ron Nipper
Assistant Stage Manager	Meredith Macdonald

176

AN IDEAL HUSBAND by Oscar Wilde

Court House Theatre
previews from May 5, opening May 24 to July 21 (46 performances)

Sir Robert Chiltern	Norman Browning
Lady Chiltern	Brigitte Robinson
Mrs Marchmont	Alison Woolridge
Countess of Basildon	Jillian Cook
Mason	Mike Shara
James	Malcolm Scott
Vicomte de Nanjac	Simon Bradbury
Earl of Caversham	Michael Ball
Miss Mabel Chiltern	Isolde O Neill
Lady Markby	Jennifer Phipps
Mrs Cheveley	Jan Alexandra Smith
Viscount Goring	Allan Gray
Mr Montford	Sandy Webster
Phipps	Jack Medley
Harold	Brian Marler

Directed by Duncan McIntosh
Designed by William Schmuck
Lighting designed by Elizabeth Asselstine

Stage Manager	Bruce MacDonald
Assistant Stage Manager	Ellen Flowers

JILLIAN COOK, ALISON WOOLRIDGE, SIMON BRADBURY, CORRINE KOSLO, AND MICHAEL BALL
IN *HOBSON'S CHOICE*, 1996 (PHOTO BY DAVID COOPER).

1996

THE SIMPLETON OF THE UNEXPECTED ISLES by Bernard Shaw
Court House Theatre
previews from June 22, opening July 10 to September 27 (48 performances)

Bernard Shaw	Al Kozlik
Maya	Lisa Waines
Janga	Dil Kainth
Vashti	Janet Lo
Kanchin	Shaun Phillips
Emigration Officer (Hyering)	Greg Spottiswood
Wilks	Guy Bannerman
Young Woman (Mrs Hyering)	Laurie Paton
Pra	Nigel Shawn Williams
Prola	Brenda Kamino
Lady Farwaters	Wendy Thatcher*
Sir Charles Farwaters	Robert Benson
The Reverend Phosphor	
Hammingtap	Ben Carlson
An Angel	Roger Honeywell

succeeded by Kelli Fox on September 14

Directed by Glynis Leyshon
Designed by Leslie Frankish
Lighting designed by Robert Thomson
Choreography by Shaun Phillips

Stage Managers	Charlotte Green
	Allan Teichman
Assistant Stage Managers	Allan Teichman
	Peter Jotkus

THE PLAYBOY OF THE WESTERN WORLD by J.M. Synge
Court House Theatre
previews from June 28, opening July 11 to September 28 (47 performances)

Pegeen Mike	Kelli Fox
Shawn Keough	Gordon Rand
Michael James Flaherty	William Webster
Philly O'Cullen	Peter Hutt
Jimmy Farrell	Andrew Gillies
Christopher Mahon	Oliver Becker
Widow Quin	Sarah Orenstein
Susan Brady	Sherri McFarlane
Honor Blake	Karen Wood
Nelly McLaughlin	Jane Johanson
Sara Tansey	Stephanie Belding
Old Mahon	Richard Farrell
Peasant	Kenneth Delaney
Peasant	William Orlowski

Directed by Jim Mezon
Designed by Cameron Porteous
Lighting designed by Elizabeth Asselstine

| Stage Manager | Carolyn Mackenzie |
| Assistant Stage Manager | Judy Farthing |

SHALL WE JOIN THE LADIES? by J.M. Barrie
Royal George Theatre
previews from June 26, opening July 12 to September 22
(37 Lunchtime performances)

Mrs Castro	Janet Lo
Miss Isit	Kelli Fox
Mr Gourlay	Shaun Phillips
Mrs Bland	Sharry Flett
Sir Joseph Wrathie	Peter Millard
Lady Jane	Alison Woolridge
The Host (Sam Smith)	David Schurmann
Lady Wrathie	Wendy Thatcher
Mr Preen	Robert Clarke
Miss Vaile	Tracey Ferencz
Captain Jennings	Ben Carlson
Mrs Preen	Lisa Waines
Mr Vaile	Douglas E. Hughes
The Butler (Dolphin)	Al Kozlik
The Maid (Lucy)	Elizabeth Inksetter
The Policeman	Tony van Bridge

Directed by Christopher Newton and Denis Johnston
Designed by Kelly Wolf
Lighting designed by Scott Henderson

| Stage Manager | Ron Nipper |
| Assistant Stage Manager | Meredith Macdonald |

1996

BELL CANADA READING SERIES

MURDER PATTERN by Herman Voaden
Royal George Theatre, July 23 (1 reading)

Narrators / Earth Voices	Kelli Fox, William Webster
First Farmer / Foreman	Gordon Rand
Second Farmer / Judge	Peter Millard
First Reporter	Andrew Gillies
Second Reporter	Isolde O Neill
Third Farmer / Guard	Kenneth Delaney
Fourth Farmer / Warden	Richard Farrell
Friendly One / Defence	Meredith McGeachie
Accusing One / Prosecutor	Jennifer Phipps
Jack Davis	Robert Clarke

Directed by Denis Johnston

Stage Manager	Ron Nipper
Assistant Stage Manager	Meredith Macdonald

WAR OF THE WORLDS by Howard Koch
Royal George Theatre, July 30 and August 6 (2 readings)

Cast: Guy Bannerman, Robert Benson, Ben Carlson, Tracey Ferencz, Sharry Flett, Douglas E. Hughes, Jane Johanson, Dil Kainth, Al Kozlik, Sherri McFarlane, Shaun Phillips, David Schurmann, Greg Spottiswood, Nigel Shawn Williams, Karen Wood

Directed by Christopher Newton

Stage Manager	Charlotte Green
Assistant Stage Manager	Judy Farthing

FARFETCHED FABLES by Bernard Shaw
Royal George Theatre, August 15 and 23 (2 readings)

Narrator / Tourist / Hermaphrodite / Raphael	Richard Binsley
Young Man / Commissioner / Student	Graham Rowat
Young Woman / Teacher	Jenny L. Wright
Middle-aged Man / Gentleman / Student	Terry Harford
Secretary / Matron / Rose / Student	Nora McLellan
Commander-in-Chief / Tramp / Shamrock	Neil Barclay
Lord Oldhand / Thistle / Student	William Vickers
Junior / Student	Maggie Blake

Directed by Denis Johnston

180

Stage Manager　　　　　　Laurie Champagne
Assistant Stage Manager　　Michelle Lagassé

TO HAVE AND TO HOLD by Jules Renard
translated by David Edney

Royal George Theatre, September 10 (1 reading)

Marthe　　　　　　　Brigitte Robinson
Pierre　　　　　　　Peter Hutt

Directed by Neil Munro

Stage Manager　　　　　　Laurie Champagne
Assistant Stage Manager　　Michelle Lagassé

NORA MCLELLAN STANDS UP TO THE REST OF THE ENSEMBLE
IN *MR CINDERS*,1996 (PHOTO BY DAVID COOPER).

1997

THIRTY-SIXTH SEASON
April 4 to October 26 (785 Performances)

WILL ANY GENTLEMAN? by Vernon Sylvaine
Festival Theatre
previews from May 13, opening May 23 to October 25 (84 performances)

Mendoza	Douglas E. Hughes
Albert Boyle	Richard Binsley
Angel*	Shauna Black
Henry Stirling	Neil Barclay
Beryl**	Mary Haney
Dr Smith	Roger Rowland
Florence Stirling	Deborah Lambie
Charley Stirling	Barry MacGregor
Detective Inspector Martin	Anthony Bekenn
Stanley Jackson	Peter Millard
Honey	Alison Woolridge
Mrs Whittle	Jennifer Phipps
Montague Billing	Sven van de Ven
Dancer	Catherine McGregor

*performed by Severn Thompson, September 16 to October 5
**performed by Shauna Black, September 16 to October 5

Directed by Christopher Newton
Designed by William Schmuck
Lighting designed by Ereca Hassell

Stage Manager	Ron Nipper
Assistant Stage Manager	Judy Farthing
Apprentice Stage Manager	Meghan Callan

MRS WARREN'S PROFESSION by Bernard Shaw
Festival Theatre
previews from April 30, opening May 21 to October 26 (83 performances)

Vivie Warren	Jan Alexandra Smith
Praed	David Schurmann
Mrs Warren	Nora McLellan
Sir George Crofts	Norman Browning
Frank Gardner	Ben Carlson
Reverend Samuel Gardner	Robert Benson
Lady of the Chorus	Severn Thompson
Gentleman of the Chorus	Jason Dietrich

Directed by Tadeusz Bradecki
Designed by Leslie Frankish
Lighting designed by Kevin Lamotte
Music directed by Roger Perkins

Stage Manager	Laurie Champagne
Assistant Stage Manager	Peter Jotkus

THE CHILDREN'S HOUR by Lillian Hellman
Court House Theatre
previews from June 12, opening July 9 to September 27 (59 performances)

Peggy Rogers	Amy Cadeau
Lois Fisher	Melissa McIntyre
Catherine	Keri Ferencz
Mrs Lily Mortar	Jillian Cook
Evelyn Munn	Shelagh Hughes
Helen Burton	Tamera Broczkowski
Rosalie Wells	Alisha Stranges
Janet	Emma Hillier
Leslie	Robin Liszak
Mary Tilford	Maggie Blake
Karen Wright	Kelli Fox
Martha Dobie	Stephanie Belding
Dr Joseph Cardin	Richard Binsley
Agatha	Deborah Lambie
Mrs Amelia Tilford	Jennifer Phipps
Grocery Boy	Malcolm Scott

Directed by Glynis Leyshon
Designed by Leslie Frankish
Lighting designed by Elizabeth Asselstine

Stage Manager	Ron Nipper
Assistant Stage Manager	Jill Beatty
Apprentice Stage Manager	Meghan Callan

HOBSON'S CHOICE by Harold Brighouse

Festival Theatre
previews from April 4, opening May 25 to June 28 (41 performances)

Delivery Boy	Jason Dietrich
Alice Hobson	Alison Woolridge
Victoria Hobson	Shauna Black
Maggie Hobson	Corrine Koslo
Albert Prosser	Mike Shara
Henry Horatio Hobson	Michael Ball
Mrs Hepworth	Jillian Cook *(until May 31)*
	Sharry Flett *(from June 1)*
Timothy (Tubby) Wadlow	Sandy Webster
Willie Mossop	Simon Bradbury
Jim Heeler	Roger Rowland
Ada Figgins	Elizabeth Inksetter
Freddy Beenstock	Brian Marler
Dr MacFarlane	Barry MacGregor

Directed by Christopher Newton
Designed by William Schmuck
Lighting designed by Kevin Lamotte

Stage Manager	Bruce MacDonald
Assistant Stage Manager	Judy Farthing

IN GOOD KING CHARLES'S GOLDEN DAYS by Bernard Shaw

Court House Theatre
previews from July 1, opening July 11 to September 27 (44 performances)

Mrs Basham	Patricia Hamilton
Sally	Laurie Paton
Isaac Newton	Andrew Gillies
King Charles II	Peter Hutt
George Fox	Guy Bannerman
Nell Gwynn	Helen Taylor
Barbara Villiers	Brigitte Robinson
Louise de Kéroualle	Philippa Domville
James, Duke of York	Gordon Rand
Godfrey Kneller	Blair Williams
Queen Catherine	Sarah Orenstein

Directed by Allen MacInnis
Designed by Charlotte Dean
Lighting designed by Robert Thomson

Stage Manager	Allan Teichman
Assistant Stage Manager	Arwen MacDonell

THE SEAGULL by Anton Chekhov
translated by David French

Festival Theatre
previews from June 20, opening July 10 to October 26 (66 performances)

Medvedenko	Simon Bradbury
Masha	Corrine Koslo
Sorin	Michael Ball
Constantine	Ben Carlson
Yakov	Brian Marler
Nina	Jan Alexandra Smith
Polina	Sharry Flett
Dorn	Robert Benson
Shamrayev	Norman Browning
Arkadina	Fiona Reid
Trigorin	Jim Mezon
Servants	Severn Thompson, Jason Dietrich

Directed by Neil Munro
Designed by Peter Hartwell
Lighting designed by Kevin Lamotte
Music composed by Christopher Donison

Stage Manager	Bruce MacDonald
Assistant Stage Manager	Peter Jotkus

ROBERT BENSON, JAN ALEXANDRA SMITH, AND NORA MCLELLAN
IN *MRS WARREN'S PROFESSION*, 1997 (PHOTO BY DAVID COOPER).

THE TWO MRS CARROLLS by Martin Vale
Royal George Theatre
previews from May 9, opening May 24 to October 25, held over to November 23
(139 performances)

Geoffrey Carroll	David Schurmann
Clémence	Philippa Domville
Denis Pennington	Blair Williams*
Sally Carroll	Laurie Paton
Mrs Latham	Patricia Hamilton
Cecily Harden	Helen Taylor
Dr Tuttle	Tony van Bridge
Harriet Carroll	Brigitte Robinson

succeeded by Richard Binsley on October 28

Directed by Joseph Ziegler
Sets designed by Peter Hartwell
Costumes designed by Kelly Wolf
Lighting designed by Bonnie Beecher

Stage Manager	Allan Teichman
Assistant Stage Manager	Michelle Lagassé

SORRY, WRONG NUMBER by Lucille Fletcher
Royal George Theatre
previews from August 7, opening August 22 to September 21
(28 Lunchtime performances)

Mrs Stevenson	Mary Haney
First Operator	Shauna Black
First Man	Anthony Bekenn
Second Man	Neil Barclay
The Client	Sven van de Ven
Second Operator	Kelli Fox
Chief Operator	Alison Woolridge
Third Operator	Deborah Lambie
Police Sergeant	Peter Millard
Delivery Boy	Kenneth Delaney
Fourth Operator	Stephanie Belding
Western Union	Douglas E. Hughes
Information	Catherine McGregor
Nurse	Jillian Cook

Directed by Dennis Garnhum
Designed by David Boechler
Lighting designed by Philip Cygan

Stage Manager	Ron Nipper
Assistant Stage Manager	Judy Farthing

THE CHOCOLATE SOLDIER
music by Oscar Straus
adapted and arranged by Ronald Hanmer
original book and lyrics by Rudolf Bernauer and Leopold Jacobson
new English book by Agnes Bernelle; new English lyrics by Adam Carstairs.

Royal George Theatre
previews from April 18, opening May 22 to October 26 (139 performances)

Colonel Kasimir Popoff	Terry Harford
Aurelia (his wife)	Jo-Anne Kirwan Clark
	Gail Hakala *(June 17, July 22, August 26)*
Nadina (his daughter)	Stephanie McNamara
	Maria Thorburn *(June 3, July 8, August 12)*
Mascha (an adopted daughter)	Karen Wood
	Ann Bisch *(July 1, August 5, October 14)*
Major Alexius Spiridoff	Sandy Winsby
	Michael Todd Cressman *(June 26 to 28, July 29, September 16)*
Lieutenant Bummerli	Stephen Simms
	David Hogan *(June 8, July 15, August 19)*
Captain Massakroff	Brian Elliott
Stephan	Patrick R. Brown
Villagers and Soldiers	Damien Atkins, Ann Bisch, Jason Chesworth, Michael Todd Cressman, Gail Hakala, David Hogan, Maria Thorburn, Jenny L. Wright (swing)

Directed by David Latham
Musical direction by Christopher Donison
Designed by Christina Poddubiuk
Lighting designed by Robert Thomson
Choreography and musical staging by William Orlowski

Stage Manager	Charlotte Green
Assistant Stage Manager	Judie M. Brokenshire

THE PLAYBOY OF THE WESTERN WORLD by J.M. Synge
Court House Theatre
previews from May 3, opening May 23 to July 18 (44 performances)

Pegeen Mike	Kelli Fox
Shawn Keogh	Malcolm Scott
Jimmy Farrell	Al Kozlik
Philly O'Cullen	George Dawson
Michael James Flaherty	Peter Hutt
Christopher Mahon	Gordon Rand
Widow Quin	Sarah Orenstein
Susan Brady	Sherri McFarlane
Nelly McLaughlin	Jane Johanson
Honor Blake	Lisa Waines
Sara Tansey	Stephanie Belding
Old Mahon	Richard Farrell
Peasants	Kenneth Delaney
	Ty Olsson

Directed by Jim Mezon
Designed by Cameron Porteous
Lighting designed by Elizabeth Asselstine

Stage Manager	Carolyn Mackenzie
Assistant Stage Manager	Jill Beatty

THE CONJUROR, PART 2 by David Ben and Patrick Watson
Royal George Theatre
previews from June 18, opening July 10 to August 3 (32 Lunchtime performances)

The Conjuror	David Ben
Conjuror's Assistant	Suleyman Fattah
Cameo 'stagehand'	Kenneth Delaney

Directed by Patrick Watson
Designed by William Schmuck
Lighting designed by Bonnie Beecher
Original set and costume designs by Kelly Wolf

Stage Manager	Carolyn Mackenzie
Assistant Stage Manager	Michelle Lagassé

THE SECRET LIFE by Harley Granville Barker
Court House Theatre
previews from August 13, opening August 22 to September 28 (21 performances)

Stephen Serocold, MP	Andrew Gillies
Sir Geoffrey Salomons	Guy Bannerman
Evan Strowde	Christopher Newton
Eleanor Strowde	Nancy Palk
Joan Westbury	Fiona Reid
Mildred Gauntlett, Countess of Peckham	Sharry Flett
Oliver Gauntlett	Mike Shara
Mr Kittredge	Sandy Webster
Susan Kittredge	Lisa Waines
Dolly Gauntlett	Elizabeth Inksetter
Sir Leslie Heriot, MP	Jim Mezon
Maid	Sherri McFarlane
Lord Clumbermere	Richard Farrell

Directed by Neil Munro
Designed by William Schmuck
Lighting designed by Robert Thomson

Stage Manager	Bruce MacDonald
Assistant Stage Manager	Arwen MacDonell

NANCY PALK, ANDREW GILLIES, CHRISTOPHER NEWTON, LISA WAINES, SHARRY FLETT, FIONA REID, AND SANDY WEBSTER IN *THE SECRET LIFE*, 1997 (PHOTO BY DAVID COOPER).

1997

BELL CANADA READING SERIES
STILL STANDS THE HOUSE by Gwen Pharis Ringwood
Royal George Theatre, July 16 (1 reading)

Narrator	Sandy Winsby
Ruth Warren	Jenny L. Wright
Arthur Manning	Patrick R. Brown
Hester Warren	Jo-Anne Kirwan Clark
Bruce Warren	Brian Elliott

Directed by Denis Johnston

Stage Manager	Charlotte Green
Assistant Stage Manager	Judie M. Brokenshire

THE TITANIC by E.J. Pratt
Royal George Theatre, July 25 (1 reading)

Cast: Damien Atkins, Michael Ball, Robert Benson, Simon Bradbury, Ben Carlson, Michael Todd Cressman, Jason Dietrich, David Hogan, Corrine Koslo, Brian Marler, Severn Thompson, Karen Wood

Directed by Christopher Newton

Production Stage Manager	Charlotte Green
Assistant Stage Manager	Judie M. Brokenshire

MR SHAW, a programme of pieces written by George Bernard Shaw, including *Why She Would Not*
Royal George Theatre, August 14 and 20 (2 readings)

Cast: Corrine Koslo, Simon Bradbury, Ty Olsson, Jo-Anne Kirwan Clark, David Hogan

Compiled and directed by Dennis Garnhum
Music directed by Logan Medland

Stage Manager	Charlotte Green
Assistant Stage Manager	Judie M. Brokenshire

THE INTRUDER by Maurice Maeterlinck
Royal George Theatre, August 29 (1 reading)

First Daughter	Elizabeth Inksetter
Second Daughter	Lisa Waines
Third Daughter	Sherri McFarlane
The Grandfather	Richard Farrell
The Father	Peter Hutt
The Uncle	Guy Bannerman
The Servant	Mike Shara

Directed by Neil Munro

Stage Manager	Charlotte Green
Assistant Stage Manager	Judie M. Brokenshire

1998

LADY WINDERMERE'S FAN by Oscar Wilde
Festival Theatre
previews from June 26, opening July 9 to October 31 (68 performances)

Parker	Richard Farrell
Lady Windermere	Colombe Demers
Lord Darlington	Gordon Rand
Duchess of Berwick	Patricia Hamilton
Lady Agatha Carlisle	Shauna Black
Lord Windermere	Ben Carlson
Mrs Guy Berkeley	Amanda Smith
Mrs Cowper-Cowper	Patty Jamieson
Lady Stutfield	Robin Hutton
Sir James Royston / Footman	Randy Ganne
Mr Charles Dumby	Neil Barclay
Mr Rufford / Footman	Patrick R. Brown
Lady Jedburgh	Mary Haney
Miss Graham	Risa Waldman
Mr Hopper	Ian Leung
Lord Augustus Lorton	Barry MacGregor
Mr Arthur Bowden / Footman	Brian Elliott
Mrs Arthur Bowden / Rosalie	Stephanie McNamara
Lord Paisley / Footman	Neil Foster
Lady Paisley	Gabrielle Jones
Mr Cecil Graham	Mike Shara
Mrs Erlynne	Fiona Reid
Lady Plymdale	Karen Wood
Lady Jansen / Alice	Catherine McGregor

Directed by Christopher Newton
Set designed by William Schmuck
Costumes designed by Christina Poddubiuk
Lighting designed by Robert Thomson

Stage Manager	Judy Farthing
Assistant Stage Manager	Arwen MacDonell

YOU CAN'T TAKE IT WITH YOU
by George S. Kaufman and Moss Hart

Festival Theatre
previews from May 2, opening May 22 to November 1 (104 performances)

Penelope Sycamore	Mary Haney
Essie Carmichael	Jenny L. Wright
Rheba	Camille James
Paul Sycamore	Peter Millard
Mr De Pinna	William Vickers
Ed Carmichael	Douglas E. Hughes
Donald	D. Garnet Harding
Martin Vanderhof	Lewis Gordon
Alice Sycamore	Colombe Demers
Wilbur Henderson	George Dawson
Tony Kirby	Mike Shara
Boris Kolenkhov	Neil Barclay
Gay Wellington	Alison Woolridge
Mr Kirby	Norman Browning
Mrs Kirby	Jillian Cook
Three Men	Al Kozlik*, Ian Leung, Mark McGrinder
Grand Duchess Olga Katrina	Brigitte Robinson

*First Man performed by John Cleland, May 12 to 24,
July 14 to August 9, August 18 to 19*

Directed by Neil Munro
Designed by Sue LePage
Lighting designed by Kevin Lamotte

Stage Manager	Carolyn Mackenzie
Assistant Stage Manager	Judy Farthing

A FOGGY DAY
words and music by George and Ira Gershwin
book by Norm Foster and John Mueller
based on the play *A Damsel in Distress* by P.G. Wodehouse and Ian Hay
original orchestrations by Christopher Donison

Royal George Theatre
previews from May 3, opening May 23 to November 1 (127 performances)

Keggs	Neil Foster
Albertina	Karen Wood
Tom	Patrick R. Brown
Steve Riker	Jeffry Denman*
Billie Dore	Nora McLellan
Lady Jessica	Stephanie McNamara

Lord Marshmorten	Richard Farrell
Lady Caroline	Gabrielle Jones
Alice Faraday	Patty Jamieson
Reggie	Todd Waite
Walter Jordan	Brian Elliott
Ensemble	Randy Ganne, Larry Herbert,**
	Robin Hutton, Risa Waldman

succeeded by Larry Herbert on September 16
**succeeded by Michael Whitehead on September 16*

Directed by Kelly Robinson
Musical direction by Christopher Donison
Choreography by William Orlowski
Set designed by Peter Hartwell
Costumes designed by Charlotte Dean
Lighting designed by Robert Thomson

Stage Manager	Bruce MacDonald
Assistant Stage Manager	M. Rebecca Miller

MAJOR BARBARA by Bernard Shaw
Festival Theatre
previews from April 16, opening May 19 to November 1 (101 performances)

Lady Britomart Undershaft	Sharry Flett
Stephen Undershaft	Joel Hechter
Morrison / Bilton	Anthony Bekenn
Barbara Undershaft	Kelli Fox
Sarah Undershaft	Lisa Waines
Charles Lomax	Malcolm Scott
Adolphus Cusins	Richard Binsley
Andrew Undershaft	Jim Mezon
Rummy Mitchens	Wendy Thatcher
Snobby Price	Blair Williams
Jenny Hill	Severn Thompson
Peter Shirley	David Schurmann
Bill Walker	Colm Magner
Mrs Baines	Jillian Cook
Army Sergeants	Chris Adams, John Cleland
Army Bandsmen	Brian Quigley, Alex Ring

Directed by Helena Kaut-Howson
Designed by William Schmuck
Lighting designed by Ereca Hassell
Music direction and sound design by Alan Laing

Stage Manager	Laurie Champagne
Assistant Stage Manager	Jill Beatty

JOY by John Galsworthy
Court House Theatre
previews from June 18, opening July 8 to September 27 (52 performances)

Colonel Hope	Michael Ball
Mrs Hope	Maralyn Ryan
Peachy Beech	Jennifer Phipps
Rose	Lisa Waines
Joy Gwyn	Severn Thompson
Dick Merton	Joel Hechter
Ernest Blunt	Colm Magner
Letty Blunt	Kelli Fox
Molly Gwyn	Sharry Flett
Maurice Lever	Richard Binsley

Directed by Neil Munro
Set designed by Cameron Porteous
Costumes designed by Kelly Wolf
Lighting designed by Ereca Hassell

Stage Manager	Ron Nipper
Assistant Stage Manager	Michelle Lagassé

THE SHOP AT SLY CORNER by Edward Percy
Royal George Theatre
previews from April 15, opening May 20 to October 31, held over to November 29
(151 performances)

Descius Heiss	Michael Ball
Archie Fellowes	Jonathan Watton
Margaret Heiss	Fiona Byrne
Joan Deal	Ann Baggley
Mathilde Heiss	Maralyn Ryan
Mrs Catt	Jennifer Phipps
Robert Graham	Simon Bradbury
Corder Morris	Guy Bannerman
Steve Hubbard	Jason Chesworth
John Elliott	Jason Dietrich

Directed by Joseph Ziegler
Designed by David Boechler
Lighting designed by Bonnie Beecher

Stage Manager	Ron Nipper
Assistant Stage Manager	Michelle Lagassé

RICHARD BINSLEY AND KELLI FOX IN *MAJOR BARBARA*, 1998 (PHOTO BY DAVID COOPER).

1998

THE LADY'S NOT FOR BURNING by Christopher Fry
Court House Theatre
previews from May 6, opening May 21 to September 27 (74 performances)

Richard	Ben Carlson
Thomas Mendip	Simon Bradbury
Alizon Eliot	Fiona Byrne
Nicholas Devize	Jason Dietrich
Margaret Devize	Patricia Hamilton
Humphrey Devize	Jonathan Watton
Hebble Tyson	Roger Rowland
Jennet Jourdemayne	Ann Baggley
The Chaplain	Barry MacGregor
Edward Tappercoom	Sandy Webster
Matthew Skipps	Tony van Bridge

Directed by Christopher Newton
Designed by Leslie Frankish
Lighting designed by Alan Brodie

Stage Manager	Allan Teichman
Assistant Stage Manager	Jane Vanstone Osborn

SIMON BRADBURY, FIONA BYRNE, AND BEN CARLSON IN *THE LADY'S NOT FOR BURNING*,
1998 (PHOTO BY DAVID COOPER).

BROTHERS IN ARMS by Merrill Denison
Royal George Theatre
previews from June 26, opening July 9 to August 1 (13 Lunchtime performances)

Dorothea Brown	Jenny L. Wright
J. Altrus Browne	Norman Browning
Syd White	Douglas E. Hughes
Charlie Henderson	Guy Bannerman

Directed by Dennis Garnhum
Designed by Peter Hartwell
Lighting designed by Kevin Lamotte

Stage Manager	Bruce MacDonald
Assistant Stage Manager	M. Rebecca Miller

WATERLOO by Arthur Conan Doyle
Royal George Theatre
previews from August 6, opening August 21 to September 19
(15 Lunchtime performances)

Norah Brewster	Shauna Black
Sergeant Archie MacDonald	Gordon Rand
Corporal Gregory Brewster	Tony van Bridge
Colonel James Midwinter	Al Kozlik

Directed by Ian Prinsloo
Set designed by Peter Hartwell
Costumes designed by Barbara Gordon
Lighting designed by Michael Kruse

Stage Manager	Laurie Champagne
Assistant Stage Manager	Arwen MacDonell

1998

JOHN BULL'S OTHER ISLAND by Bernard Shaw
Court House Theatre
previews from July 4, opening July 10 to September 26 (47 performances)

Hodson	Anthony Bekenn
Tom Broadbent	David Schurmann
Timothy Haffigan	Peter Millard
Larry Doyle	Blair Williams
Peter Keegan	Peter Hutt
Patsy Farrell	Malcolm Scott
Nora Reilly	Alison Woolridge
Cornelius Doyle	William Vickers
Father Dempsey	George Dawson
Matthew Haffigan	Peter Millard
Aunt Judy	Wendy Thatcher
Barney Doran	Lewis Gordon
Local lads	John Cleland, Chris Adams

Directed by Jim Mezon
Set designed by Kelly Wolf
Costumes designed by Cameron Porteous
Lighting designed by Kevin Lamotte

Stage Manager	Carolyn Mackenzie
Assistant Stage Manager	Jill Beatty

PASSION, POISON, AND PETRIFACTION by Bernard Shaw
Royal George Theatre
previews from June 19, opening July 10 to September 20
(37 Lunchtime performances)

Lady Magnesia Fitztollemache	Camille James
Phyllis	Brigitte Robinson
George Fitztollemache	D. Garnet Harding
Adolphus Bastable	Todd Waite
The Landlord	Roger Rowland
Police Constable	Mark McGrinder
The Doctor	Sandy Webster
Choir of Angels	Jason Chesworth, Keri Ferencz, Catherine McGregor
The Foley	Larry Herbert
The Pianist	Logan Medland

Directed by Gyllian Raby
Designed by Peter Hartwell
Lighting designed by Kevin Lamotte
Choreography by Jane Johanson
Music composed, arranged and directed by Logan Medland

Stage Manager	Allan Teichman
Assistant Stage Manager	Jane Vanstone Osborn

198

BELL CANADA READING SERIES

TRIFLES by Susan Glaspell
Royal George Theatre, July 16 (1 reading)

Narrator	Blair Williams
County Attorney Henderson	Ben Carlson
Mrs Peters	Wendy Thatcher
Sheriff Henry Peters	David Schurmann
Mr Hale	Barry MacGregor
Mrs Hale	Patricia Hamilton

Directed by Denis Johnston

Stage Manager	Allan Teichman
Assistant Stage Manager	Jane Vanstone Osborn

MR SHAW INTERVIEWS HIMSELF
readings from the works of Bernard Shaw

Royal George Theatre, July 30 (1 reading)

Cast: Richard Binsley, Sharry Flett, Larry Herbert, Mark McGrinder,
Nora McLellan, Jim Mezon, Lisa Waines

Compiled and directed by Gyllian Raby
Music directed by Logan Medland

Stage Manager	Laurie Champagne
Assistant Stage Manager	Jane Vanstone Osborn

THE BALLAD OF OSCAR WILDE
a compilation of The Ballad of Reading Gaol and Wilde's three trials of 1895

Royal George Theatre, August 14 (1 reading)

Narrator #1	Al Kozlik
Narrator #2	Ian Leung
Narrator #3	Mark McGrinder
Clarke	Michael Ball
Carson	Guy Bannerman
Judge	Lewis Gordon
Balladeer #1	Mike Shara
Balladeer #2	Peter Millard
Oscar Wilde	Neil Barclay

Adapted and directed by Neil Munro

Stage Manager	Judy Farthing
Assistant Stage Manager	Michelle Lagassé

1998

STORIES BY ETHEL WILSON
Royal George Theatre, August 27 (1 reading)

We Have to Sit Opposite

Narrator	Fiona Reid
Mrs Montrose	Jenny L. Wright
Blue Tooth Man	George Dawson
Mrs Forrester	Mary Haney

Fog

Narrator A	Norman Browning
Narrator B / Policeman / Hoodlum	Jason Chesworth
Mrs Bylow	Mary Haney
Child / Miss Casey	Jenny L. Wright
Mrs Wong Kee / Mrs Merkle	Fiona Reid
Customer / Parent	George Dawson

A Drink with Adolphus

Narrator	Mary Haney
Anne / Maid / Mabel	Jenny L. Wright
Mrs Gormley	Fiona Reid
Ah Sing / Adolphus	George Dawson
Jonathan / Waiter / Ozzie	Jason Chesworth
Mr Leaper	Norman Browning

Adapted and directed by Christopher Newton

Stage Manager	Carolyn Mackenzie
Assistant Stage Manager	Arwen MacDonell

1999

April 9 to November 28 (811 Performances)

EASY VIRTUE by Noel Coward
Festival Theatre
previews from July 2, opening July 9 to October 30, held over to November 14
(74 performances)

Mrs Whittaker	Patricia Hamilton
Marion	Kelli Fox
Colonel Whittaker	David Schurmann
Hilda	Fiona Byrne
Furber	Richard Farrell
John Whittaker	Kevin Bundy
Larita	Goldie Semple
Sarah Hurst	Glynis Ranney*
Charles Burleigh	Todd Waite
Philip Borden	Brian Elliott
Mr Harris	Patrick R. Brown
Hugh Petworth	Larry Herbert
Nina Vansittart	Patty Jamieson
Bobby Coleman	Randy Ganne
Letty Austin	Risa Waldman
Algy Prynne	Alistair James Harlond
Lucy Coleman	Karen Wood
Henry Furley	Allan Craik
Mrs Hurst	Nora McLellan
Mrs Phillips	Gabrielle Jones
Mary Banfield	Robin Hutton

succeeded by Jenny L. Wright on November 3

Directed by Christopher Newton
Designed by William Schmuck
Lighting designed by Alan Brodie

Stage Manager	Bruce MacDonald
Assistant Stage Manager	Meredith Macdonald

FIONA BYRNE AND DOUGLAS RAIN IN *HEARTBREAK HOUSE*, 1999 (PHOTO BY DAVID COOPER).

HEARTBREAK HOUSE by Bernard Shaw
Festival Theatre
previews from May 1, opening May 25 to October 31 (101 performances)

Ellie Dunn	Fiona Byrne
Nurse Guinness	Patricia Hamilton
Captain Shotover	Douglas Rain
Ariadne, Lady Utterword	Kelli Fox
Hesione Hushabye	Sarah Orenstein
Mazzini Dunn	David Schurmann
Hector Hushabye	Gordon Rand
Boss Mangan	Jim Mezon
Randall Utterword	Kevin Bundy
William Dunn	Barry MacGregor

Directed by Tadeusz Bradecki
Set designed by Peter Hartwell
Costumes designed by Christina Poddubiuk
Lighting designed by Kevin Lamotte

Stage Manager	Laurie Champagne
Assistant Stage Manager	M. Rebecca Miller

YOU CAN'T TAKE IT WITH YOU
by George S. Kaufman and Moss Hart

Festival Theatre

previews from April 9, opening May 28 to July 24 (57 performances)

Penelope Sycamore	Mary Haney
Essie Carmichael	Jenny L. Wright
Rheba	Camille James
Paul Sycamore	Peter Millard
Mr De Pinna	William Vickers
Ed Carmichael	Douglas E. Hughes
Donald	D. Garnet Harding
Martin Vanderhof	Bernard Behrens
Alice Sycamore	Catherine McGregor
Wilbur Henderson	George Dawson
Tony Kirby	Ben Carlson
Boris Kolenkhov	Neil Barclay
Gay Wellington	Lynne Cormack
Mr Kirby	Norman Browning
Mrs Kirby	Jillian Cook
Three Men	Jason Chesworth, Craig Erickson, Mark McGrinder
Grand Duchess Olga Katrina	Jennifer Phipps

Directed by Neil Munro
Designed by Sue LePage
Lighting designed by Kevin Lamotte

Stage Manager	Judy Farthing
Assistant Stage Manager	Michelle Lagassé

S.S. TENACITY by Charles Vildrac

Court House Theatre

previews from June 24, opening July 8 to September 25 (46 performances)

Hidoux	Al Kozlik
Madame Cordier	Jennifer Phipps
Thérèse	Catherine McGregor
Bastien	Craig Erickson
Ségard	Jason Chesworth
English Sailor	Matthew MacFadzean
Workmen / Sailors / Swimmers / Travellers	Aaron Fry, Thomas Grant, Cyrus Lane, Mark McGrinder, Duncan Stewart
Boy	Henry Lamotte

Directed by Dennis Garnhum
Designed by Kelly Wolf
Lighting designed by Kevin Lamotte

Stage Manager	Allan Teichman
Assistant Stage Managers	Meghan Callan

1999

GETTING MARRIED by Bernard Shaw
Court House Theatre
previews from May 14, opening May 29 to September 26 (63 performances)

William Collins	Guy Bannerman
Alice (Mrs Alfred) Bridgenorth	Donna Belleville
General "Boxer" Bridgenorth	Roger Rowland *(until June 9)*
	Aaron Fry *(June 11 to July 6)*
	Rodger Barton *(from July 9)*
Lesbia Grantham	Sarah Orenstein
Reginald Bridgenorth	Barry MacGregor
Leo (Mrs Reginald) Bridgenorth	Laura de Carteret
Alfred Bridgenorth, Bishop of Chelsea	Anthony Bekenn
St John Hotchkiss	Gordon Rand
Cecil Sykes	Ian Leung
Edith Bridgenorth	Severn Thompson
Reverend Oliver Cromwell Soames	Simon Bradbury
The Beadle	Al Kozlik
Mrs George Collins	Sharry Flett

Directed by Jim Mezon
Designed by David Boechler
Lighting designed by Ereca Hassell

Stage Manager — Allan Teichman
Assistant Stage Manager — Meghan Callan

ALL MY SONS by Arthur Miller
Festival Theatre
previews from August 13, opening August 21 to October 31 (41 performances)

Dr Jim Bayliss	William Vickers
Joe Keller	Norman Browning
Frank Lubey	Douglas E. Hughes
Sue Bayliss	Brigitte Robinson
Lydia Lubey	Jenny L. Wright
Chris Keller	Ben Carlson
Bert	Patrick O'Hearn *or* Sean Porter
Kate Keller	Mary Haney
Ann Deever	Laurie Paton
George Deever	Peter Krantz

Directed by Neil Munro
Designed by Leslie Frankish
Lighting designed by Kevin Lamotte

Stage Manager — Judy Farthing
Assistant Stage Managers — Jill Beatty

MARY HANEY, LAURIE PATON, BEN CARLSON, AND NORMAN BROWNING IN *ALL MY SONS*, 1999
(PHOTO BY DAVID COOPER).

THE MADRAS HOUSE by Harley Granville Barker
Court House Theatre
previews from June 11, opening July 7 to September 26 (43 performances)

Philip Madras	Blair Williams
Major Hippisley Thomas	Ben Carlson
Maid / Clara / Mannequin	Jenny L. Wright
Julia / Mrs Brigstock	Lynne Cormack
Laura / Miss Chancellor / Mannequin	Laurie Paton
Emma / Mannequin / Maid	Jane Perry
Jane / Miss Yates / Mannequin	Shauna Black
Mrs Katherine Huxtable	Donna Belleville
Mr Henry Huxtable	Michael Ball
Mrs Amelia Madras	Jillian Cook
Minnie / Jessica Madras	Philippa Domville
Mr Brigstock	William Vickers
Belhaven	Mark McGrinder
Mr Windlesham	George Dawson
Eustace Perrin State	Douglas E. Hughes
Constantine Madras	Peter Millard

Directed by Neil Munro
Set designed by Peter Hartwell
Costumes designed by Christina Poddubiuk
Lighting designed by Ereca Hassell
Music composed by Paul Sportelli

Stage Manager	Judy Farthing
Assistant Stage Manager	Michelle Lagassé

205

1999

REBECCA by Daphne du Maurier
Royal George Theatre
previews from April 14, opening May 27 to November 28 (163 performances)

Frith	Roger Rowland *(until June 9)*
	Thomas Grant *(June 11 to June 30)*
	James Mainprize *(from July 2)*
Beatrice Lacy	Brigitte Robinson
Giles Lacy	Anthony Bekenn
Frank Crawley	Jason Dietrich
Maxim de Winter	Peter Krantz
Mrs de Winter	Severn Thompson
Mrs Danvers	Sharry Flett
Robert	Ian Leung
Alice	Joanne Marrella
Jack Favell	Simon Bradbury
Colonel Julyan	Tony van Bridge
William Tabb	Guy Bannerman

Directed by Christopher Newton
Designed by William Schmuck
Lighting designed by Elizabeth Asselstine

Stage Manager	Ron Nipper
Assistant Stage Manager	Jill Beatty

A FOGGY DAY
words and music by George and Ira Gershwin
book by Norm Foster and John Mueller
based on the play *A Damsel in Distress* by P.G. Wodehouse and Ian Hay
music arranged and orchestrated by Christopher Donison
with additional arrangements and orchestrations by Paul Sportelli

Royal George Theatre
previews from April 29, opening May 26 to October 31, held over to November 14
(136 performances)

Keggs	Patrick R. Brown
Albertina	Karen Wood
Steve Riker	Larry Herbert
Billie Dore	Nora McLellan
Lady Jessica*	Glynis Ranney
Thomas	Brian Elliott
Lord Marshmoreton	Richard Farrell
Lady Caroline	Gabrielle Jones
Alice Faraday	Patty Jamieson
Reggie	Todd Waite
Walter Jordan	Allan Craik *(until May 6)*
	Sandy Winsby *(May 7 to June 13)*
	Craig Gardner *(from June 15)*

Ensemble	Allan Craik, Randy Ganne,
	Alistair James Harlond,
	Robin Hutton, Risa Waldman

performed by Robin Hutton on November 10 and 12

Directed by Kelly Robinson
Musical direction by Paul Sportelli
Choreography by William Orlowski
Sets designed by Peter Hartwell
Costumes designed by Charlotte Dean
Lighting designed by Robert Thomson

| Stage Manager | Bruce MacDonald |
| Assistant Stage Manager | Meredith Macdonald |

VILLAGE WOOING by Bernard Shaw
Royal George Theatre
previews from July 1, opening July 9 to September 19 (40 Lunchtime performances)

'A'	Neil Barclay
'Z'	Camille James
Steward	Duncan Stewart

Directed by Nikki Lundmark
Designed by Barbara Gordon
Lighting designed by Michael Kruse

| Stage Manager | Joanna Jurychuk |
| Apprentice Stage Manager | Amy Jewell |

WATERLOO by Arthur Conan Doyle
Royal George Theatre
previews from June 5, opening July 8 to July 25 (21 Lunchtime performances)

Norah Brewster	Shauna Black
Sergeant Archie MacDonald	Jason Dietrich
Corporal Gregory Brewster	Tony van Bridge
Colonel James Midwinter	Al Kozlik

Directed by Ian Prinsloo
Set designed by Peter Hartwell
Costumes designed by Barbara Gordon
Lighting designed by Michael Kruse

| Stage Manager | Joanna Jurychuk |
| Apprentice Stage Manager | Amy Jewell |

1999

UNCLE VANYA by Anton Chekhov
Court House Theatre
previews from August 6, opening August 20 to September 25 (23 performances)

Marina	Amanda Smith
Dr Astrov (Mikhail Lvovich Astrov)	Jim Mezon
Vanya (Ivan Petrovich Voinitsky)	Michael Ball
Professor Serebriakov	
(Alexander Vladimirovich Serebriakov)	Bernard Behrens
Elena (Elena Andreyevna Serebriakov)	Philippa Domville
Sonya	
(Sophia Alexandrovna Serebriakov)	Shauna Black
Waffles (Ilya Ilyitch Telyegin)	Blair Williams
Mrs Maria Voinitsky	Jillian Cook
Yefim	Cyrus Lane
Nikita	Duncan Stewart
Petruschka	Matthew MacFadzean

Directed by Ian Prinsloo
Designed by Sue LePage
Lighting designed by Alan Brodie

Stage Manager	Laurie Champagne
Assistant Stage Manager	M. Rebecca Miller

BELL CANADA READING SERIES

THE BLACK GIRL IN SEARCH OF GOD by Bernard Shaw
arranged for reading performance by Dan H. Laurence

Royal George Theatre, July 16 (1 reading)

Black Girl	Camille James
Narrator	Jane Perry
Missionary / First Woman	Donna Belleville
Lord of Hosts / Myop (Dr Pavlov) /	
Churchman No. 1 / First Gentleman	George Dawson
Nailor (God of Job) / Churchman	
No. 3 / Mr Croker / Old Gentleman	
(Voltaire)	Neil Barclay
Koheleth (Ecclesiastes) /Fisherman /	
Third Gentleman / Image Maker /	
Leader of the Bearers	D. Garnet Harding
Micah / Second Gentleman / Arab	Michael Ball
Conjurer / Wandering Jew / Irishman	Peter Millard
Churchman No. 2 / Second Woman	Lynne Cormack

Directed by Nikki Lundmark

Stage Manager	Joanna Jurychuk
Apprentice Stage Manager	Amy Jewell

LESSONS FROM LEACOCK by Stephen Leacock
Royal George Theatre, July 22 (1 reading)

My Remarkable Uncle	Douglas Rain
Maddened by Mystery	Kelli Fox, David Schurmann, Kevin Bundy, Goldie Semple, Douglas Rain, Thomas Grant
The Marine Excursion of the Knights of Pythias	David Schurmann, Goldie Semple, Kelli Fox, Douglas Rain, Kevin Bundy, Thomas Grant

Adapted and directed by Christopher Newton

Stage Manager	Joanna Jurychuk
Apprentice Stage Manager	Amy Jewell

THE APOLLO OF BELLAC by Jean Giraudoux
translated by Carole Galloway

Royal George Theatre, August 5 (1 reading)

Narrator	Neil Barclay
Agnès	Fiona Byrne
Reception Clerk	George Dawson
The Man from Bellac	Peter Millard
Managing Director	Aaron Fry
Council members	Kevin Bundy
President	David Schurmann
Chevredent	Patricia Hamilton
Thérèse	Lynne Cormack

Directed by Denis Johnston

Stage Manager	Joanna Jurychuk
Apprentice Stage Manager	Amy Jewell

THE BIRDS by Daphne du Maurier
Royal George Theatre, August 26 (1 reading)

Cast: Shauna Black, Ben Carlson, Jillian Cook, Philippa Domville, Randy Ganne, Laurie Paton, Jane Perry, Blair Williams, Jenny L. Wright

Adapted and directed by Neil Munro

Stage Manager	Joanna Jurychuk
Apprentice Stage Manager	Amy Jewell

2000

THIRTY-NINTH SEASON
March 31 to November 11 (811 Performances)

EASY VIRTUE by Noel Coward
Festival Theatre
previews from March 31, opening May 27 to July 21 (62 performances)

Mrs Whittaker	Patricia Hamilton
Marion	Kelli Fox
Colonel Whittaker	David Schurmann
Hilda	Fiona Byrne
Furber	Richard Farrell
John Whittaker	Ben Carlson
Larita	Goldie Semple
Charles Burleigh	Patrick R. Brown
Philip Borden	Brian Elliott
Mr Harris	Barry MacGregor
Hugh Petworth	Jay Turvey
Nina Vansittart	Blythe Wilson
Bobby Coleman	Randy Ganne
Letty Austin	Imali Perera
Algy Prynne	Alistair James Harlond
Lucy Coleman	Tracy Dawson
Henry Furley	Allan Craik
Mrs Hurst	Amanda Smith
Mrs Phillips	Patty Jamieson
Mary Banfield	Risa Waldman

Directed by Christopher Newton
Designed by William Schmuck
Lighting designed by Alan Brodie

Stage Manager	Bruno Gonsalves
Assistant Stage Manager	M. Rebecca Miller

210

THE ENTR'ACTES FROM *THE DOCTOR'S DILEMMA*, 2000 (PHOTO BY DAVID COOPER).

THE DOCTOR'S DILEMMA by Bernard Shaw
Festival Theatre
previews from May 4, opening May 24 to October 29 (103 performances)

Redpenny	Duncan Stewart
Emmy	Jennifer Phipps
Sir Colenso Ridgeon	Blair Williams
Dr Leo Schutzmacher	Neil Barclay
Sir Patrick Cullen	Bernard Behrens
Mr Cutler Walpole	Lorne Kennedy
Sir Ralph Bloomfield	
Bonington	Jim Mezon
Dr Blenkinsop	Guy Bannerman
Jennifer Dubedat	Severn Thompson
Louis Dubedat	Mike Shara
Minnie Tinwell	Catherine McGregor
The Waiter	Pete Treadwell
The Newspaper Man	Jeff Meadows
Mr Danby	Jason Chesworth
Entr'actes	Cast, plus
	John Cleland *(May 18 to June 8)*
	Cyrus Lane *(June 9 to October 29)*

Directed by Christopher Newton
Designed by Sue LePage
Lighting designed by Kevin Lamotte
Entr'actes staged by Jane Johanson

Stage Manager	Laurie Champagne
Assistant Stage Manager	Thom Payne

211

2000

LORD OF THE FLIES
adapted for the stage by Nigel Williams
from the novel by William Golding

Festival Theatre
previews from July 5, opening July 14 to October 29 (52 performances)

Ralph	Craig Erickson
Piggy	Pete Treadwell
Jack	Mike Shara
Simon	Dylan Trowbridge
Sam	John Cleland
Eric	Duncan Stewart
Henry	Joel Hechter
Maurice	Jason Chesworth
Bill	Cyrus Lane
Roger	Matthew MacFadzean
Perceval	Devon Tullock
Naval Officer	Peter Krantz

Directed by Neil Munro
Designed by Cameron Porteous
Lighting designed by Kevin Lamotte
Original music composed by Paul Sportelli
Movement directed by Jane Johnson
Fights directed by John Stead

Stage Manager	Judy Farthing
Assistant Stage Manager	Thom Payne
Apprentice Stage Manager	Mike Deschambeault

THE MATCHMAKER by Thornton Wilder
Festival Theatre
previews from August 12, opening August 18 to November 11 (66 performances)

Joe Scanlon	Peter Millard
Horace Vandergelder	Michael Ball
Ambrose Kemper	Craig Erickson
Gertrude	Wendy Thatcher
Cornelius Hackl	Kevin Bundy
Ermengarde	Fiona Byrne*
Malachi Stack	George Dawson
Mrs Dolly Levi	Goldie Semple
Barnaby Tucker	Dylan Trowbridge
Mrs Irene Molloy	Corrine Koslo
Minnie Fay	Lisa Norton
Cabman	Anthony Bekenn

212

Rudolph *   Al Kozlik
August   Sandy Webster
Luigi   Craig Gardner
Miss Flora Van Huysen Patricia Hamilton
Cook   Camille James

succeeded by Catherine McGregor on September 26

Directed by Christopher Newton
Designed by William Schmuck
Lighting designed by Kevin Lamotte

Stage Manager   Bruno Gonsalves
Assistant Stage Manager Arwen MacDonell
Apprentice Stage Manager Patricia Levert

A WOMAN OF NO IMPORTANCE by Oscar Wilde

Court House Theatre
previews from May 16, opening May 27 to September 24 (62 performances)

Lady Caroline Pontefract Jennifer Phipps
Sir John Pontefract Norman Browning
Miss Hester Worsley Severn Thompson
Lady Hunstanton   Sharry Flett
Francis, a footman   Thomas Grant
Gerald Arbuthnot   Mike Wasko
Mrs Allonby   Brigitte Robinson
Lady Stutfield   Jillian Cook
Mr Kelvin, MP   Lorne Kennedy
Lord Illingworth   Jim Mezon
Lord Alfred Rufford Tony van Bridge
Butler   Scott Roberts
Farquhar   Guy Bannerman
Maid   Lisa Norton*
Mrs Arbuthnot   Mary Haney
Archdeacon Daubeny, DD Bernard Behrens
Alice   Catherine McGregor

succeeded by Joanne Marrella on June 13

Directed by Susan Ferley
Designed by William Schmuck
Lighting designed by Michael Kruse

Stage Manager   Allan Teichman
Assistant Stage Manager Jane Vanstone Osborn

THE APPLE CART by Bernard Shaw

Court House Theatre

previews from June 9, opening July 13 to September 23 (50 performances)

Pamphilius	Roger Rowland
Sempronius	Kevin Bundy
Boanerges (President of the Board of Trade)	Michael Ball
Magnus (King of England)	David Schurmann
Alice (The Princess Royal)	Fiona Byrne
Proteus (Prime Minister)	Peter Millard
Balbus (Home Secretary)	Anthony Bekenn
Nicobar (Foreign Secretary)	George Dawson
Crassus (Transport Secretary)	Sandy Webster
Pliny (Chancellor of the Exchequer)	Craig Gardner
Lysistrata (Energy Secretary)	Corrine Koslo
Amanda (Communications Secretary)	Camille James
Orinthia	Pamela Rabe
Queen Jemima	Wendy Thatcher
Ms Vanhattan (American Ambassador)	Lynne Cormack
Pages	Joanne Marrella, Lisa Norton, Scott Roberts

Directed by Richard Greenblatt
Designed by Kelly Wolf
Lighting designed by Bonnie Beecher
Music composed / arranged by John Millard

Stage Manager	Bruno Gonsalves
Assistant Stage Manager	Michelle Lagassé

SIX CHARACTERS IN SEARCH OF AN AUTHOR

by Luigi Pirandello

in a new translation by Domenico Pietropaolo

Court House Theatre

previews from August 11, opening August 19 to September 23 (19 performances)

The Father	Norman Browning
The Mother	Sharry Flett
The Stepdaughter	Kelli Fox
The Son	Joel Hechter
The Boy	Devon Tullock
Rosetta	Celeste Cairns / Zoe Roycroft
Madama Pace	Mary Haney
The Director	Barry MacGregor
The Stage Manager	Jillian Cook

The Prompter	Cameron MacDuffee
The Leading Man	Ben Carlson
The Leading Lady	Brigitte Robinson
A Young Actor	Mark McGrinder
An Ingénue	Imali Perera
An Actor	John Cleland
An Actor	Alistair James Harlond
An Actor	Amanda Smith
An Actor	Mike Wasko
A Technician	Matthew MacFadzean
The Doorman	Thomas Grant

Directed by Tadeusz Bradecki
Designed by Peter Hartwell
Lighting designed by Robert Thomson

Stage Manager	Allan Teichman
Assistant Stage Manager	Jane Vanstone Osborn
Apprentice Stage Manager	Mike Deschambeault

STILL LIFE by Noel Coward

Royal George Theatre
previews from June 17, opening July 14 to September 10
(38 Lunchtime performances)

Stanley	Blair Williams
Myrtle Bagot	Nora McLellan
Beryl Waters	Jenny L. Wright
Albert Godby	Neil Barclay
Alec Harvey	Simon Bradbury
Laura Jesson	Jan Alexandra Smith
A Customer	Susie Burnett
Bill	Bruce Davies
Johnnie	Douglas E. Hughes
Mildred	Jane Perry
Dolly Messiter	Laurie Paton

Directed by Dennis Garnhum
Designed by Barbara Gordon
Lighting designed by Jeff Logue

Stage Manager	Laurie Champagne
Assistant Stage Manager	Ingrid Kottke

CAMERON MACDUFFEE, PATTY JAMIESON, BEN CARLSON, MARK MCGRINDER, AND JAY TURVEY IN *SHE LOVES ME*, 2000 (PHOTO BY DAVID COOPER).

SHE LOVES ME

book by Joe Masteroff
music by Jerry Bock
lyrics by Sheldon Harnick

Royal George Theatre
previews from May 9, opening May 25 to October 29, held over to December 10 (170 performances)

Arpad Laszlo	Mark McGrinder
Ladislav Sipos	Jay Turvey
Ilona Ritter	Patty Jamieson
Steven Kodaly	Cameron MacDuffee
Georg Nowack	Ben Carlson*
Mr Maraczek	Richard Farrell
Three Customers	Tracy Dawson, Risa Waldman, Blythe Wilson
Amalia Balash	Glynis Ranney
Mr Keller	Allan Craik
Maitre d'	Patrick R. Brown
Waitress	Imali Perera
Mr Liszt	Brian Elliott**
Tango Dancers	Randy Ganne, Alistair James Harlond, Risa Waldman
Café Patrons, Carolers	Members of the Cast

succeeded by Brian Elliott on October 17
**succeeded by Mark Harapiak on October 14*

216

Directed by Roger Hodgman
Musical direction and orchestral adaptation
    by Paul Sportelli
Choreographed by William Orlowski
Designed by Patrick Clark
Lighting designed by Michael J. Whitfield

Stage Manager	Bruce MacDonald
Assistant Stage Manager	M. Rebecca Miller

TIME AND THE CONWAYS by J.B. Priestley

Royal George Theatre
previews from April 13, opening May 26 to October 28 (144 performances)

Hazel	Jane Perry
Carol	Susie Burnett
Alan	Peter Krantz
Madge	Laurie Paton
Kay	Jenny L. Wright
Mrs Conway	Nora McLellan
Joan Helford	Jan Alexandra Smith
Gerald Thornton	Douglas E. Hughes
Ernest Beevers	Simon Bradbury
Robin	Bruce Davies

Directed by Neil Munro
Sets designed by Brian Perchaluk
Costumes designed by David Boechler
Lighting designed by Ereca Hassell

Stage Manager	Judy Farthing
Assistant Stage Manager	Ingrid Kottke

A ROOM OF ONE'S OWN

adapted for the stage by Patrick Garland
from the essay by Virginia Woolf

Court House Theatre
previews from June 27, opening July 15 to September 22 (39 performances)

Virginia Woolf	Pamela Rabe

Directed by Micheline Chevrier
Designed by Judith Bowden
Lighting designed by Elizabeth Asselstine
Music composed and sound designed
    by Marc Desormeaux

Stage Manager	Joanna Jurychuk
Assistant Stage Manager	Michelle Lagassé

2000

BELL CANADA READING SERIES

THE DIARY OF SAMUEL MARCHBANKS by Robertson Davies
Royal George Theatre, July 20 (1 reading)

Cast: Michael Ball, Kevin Bundy, Lynne Cormack, George Dawson

Adapted and directed by Denis Johnston

Stage Manager   Ron Nipper
Assistant Stage Manager   Joanna Jurychuk

TO THE LIGHTHOUSE by Virginia Woolf
adapted by Lindsay Bell

Royal George Theatre, August 3 (1 reading)

Cast: Guy Bannerman, Bernard Behrens, Sharry Flett, Catherine McGregor,
Jeff Meadows, Severn Thompson

Directed by Ann Hodges

Stage Manager   Ron Nipper
Assistant Stage Manager   Joanna Jurychuk

HEART OF DARKNESS by Joseph Conrad
Royal George Theatre, August 17 (1 reading)

Marlow	Jim Mezon
Female Chorus	Lynne Cormack, Catherine McGregor, Severn Thompson
Male Chorus	Guy Bannerman, Bernard Behrens, Lorne Kennedy

Adapted and directed by Neil Munro

Stage Manager   Ron Nipper
Assistant Stage Manager   Joanna Jurychuk

DEAR SIR by Bernard Shaw
adapted by Alan Andrews

Royal George Theatre, August 24 (1 reading)

Cast: Michael Ball, Anthony Bekenn, Patricia Hamilton, Roger Rowland

Directed by Christopher Newton

Stage Manager   Ron Nipper
Assistant Stage Manager   Joanna Jurychuk

MUSICAL READING SERIES
WHAT A SWELL PARTY
words and music by Cole Porter
musical direction by Paul Sportelli

Royal George Theatre, August 12 (1 reading)

Cast: Patrick R. Brown, Allan Craik, Tracy Dawson, Brian Elliott,
Richard Farrell, Randy Ganne, Patty Jamieson, Imali Perera,
Glynis Ranney, Jay Turvey, Risa Waldman, Blythe Wilson

Staging by Christopher Newton

| Stage Manager | Bruce MacDonald |
| Assistant Stage Manager | M. Rebecca Miller |

SADIE THOMPSON
music by Vernon Duke
lyrics by Howard Dietz
book by Howard Dietz and Rouben Mamoulian

Royal George Theatre, August 3 (1 reading)

John Horn, owner of general store and hotel	Patrick R. Brown
Sergeant Tim O'Hara	Brian Elliott
Private Griggs	Alistair James Harlond
Ameena Horn, native wife of Joe Horn	Glynis Ranney
Corporal Hodgson	Randy Ganne
Mrs Davidson, wife of Reverend Davidson	Risa Waldman
Dr Cicely MacPhail, an anthropologist	Tracy Dawson
Sadie Thompson	Patty Jamieson
Quartermaster Bates (of the *S.S. Orduna*)	Allan Craik
Reverend Davidson	Jay Turvey
Marines / Islanders	Cameron MacDuffee, Mark McGrinder
Islanders	Imali Perera, Blythe Wilson

Adapted by Paul Sportelli and Christopher Newton
Directed by Christopher Newton
Music directed by Paul Sportelli

| Stage Manager | Bruce MacDonald |
| Assistant Stage Manager | M. Rebecca Miller |

2001

FORTIETH SEASON

April 5 to November 25 (758 Performances)

SIX CHARACTERS IN SEARCH OF AN AUTHOR
by Luigi Pirandello

Court House Theatre
previews from June 30, opening July 7 to September 22 (35 performances)

The Father	Norman Browning
The Mother	Sharry Flett
The Stepdaughter	Kelli Fox
The Son	Jason Chesworth
The Boy	Devon Tullock
Rosetta	Celeste Cairns / Stephanie Tope
Madama Pace	Sarah Orenstein
The Director	Blair Williams
The Stage Manager	John Cleland
The Prompter	Tony van Bridge*
The Leading Man	Nigel Shawn Williams
The Leading Lady	Brigitte Robinson
A Young Actor	Jason Jazrawy
An Ingénue	Susie Burnett
An Actor	Jamie Burnett
An Actor	Stephen McQuigge
An Actor	Duncan Stewart
A Technician	Dylan Trowbridge
The Doorman	Joe Wynne

succeeded by Stephen McQuigge on August 8

Directed by Tadeusz Bradecki
Designed by Peter Hartwell
Lighting designed by Robert Thomson

Stage Manager	Judy Farthing
Assistant Stage Manager	Meredith MacDonald

PETER PAN by J.M. Barrie

Festival Theatre
previews from April 18, opening May 26 to October 28 (108 performances)

Liza	Sherry Smith
Mrs Darling	Goldie Semple
Mr Darling	Jim Mezon
Wendy Darling	Fiona Byrne
John Darling	Pete Treadwell
Michael Darling	Devon Tullock
Nana / Dancer / Turley	Jeff Lillico
Peter Pan	Dylan Trowbridge
Tinker Bell / Mermaid	Jenny L. Wright*
Noodler / Dancer	Cameron MacDuffee
Tootles	Mike Wasko
Slightly	Neil Barclay
Curly	Duncan Stewart
First Twin	Joe Wynne
Second Twin	Jason Jazrawy
Nibs	Jason Chesworth
Captain James Hook	Jim Mezon
Starkey	Norman Browning
Smee	Bernard Behrens
Cecco / Dancer	Micheal Querin
Bill Jukes	Douglas E. Hughes
Indian / Whibbles / The Crocodile	Jamie Burnett
Skylights / Great Big Little Panther	Brian Elliott
Robert Mullins / Soldier	Mark McGrinder
Cookson / Cabbie	Anthony Bekenn
Tiger Lily	Goldie Semple
Canary Robb / Lone Wolf / Dancer	Adrian Marchuk
Mermaids / Indians	Tracy Michailidis, Leah Oster, Katherine Slater
Jane	Michelle Bauer / Leanne Browning

*succeeded by Jane Johanson on May 31

Directed by Christopher Newton
Designed by Sue LePage
Lighting designed by Kevin Lamotte
Fights directed by John Stead
Choreography by Jane Johanson

Stage Manager	Judy Farthing
Assistant Stage Managers	Jane Vanstone Osborn
	Thom Payne

2001

THE MILLIONAIRESS by Bernard Shaw
Festival Theatre
previews from May 3, opening May 23 to October 28 (100 performances)

Julius Sagamore	Peter Millard
Epifania Ognisanti di Parerga	Sarah Orenstein
Alastair Fitzfassenden	Peter Krantz
Patricia Smith	Severn Thompson*
Adrian Blenderbland	David Schurmann
The Manager	John Cleland
The Doctor	Nigel Shawn Williams
The Old Man	William Vickers
The Old Lady	Donna Belleville

succeeded by Caroline Cave on September 25

Directed by Allen MacInnis
Designed by William Schmuck
Lighting designed by Michael Kruse
Music and lyrics by Paul Sportelli and Jay Turvey
Fights directed by John Stead

Stage Manager	Bruce MacDonald*
Assistant Stage Manager	Michelle Lagassé**

succeeded by Michelle Lagassé on October 3
**succeeded by Jane Vanstone Osborn on September 25*

THE MAN WHO CAME TO DINNER
by Moss Hart and George S. Kaufman
Festival Theatre
previews from June 28, opening July 6 to November 10 (73 performances)

Harriet Stanley	Mary Haney
Mrs Stanley	Nora McLellan
Miss Preen	Patty Jamieson
Richard Stanley	Matthew Edison
John	Al Kozlik
June Stanley	Caroline Cave
Sarah	Jillian Cook
Mrs McCutcheon	Lynne Cormack
Mrs Dexter	Katey Wright*
Mr Stanley	Lorne Kennedy
Maggie Cutler	Laurie Paton
Dr Bradley	Richard Farrell
Sheridan Whiteside	Michael Ball
Professor Adolph Metz	George Dawson
Bert Jefferson	Kevin Bundy
Prisoner / Expressman / Technician / Officer	David Leyshon

222

Sandy / Prisoner	Jeff Meadows
Baker / Technician /	
Expressman / Deputy	Leo Vernik
Prisoner / Expressman /	
Deputy	Todd Witham
Lorraine Sheldon	Jane Perry
Beverly Carlton	Patrick R. Brown
Westcott	Robert Benson
Banjo	Simon Bradbury

succeeded by Severn Thompson, July 17; then by Helen Taylor, July 25

Directed by Neil Munro
Set designed by David Boechler
Costumes designed by Christina Poddubiuk
Lighting designed by Kevin Lamotte

Stage Manager	Laurie Champagne
Assistant Stage Manager	Dora Tomassi Corrigan
Apprentice Stage Manager	Dana Pew

FANNY'S FIRST PLAY by Bernard Shaw

Court House Theatre
previews from June 7, opening July 5 to September 22 (56 performances)

Footman	Christopher Blake
Cecil Savoyard	Robert Benson
Count O'Dowda	David Schurmann
Fanny O'Dowda /	
Margaret Knox	Severn Thompson
Mr Trotter	William Vickers
Mr Vaughan	George Dawson
Mr Gunn	Jeff Meadows
Flawner Bannal	Todd Witham
Mrs Gilbey	Nora McLellan
Mr Gilbey	Peter Millard
Juggins	Peter Krantz
Dora Delaney	Caroline Cave
Mrs Knox	Donna Belleville
Mr Knox	Roger Rowland
Duvallet	Simon Bradbury
Bobby Gilbey	Matthew Edison
The Producer	William Arthur

Directed by Todd Hammond
Designed by Teresa Przybylski
Lighting designed by Kevin Lamotte

Stage Manager	Bruce MacDonald
Assistant Stage Manager	Michelle Lagassé

2001

PICNIC by William Inge
Court House Theatre
previews from May 17, opening May 26 to September 21 (62 performances)

Hal Carter	Mike Wasko
Helen Potts	Jennifer Phipps
Millie Owens	Lisa Norton
Bomber	Pete Treadwell
Madge Owens	Fiona Byrne
Flo Owens	Wendy Thatcher
Rosemary Sydney	Goldie Semple
Alan Seymour	Mike Shara
Irma Kronkite	Sherry Smith
Christine Schoenwalder	Jane Johanson
Howard Bevans	Jim Mezon

Directed by Jackie Maxwell
Designed by Christina Poddubiuk
Lighting designed by Robert Thomson
Music by Paul Sportelli
Choreography by Jane Johanson

Stage Manager	Joanna Jurychuk
Assistant Stage Manager	Jane Vanstone Osborn

LAURA by Vera Caspary and George Sklar
Royal George Theatre
previews from April 5, opening May 24 to July 14 (68 performances)

Mark McPherson	Ben Carlson
Danny Dorgan	Stephen McQuigge
Waldo Lydecker	Michael Ball
Shelby Carpenter	Kevin Bundy
Bessie Clary	Mary Haney
Mrs Dorgan	Patricia Hamilton
The Woman	Jane Perry
Olsen	Al Kozlik

Directed by Neil Munro
Designed by Yvonne Sauriol
Lighting designed by Ereca Hassell

Stage Manager	Laurie Champagne
Assistant Stage Manager	Christine Oakey

THE RETURN OF THE PRODIGAL by St John Hankin

Court House Theatre

previews from August 5, opening August 18 to September 23 (21 performances)

Mrs Jackson	Patricia Hamilton
Lady Faringford	Brigitte Robinson
Stella Faringford	Susie Burnett
Violet Jackson	Kelli Fox
Mrs Pratt	Sharry Flett
Baines	Terrence Bryant
Mr Samuel Jackson	Bernard Behrens
The Reverend Cyril Pratt	Anthony Bekenn
Henry Jackson	Blair Williams
Sir John Faringford	Christopher Blake
Eustace Jackson	Ben Carlson
Dr Glaisher	Roger Rowland
Footman	William Arthur
Footman	Stephen McQuigge

Directed by Christopher Newton
Designed by William Schmuck
Lighting designed by Kevin Lamotte

Stage Manager	Thom Payne
Assistant Stage Manager	Meredith Macdonald
Apprentice Stage Manager	Lisa Whittaker

LOVE FROM A STRANGER by Frank Vosper

based on a story by Agatha Christie

Royal George Theatre

previews from August 1, opening August 17 to November 25 (63 performances)

Auntie Loo-Loo	Jennifer Phipps
Mavis Wilson	Laurie Paton
Cecily Harrington	Lisa Norton
Bruce Lovell	Mike Shara
Nigel Lawrence	Leo Vernick
Hodgson	Richard Farrell
Ethel	Helen Taylor
Dr Gribble	Lorne Kennedy

Directed by Micheline Chevrier
Designed by Brian Perchaluk
Lighting designed by Ereca Hassell

Stage Manager	Joanna Jurychuk
Assistant Stage Manager	Dora Tomassi Corrigan

THE MYSTERY OF EDWIN DROOD a musical by Rupert Holmes
based on the unfinished novel by Charles Dickens

Royal George Theatre
previews from May 10, opening May 25 to October 27 (119 performances)

Your Chairman	Neil Barclay
The Stage Manager	Mark McGrinder
John Jasper	Micheal Querin
Edwin Drood	Blythe Wilson
Rosa Bud	Tracy Michailidis
Wendy, a schoolgirl	Leah Oster
Beatrice, a schoolgirl	Katherine Slater
The Reverend Mr Crisparkle	Douglas E. Hughes
Neville Landless	Jeff Madden
Helena Landless	Jenny L. Wright
The Princess Puffer	Corrine Koslo
Durdles	Cameron MacDuffee
Deputy	Jeff Lillico
Bazzard	Guy Bannerman
Horace, a policeman	Brian Elliott
Robert, a citizen of Cloisterham	Gabriel Burrafato
Violet, a citizen of Cloisterham	Karen Wood
Christopher, a citizen of Cloisterham	Adrian Marchuk

Directed by Dennis Garnhum
Musical direction and
   orchestral adaptation by Paul Sportelli
Choreography by Timothy French
Set and lighting designed by Allan Stichbury
Costumes designed by Kelly Wolf

Stage Manager	Allan Teichman
Assistant Stage Manager	Amy Jewell

SHADOW PLAY by Noel Coward
Royal George Theatre
previews from April 18, opening May 22 to October 26 (47 Lunchtime performances)

Lena	Karen Wood
Hodge	Gabriel Burrafato
Victoria Gayforth	Patty Jamieson
Martha Cunningham	Jillian Cook
Simon Gayforth	Patrick R. Brown
Sibyl Heston	Blythe Wilson
Michael Doyle	Jeff Madden
Young Man	David Leyshon
George Cunningham	Guy Bannerman

Directed by David Savoy
Musical direction, arrangements,
  and orchestrations by Paul Sportelli
Choreography by William Orlowski
Designed by Judith Bowden
Lighting designed by Jeff Logue

| Stage Manager | Allan Teichman |
| Assistant Stage Manager | Amy Jewell |

BELL CANADA READING SERIES

THE MAN WITH THE FLOWER IN HIS MOUTH by Luigi Pirandello
translated by William Murray

Royal George Theatre, July 13 (1 reading)

Cecè

Narrator	Peter Millard
Cecè	David Schurmann
Squatriglia	William Vickers
Nada	Severn Thompson

The Man with the Flower in His Mouth

Narrator	Severn Thompson
The Man	Peter Millard
The Traveller	William Vickers

Directed by Denis Johnston

| Stage Manager | Michelle Lagassé |
| Assistant Stage Manager | Christine Oakey |

GBS VERSUS GKC
Royal George Theatre, August 3 (1 reading)

Shaw	Simon Bradbury
Chesterton	Neil Barclay
Narrator	Corrine Koslo
Belloc	Kevin Bundy

Adapted and directed by Jean Morpurgo

| Stage Manager | Laurie Champagne |
| Assistant Stage Manager | Jane Vanstone Osborn |

2001

LE GRAND MEAULNES by Alain-Fournier
Royal George Theatre, August 23 (1 reading)

Meaulnes	Joe Wynne
François	Dylan Trowbridge
Female Chorus	Fiona Byrne, Jane Johanson Jenny L. Wright
Male Chorus	Guy Bannerman, Douglas E. Hughes, Micheal Querin

Adapted and directed by Neil Munro

Stage Manager	Jane Vanstone Osborn
Apprentice Stage Manager	Amy Jewell

KLEE WYCK by Emily Carr
adapted by Lindsay Bell

Royal George Theatre, August 31 (1 reading)

Cast: Lynne Cormack, Sharry Flett, Kelli Fox, Patricia Hamilton, Corrine Koslo

Directed by Christopher Newton

Stage Manager	Allan Teichman
Assistant Stage Manager	Amy Jewell

MUSICAL READING SERIES

OVER THE RAINBOW the music of Harold Arlen
Royal George Theatre, August 17 (1 reading)

Cast: Neil Barclay, Jeff Lillico, Adrian Marchuk, Tracy Michailidis, Leah Oster, Goldie Semple

Musical direction by Paul Sportelli

Stage Manager	Judy Farthing
Assistant Stage Manager	Jane Vanstone Osborn

ARCHY AND MEHITABEL
book by Joe Darion and Mel Brooks
music by George Kleinsinger
lyrics by Joe Darion

Royal George Theatre, October 6 (1 reading)

The Newspaperman (Don Marquis)	Guy Bannerman
Archy, the cockroach with a soul	Jeff Madden
Mehitabel, a free soul and the queen of shinbone alley	Patty Jamieson
Big Bill, the big tom, tough, mean, brave	Neil Barclay

Mehitabel's cohorts, a gang
of rakish, bedraggled,
low-down alley cats   Leah Oster, Katherine Slater,
                                       Blythe Wilson, Karen Wood

Directed by Christopher Newton
Music directed by Paul Sportelli

Stage Manager   Allan Teichman
Assistant Stage Manager   Amy Jewell

Post-Season Tour

A ROOM OF ONE'S OWN

Brescia College (University of Western Ontario), London, September 29
(1 performance)

National Arts Centre, Ottawa, October 2 to 13 (14 performances)

For the above tours Kelli Fox appeared as Virginia Woolf. The Stage
Manager was Meredith Macdonald, and Stephen McQuigge was
an Apprentice Stage Manager.

Prairie Theatre Exchange, Winnipeg, October 17 to November 4 (20 performances)

For this tour Kelli Fox appeared as Virginia Woolf. The Stage Manager
was Meredith Macdonald, and Amanda Smart was an Apprentice
Stage Manager.

A SCENE FROM *PICNIC*, 2001 (PHOTO BY DAVID COOPER).

2002

FORTY-FIRST SEASON
April 4 to November 24 (773 Performances)

MERRILY WE ROLL ALONG
music and lyrics by Stephen Sondheim
book by George Furth
based on the original play by George S. Kaufman and Moss Hart

Royal George Theatre
previews from May 11, opening May 24 to October 26 (118 performances)

Franklin Shepard	Tyley Ross
Charley Kringas	Jay Turvey
Mary Flynn	Jenny L. Wright
Gussie Carnegie	Charlotte Moore
Joe Josephson	Gary Krawford
Beth Spencer	Glynis Ranney
Frank, Jr	Kurtis M.L. Baker / Kevin Morris
Tyler	Jeff Madden
Terry / Mr Spencer	Peter Millard
Scotty	Mark McGrinder
Dory / Evelyn	Jane Johanson
Ru	Jeff Lillico
Jerome	Patrick R. Brown
KT	Patty Jamieson
Meg Kincaid	Tracy Thomas
Bunker / Make-up Artist	Wayne Sujo
Mrs Spencer / Newswoman	Nora McLellan
Newswoman / Photographer / Pianist	Adrian Marchuk
Script Girl / Waitress	Nadia Hovan
Minister	Karim Morgan

Directed by Jackie Maxwell
Musical direction and orchestral adaptation
by Paul Sportelli
Choreography by Valerie Moore
Designed by Judith Bowden
Lighting designed by Robert Thomson

Stage Manager	Allan Teichman
Assistant Stage Manager	Christine Oakey
Rehearsal Apprentice Stage Manager	Stéfanie Séguin

HIS MAJESTY by Harley Granville Barker
Court House Theatre
previews from June 28, opening July 6 to September 21 (38 performances)

Henry Dwight Osgood	Robert Benson
Colonel Guastalla	Lorne Kennedy
The King	David Schurmann
Count Zapolya	Terrence Bryant
The Queen	Mary Haney
Dominica	Severn Thompson
Countess Czernyak	Sharry Flett
Ella	Lisa Norton
Colonel Hadik	Richard Farrell
Madrassy	Michael Ball
General Horvath	Al Kozlik
Captain Papp	Dylan Trowbridge
Stephen Czernyak	Ben Carlson
Mr Bruckner	George Dawson
Captain Dod	Jeff Meadows
Young Officer	Kevin Bundy
George Nagy, Mayor of Zimony	William Vickers
Lieutenant Vida	Christopher Blake (until August 25)
	Andrew Bunker (after August 25)
Sergeant-Major Bakay	Peter Krantz
Sir Charles Cruwys	Anthony Bekenn
Jakab, a farmer	Roger Rowland
Orderly	Andrew Bunker

Directed by Neil Munro
Designed by Sue LePage
Lighting designed by Ereca Hassell
Music composed by Paul Sportelli

Stage Manager	Thom Payne
Assistant Stage Manager	Amy Jewell
Rehearsal Apprentice Stage Manager	Stéfanie Séguin

THE RETURN OF THE PRODIGAL by St John Hankin
Court House Theatre
previews from May 17, opening May 25 to October 5 (70 performances)

Mrs Jackson	Patricia Hamilton
Lady Faringford	Brigitte Robinson
Stella Faringford	Susie Burnett
Violet Jackson	Kelli Fox
Mrs Pratt	Sharry Flett
Baines	Terrence Bryant
Mr Samuel Jackson	Bernard Behrens
The Reverend Cyril Pratt	Anthony Bekenn
Henry Jackson	Blair Williams
Sir John Faringford	Christopher Blake
Eustace Jackson	Ben Carlson
Dr Glaisher	Roger Rowland
Footman	Andrew Bunker
Footman	Todd Witham

Directed by Christopher Newton
Designed by William Schmuck
Lighting designed by Kevin Lamotte
Associate Lighting Designer: Jeff Logue

Stage Manager	Meredith Macdonald
Apprentice Stage Manager	Amy Jewell

CAESAR AND CLEOPATRA by Bernard Shaw
Festival Theatre
previews from April 13, opening May 21 to October 27 (95 performances)

Cleopatra VII	Caroline Cave
Ftatateeta	Sarah Orenstein
Charmian	Glynis Ranney
Iras	Jane Johanson
Lady in Waiting	Juliet Dunn
Harpist	Tracy Thomas
Nubian Slave	Karim Morgan
Professor of Music	Jay Turvey
Apollodorus	Patrick R. Brown
Ptolemy XIII	Jeff Lillico
Pothinus	Neil Barclay
Theodotus	Peter Millard
Achillas	Tyley Ross
Aide de Camp	Adrian Marchuk
Lucius Septimius	Mike Wasko

Belzanor	Gary Krawford
The Persian	Jeff Madden
Julius Caesar	Jim Mezon
Rufio	Guy Bannerman
Britannus	Norman Browning
Centurion	Douglas E. Hughes
Roman Sentinel	Jeffrey Renn
Bel Affris	Pete Treadwell
Roman Soldier	Jamie Burnett
First Porter	David Leyshon
Wounded Soldier	Mark McGrinder
Second Major Domo	Stephen McQuigge
Boatman	Micheal Querin
Priest	Wayne Sujo
First Major Domo	Duncan Stewart
Auxiliary Sentinel	Corey Turner
Third Sentinel	Alex Ring

Directed by Christopher Newton
Designed by William Schmuck
Lighting designed by Kevin Lamotte

Stage Manager	Laurie Champagne
Assistant Stage Manager	Christine Oakey
Apprentice Stage Manager	Heather Lewis

THE OLD LADY SHOWS HER MEDALS by J.M. Barrie

Royal George Theatre
previews from July 19, opening August 17 to September 21
(31 Lunchtime performances)

Mrs Dowey	Jennifer Phipps
Mrs Twymley	Maria Vacratsis
Mrs Haggerty	Wendy Thatcher
Mrs Mickleham	Donna Belleville
Mr Willings	Douglas E. Hughes
Private Kenneth Dowey	Pete Treadwell

Directed by Todd Hammond
Designed by Deeter Schurig
Lighting designed by Melinda Sutton

Stage Manager	Joanna Jurychuk
Assistant Stage Manager	Marinda de Beer
Rehearsal Apprentice Stage Manager	Heather Lewis

2002

DETECTIVE STORY by Sidney Kingsley
Festival Theatre
previews from May 2, opening May 23 to September 21 (63 performances)

Detective Dakis	Norman Browning
Shoplifter	Sarah Orenstein
Detective Gallagher	Douglas E. Hughes
Patrolman Keogh	Pete Treadwell
Mrs Farragut	Jennifer Phipps
Patrolman Baker	Corey Turner
Joe Feinson	William Vickers
Detective Callahan	Mike Wasko
Detective O'Brien	Guy Bannerman
Detective Brody	Robert Benson
Endicott Sims	Neil Barclay
Detective McLeod	Peter Krantz
Arthur Kindred	Jeff Meadows
Patrolman Barnes	Leo Vernik
Lewis Abbott	Dylan Trowbridge
Charlie Gennini	George Dawson
Mrs Bagatelle	Helen Taylor
Willy	Stephen McQuigge
Kurt Schneider	Lorne Kennedy
Lieutenant Monoghan	Jim Mezon
Susan Carmichael	Fiona Byrne
Miss Hatch	Goldie Semple
Mrs Feeney	Caroline Cave
Mr Feeney	Jamie Burnett
Crumb-Bum	Micheal Querin
Mr Gallantz / Photographer	David Leyshon
Mr Pritchett	Al Kozlik
Mary McLeod	Jane Perry
Tami Giacoppetti	Simon Bradbury
Classy Gentleman	Richard Farrell
Classy Lady	Jillian Cook
Mr Bagatelle	Jeffrey Renn
Indignant Citizen	Duncan Stewart

Directed by Neil Munro
Designed by Cameron Porteous
Lighting designed by Alan Brodie

Stage Manager	Judy Farthing
Assistant Stage Manager	Jane Vanstone Osborn

THE HOUSE OF BERNARDA ALBA by Federico García Lorca
in a new translation by Richard Sanger

Court House Theatre
previews from June 8, opening July 4 to October 5 (56 performances)

Maid	Patty Jamieson
La Poncia	Patricia Hamilton
Beggar	Catherine McGregor
Young Girl	Danielle Baker / Stephanie Tope
Mourner / Prudencia	Brigitte Robinson
Mourner / María Josefa	Jillian Cook
Mourner	Jenny L. Wright
Mourner	Nadia Hovan
Mourner	Charlotte Moore
Angustias	Lynne Cormack
Magdalena	Helen Taylor
Amelia	Jane Perry
Martirio	Susie Burnett
Adela	Fiona Byrne
Bernarda Alba	Nora McLellan

Directed by Tadeusz Bradecki
Designed by Teresa Przybylski
Lighting designed by Kevin Lamotte

Stage Manager	Allan Teichman
Assistant Stage Manager	Jane Vanstone Osborn

CANDIDA by Bernard Shaw
Festival Theatre
previews from June 26, opening July 5 to November 23 (59 performances)

Miss Proserpine Garnett	Laurie Paton
The Reverend James Mavor Morell	Blair Williams
The Reverend Lexy Mill	Todd Witham
Mr Burgess	Bernard Behrens
Candida Morell	Kelli Fox
Eugene Marchbanks	Mike Shara

Directed by Jackie Maxwell
Set designed by Sue LePage
Costumes designed by Christina Poddubiuk
Lighting designed by Kevin Lamotte
Music composed by Paul Sportelli

Stage Manager	Meredith Macdonald
Assistant Stage Manager	Dora Tomassi

THE OLD LADIES by Rodney Ackland

Royal George Theatre

previews from April 4, opening May 22 to October 27 (152 performances)

May Beringer	Wendy Thatcher
Lucy Amorest	Donna Belleville
Agatha Payne	Maria Vacratsis

Directed by James MacDonald
Designed by David Boechler
Lighting designed by Andrea Lundy

Stage Manager	Joanna Jurychuk
Assistant Stage Manager	Marinda de Beer

HAY FEVER by Noel Coward

Festival Theatre

previews from July 31, opening August 16 to November 24 (55 performances)

Sorel Bliss	Severn Thompson
Simon Bliss	Mike Shara
Clara	Mary Haney
Judith Bliss	Fiona Reid
David Bliss	Michael Ball
Sandy Tyrell	Kevin Bundy
Myra Arundel	Laurie Paton
Richard Greatham	David Schurmann
Jackie Coryton	Lisa Norton

Directed by Christopher Newton
Designed by William Schmuck
Lighting designed by Alan Brodie

Stage Manager	Thom Payne
Assistant Stage Manager	Dora Tomassi

CHAPLIN by Simon Bradbury

Court House Theatre

previews from August 10, opening August 17 to October 6 (29 performances)

Chaplin	Simon Bradbury

Voices:

Elsie	Nora McLellan
Alf Reeves	Michael Ball
Sump pump man	Jamie Burnett
Take-out lady	Caroline Cave
Rollie Totheroh	Leo Vernik
Assistant Director	Duncan Stewart
Joe Schenck	Norman Browning

Bob Meltzer	Micheal Querin
Dan James	Mike Wasko
Sydney	Douglas E. Hughes
Young Chaplin	Malcolm Bradbury
Reporter 1	Jim Mezon
Reporter 2	Corey Turner
Reporter 3	Sarah Orenstein

On Screen:

Camera Assistant	Jeffrey Renn
Props Person	Lisa Norton
Hynkel Secretary	Juliet Dunn
Hynkel Secretary	Tracy Thomas
Hynkel Secretary	Wayne Sujo
Young Chaplin	Thomas Bradbury

Directed by Neil Munro
Designed by David Boechler
Lighting designed by Kevin Lamotte
Sound designed by Trevor Hughes
Multimedia and video projection
  designed by Simon D. Clemo
Original piano music by Paul Sportelli
Movement coach and Chaplin consultant: Dan Kamin

| Stage Manager | Judy Farthing |
| Apprentice Stage Manager | Stéfanie Séguin |

BELL CANADA READING SERIES

QUEENS OF FRANCE a reading of two plays by Thornton Wilder
Royal George Theatre, July 20 (1 reading)

Queens of France

Narrator	David Leyshon
Cahusac	Guy Bannerman
Mlle Cressaux	Fiona Byrne
Mme Pugeot	Helen Taylor
Mlle Pointevin	Goldie Semple

Love and How to Cure It

Narrator	Helen Taylor
Rowena	Goldie Semple
Linda	Fiona Byrne
Joe	Guy Bannerman
Arthur	David Leyshon

Directed by Denis Johnston

| Stage Manager | Jane Vanstone Osborn |
| Apprentice Stage Manager | Stéfanie Séguin |

THE BEAR and THE PROPOSAL
a reading of two plays by Anton Chekhov

Royal George Theatre, August 2 (1 reading)

The Bear

Luka	Guy Bannerman
Yelena	Helen Taylor
Smirnov	Jim Mezon

The Proposal

Chubukov	Robert Benson
Lomov	Mike Wasko
Natalya	Caroline Cave

Directed by Jackie Maxwell

Stage Manager	Jane Vanstone Osborn
Apprentice Stage Manager	Heather Lewis

GKC by Tony van Bridge
based on the writings of G.K. Chesterton

Royal George Theatre, August 22 (1 reading)

Chesterton	Neil Barclay

Adapted and directed by
Tony van Bridge and Christopher Newton

Stage Manager	Christine Oakey
Apprentice Stage Manager	Stéfanie Séguin

THE PLACE OF THE LION by Charles Williams
Royal George Theatre, September 6 (1 reading)

Damaris Tighe	Susie Burnett
Anthony	Ben Carlson
Mrs Rockbotham	Jillian Cook
Nurse / Maid / Mrs Portman	Lynne Cormack
Dora Wilmot	Sharry Flett
Mr Foster / Dr Rockbotham	Lorne Kennedy
Mr Tighe / Mr Richardson / Lorrigan	Duncan Stewart
Quentin	William Vickers

Adapted and directed by Neil Munro

Stage Manager	Amy Jewell
Apprentice Stage Manager	Heather Lewis

MUSICAL READING SERIES
ARCHY AND MEHITABEL
book by Joe Darion and Mel Brooks
music by George Kleinsinger
lyrics by Joe Darion

Royal George Theatre, July 5 (1 reading)

The Newspaperman (Don Marquis)	Guy Bannerman
Archy, the cockroach with a soul	Jeff Madden
Mehitabel, a free soul and the queen of shinbone alley	Patty Jamieson
Big Bill, the big tom, tough, mean, brave	Neil Barclay
Mehitabel's cohorts, a gang of rakish, bedraggled, low-down alley cats	Caroline Cave, Juliet Dunn, Glynis Ranney, Tracy Thomas

Directed by Christopher Newton
Music directed by Paul Sportelli

Stage Manager	Laurie Champagne
Apprentice Stage Manager	Heather Lewis

HELLO AGAIN by Michael John Lachiusa
based on the play *La Ronde* by Arthur Schnitzler

Royal George Theatre, August 29 (1 reading)

The Whore	Juliet Dunn
The Soldier	Adrian Marchuk
The Nurse	Glynis Ranney
The College Boy	Jeff Lillico
The Young Wife	Patty Jamieson
The Husband	Patrick R. Brown
The Young Thing	Jeff Madden
The Writer	Tyley Ross
The Actress	Caroline Cave
The Senator	Jay Turvey

Directed by Christopher Newton
Musically directed by Paul Sportelli

Stage Manager	Allan Teichman
Apprentice Stage Manager	Heather Lewis

PANAMA HATTIE
music and lyrics by Cole Porter
book by Herbert Fields and B.G. DeSylva

Royal George Theatre, July 17 (1 reading)
Jackson-Triggs Niagara Estate Winery, August 10 (1 reading)

Woozy Hogan, sailor from the *S.S. Idaho*	Neil Barclay
Skat Briggs, sailor from the *S.S. Idaho*	Jeff Lillico
Windy Deegan, sailor from the *S.S. Idaho*	Mark McGrinder
Mac, hostess of The Tropical Shore Cabaret	Juliet Dunn
Tim, U.S. soldier	Wayne Sujo
Tom, U.S. soldier	Karim Morgan
Hattie Maloney, owner of and singer at The Tropical Shore Cabaret	Karen Wood
Leila Tree	Charlotte Moore
Mildred von Hunter	Nadia Hovan
Nick Bullett	Micheal Querin
Florrie	Jane Johanson
Geraldine Bullett (Jerry), Nick's daughter	Tracy Thomas
Vivian Budd, Geraldine's English butler and chaperone	David Schurmann
Whitney Randolph, chairman of the Panama Canal works	Michael Ball

Adapted and directed by
Christopher Newton and Paul Sportelli

Stage Manager	Allan Teichman
Apprentice Stage Manager	Stéfanie Séguin

Post-Season Tour

CANDIDA

National Arts Centre, Ottawa, November 27 to December 14 (19 performances)

> For this tour Severn Thompson appeared as Miss Proserpine Garnett and Laurie Paton appeared as Candida Morell.

Meadow Brook Theatre, Rochester, Michigan, January 8 to February 2, 2003 (27 performances)

> For this tour Severn Thompson appeared as Miss Proserpine Garnett and Laurie Paton appeared as Candida Morell. The Assistant Stage Manager was Sarah Warren.

2003

FORTY-SECOND SEASON
April 3 to November 30 (830 Performances)

ON THE TWENTIETH CENTURY
book and lyrics by Betty Comden and Adolph Green
music by Cy Coleman

Royal George Theatre
previews from April 3, opening May 22 to November 2 (129 performances)

Congressman Grover Lockwood	Guy Bannerman
Owen O'Malley	Patrick R. Brown
Bruce Granit	Evan Buliung
Dr Johnson	Juliet Dunn
Imelda Thornton	Lisa Horner
Train Secretary	Nadia Hovan
Conductor Flanagan	Douglas E. Hughes
Lily Garland	Patty Jamieson
Oscar Jaffee	Gary Krawford
Porter	Richard MacDonagh
Max Jacobs	Jeff Madden
Porter	Shawn Meunier
Porter	Mike Nadajewski
Letitia Peabody Primrose	Brigitte Robinson
Anita	Katherine Slater
Porter	Sam Strasfeld
Agnes	Severn Thompson
Oliver Webb	William Vickers
Paper Girl / Photographer	Leslie-Anne Wickens

Directed by Valerie Moore and Patricia Hamilton
Musical direction and orchestral adaptation
   by Paul Sportelli
Choreography by Valerie Moore
Designed by Yvonne Sauriol
Lighting designed by Harry Frehner

Stage Manager	Allan Teichman
Assistant Stage Manager	Jane Vanstone Osborn

2003

THREE SISTERS by Anton Chekhov
a new version by Susan Coyne

Festival Theatre

previews from April 26, opening May 24 to August 2 (50 performances)

Olga	Kelli Fox
Masha	Tara Rosling
Irina	Caroline Cave
Andrei	Ben Carlson
Chebutykin, a military doctor	David Schurmann
Baron Tuzenbach, first lieutenant	Jeff Meadows
Solyony, subaltern	Peter Krantz
Anfisa, an old nanny	Jennifer Phipps
Ferapont, Dirstrict Council caretaker	Richard Farrell
Vershinin, battery commander	Kevin Bundy
Kulygin, Masha's husband	Douglas E. Hughes
Natasha, a local girl	Fiona Byrne
Fedotik, second lieutenant	Jeff Madden
Rohde, second lieutenant	Andrew Bunker
Maid / Musician's Girl	Katherine Slater
Houseboy / Soldier	Jared Brown
Orderly / Soldier	Sam Strasfeld
Musician / Soldier	George Dawson
Soldier	Mark Adriaans

Directed by Jackie Maxwell
Designed by Sue LePage
Lighting designed by Kevin Lamotte
Music composed by Paul Sportelli

Stage Manager	Thom Payne
Assistant Stage Manager	Marinda de Beer

MISALLIANCE by Bernard Shaw
Festival Theatre

previews from April 10, opening May 20 to November 2 (106 performances)

Johnny Tarleton	Mike Shara
Bentley Summerhays	David Leyshon
Hypatia	Jane Perry
Mrs Tarleton	Sharry Flett
Lord Summerhays	Michael Ball
John Tarleton	Lorne Kennedy
Joey Percival	Graeme Somerville
Lina Szczepanowska	Laurie Paton
Gunner	Pete Treadwell
Aviators	Mark Adriaans, Jared Brown

Directed by Neil Munro
Designed by Peter Hartwell
Lighting designed by Alan Brodie

Stage Manager	Judy Farthing
Assistant Stage Manager	Amy Jewell
Apprentice Stage Manager	Kathryn Brown

HAPPY END

lyrics by Bertolt Brecht
music by Kurt Weill
original German play by Dorothy Lane
books and lyrics adapted by Michael Feingold

Royal George Theatre
previews from August 5, opening August 15 to October 31 (43 performances)

Bill Cracker	Benedict Campbell
Sammy "Mammy" Wurlitzer	Neil Barclay
Dr Nakamura ("The Governor")	Jay Turvey
Jimmy Dexter ("The Reverend")	Guy Bannerman
Bob Marker ("The Professor")	Peter Millard
Johnny Flint ("Baby Face")	Jeff Lillico
A Lady in Gray ("The Fly")	Glynis Ranney
Miriam	Wendy Thatcher
Major Stone	Donna Belleville
Lieutenant Lillian Holiday ("Hallelujah Lil")	Blythe Wilson
Captain Hannibal Jackson	Mike Nadajewski
Sister Mary	Trish Lindström
Sister Jane	Jenny L. Wright
Brother Ben Owens	Kevin Dennis
The Cop	Robert Benson
Members of the Fold	Nadia Hovan, Jeff Irving, Richard MacDonagh, Leslie-Anne Wickens

Directed by Tadeusz Bradecki
Musical direction by Paul Sportelli
Choreography by Jane Johanson
Set designed by Peter Hartwell
Costumes designed by Teresa Przybylski
Lighting designed by Jeff Logue

Stage Manager	Joanna Jurychuk
Assistant Stage Manager	Jane Vanstone Osborn
Apprentice Stage Manager	Jaime-Rose de Pippo

2003

THE CORONATION VOYAGE by Michel Marc Bouchard
translated by Linda Gaboriau

Festival Theatre
previews from June 24, opening July 5 to November 1 (64 performances)

The Biographer	George Dawson
The Diplomat	Peter Krantz
Sandro	Jeff Lillico
The Chief	Jim Mezon
Etienne	Dylan Trowbridge
Minister Joseph Gendron	David Schurmann
Alice Gendron	Donna Belleville
Marguerite Gendron	Susie Burnett
Mademoiselle Lavallée	Glynis Ranney
Elisabeth Turcotte	Tara Rosling
Elisabeth Ménard	Lisa Norton
Elisabeth Pennington	Jenny L. Wright
Willy	Richard Farrell
Jeremy	Andrew Bunker
Passengers	Catherine O'Brien, Micheal Querin

Directed by Jackie Maxwell
Set designed by Ken MacDonald
Costumes designed by William Schmuck
Lighting designed by Alan Brodie
Original music composed by Allen Cole

Stage Manager	Thom Payne
Assistant Stage Manager	Christine Oakey

WIDOWERS' HOUSES by Bernard Shaw

Court House Theatre
previews from May 15, opening May 23 to October 4 (74 performances)

Waiter	Kevin Dennis
Dr Harry Trench	Dylan Trowbridge
Mr William de Burgh Cokane	Patrick Galligan
Sartorius	Jim Mezon
Blanche	Lisa Norton
Porter	Jeff Irving
Lickcheese	Peter Millard
Parlourmaid	Susie Burnett

Directed by Joseph Ziegler
Designed by Christina Poddubiuk
Lighting designed by Alan Brodie

Stage Manager	Joanna Jurychuk
Assistant Stage Manager	Christine Oakey

THE ROYAL FAMILY by George S. Kaufman and Edna Ferber
Festival Theatre
previews from August 8, opening August 16 to November 23 (68 performances)

Della	Jillian Cook
Jo	Anthony Bekenn
Hallboy	Jared Brown
McDermott	Jeff Meadows
Herbert Dean	Norman Browning
Kitty LeMoyne Dean	Nora McLellan
Gwen Cavendish	Caroline Cave
Perry Stewart	David Leyshon
Fanny Cavendish	Patricia Hamilton
Oscar Wilde	Robert Benson
Julie Cavendish	Goldie Semple
Tony Cavendish	Peter Hutt
Hallboy	Mark Adriaans
Chauffeur / Gunga	Al Kozlik
Gilbert Marshall	Ric Reid
Miss Peake	Diana Donnelly

Directed by Martha Henry
Designed by William Schmuck
Lighting designed by Kevin Lamotte

Stage Manager	Meredith Macdonald
Assistant Stage Manager	Dora Tomassi

LISA NORTON AND DYLAN TROWBRIDGE IN *WIDOWERS' HOUSES*, 2003 (PHOTO BY DAVID COOPER).

2003

THE PLOUGH AND THE STARS by Seán O'Casey
Court House Theatre
previews from June 20, opening July 4 to October 5 (61 performances)

Fluther Good	Benedict Campbell
Peter Flynn	Simon Bradbury
Mrs Gogan	Kelli Fox
The Young Covey	Ben Carlson
Nora Clitheroe	Fiona Byrne
Mrs Bessie Burgess	Wendy Thatcher
Jack Clitheroe	Mike Shara
Captain Brennan	Kevin Bundy
Mollser	Trish Lindstrom
Barman	Neil Barclay
Rosie Redmond	Helen Taylor
Figure of the Tall Man	Patrick Galligan
Lieutenant Langon	Pete Treadwell
The Woman	Blythe Wilson
Corporal Stoddart	Jay Turvey
Sergeant Tinley	Graeme Somerville

Directed by Neil Munro
Designed by Cameron Porteous
Lighting designed by Kevin Lamotte
Original music composed by Paul Sportelli

Stage Manager	Alison Peddie
Assistant Stage Manager	Marinda de Beer

DIANA OF DOBSON'S by Cicely Hamilton
Court House Theatre
previews from June 3, opening July 3 to October 4 (69 performances)

Miss Smithers	Lisa Horner
Kitty Brant	Diana Donnelly
Miss Jay	Patty Jamieson
Diana Massingberd	Severn Thompson
Miss Morton	Juliet Dunn
Miss Pringle / Old Woman	Jillian Cook
Mrs Cantelupe	Goldie Semple
Mrs Whyte-Fraser	Patricia Hamilton
Waiter / Vagrant	Shawn Meunier
Sir Jabez Grinley	Peter Hutt
Captain Victor Bretherton, late of the Welsh Guards	Evan Buliung
Police Constable Fellowes	Al Kozlik

Directed by Alisa Palmer
Sets designed by Judith Bowden
Costumes designed by David Boechler
Lighting designed by Andrea Lundy

Stage Manager	Allan Teichman
Assistant Stage Manager	Dora Tomassi

BLOOD RELATIONS by Sharon Pollock

Royal George Theatre
previews from May 1, opening May 21 to November 30 (120 performances)

The Actress / Lizzie	Laurie Paton
Miss Lizzie / Bridget	Jane Perry
The Defense / Dr Patrick	Anthony Bekenn
Harry	Lorne Kennedy
Emma	Sharry Flett
Abigail Borden	Nora McLellan
Andrew Borden	Michael Ball

Directed by Eda Holmes
Designed by William Schmuck
Lighting designed by Andrea Lundy

Stage Manager	Meredith Macdonald
Assistant Stage Manager	Amy Jewell

AFTERPLAY by Brian Friel

Court House Theatre
previews from July 11, opening August 16 to September 20
(31 Lunchtime performances)

Sonya Serebriakova	Helen Taylor
Andrey Prozorov	Simon Bradbury

Directed by Daryl Cloran
Designed by Judith Bowden
Lighting designed by Kevin Lamotte
Music composed by Alan Moon

Stage Manager	Alison Peddie
Apprentice Stage Manager	Kathryn Brown

2003

BELL CANADA READING SERIES

THE SHEWING-UP OF BLANCO POSNET by Bernard Shaw
Royal George Theatre, July 18 (1 reading)

Narrator	Gary Krawford
Babsy	Katherine Slater
Lottie	Lisa Norton
Hannah	Jennifer Phipps
Jessie	Tara Rosling
Elder Daniels	David Schurmann
Blanco Posnet	Peter Krantz
Strapper Kemp	Micheal Querin
Feemy Evans	Susie Burnett
Sheriff Kemp	Anthony Bekenn
The Foreman	Richard Farrell
Wagonner Jo	Sam Strasfeld
The Woman	Catherine O'Brien

Directed by Denis Johnston

Stage Manager	Christine Oakey
Apprentice Stage Manager	Kathryn Brown

A THEATRICAL TRIP FOR A WAGER
based on the travel memoir by Captain Horton Rhys

Royal George Theatre, August 7 (1 reading)

Adapted and performed by Christopher Newton

Stage Manager	Judy Farthing
Apprentice Stage Manager	Jaime-Rose de Pippo

VOYAGE IN THE DARK by Jean Rhys
Royal George Theatre, August 22 (1 reading)

Maudie	Fiona Byrne
Anna	Caroline Cave
Mother St Anthony / Mrs Dawes	Kelli Fox
Judd Street Landlady / Ethel	Nora McLellan
Landlady / Laurie / Germaine	Lisa Norton
Mrs Flowers / Mrs Robinson	Tara Rosling
Jeffries / Joe / Doctor	Andrew Bunker
Jones / Waiter / Vincent / Carl	Douglas E. Hughes

Adapted and directed by Neil Munro

Stage Manager	Marinda de Beer
Apprentice Stage Manager	Kathryn Brown

THE WORDS UPON THE WINDOW-PANE and PURGATORY
a reading of two plays by W.B. Yeats

Royal George Theatre, August 29 (1 reading)

The Words upon the Window-Pane

Dr Trench	David Schurmann
Miss Mackenna	Jenny L. Wright
John Corbet	Simon Bradbury
Abraham Johnson	Graeme Somerville
Mrs Mallet	Catherine O'Brien
Cornelius Patterson	Richard Farrell
Mrs Henderson	Jennifer Phipps

Purgatory

Boy	Jared Brown
Old Man	Bernard Behrens

Directed by Jackie Maxwell

Stage Manager	Alison Peddie
Apprentice Stage Manager	Jaime-Rose de Pippo

MUSICAL READING SERIES

JUBILEE
music and lyrics by Cole Porter
book by Moss Hart

Royal George Theatre, September 21 (1 reading)

Prime Minister / Narrator	Guy Bannerman
Eric Dare	Patrick R. Brown
Charlie Rausmiller	Evan Buliung
Cabinet Minister	Juliet Dunn
Eva Standing	Lisa Horner
Mrs Watkins	Nadia Hovan
The King	Douglas E. Hughes
Karen O'Kane	Patty Jamieson
The Prince	Jeff Madden
Prince Peter	Mike Nadajewski
The Queen	Brigitte Robinson
The Princess	Katherine Slater
Prince Rudolf	Sam Strasfeld
Laura	Severn Thompson

Adapted and directed by
Christopher Newton and Paul Sportelli

Stage Manager	Allan Teichman
Assistant Stage Manager	Joanna Jurychuk

2004

FORTY-THIRD SEASON
April 2 to December 4 (857 Performances)

MAN AND SUPERMAN by Bernard Shaw
Festival Theatre
previews from June 26, opening July 3 to October 9 (43 performances)

Roebuck Ramsden	David Schurmann
Maid	Jessica Lowry
Octavius Robinson	Evan Buliung
John Tanner	Ben Carlson
Ann Whitefield	Fiona Byrne
Mrs Whitefield	Sharry Flett
Miss Ramsden	Wendy Thatcher
Violet Robinson	Lisa Norton
Henry Straker	Patrick Galligan
Hector Malone	Graeme Somerville
Mendoza	Benedict Campbell
Anarchist	Jay Turvey
Rowdy Social Democrat	Jeff Madden
Sulky Social Democrat	Jeff Meadows
Duval	George Dawson
Brigands	Mark Adriaans, Jared Brown, Martin Happer, Evert Houston, Jeff Irving
Old Woman	Jennifer Phipps
Officer	Andrew Bunker
Mr Malone	Guy Bannerman

The *Don Juan in Hell* scene was added to Act III for eleven performances from June 26 to July 25.

Old Woman	Jennifer Phipps
Don Juan	Ben Carlson
Doña Ana	Fiona Byrne
The Statue	David Schurmann
The Devil	Benedict Campbell

Directed by Neil Munro
Designed by Peter Hartwell
Lighting designed by Kevin Lamotte
Original music composed by Paul Sportelli

Stage Manager	Judy Farthing
Assistant Stage Manager	Dora Tomassi
Apprentice Stage Manager	Patti Neice

THE TINKER'S WEDDING by J.M. Synge
Court House Theatre
previews from June 16, opening July 3 to September 5 (31 Lunchtime performances)

Michael Byrne	David Leyshon
Sarah Casey	Trish Lindström
A Priest	William Vickers
Mary Byrne	Nora McLellan

Directed by Micheline Chevrier
Designed by Deeter Schurig
Lighting designed by Peter Debreceni

Stage Manager	Thom Payne
Assistant Stage Manager	Lisa Whittaker

AH, WILDERNESS! by Eugene O'Neill
Court House Theatre
previews from May 13, opening May 29 to October 8 (80 performances)

Tommy	Zachary Thomson / Christopher Wowk
Mildred	Tamara Kit
Arthur	Jeff Irving
Essie Miller	Wendy Thatcher
Lily Miller	Mary Haney
Nat Miller	Norman Browning
Sid Davis	William Vickers
Richard	Jared Brown
David McComber	George Dawson
Norah	Jessica Lowry
Wint Selby	Martin Happer
Belle	Lisa Norton
Bartender	Graeme Somerville
Salesman	Michael Ball
Muriel McComber	Maggie Blake

Directed by Joseph Ziegler
Designed by Christina Poddubiuk
Lighting designed by Alan Brodie
Musical direction and original music
composed by John Tute

Stage Manager	Joanna Jurychuk
Assistant Stage Manager	Barry Burns

2004

THREE MEN ON A HORSE by John Cecil Holm and George Abbott

Festival Theatre

previews from April 24, opening May 8 to October 29 (95 performances)

Audrey Trowbridge	Catherine McGregor
Erwin Trowbridge	Kevin Bundy
Clarence Dobbins	Douglas E. Hughes
Tailor / Delivery Boy / Al	Al Kozlik
Harry	Peter Millard
Charlie	Peter Hutt
Frankie	Jeff Lillico
Patsy	Simon Bradbury
Mabel	Glynis Ranney
Moses	Kevin Dennis
Gloria Gray	Jillian Cook
Hotel maid	Darcy Dunlop
Mr Carver	Anthony Bekenn

Directed by Jim Mezon
Designed by Cameron Porteous
Lighting designed by Louise Guinand

Stage Manager	Meredith Macdonald
Assistant Stage Manager	Amy Jewell
Apprentice Stage Manager	Kinnon Elliott

PYGMALION by Bernard Shaw

Festival Theatre

previews from April 8, opening May 6 to November 27 (123 performances)

Clara Eynsford Hill	Catherine McGregor
Mrs Eynsford Hill	Jillian Cook***
Freddy Enysford Hill	Adam Brazier*****
Eliza Doolittle	Tara Rosling
Colonel Pickering*	Lorne Kennedy
Henry Higgins	Jim Mezon
Mrs Pearce	Nora McLellan****
Alfred Doolittle	Simon Bradbury
Mrs Higgins	Patricia Hamilton
Parlourmaid**	Shannon McCaig
Nepommuck	Neil Barclay

Londoners: Anthony Bekenn, Richard Farrell, Elodie Gillett,
Mark Harapiak, Lisa Horner, Evert Houston, Patty Jamieson, Al Kozlik,
Joanne Mendioro, Micheal Querin, Kiera Sangster, Ashley Taylor

performed by Micheal Querin, June 20 to July 3
**performed by Elodie Gillett, September 4 to 25*
***succeeded by Sharry Flett on October 26*
****succeeded by Jillian Cook on October 26*
*****succeeded by Jeff Meadows on November 16*

252

Directed by Jackie Maxwell
Designed by Sue LePage
Lighting designed by Kevin Lamotte
Original music and sound designed by Marc Desormeaux

| Stage Manager | Thom Payne |
| Assistant Stage Manager | Amy Jewell |

PAL JOEY

music by Richard Rodgers, lyrics by Lorenz Hart, book by John O'Hara

Royal George Theatre
previews from May 11, opening May 28 to October 30 (108 performances)

Joey Evans	Adam Brazier
Mike Spears*	Lorne Kennedy
The Kid***	Ashley Taylor
Gladys Bumps	Jenny L. Wright
Diane	Kiera Sangster
Terry	Joanne Mendioro
Tilda	Lisa Horner
Valerie	Helen Taylor
Claire	Elodie Gillett
Linda English	Shannon McCaig****
Mrs Vera Simpson	Laurie Paton
Ernest the tailor**	Marcus Nance
Victor	Sam Strasfeld
Louis the tenor / Mr Hoople	Mark Harapiak
Melba Snyder	Patty Jamieson
Ludlow Lowell	Neil Barclay
Waldo	Andrew Kushnir
Deputy Commissioner O'Brien	Cameron MacDuffee

performed by Marcus Nance, July 21 to August 1
**performed by Joanne Mendioro (as Ernestina), July 21 to August 1*
***performed by Elodie Gillett, September 4 to 19*
****succeeded by Ashley Taylor on September 4*

Directed by Alisa Palmer
Musical direction and
   orchestral adaptation by Paul Sportelli
Choreography by Amy Wright
Designed by William Schmuck
Lighting designed by Andrea Lundy

| Stage Manager | Alison Peddie |
| Assistant Stage Manager | Christine Oakey* |

succeeded by Barry Burns on September 30

2004

RUTHERFORD AND SON by Githa Sowerby

Court House Theatre

previews from June 8, opening June 18 to October 9 (69 performances)

Ann	Mary Haney
Mary	Nicole Underhay
Janet	Kelli Fox
John	Dylan Trowbridge
Richard	Mike Shara
Rutherford	Michael Ball
Martin	Peter Krantz
Mrs Henderson	Donna Belleville

Directed by Jackie Maxwell

Designed by William Schmuck

Lighting designed by Louise Guinand

Stage Manager	Joanna Jurychuk
Assistant Stage Manager	Beatrice Campbell

NICOLE UNDERHAY IN *RUTHERFORD AND SON*, 2004 (PHOTO BY DAVID COOPER).

THE IMPORTANCE OF BEING EARNEST by Oscar Wilde
Royal George Theatre
previews from April 2, opening May 7 to December 4 (152 performances)

Lane	Robert Benson
Algernon Moncrieff	David Leyshon
John Worthing, J.P.	Evan Buliung
Lady Bracknell	Goldie Semple
Honourable Gwendolen Fairfax	Fiona Byrne
Miss Prism	Brigitte Robinson
Cecily Cardew	Diana Donnelly
Reverend Canon	
Chasuble, D.D.	Bernard Behrens
Merriman	Guy Bannerman

Directed by Christopher Newton
Designed by Judith Bowden
Lighting designed by Jeff Logue

Stage Manager	Allan Teichman*
Assistant Stage Manager	Lisa Whittaker

succeeded by Judy Farthing on November 22

NOTHING SACRED by George F. Walker
Festival Theatre
previews from August 14, opening August 25 to October 30 (35 performances)

Bailiff	Patrick Galligan
Gregor	Andrew Bunker
Yevgeny Bazarov	Mike Shara
Arkady Kirsanov	Jeff Meadows
Piotr	Richard Farrell
Nikolai Kirsanov	Jim Mezon
Fenichka	Trish Lindström
Pavel Kirsanov	Benedict Campbell
Viktor Sitnikov	Dylan Trowbridge
Anna Odintsov	Tara Rosling
Sergei	Micheal Querin
Peasants	Mark Adriaans, Evert Houston

Directed by Morris Panych
Set designed by Ken MacDonald
Costumes designed by David Boechler
Lighting designed by Alan Brodie

Stage Manager	Judy Farthing
Assistant Stage Manager	Beatrice Campbell

HARLEQUINADE by Terence Rattigan
Royal George Theatre
previews from August 11, opening August 26 to September 19 (17 performances)

Arthur Gosport	Peter Hutt
Edna Selby	Goldie Semple
Jenny	Maggie Blake
Dame Maud Gosport	Jennifer Phipps
Jack Wekefield	Kevin Bundy
George Chudleigh	Bernard Behrens
First Halberdier	Mark Adriaans
Second Halberdier	Jeff Irving
Miss Fishlock	Brigitte Robinson
Frederick Ingram	Peter Krantz
Muriel Palmer	Diana Donnelly
Tom Palmer	Graeme Somerville
Mr Burton	David Schurmann
Joyce Langland	Nicole Underhay
Policeman	Robert Benson

Directed by Neil Munro
Designed by Judith Bowden
Lighting designed by Sandra Marcroft

Stage Manager	Allan Teichman
Assistant Stage Manager	Barry Burns

WAITING FOR THE PARADE by John Murrell
Royal George Theatre
previews from June 4, opening June 19 to October 9 (60 performances)

Janet	Helen Taylor
Catherine	Kelly Fox
Margaret	Donna Belleville
Marta	Laurie Paton
Eve	Jenny L. Wright

Directed by Linda Moore
Designed by William Schmuck
Lighting designed by Andrea Lundy
Musical direction and original music
composed by Allen Cole

Stage Manager	Meredith Macdonald
Assistant Stage Manager	Christine Oakey*

succeeded by Lisa Whittaker on September 28

JEFF LILLICO AND JAY TURVEY IN *FLOYD COLLINS*, 2004 (PHOTO BY DAVID COOPER).

FLOYD COLLINS
music and lyrics by Adam Guettel, book by Tina Landau
additional lyrics by Tina Landau

Court House Theatre
previews from August 3, opening August 26 to October 9 (39 performances)

Jewell Estes	Kevin Dennis
Nellie Collins	Glynis Ranney
Homer Collins	Jeff Madden
Miss Jane	Sharry Flett
Skeets Miller	Jeff Lillico
Floyd Collins	Jay Turvey
Ed Bishop	Cameron MacDuffee
Lee Collins	Peter Millard
Bee Doyle	Ben Carlson
H.T. Carmichael	Douglas E. Hughes
Cliff Roney / Reporter	Sam Strasfeld
Dr Hazlett / Reporter	Marcus Nance
Frederick Jordan / Reporter	Andrew Kushnir

Directed and choreographed by Eda Holmes
Musical direction by Paul Sportelli
Designed by William Schmuck
Lighting designed by Kevin Lamotte

Stage Manager	Alison Peddie
Assistant Stage Manager	Dora Tomassi

BELL CANADA READING SERIES

THREE KINDS OF BLISS stories by Katherine Mansfield
Royal George Theatre, July 15 (1 reading)

The Wind Blows

Matilda	Maggie Blake
Mother	Nora McLellan
Bogey	Jeff Lillico
Mr Bullen	Simon Bradbury
Marie	Diana Donnelly

Feuille d'Album

Woman 1	Trish Lindström
Woman 2	Maggie Blake
Woman 3	Brigitte Robinson
Ian	Jeff Lillico
Yvette	Diana Donnelly

Bliss

Bertha	Glynis Ranney
Mary	Diana Donnelly
Nurse	Nora McLellan
Harry	Kevin Bundy
Mrs Norman Knight	Brigitte Robinson
Norman Knight	Simon Bradbury
Eddie Warren	David Leyshon
Miss Fulton	Trish Lindström

Adapted by Morwyn Brebner
Directed by Daryl Cloran

Stage Manager	Barry Burns
Apprentice Stage Manager	Kinnon Elliott

HOW THE VOTE WAS WON
Royal George Theatre, July 23 (1 reading)

The Rally by Elizabeth Robins

Mr Pilcher	David Schurmann
Winifred	Helen Taylor
Working woman	Donna Belleville
Protesters	The Ensemble

A Chat with Mrs Chicky by Evelyn Glover

Mrs Chicky	Lisa Horner
Mrs Holbrook	Jennifer Phipps

How the Vote Was Won
by Cecily Hamilton and Christopher St John

Horace Cole	David Schurmann
Ethel	Sharry Flett
Winifred	Helen Taylor
Agatha	Jenny L. Wright
Molly	Shannon McCaig
Madame Christine	Jennifer Phipps
Maudie	Lisa Horner
Lily / Aunt Lizzie	Donna Belleville
Gerald Williams	Jeff Madden

Directed by Barbara Worthy

Stage Manager	Christine Oakey
Apprentice Stage Manager	Patti Neice

THE WEATHER BREEDER by Merrill Denison
Royal George Theatre, July 28 (1 reading)

Jim	Dylan Trowbridge
Lize	Lisa Norton
Levi	Martin Happer
John	Michael Ball
Murl	David Leyshon

Directed by Valerie Moore

Stage Manager	Lisa Whittaker
Apprentice Stage Manager	Patti Neice

THE DUNWICH HORROR by H.P. Lovecraft
Royal George Theatre, August 20 (1 reading)

Cast: Jillian Cook, Patricia Hamilton, Douglas E. Hughes, Catherine McGregor, Peter Millard, Micheal Querin, Glynis Ranney, William Vickers

Adapted and directed by Neil Munro

Stage Manager	Amy Jewell
Apprentice Stage Manager	Kinnon Elliott

MUSICAL READING SERIES

BLOOMER GIRL
music by Harold Arlen
lyrics by E.Y. Harburg
Royal George Theatre, October 2 (1 reading)

Narrator	Patricia Hamilton
Serena	Sherry Flett
Octavia / Hetty	Jenny L. Wright
Delia / Bloomer Girl	Joanne Mendioro
Julia / Bloomer Girl	Elodie Gillett
Daisy	Lisa Horner
Horatio	Lorne Kennedy
Evalina	Shannon McCaig
Dolly	Laurie Paton
Jeff	Adam Brazier
Prudence	Kiera Sangster
Paula	Ashley Taylor
Gus / Deputy / Governor's Aide	Mark Harapiak
Pompey	Marcus Nance
Sheriff	Neil Barclay
Ebenezer / Auctioneer	Andrew Kushnir
Herman / Deputy	Cameron MacDuffee
Hamilton / Governor	David Schurmann
Joshua / Deputy	Sam Strasfeld

Directed by Jackie Maxwell
Musical direction by Noreen Waibel

Stage Manager	Thom Payne
Apprentice Stage Manager	Patti Neice

Post-Season Tour

RUTHERFORD AND SON
National Arts Centre, Ottawa, November 10 to 27 (19 performances)

2005

MAJOR BARBARA by Bernard Shaw
Festival Theatre
previews from June 10, opening June 24 to October 29 (68 performances)

Lady Britomart Undershaft	Mary Haney
Stephen Undershaft	David Leyshon
Morrison / Bilton	Micheal Querin
Barbara Undershaft	Diana Donnelly
Sarah Undershaft	Charlotte Gowdy
Charles Lomax	Evan Buliung
Adolphus Cusins	Ben Carlson
Andrew Undershaft	Benedict Campbell
Rummy Mitchens	Sharry Flett
Snobby Price	Andrew Bunker
Jenny Hill	Jenny L. Wright
Peter Shirley	Jay Turvey
Bill Walker	Patrick Galligan
Mrs Baines	Patty Jamieson
Army Members	Cathy Current, Evert Houston, Chilina Kennedy

Directed by Joseph Ziegler
Designed by Christina Poddubiuk
Lighting designed by Kevin Lamotte
Musical direction and original music
composed by Allen Cole

Stage Manager	Allan Teichman
Assistant Stage Manager	Beatrice Campbell

2005

HAPPY END
lyrics by Bertolt Brecht
music by Kurt Weill
original German play by Dorothy Lane
books and lyrics adapted by Michael Feingold

Royal George Theatre
previews from May 15, opening May 28 to October 28 (82 performances)

Bill Cracker	Benedict Campbell
Sammy "Mammy" Wurlitzer	Neil Barclay
Dr Nakamura ("The Governor")	Jay Turvey
Jimmy Dexter ("The Reverend")	Ben Carlson
Bob Marker ("The Professor")	Peter Millard
Johnny Flint ("Baby Face")	Jeff Madden
A Lady in Gray ("The Fly")	Patty Jamieson
Miriam	Gabrielle Jones
Major Stone	Donna Belleville
Lieutenant Lillian Holiday ("Hallelujah Lil")	Glynis Ranney
Captain Hannibal Jackson	David Leyshon
Sister Mary	Jenny L. Wright
Sister Jane	Julie Martell
Brother Ben Owens	Kevin Dennis
The Cop	Al Kozlik
Members of the Fold	Elodie Gillett, Jeff Irving, Kiera Sangster, Darren Voros*

succeeded by Devon Tullock on August 16

Directed by Tadeusz Bradecki
Musical direction by Paul Sportelli
Choreography by Jane Johanson
Set designed by Peter Hartwell
Costumes designed by Teresa Przybylski
Lighting designed by Jeff Logue

Stage Manager	Allan Teichman
Assistant Stage Manager	Dora Tomassi
Apprentice Stage Manager	Eamonn Reil

YOU NEVER CAN TELL by Bernard Shaw
Festival Theatre
previews from April 24, opening May 5 to November 26 (97 performances)

Valentine	Mike Shara
Dolly	Nicole Underhay
The Parlourmaid	Jessica Lowry
Philip	Harry Judge
Mrs Lanfrey Clandon	Goldie Semple
Gloria	Fiona Byrne
Fergus Crampton	Norman Browning
Jo, a Waiter	Martin Happer
The Cook	Mark Adriaans
The Waiter (William)	David Schurmann
Finch M'Comas	Guy Bannerman
Bohun	Graeme Somerville

Directed by Morris Panych
Set designed by Ken MacDonald
Costumes designed by Nancy Bryant
Lighting designed by Paul Mathiesen

Stage Manager	Meredith Macdonald
Assistant Stage Manager	Amy Jewell

JOURNEY'S END by R.C. Sherriff
Court House Theatre
previews from May 13, opening May 27 to October 8 (74 performances)

Captain Hardy	Blair Williams
Lieutenant Osborne	Patrick Galligan
Private Mason	Simon Bradbury
Second Lieutenant Raleigh	Jeff Lillico
Captain Stanhope	Evan Buliung
Second Lieutenant Trotter	William Vickers
Bert	Andrew Bunker
Second Lieutenant Hibbert	Jeff Meadows
Company Sergeant-Major	Douglas E. Hughes
The Colonel	Anthony Bekenn
German Soldier	Evert Houston
Broughton	Sam Strasfeld

Directed by Christopher Newton
Designed by Cameron Porteous
Lighting designed by Louise Guinand

Stage Manager	Joanna Jurychuk
Assistant Stage Manager	Barry Burns
Rehearsal Apprentice Stage Manager	Michael Haltrecht

GYPSY
book by Arthur Laurents
music by Jule Styne
lyrics by Shephen Sondheim

Festival Theatre
previews from April 12, opening May 7 to October 30 (127 performances)

Uncle Jocko	William Vickers
George	Neil Barclay
Baby June	Alexandra Beaton / Michaela Bekenn
Baby Louise	Melissa Peters / Jessica Benevides
Balloon Girl	Katie Cambone-Mannell / Jessie Hernder
Ricky (and his recorder)	Jacob Stokl / Nigel Inneo
Rose	Nora McLellan
Rose alternate	Kate Hennig*
Pop	Bernard Behrens
Weber	Anthony Bekenn
Herbie	Ric Reid
Newsboys	David Aiello, Matthew Langelaan, Jacob Stokl / Nigel Inneo, Zachary Murphy, Alex Race
Louise	Julie Martell
June	Trish Lindström
Tulsa	Jeff Lillico
Yonkers	Jeff Irving
Angie	Darren Voros**
L.A.	Sam Strasfeld
Kringelein	Anthony Bekenn
Mr Goldstone	William Vickers
Miss Cratchitt	Kate Hennig
Miss Cratchitt alternate	Patricia Vanstone*
Agnes	Chilina Kennedy
Thelma	Elodie Gillett
Marjorie May	Kiera Sangster
Dolores	Cathy Current
Cigar	Neil Barclay
Pastey	Kevin Dennis
Tessie Tura	Lisa Horner
Mazeppa	Gabrielle Jones
Electra	Patricia Vanstone
Renee	Cathy Current
Phil	William Vickers
Bourgeron-Cochon	Micheal Querin
Stage Hands and Showgirls	Ensemble

on the following dates, Kate Hennig played Rose and Patricia Vanstone
played Miss Cratchitt: May 13, 22; June 5, 10, 23, 29; July 6, 22; August
4, 10, 24; September 1, 18, 23, 28; October 6, 13, 20, 28
**succeeded by Devon Tullock on August 16*

Directed by Jackie Maxwell
Musical direction and orchestral adaptation
   by Paul Sportelli
Choreography and associate direction by Valerie Moore
Set designed by Peter Hartwell
Costumes designed by Judith Bowden
Lighting designed by Kevin Lamotte
Sound designed by Peter McBoyle

Stage Manager	Judy Farthing
Assistant Stage Manager	Dora Tomassi
Rehearsal Assistant	
Stage Manager	Leigh Hurst Kerr
Apprentice Stage Manager	Michael Haltrecht

THE CONSTANT WIFE by Somerset Maugham

Royal George Theatre
previews from April 1, opening May 6 to October 9 (99 performances)

Mrs Culver	Patricia Hamilton
Bentley	Al Kozlik
Martha Culver	Catherine McGregor
Barbara Fawcett	Wendy Thatcher
Constance Middleton	Laurie Paton
Marie-Louise Durham	Glynis Ranney
John Middleton, FRCS	Blair Williams
Bernard Kersal	Peter Krantz
Mortimer Durham	Michael Ball

Directed by Neil Munro
Designed by William Schmuck
Lighting designed by Andrea Lundy

Stage Manager	Alison Peddie
Assistant Stage Manager	Barry Burns

2005

SOMETHING ON THE SIDE
by Georges Feydeau and Maurice Desvallières
adapted by Neil Munro
based on a new translation by Maureen LaBonté

Royal George Theatre
previews from June 10, opening June 25 to September 25
(46 Lunchtime performances)

Henry	Harry Judge
Alfred	Simon Bradbury
Jen	Trish Lindström
Tom-Pop	Ric Reid
H.B.S.	Douglas E. Hughes
Rosaline	Kate Hennig
Laurette	Lisa Horner

Directed by Neil Munro
Designed by Sue LePage
Lighting designed by Peter Debreceni
Music composed by Jason Jestadt

Stage Manager	Judy Farthing
Assistant Stage Manager	Amy Jewell

BUS STOP by William Inge
Royal George Theatre
previews from June 28, opening July 15 to November 27 (76 performances)

Elma Duckworth	Diana Donnelly
Grace	Mary Haney
Will Masters	Michael Ball
Cherie	Nicole Underhay
Dr Gerald Lyman	Norman Browning
Carl	Guy Bannerman
Virgil Blessing	Peter Krantz
Bo Decker	Martin Happer

Directed by Jackie Maxwell
Designed by Sue LePage
Lighting designed by Andrea Lundy

Stage Manager	Meredith Macdonald
Assistant Stage Manager	Beatrice Campbell

THE AUTUMN GARDEN by Lillian Hellman
Court House Theatre
previews from June 11, opening June 25 to October 8 (69 performances)

Rose Griggs	Wendy Thatcher
General Benjamin Griggs	David Schurmann
Carrie Ellis	Goldie Semple*
Frederick Ellis	Mike Shara
Mrs Mary Ellis	Patricia Hamilton
Edward Crossman	Jim Mezon
Sophie Tuckerman	Charlotte Gowdy
Leon	Mark Adriaans
Constance Tuckerman	Sharry Flett
Nicholas Denery	Peter Hutt
Nina Denery	Laurie Paton
Hilda	Catherine McGregor

*succeeded by Brigitte Robinson** on August 10*
**succeeded by Barbara Worthy on August 24*

Directed by Martha Henry
Designed by William Schmuck
Lighting designed by Louise Guinand

Stage Manager	Alison Peddie
Assistant Stage Manager	Christine Oakey

BELLE MORAL: A Natural History by Ann-Marie MacDonald
Court House Theatre
previews from July 7, opening July 16 to October 7 (46 performances)

The Bride / Creature / Claire	Jessica Lowry
The Jackal / Wee Farleigh	Jeff Madden
Pearl MacIsaac	Fiona Byrne
Flora MacIsaac	Donna Belleville
Victor MacIsaac	Jeff Meadows
Young Farleigh	Bernard Behrens
Dr Seamus Reid	Peter Millard
Mr Abbott	Graeme Somerville

Directed by Alisa Palmer
Designed by Judith Bowden
Lighting designed by Kevin Lamotte
Original music composed by Paul Sportelli

Stage Manager	Joanna Jurychuk
Assistant Stage Manager	Christine Oakey
Rehearsal Apprentice Stage Manager	Eamonn Reil

READING SERIES

THE DARK LADY OF THE SONNETS by Bernard Shaw

Royal George Theatre, July 22 (1 reading)

The Beefeater	Anthony Bekenn
Shakespear	Martin Happer
Queen Elizabeth	Kate Hennig
The Dark Lady	Lisa Horner

Directed by Jim Mezon

Stage Manager	Dora Tomassi

A CERTAIN LADY: Dorothy Parker

Royal George Theatre, August 12 (1 reading)

Big Blonde

Hazel	Kate Hennig
Narrator	Peter Hutt
Mrs Martin / Mrs Riley	Catherine McGregor
Herbie / Art	Jim Mezon
Ed / Doctor	Micheal Querin
Nettie / Mrs Miller	Wendy Thatcher

Here We Are

She	Catherine McGregor
He	Jim Mezon

Adapted and directed by Barbara Worthy

Stage Manager	Christine Oakey

THE LOVED ONE: An Anglo-American Tragedy
by Evelyn Waugh

Royal George Theatre, September 2 (1 reading)

Cast: Michael Ball, Bernard Behrens, Diana Donnelly, Sharry Flett, Patricia Hamilton, Peter Krantz, Trish Lindström

Adapted and directed by Neil Munro

Stage Manager	Christine Oakey

MUSICAL READING SERIES

TRISTAN book, music and lyrics by Jay Turvey and Paul Sportelli
based on the story *Tristan* by Thomas Mann

Festival Theatre, August 21 and September 1 (2 readings)

Fraulein von Osterloh	Patty Jamieson
Doctor Leander	Graeme Somerville
Frau Hohlenrauch	Fiona Byrne
The General	Peter Millard
Frau Spatz	Donna Belleville
Natalia	Jenny L. Wright
Vladimir	Blair Williams
Heinrich Kloterjahn	Ben Carlson
Gabrielle Kloterjahn	Glynis Ranney
Detlev Spinell	Jeff Madden
Frida	Jessica Lowry

Directed by Jackie Maxwell
Musical direction by Paul Sportelli

Stage Manager   Allan Teichman

BENEDICT CAMPBELL, DIANA DONNELLY, AND BEN CARLSON IN *MAJOR BARBARA*, 2005
(PHOTO BY DAVID COOPER).

2006

FORTY-FIFTH SEASON

March 30 to November 19 (813 Performances)

HIGH SOCIETY
music and lyrics by Cole Porter
book by Arthur Kopit
additional lyrics by Susan Birkenhead

Festival Theatre
previews from April 26, opening May 6 to November 19 (120 performances)

Maids	Elodie Gillett, Melanie Janzen, Jane Johanson, Marla McLean, Jenny L. Wright*
Butlers	Jeff Irving, David Lopez, Cameron MacDuffee, Jeff Madden, Sam Strasfeld
Mrs Lord	Sharry Flett
Dinah Lord	Melissa Peters
Tracy Lord	Camilla Scott
Uncle Willie	Neil Barclay
Dexter Haven	Dan Chameroy
Liz Imbrie	Patty Jamieson
	Lisa Horner *(May 24 to September 23)*
Mike Connor	Jay Turvey
George Kittredge	David Leyshon
Seth Lord	Lorne Kennedy

succeeded by Julie Martell on October 18

Directed by Kelly Robinson
Musical direction and orchestral adaptation
   by Paul Sportelli
Choreography by John MacInnis
Designed by William Schmuck
Lighting designed by Kevin Lamotte
Sound designed by Peter McBoyle

Stage Manager	Judy Farthing
Assistant Stage Managers	Barry Burns
	Beatrice Campbell

270

THE CRUCIBLE by Arthur Miller
Festival Theatre
previews from June 3, opening June 23 to October 14 (63 performances)

Betty Parris	Katie Cambone-Mannell
Reverend Samuel Parris	Ric Reid
Tituba	Lisa Berry
Abigail Williams	Charlotte Gowdy
Susanna Wallcott	Nelly Scott
Ann Putnam	Mary Haney
Thomas Putnam	Norman Browning
Mercy Lewis	Taylor Trowbridge
Mary Warren	Trish Lindström
John Proctor	Benedict Campbell
Rebecca Nurse	Jennifer Phipps
Giles Corey	Bernard Behrens
Reverend John Hale	Peter Krantz
Elizabeth Proctor	Kelli Fox
Francis Nurse	Al Kozlik
Ezekiel Cheever	Guy Bannerman
Marshal Herrick	Jeff Meadows
Judge Hathorne	David Schurmann
Deputy Governor Danforth	Jim Mezon
Sarah Good	Wendy Thatcher
Hopkins	Anthony Bekenn
Townsperson	Evert Houston
Guard	Micheal Querin

Directed by Tadeusz Bradecki
Set designed by Peter Hartwell
Costumes designed by Teresa Przybylski
Lighting designed by Kevin Lamotte
Original music composed by Paul Sportelli

Stage Manager	Meredith Macdonald
Assistant Stage Manager	Amy Jewell
Rehearsal Apprentice	
Stage Manager	Eamonn Reil

THE INVISIBLE MAN by Michael O'Brien
adapted from the novel by H.G. Wells

Royal George Theatre
previews from May 13, opening May 27 to October 29 (78 performances)

Gould	Micheal Querin
Fearenside	Anthony Bekenn
Henfry	Guy Bannerman
Mrs Hall	Wendy Thatcher
Millie	Trish Lindström
Huxter	Douglas E. Hughes
James Griffin	Peter Krantz
Dr Cuss	Al Kozlik
Mr Bunting	David Leyshon
Constable Jaffers	Cameron MacDuffee
Dr David Kemp	Jeff Meadows
Catherine Kemp	Jenny L. Wright
Mr Thomas Marvel	Neil Barclay
Mariner	Bernard Behrens
Women	Lisa Berry, Taylor Trowbridge
Colonel Adye	David Schurmann
Harris	Jeff Irving
Walters	Evert Houston
Helen	Charlotte Gowdy

Directed by Neil Munro
Designed by Judith Bowden
Lighting designed by Kevin Lamotte
Original music composed by Allen Cole
Effects designed by Marshall Magoon

Stage Manager	Meredith Macdonald
Assistant Stage Manager	Barry Burns
Apprentice Stage Manager	Rachael King

DESIGN FOR LIVING by Noel Coward
Royal George Theatre
previews from June 15, opening July 14 to November 18 (87 performances)

Gilda	Nicole Underhay
Ernest Friedman	Lorne Kennedy
Otto	Graeme Somerville
Leo	David Jansen
Miss Hodge	Jane Johanson
Mr Birbeck	Harry Judge
Photographer	Sam Strasfeld
Grace Torrence	Camilla Scott
Henry Carver	Jeff Madden
Helen Carver	Jessica Lowry
Matthew	David Lopez

Directed by Morris Panych
Set designed by Ken MacDonald
Costumes designed by Charlotte Dean
Lighting designed by Alan Brodie

Stage Manager   Beatrice Campbell
Assistant Stage Manager   Evan R. Klassen

ARMS AND THE MAN by Bernard Shaw
Festival Theatre
previews from March 30, opening May 4 to October 29 (119 performances)

Raina Petkoff	Diana Donnelly
Catherine Petkoff	Nora McLellan
Louka	Catherine McGregor
Captain Bluntschli	Patrick Galligan
A Russian Officer	Martin Happer
A Soldier	Michael Strathmore
Nicola	Peter Millard
Major Paul Petkoff	Peter Hutt
Major Sergius Saranoff	Mike Shara

Directed by Jackie Maxwell
Set designed by Sue LePage
Costumes designed by William Schmuck
Lighting designed by Louise Guinand
Music composed by Paul Sportelli

Stage Manager   Alison Peddie
Assistant Stage Manager   Dora Tomassi

THE HEIRESS by Ruth Goetz and Augustus Goetz
Royal George Theatre
previews from April 12, opening May 5 to October 7 (100 performances)

Maria	Krista Colosimo
Dr Austin Sloper	Michael Ball
Lavinia Penniman	Donna Belleville
Catherine Sloper	Tara Rosling
Elizabeth Almond	Nora McLellan
Arthur Townsend	Harry Judge
Marian Almond	Jessica Lowry
Morris Townsend	Mike Shara
Mrs Montgomery	Catherine McGregor
Coachman	Michael Strathmore

Directed by Joseph Ziegler
Designed by Christina Poddubiuk
Lighting designed by Louise Guinand

Stage Manager   Allan Teichman
Assistant Stage Manager   Evan Klassen

A SCENE FROM *THE MAGIC FIRE*, 2006 (PHOTO BY DAVID COOPER).

THE MAGIC FIRE by Lillian Groag
Court House Theatre
previews from June 11, opening June 24 to September 24 (64 performances)

Lise Berg	Tara Rosling
Young Lise	Lila Bata-Walsh
Otto Berg (Lise's father)	Ric Reid
Amalia Berg (his wife)	Sharry Flett
Elena Guarneri (Amalia's sister)	Goldie Semple
Paula Guarneri (Amalia's aunt)	Donna Belleville
Gianni "Juan" Guarneri	
(Amalia's father)	Michael Ball
Maddalena "Nonna" Guarneri	
(Juan's mother)	Jennifer Phipps
General Henri Fontannes	Dan Chameroy
Alberto Barcos	Jay Turvey
Clara Stepaneck (Otto's aunt)	Patricia Hamilton
Rose Arrúa	Waneta Storms

Directed by Jackie Maxwell
Designed by Sue LePage
Lighting designed by Louise Guinand
Sound designed by John Gzowski

Stage Manager	Allan Teichman
Assistant Stage Manager	Christine Oakey
Apprentice Stage Manager	Eamonn Reil

274

TOO TRUE TO BE GOOD by Bernard Shaw
Court House Theatre
previews from May 9, opening May 26 to October 7 (78 performances)

The Microbe	William Vickers
The Patient	Nicole Underhay
The Elderly Lady	Mary Haney
The Doctor	David Jansen
The Nurse	Kelli Fox
The Burglar	Blair Williams
Colonel Tallboys, VC, DSO	Benedict Campbell
Private Napoleon Alexander Trotsky Meek	Andrew Bunker
Sergeant Fielding	Graeme Somerville
The Elder	Norman Browning

Directed by Jim Mezon
Designed by Kelly Wolf
Lighting designed by Alan Brodie

Stage Manager	Bill Jamieson
Assistant Stage Manager	Amy Jewell

ROSMERSHOLM by Henrik Ibsen
adapted by Neil Munro

Court House Theatre
previews from July 5, opening July 15 to October 7 (49 performances)

Mrs Helseth	Patricia Hamilton
Rebecca West	Waneta Storms
Alex Kroll	Peter Hutt
John Rosmer	Patrick Galligan
Ulrich Brendel	Peter Millard
Peter Morten	Douglas E. Hughes

Adapted and directed by Neil Munro
Designed by Peter Hartwell
Lighting designed by Kevin Lamotte
Video designed by Simon Clemo

Stage Manager	Alison Peddie
Assistant Stage Manager	Christine Oakey
Rehearsal Apprentice Stage Manager	Rachael King

2006

LOVE AMONG THE RUSSIANS by Anton Chekhov
adapted by Morwyn Brebner

Court House Theatre
previews from June 10, opening June 24 to September 24
(50 Lunchtime performances)

THE BEAR

Luka	William Vickers
Elena Ivanovna Popova	Diana Donnelly
Grigory Stepanovich Smirnov	Blair Williams

THE PROPOSAL

Stephan Stepanovich Chubukov	William Vickers
Ivan Vasylievich Lomov	Martin Happer
Natalya Stepanovna	Diana Donnelly

Musical Peasants: Andrew Bunker, Krista Colosimo, Elodie Gillett

Directed by Eda Holmes
Designed by William Schmuck
Lighting designed by Julia Vandergraaf
Music composed by Paul Sportelli and Jay Turvey

Stage Manager	Bill Jamieson
Assistant Stage Manager	Dora Tomassi

READING SERIES

THE DIGESTIBLE AND INTERACTIVE SHAW
Festival Theatre, July 9 (1 reading)

The Appetizer
(loosely based on the essay *The Life of Bernard Shaw* by Brooke Allen)

Cast: Anthony Bekenn, Diana Donnelly, Jeff Meadows, Jennifer Phipps, Ric Reid, Wendy Thatcher

The Main Course
Press Cuttings by Bernard Shaw

General Mitchener	Anthony Bekenn
Prime Minister	Ric Reid
An Orderly	Jeff Meadows
Mrs Farrell	Jennifer Phipps
Mrs Rosa Carmina Banger	Wendy Thatcher
Lady Corinthia Fanshawe	Diana Donnelly

Adapted and directed by Barbara Worthy

Stage Manager	Dora Tomassi

276

IBSEN: IN EXTREME
Festival Theatre, August 13 (1 reading)

Part I: Poetry / Music

    Cast: Carol Forte, Patrick Galligan, Douglas E. Hughes, Trish Lindström, Peter Millard, Micheal Querin, Goldie Semple, Waneta Storms

Part II: The Plays

(Introduction: Ibsen's Men and Women; *A Doll's House*: Wife – Mother Sees the Light; *Ghosts*: Mother – Woman Gone Wrong; *Hedda Gabler*: The Unwomanly Woman; *The Master Builder*: Woman as Rejuvenating Spirit; *Little Eyolf*: When what is meant to be... isn't)

    Cast: Patrick Galligan, Douglas E. Hughes, Trish Lindström, Peter Millard, Micheal Querin, Goldie Semple, Waneta Storms

Adapted and directed by Neil Munro

Stage Manager	Christine Oakey
Composer / Pianist	Paul Sportelli

LA NONA by Roberto M. Cossa
translated by Raul Moncada

Festival Theatre, September 10 (1 reading)

Nona	Michael Ball
Anyula	Goldie Semple
Chicho	Mike Shara
Carmelo	Blair Williams
Maria	Tara Rosling
Marta	Krista Colosimo
Don Francisco	William Vickers

Directed by Jackie Maxwell

Stage Manager	Judy Farthing

BENEDICT CAMPBELL, BLAIR WILLIAMS, AND KELLI FOX IN *TOO TRUE TO BE GOOD*, 2006 (PHOTO BY DAVID COOPER).

MUSICAL READING SERIES

THE GOLDEN APPLE
music by Jerome Moross
book and lyrics by John Latouche

Festival Theatre, October 1 and October 7 (2 readings)

Helen	Elodie Gillett
Lovey Mars / The Siren	Melanie Janzen
Mrs Juniper / Calypso	Krista Colosimo
Miss Minerva Olliver /	
The Lady Scientist	Sharry Flett
Mother Hare / Circe	Diana Donnelly
Penelope	Marla McLean
Menelaus / Scylla	Cameron MacDuffee
The Heroes (Ulysses' Men)	Andrew Bunker, Jeff Irving,
	Michael Strathmore
Ulysses	David Leyshon
Paris	Martin Happer
Hector / Charybdis	Neil Barclay

Adapted and directed by Paul Sportelli
Musical director / pianist: Ryan deSouza

Stage Manager	Barry Burns
Rehearsal Pianist	Greg Gibson

278

2007

HOTEL PECCADILLO
adapted by Morris Panych
based on the play *L'Hôtel du Libre-Echange*
by Georges Feydeau and Maurice Desvallières

Festival Theatre
previews from May 31, opening June 16 to October 7 (67 performances)

Dr Pinglet	Patrick Galligan
Paillardin	Benedict Campbell
Georges Feydeau	Lorne Kennedy
Madame Angelique Pinglet	Goldie Semple
Dr Heindlich / Father Chervet	Anthony Bekenn
Victoire	Trish Lindström
Madame Marcelle Paillardin	Charlotte Gowdy
Maxime	Jeff Irving
Mathieu	David Leyshon
Tanya (Flygirl)	Melanie Phillipson
Katya (Flygirl)	Catherine Braund
Raina (Flygirl) / Dancer	Kiera Sangster
Ludmila	Laurie Paton
Boulot	Mike Nadajewski
Newlywed / Constable /	
Detective / Dancer	Devon Tullock
Newlywed / Dancer	Katrina Reynolds
Inspector Boucard	William Vickers

Directed by Morris Panych
Set designed by Ken MacDonald
Costumes designed by Nancy Bryant
Lighting designed by Alan Brodie
Sound designed by John Lott
Music composed and directed by Ryan deSouza

Stage Manager	Beatrice Campbell
Assistant Stage Manager	Dora Tomassi
Apprentice Stage Manager	Rachael King

MACK AND MABEL
book by Michael Stewart, music and lyrics by Jerry Herman
revised by Francine Pascal

Festival Theatre
previews from April 3, opening May 12 to October 28 (123 performances)

Mack Sennett	Benedict Campbell
Lottie Ames	Gabrielle Jones
Frank	Jeff Madden
Fatty Arbuckle	Neil Barclay
Mabel Normand	Glynis Ranney
Andy / Keystone Kop	Jeff Irving
Ella	Patty Jamieson
Mr Kessel	Jay Turvey
Mr Bauman	William Vickers
Swain / William Desmond Taylor	Peter Millard
Charlie Chaplin / Keystone Kop	Kawa Ada
Ben Turpin / Keystone Kop	Mike Nadajewski
Buster Keaton / Keystone Kop	Devon Tullock
Cameraman / Keystone Kop	Mark Uhre
Script Girl / Bathing Beauty / Keystone Kop	Catherine Braund
Make-up Girl / Bathing Beauty / Keystone Kop	Katrina Reynolds
Secretary / Bathing Beauty / Keystone Kop	Jane Johanson
Mae Busch / Bathing Beauty / Keystone Kop	Chilina Kennedy
Wig Girl / Bathing Beauty / Keystone Kop	Melanie Phillipson
Wardrobe Girl / Bathing Beauty / Keystone Kop	Kiera Sangster
Swings	Melanie Janzen, Micheal Querin

Directed by Molly Smith
Musical direction and orchestral adaptation
by Paul Sportelli
Choreography by Baayork Lee
Designed by William Schmuck
Lighting designed by Jock Munro
Sound designed by John Lott
Dance supervision by Parker Esse

Stage Manager	Alison Peddie
Assistant Stage Managers	Beatrice Campbell
	Dora Tomassi
Rehearsal Apprentice Stage Manager	Rachael King

THE CASSILIS ENGAGEMENT by St John Hankin

Court House Theatre

previews from May 29, opening June 15 to October 5 (66 performances)

Mrs Herries	Wendy Thatcher
The Reverend Hildebrand	
Herries	Lorne Kennedy
Watson, the Butler	Al Kozlik
The Countess of Remenham	Donna Belleville
Lady Mabel Venning	Charlotte Gowdy
Mrs Cassilis	Goldie Semple
Arthur, a footman	Ken James Stewart
James, a footman	Gray Powell
Lady Marchmont	Laurie Paton
Geoffrey Cassilis	David Leyshon
Mrs Borridge	Mary Haney
Ethel Borridge	Trish Lindström
Dorset, the Maid	Krista Colosimo
Major Warrington	Patrick Galligan

Directed by Christopher Newton
Designed by William Schmuck
Lighting designed by Kevin Lamotte

Stage Manager	Meredith Macdonald
Assistant Stage Manager	Evan R. Klassen

TRISH LINDSTROM, PATRICK GALLIGAN, MARY HANEY, GOLDIE SEMPLE, LAURIE PATON, AND
DONNA BELLEVILLE IN *THE CASSILIS ENGAGEMENT*, 2007 (PHOTO BY DAVID COOPER).

2007

THE PHILANDERER by Bernard Shaw

Royal George Theatre
previews from May 1, opening May 12 to October 7 (92 performances)

Grace Tranfield	Deborah Hay
Leonard Charteris	Ben Carlson
Julie Craven	Nicole Underhay
Mr Joseph Cuthbertson	Norman Browning
Colonel Daniel Craven	Peter Hutt
Dr Paramore	Peter Krantz
Sylvia Craven	Nicolá Correia-Damude
The Page (Spedding)	Michael Strathmore

Directed by Alisa Palmer
Designed by Judith Bowden
Lighting designed by Louise Guinand

Stage Manager	Bill Jamieson
Assistant Stage Manager	Barry Burns

Fifteen performances between May 25 and July 15 included Shaw's original Act III, which followed (as Act IV, with no intermission) the regular Act III.

SUMMER AND SMOKE by Tennessee Williams

Royal George Theatre
previews from June 23, opening July 6 to October 27 (62 performances)

Reverend Winemiller	Peter Hutt
Mrs Winemiller	Sharry Flett
John Buchanan, Jr	Jeff Meadows
Alma Winemiller	Nicole Underhay
Rosa Gonzales	Nicolá Correia-Damude
Nellie Ewell	Chilina Kennedy
Roger Doremus	Jay Turvey
Dr John Buchanan, Sr	Guy Bannerman
Vernon / Dusty	Kawa Ada
Mrs Bassett	Brigitte Robinson
Rosemary	Melanie Janzen
Gonzales	Micheal Querin
Archie Kramer	Jonathan Gould

Directed by Neil Munro
Set designed by Peter Hartwell
Costumes designed by Christina Poddubiuk
Lighting designed by Alan Brodie
Original music by Marc Desormeaux

Stage Manager	Bill Jamieson
Assistant Stage Manager	Heather Lewis
Rehearsal Apprentice Stage Manager	Marisa Vest

TRISTAN
book, music and lyrics by Paul Sportelli and Jay Turvey
adapted from the story "Tristan" by Thomas Mann

Court House Theatre
previews from July 12, opening July 28 to October 6 (41 performances)

Fraulein von Osterloh	Patty Jamieson
Doctor Leander	Graeme Somerville
Frieda	Krista Colosimo
The General	Neil Barclay
Frau Hohlenrauch	Jane Johanson
Frau Spatz	Donna Belleville
Natalia Brodyagina	Gabrielle Jones
Vladimir Brodyagin	Peter Millard
Heinrich Kloterjahn	Mark Uhre
Gabrielle Kloterjahn	Glynis Ranney
Detlev Spinell	Jeff Madden

Directed by Eda Holmes
Musical direction and orchestration by Paul Sportelli
Dramaturgy by Jackie Maxwell
Set designed by Judith Bowden
Costumes designed by William Schmuck
Lighting designed by Kevin Lamotte

Stage Manager	Alison Peddie
Assistant Stage Manager	Evan R. Klassen

THE CIRCLE by Somerset Maugham
Royal George Theatre
previews from April 10, opening May 10 to October 28 (117 performances)

Arnold Champion-Cheney, M.P.	David Jansen
Footman	Ken James Stewart
Mrs Anna Shenstone	Deborah Hay
Elizabeth Champion-Cheney	Moya O'Connell
Edward Luton	Gray Powell
Clive Champion-Cheney	David Schurmann
Butler	Al Kozlik
Lady Chatherine Champion-Cheney	Wendy Thatcher
Lord Porteous	Michael Ball

Directed by Neil Munro
Designed by Christina Poddubiuk
Lighting designed by Louise Guinand

Stage Manager	Meredith Macdonald
Assistant Stage Manager	Barry Burns

2007

A MONTH IN THE COUNTRY (after Turgenev) by Brian Friel
Court House Theatre
previews from April 29, opening May 11 to October 6 (77 performances)

Herr Schaaf (a tutor)	David Schurmann
Lizaveta Bogdanovna (Anna's companion)	Sharry Flett
Anna Semyonovna Islayeva (Arkady's widowed mother)	Patricia Hamilton
Natalya Petrovna (Arkady's wife)	Fiona Byrne
Katya (a servant)	Moya O'Connell
Michel Aleksandrovich Rakitin (a family friend)	David Jansen
Aleksey Nikolayevich Belyayev (a student/tutor)	Martin Happer
Matvey (a servant)	Thom Marriott
Doctor Ignaty Ilyich Shpigelsky	Ric Reid
Vera Aleksandrovna (Natalya's ward)	Marla McLean
Arkady Sergeyevich Islayev (a rich landlord)	Blair Williams
Afanasy Ivanovich Bolshintsov (a neighbouring landlord)	Michael Ball
Peasants	Billy Lake, Jesse Martyn

Directed by Tadeusz Bradecki
Designed by Peter Hartwell
Lighting designed by Jeff Logue

Stage Manager	Judy Farthing
Assistant Stage Manager	Heather Lewis
Apprentice Stage Manager	Marisa Vest

THE KILTARTAN COMEDIES by Lady Augusta Gregory
Court House Theatre
previews from June 20, opening July 7 to October 6 (49 Lunchtime performances)

THE RISING OF THE MOON

Policeman B	Harry Judge
Policeman X	Andrew Bunker
Sergeant	Douglas E. Hughes
Ragged Man	Patrick McManus

SPREADING THE NEWS

Magistrate	Douglas E. Hughes
Policeman Jo Muldoon	Andrew Bunker
Mrs Tarpey	Mary Haney
James Ryan	Jonathan Gould
Bartley Fallon	Guy Bannerman

284

Mrs Fallon	Tara Rosling
Jack Smith	Patrick McManus
Tim Casey	Jeff Meadows
Mrs Tully	Brigitte Robinson
Shawn Early	Harry Judge

Directed by Micheline Chevrier
Designed by Deeter Schurig
Lighting designed by Julie Vandergraaf

| Stage Manager | Allan Teichman |
| Assistant Stage Manager | Amy Jewell |

SAINT JOAN by Bernard Shaw
Festival Theatre
previews from April 21, opening May 9 to October 27 (99 performances)

Archbishop of Rheims / The Executioner	Norman Browning
Bertrand de Poulengey / Brother Martin Ladvenu	Andrew Bunker
Peter Cauchon, Bishop of Beauvais	Ben Carlson
Gilles de Rais (Bluebeard) / Canon de Courcelles	Martin Happer
Captain La Hire / English Soldier	Douglas E. Hughes
Dauphin (later Charles VII)	Harry Judge
Chaplain John de Stogumber	Peter Krantz
Steward / Soldier	Billy Lake
La Trémouille / Canon d'Estivet	Thom Marriott
Warwick's Page / Soldier	Jesse Martyn
Page / Soldier	Marla McLean
Dunois	Patrick McManus
Robert de Baudricourt / The Inquisitor	Ric Reid
Joan	Tara Rosling
Dunois' Page / Soldier	Michael Strathmore
Richard, Earl of Warwick	Blair Williams

Directed by Jackie Maxwell
Designed by Sue LePage
Lighting designed by Kevin Lamotte
Music composed by Paul Sportelli

| Stage Manager | Allan Teichman* |
| Assistant Stage Manager | Amy Jewell |

succeeded by Alison Peddie on October 12

READING SERIES

LILIES by Michel Marc Bouchard
Festival Theatre, July 13 (1 reading)

Simon Doucet (in 1952)	Ric Reid
Bishop Bilodeau	Guy Bannerman
Simon Doucet (in 1912)	Jonathan Gould
Count Vallier	Kawa Ada
Father Saint-Michel	Patrick McManus
Student	Billy Lake
Jean Bilodeau	Martin Happer
Countess Marie-Laure de Tilly	Blair Williams
Timothée Doucet	Thom Marriott
Baron de Hüe	Douglas E. Hughes
Madame Lydie-Anne de Rozier	Andrew Bunker
Baroness de Hüe	Jesse Martyn

Directed by Jackie Maxwell

Stage Manager	Judy Farthing

AN EXPERIMENT WITH AN AIR PUMP by Shelagh Stephenson
Festival Theatre, August 11 (1 reading)

Joseph Fenwick / Tom	David Schurmann
Susannah Fenwick / Ellen	Patricia Hamilton
Harriet / Kate	Fiona Byrne
Maria	Melanie Phillipson
Peter Mark Roget	Graeme Somerville
Thomas Armstrong / Phil	David Jansen
Isobel Bridie	Moya O'Connell

Directed by Eda Holmes

Stage Manager	Judy Farthing

HOMEBODY / KABUL by Tony Kushner
Festival Theatre, September 10 (1 reading)

The Homebody	Goldie Semple
Dr Qari Shah	David Leyshon
Mullah Aftar Ali Durrani / Zai Garshi	Gray Powell
Milton Ceiling	Lorne Kennedy
Quango Twistleton	Anthony Bekenn
Priscilla Ceiling	Krista Colosimo
The Munkrat / A Border Guard	Ken James Stewart
Khwaja Aziz Mondanabosh	Patrick Galligan
Mahala	Laurie Paton

Directed by Neil Munro

Stage Manager	Meredith Macdonald

TWO BROTHERS by Hannie Rayson
Festival Theatre, September 15 (1 reading)

Hazem Al Ayad	Neil Barclay
James 'Eggs' Benedict	Benedict Campbell
Tom Benedict	Michael Ball
Fiona Benedict	Deborah Hay
Angela Sidoropoulous	Gabrielle Jones
Harry Benedict	Jeff Irving
Jamie Savage	Patty Jamieson
Eric / Reporter	Mark Uhre
The Therapist / Reporter	Jane Johanson
Lachan Benedict	Graeme Somerville

Directed by Eda Holmes

Stage Manager   Judy Farthing

Post-Season Tour

SAINT JOAN
Chicago Shakespeare Theatre, January 8 to 20 (16 performances)

For this tour Patrick Galligan appeared as Richard, Earl of Warwick.

MICHAEL BALL AND WENDY THATCHER IN *THE CIRCLE*, 2007 (PHOTO BY DAVID COOPER).

APPENDIX I
THE TORONTO PROJECT

The Toronto Project was an initiative to extend the Shaw Festival's presence into Toronto during the winter season, and also to extend its mandate into contemporary work in collaboration with Toronto theatre companies.

1982

DREAMING AND DUELLING by John Lazarus
in collaboration with Joa Lazarus
Co-production with Young People's Theatre

previews February 2 to 3, 1982, opening February 4 to 28 (28 performances)

Eric Cullen	Peter Krantz
Joel Goldner	Dan Lett
Mrs Thorpe	Patricia Hamilton
Skelly	Andrew Lewarne
Louise	Ann-Marie Macdonald

Directed by Christopher Newton
Designed by Mary Kerr
Lighting designed by Harry Frehner
Fights choreographed by F. Braun McAsh

Stage Manager   Janine Ralph

1984

DELICATESSEN by François-Louis Tilly
adapted by Derek Goldby and David Hemblen
Co-production with Toronto Free Theatre

previews January 6 to 10, 1984, opening January 11 to February 26 (51 performances)

The Father	Al Kozlik
The Mother	Marion Gilsenan
The Son	Dan Lett
Francine	Joyce Campion
The Boy	Daniel Allman

Directed by Derek Goldby and David Hemblen
Designed by Terry Gunvordahl
Lighting designed by Donald Finlayson

Stage Manager   Shirley Third

1985

GOODNIGHT DISGRACE by Michael Mercer

Co-production with Toronto Free Theatre

previews March 2 to 5, 1985,   opening March 6 to 31 (30 performances)

Conrad Aiken	Matthew Walker
Nurse	Carole Galloway
Malcolm Lowry	Geraint Wyn Davies
Clarissa Lorenz	Wendy Thatcher
Arthur O. Lowry	Ron Hartmann
Ed Burra	David Schurmann
Jan Gabriel	Caroline Yeager

Directed by Leon Pownall
Designed by Diz Marsh
Lighting designed by Donald Finlayson
Artwork and slides by Paul Kuzma

Stage Manager   Winston Morgan
Assistant Stage Manager   Christine Leacock

1985-86

SOUVENIRS by Sheldon Rosen

Co-production with Factory Theatre

previews December 27 to 30, 1985, opening December 31 to January 26, 1986
(34 performances)

Daniel	Ted Dykstra
Ralph	Richard Farrell
Vicki	Donna Goodhand
Mrs Harold	Patricia Hamilton
The Director	Peter Hutt
Peter	Ricardo Keens-Douglas
John	Jim Mezon
The Cellist	Francesca Thorneycroft

Directed by Duncan McIntosh
Designed by Patsy Lang
Lighting designed by Jeffrey Dallas

Stage Manager   Peter Freund

1986

AS IS by William M. Hoffman
Co-production with Toronto Free Theatre

previews January 2 to 5, 1986, opening January 8 to February 22 (53 performances)

Hospice Worker	Joyce Campion
Rich	John Moffat
Saul	Brian Torpe
Chet	Andrew Jackson
Lily	Ann Turnbull
Business Partner	Joyce Campion
Brother	Allan Gray
Clones	Philip Akin, Joe-Norman Shaw
Pat	Joe-Norman Shaw
Barney	Allan Gray
Nurse	Joyce Campion
Hospital Worker	Philip Akin

Also Doctors, Pick-ups, Bartender, Bookstore Patrons

Directed by Margaret Bard
Set designed by Allan Stichbury
Costumes designed by Michael Eagan
Lighting designed by David Gibbons

Stage Manager	Christine Leacock
Assistant Stage Manager	Melissa Veal

1986

BREAKING THE SILENCE by Stephen Poliakoff
Co-production with Toronto Workshop Productions

previews October 27 to 30, 1986, opening October 29 to November 30
(39 performances)

Polya	Deborah Taylor
Alexander (Sasha) Nikolaivitch Pesiakoff	Richard Waugh
Eugenia Mikhailovna Pesiakoff	Fiona Reid
Alexei Verkoff	Jim Mezon
Nikolai Semenovitch Pesiakoff	Christopher Newton
Guards	Ted Dykstra, Al Kozlik

Directed by Marti Maraden
Designed by Cameron Porteous
Lighting designed by Patsy Lang
Sound designed by Walter Lawrence

Stage Manager	Debra McKay
Assistant Stage Manager	Jennifer White

1987

B-MOVIE THE PLAY by Tom Wood
Co-production with Toronto Workshop Productions

previews January 17 to 20, 1987, opening January 21 to March 15 (54 performances)

Gloria Hunt	Dana Brooks
Lottie Purdum	Corrine Koslo
Stan Purdum	Steven Ouimette
Art Findell	Tom Wood
Dick	David Elliott

Directed by Bob Baker
Set and lighting designed by Stancil Campbell
Costumes designed by Leslie Frankish
Music and sound by Michael Becker

Stage Manager	Candace Burley
Assistant Stage Manager	Sandra McEwing

1987

PATRIA I: THE CHARACTERISTICS MAN by R. Murray Schafer
Co-production with the Canadian Opera Company (Tannenbaum Opera Centre)

opening November 21 to 28, 1987 (6 performances)

Ariadne (at 6)	Inga Braunstein
Sir Percival Schöps	Grant Carmichael
Ariadne (the Party Girl)	Martha Collins
Illich P. Vogler	Steven Cumyn
Ovid Klein	George Dawson
Thaddeus J. McGuire	Kerry Dorey
Henry Judah Treece	Ross Driedger
Amadeus Nagy / Toth-Toth	Peter Hutt
Charlie Chereptnin	Jim Jones
Nellie Frencheater	Gabrielle Jones
Mimi Mippipopolous	Jo-Anne Kirwan Clark
Hvar Mullin	Al Kozlik
Ron Muck	Paul Larocque
Mercedes Jardine	Patric Masurkevitch
Glen Frever	Lance McDayter
D.P, the Characteristics Man	Peter Millard
Massimo Quigg	Paul Mulloy
Primavera Nicolson	Carole Pope
Reverend Rabbindranath / Le Meul	Ian Prinsloo
Syball Wong Schöps Fu	Brigitte Robinson

(cont'd)

Muhammed ben Muslim al Zuhri	Alec Tebbutt
Sass Boomga	Richard Thorne
Eddie Le Chasseur	Richard Waugh
Voiceover	R. Murray Schafer

Directed by Christopher Newton
Musical direction by Robert Aitken
Designed by Jerrard and Diana Smith
Lighting designed by Stephen Ross

Stage Manager	Isolde Pleasants-Faulkner
Assistant Stage Manager	Fiona MacGregor

1988

FIRE by Paul Ledoux and David Young
Co-production with Theatre Passe Muraille

previews October 25 to 27, 1988, opening October 28 to December 4 (46 performances)

Cale Blackwell	Ted Dykstra
Herschel Blackwell	Michael Riley
Molly King	Helen Taylor
Truman King	Peter Millard
J.D. Blackwell	Denny Doherty
A Small Town Radio Producer / Shelly Grant / Dave Mitchell / Jim the TV Producer / A Northerner / Orville Jackson / James the Hairdresser / Members of the Auxiliary	Alec Willows, Melanie Doane, Paula Wolfson, Pat Perez

Directed by Brian Richmond
Designed by John Ferguson
Lighting designed by Jeffrey Dallas
Musical direction by Don Horsburgh and Pat Perez

Stage Manager	Hilary Blackmore

Music provided by the cast (piano: Ted Dykstra; bass: Peter Millard; sax: Pat Perez; fiddle, doublebass, mandolin: Melanie Doane; lead guitar: Denny Doherty; drums: Alec Willows; acoustic and bottle neck guitar, auto harp: Paula Wolfson).
Lead vocals by Helen Taylor, Michael Riley, Ted Dykstra, and Denny Doherty; backup vocals by balance of cast.

TARA ROSLING IN *PYGMALION*, 2004 (PHOTO BY DAVID COOPER).

APPENDIX II
THE DIRECTORS PROJECT

The Directors Project provides an opportunity for intern directors and assistant designers at the Festival to present one-act plays, featuring members of the company ensemble, to an audience of company members and invited theatre professionals.

1988 September 24 to 25

CONTRACT (Act I) by Merrill Denison

Maid	Stephanie Kerr
Constance Huston	Sherry Smith
Nono Marshall	Sarah Orenstein
Bert Marshall	Shawn Wright
Jane Gormley	Tracey Ferencz
Mrs Gormley	Nancy Kerr
Jim Musgrave	Peter Krantz
Oliver Stillwater	Blair Williams
Norman Canfield	Jon Bryden

Directed by Heather Jones-Barker

Stage Manager   Paul Mulloy

HURLY BURLY (Act III) by David Rabe

Mickey	Peter Windrem
Darlene	Sharry Flett
Eddie	Andrew Gillies
Artie	Rod Campbell
Donna	Karen Bernstein

Directed by Randy Maertz

Stage Manager   Allan Teichman

THE BAY AT NICE by David Hare

Valentina Nrovka	Irene Hogan
Sophia Yepileva	Mary Haney
Assistant Curator	Adrian Griffin
Peter Linisky	Craig Davidson

Directed by Kathryn Allison

Stage Manager   Susann Krantz

JENNIE'S STORY (Act II) by Betty Lambert

Molly Dorval	June Crowley
Harry McGrain	Richard Partington
Jennie McGrain	Jane Wheeler
Edna Delevault	Lorna Wilson
Father Edward Fabrizeau	Patric Masurkevitch

Directed by Suzanne Turnbull

Stage Manager	Ian Simpson

THE RULING CLASS by Peter Barnes

13th Earl	George Dawson
Daniel Tucker	Sven van de Ven
Bishop Lambton	Al Kozlik
Sir Charles Gurney	Guy Bannerman
Dinsdale Gurney	Mark Burgess
Lady Claire Gurney	Barbara Worthy
Matthew Peake	Declan Hill
14th Earl of Gurney	Duncan Ollerenshaw
Dr Paul Herder	Todd Stewart
Mrs Treadwell	Gabrielle Jones
Mrs Pigott-Wells	Deann DeGruijter
Grace Shelly	Susan Johnston
Mr McKyle	Richard Waugh
Mr McKyle's Assistant	Dean Cooney

Directed by Michel Lefebvre

Stage Manager	Laurie Champagne

Designed by Christine Plunkett
Lighting designed by Matthew Flawn and Colin Hughes

1989 September 24

27 WAGONS FULL OF COTTON by Tennessee Williams

Jake	Sven van de Ven
Flora	Monica Dufault
Silva	Peter Krantz
Voices	Paula Grove
	Jane Wheeler
	Dean Cooney

Directed by David Ferry

Stage Manager	Kim Barsanti

Appendix II: The Directors Project

THE BALD SOPRANO by Eugene Ionesco

Mrs Smith	Susan Johnston
Mr Smith	Mark Burgess
Mrs Martin	Julie Stewart
Mr Martin	Patric Masurkevitch
Maid	Michelle Todd
Fire Chief	Doug Adler

Directed by Paul Lampert

Stage Manager	Christian Chenier
Assistant Stage Manager	Michelle Lagassé

Designed by Dot Moore
Lighting designed by Matthew Flawn and Les Sanderson

1990 September 23

WOYZECK by Georg Büchner

Woyzeck	Hugo Dann
Captain	Simon Bradbury
Andres / Monkey	Murray Oliver
Marie	Janet Snetsinger
Kathe	Deborah Lambie
Drum Major	Peter Krantz
Showman / Apprentice / Student / Pawnbroker	Neil Barclay
Horse / Karl	Steven Sutcliffe
Barker's Assistant / Tavern Girl / Grandma	Julie Stewart
Sergeant / Apprentice / Student / Landlord	Bart Anderson
Doctor	Blair Williams

Directed by Jon Michaelson
Music and sound effects by Richard March

Stage Manager	Michelle Lagassé

SALOME by Oscar Wilde

First Soldier	Susan Johnston
Second Soldier	Charlotte Moore
Nubian / Nazarene	Bernadette Taylor
Naaman / Nazarene	Bart Anderson
A Cappadocian / Jew	Neil Barclay
The Page of Herodias	Mark Burgess

The Young Syrian	Murray Oliver
Salome, daughter of Herodias	Ann Baggley
A Slave	Michelle C. Martin
Jokanaan the Prophet	Simon Bradbury
Herodias, wife of Herod	Diana Leblanc
Herod Antipas	Robert Benson
Tigellinus	David Hogan

Directed by Sandhano Schultze
Music composed by Frederic Chopin and Jeff Corness

Stage Manager — Meredith Macdonald

Designed by Elizabeth Raap-Wolski
Lighting designed by Matthew Flawn

1991 August 18

EMBERS by Samuel Beckett
a stage adaptation of Beckett's radio play

Sound Dog	William Vickers
Henry	Robert Persichini
Ada	Sarah Orenstein
On tape:	
Addie	Karen Skidmore
Music Maker	David Adams
Horse Master	Stephen Flett

Directed and designed by Lindsey Robinson
Choreographed by Paul Kuzma

Stage Manager	Andrew Mestern
Assistant Stage Managers	Rachel Druker
	George Galanis

THE MAIDS by Jean Genet

Solange	Elizabeth Brown
Claire	Sherry Smith
Madame	Deborah Lambie
Special Appearance by	Matthew Heney

Directed by Colin Taylor

Stage Manager	Meredith Macdonald
Assistant Stage Manager	Joy Swain

Lighting designed by Matthew Flawn

Appendix II: The Directors Project

1992 August 30

THE DRAPES COME by Charles Dizenzo

Barbara   Janet Martin
Mrs Fiers   Jeffrey Prentice

Directed by Conrad Alexandrowicz

Stage Manager   Season Osborne

THE LOVE OF DON PERLIMPLIN
AND BELISA IN THE GARDEN by Federico García Lorca
translated by Gwynne Edwards

Sprite #1   Mario Marcil
Sprite #2   Sherri McFarlane
Don Perlimplin   David Adams
Marcolfa   Wendy Thatcher
Belisa   Elizabeth Brown
Belisa's Mother   Bridget O'Sullivan

Directed by Sally Han
Choreographed by Cassel Miles
Music composed and directed by Christopher Mounteer

Stage Manager   Todd Bricker

Lighting designed by Bonnie Beecher
Designed by Monika Heredi

1993 September 19

A PHOENIX TOO FREQUENT by Christopher Fry

Dynamene   Tracey Ferencz
Doto   Jane Johanson
Tegeus-Chromis   Troy Skog

Directed by Hans Engel
Designed by Pamela Gallop

Stage Manager   Todd Bricker

298

IN THE ZONE by Eugene O'Neill

Davis	David Adams
Cocky	Roger Honeywell
Driscoll	Dick Murphy
Jack	Gordon Rand
Scotty	Andrew Skelly
Swanson	Ian Vandeburgt
Smitty	Cavan Young

Directed by Mark Cassidy
Designed by Tania Etienne
Music composed by Karl Mohr

Stage Manager   Ellen Flowers

Lighting designed by John Stephenson

1994 September 9

ESCURIAL by Michel de Ghelderode

The King	William Vickers
Folial	Peter Millard
The Monk	Robert Clarke
The Executioner	Roger Honeywell

Directed by Lise Ann Johnson

Stage Manager   Ellen Flowers

THE MEADOW by Ray Bradbury

Douglas	Robert Benson
Smith	Dick Murphy
Narrator	Patric Masurkevitch
Young	Christopher Royal
Man 1	Matt Handy
Man 2	Bruce Davies
Foley	Jillian Cook

Directed by David Oiye

Stage Manager   Meredith Macdonald

Designed by Elizabeth Raap-Wolski
Lighting designed by Christopher L. Dennis

Appendix II: The Directors Project

1995 August 25

FRESHWATER by Virginia Woolf

Julia Margaret Cameron	Nuala FitzGerald
Charles Hay Cameron	Peter Millard
Alfred Tennyson	Andrew Gillies
George F. Watts	William Vickers
Ellen Terry	Ann Baggley
John Craig	Ben Carlson
Mary Magdalene	Stephanie Belding
Queen Victoria	Irene Hogan
Porpoise	Mac Hillier

Directed by Paulina B. Abarca

Stage Manager	Bruce MacDonald

JUDGMENT DAY by Odon von Horvath

Thomas Hudetz	Robert Clarke
Mrs Hudetz	Wendy Thatcher
Alphons	Douglas E. Hughes
Anna Lechner	Shauna Black
Landlord	Richard Farrell
Leni	Laurie Paton
Mrs Leimgruber	Nora McLellan
Policeman	Neil Barclay
Ferdinand / Detective	Gordon Rand
Forestry Worker / Prosecutor / Pokorny	Bruce Davies
Salesman / Fireman / Customer / Brakeman	Matt Handy

Directed by Craig Walker

Stage Manager	Lorie Abernethy
Assistant Stage Managers	Victoria Mainprize
	Carol Nesbitt

Designed by Kelly Wolf
Lighting designed by Joel Thoman

1996 September 13

THE BROWNING VERSION by Terence Rattigan

Taplow	Todd Witham
Frank Hunter	Ben Carlson
Millie Crocker-Harris	Jane Johanson
Andrew Crocker-Harris	Peter Millard
Frobisher	William Webster
Peter Gilbert	Dil Kainth
Mrs Gilbert	Meredith McGeachie

Directed by Karen Rickers

Stage Manager	Elaine Lumley

SOMETIME EVERY SUMMERTIME by Fletcher Markle

Mary Thomas	Lisa Waines
Fran Howard	Jenny L. Wright
Helen Rowley	Janet Lo
Clem Waldron	Graham Rowat
Mac McFedries	Robert Clark
Charlie Hayes	Kenneth Delaney
George Thomas	Malcolm Scott
Mr Thomas	Robert Benson

Directed by Dennis Garnhum

Stage Manager	Jennifer McKenna
Assistant Stage Manager	Rachel Marks

Designed by Kelly Wolf
Lighting designed by Philip Cygan

1997 September 26

THE ASTONISHED HEART by Noel Coward

Barbara Faber	Sarah Orenstein
Susan Birch	Lisa Waines
Tim Verney	Brian Marler
Ernest	Roger Rowland
Sir Reginald French	Robert Benson
Leonora Vail	Philippa Domville
Christian Faber	Gordon Rand

Directed by Ian Prinsloo

Stage Manager	Meghan Callan

Appendix II: The Directors Project

THE PURGING, OR BABY WON'T GO by Georges Feydeau

Follavoine	Blair Williams
Rose	Severn Thompson
Julie	Laurie Paton
M'sieur Chouilloux	Sandy Winsby
Toto	Adam Robinson Hutt
Madame Chouilloux	Helen Taylor
Truchet	Ty Olsson

Directed by Gyllian Raby

Stage Manager	Arwen MacDonell

Designed by Barbara Gordon
Lighting designed by Michael Kruse

1998 September 18

SHADOW PLAY by Noel Coward

Victoria Gayforth	Patty Jamieson
Simon Gayforth	Patrick R. Brown
Martha Cunningham	Jillian Cook
George Cunningham	Neil Foster
Sibyl Heston	Jenny L. Wright
Michael Doyle	Brian Elliott
A Young Man	John Cleland

Directed by David Savoy
Music directed by Jason Chesworth
Choreographed by Jenny L. Wright

Stage Manager	Amy Jewell

A DEBT OF HONOUR by Sydney Grundy

Sir George Carlyon	Peter Millard
Lady Carlyon	Lisa Waines
Philip Graham	Ian Leung
Rose Dalrymple	Fiona Byrne

Directed by Nikki Lundmark

Stage Manager	Jenny Sinclair

Designed by David Wootton
Lighting designed by Jeff Logue

1999 September 17

RIDERS TO THE SEA by J.M. Synge

Maurya, an old woman	Jennifer Phipps
Bartley, her son	Thomas Grant
Cathleen, her daughter	Laura de Carteret
Nora, a younger daughter	Fiona Byrne
Men and women	Allan Craik, Al Kozlik, Joanne Marrella, Catherine McGregor

Directed by Richard Wolfe

Stage Manager	M. Rebecca Miller

PLAYING WITH FIRE by August Strindberg

The Son	Matthew MacFadzean
The Daughter-in-Law	Philippa Domville
The Mother	Gabrielle Jones
The Father	Guy Bannerman
The Cousin	Severn Thompson
The Friend	Jason Dietrich

Directed by Ann Hodges

Stage Manager	Patricia Levert

Designed by Brian Smith
Lighting designed by Matt Flawn

2000 September 22

THE OLD LADY SHOWS HER MEDALS by J.M. Barrie

Mrs Dowey	Mary Haney
Mrs Twymley	Lynne Cormack
The Haggerty Woman	Amanda Smith
Mrs Mickleham	Jillian Cook
Mr Willings	Kevin Bundy
Private Dowey	Mike Wasko

Directed by Todd Hammond

Stage Manager	Patricia Levert

Designed by Deeter Schurig
Lighting designed by M. Rebecca Miller
Sound designed by Fred Gabrsek

Appendix II: The Directors Project

OVERLAID by Robertson Davies

Pop	Richard Farrell
Milton Cross	Mark Wiedman
Mrs August Belmont	Joanne Marrella
Ethel	Patty Jamieson
Jimmy	Devon Tullock
George Bailey	Douglas E. Hughes

Directed by Jean Morpurgo

Stage Manager   Mike Deschambeault

Designed by Deeter Schurig
Lighting designed by M. Rebecca Miller
Sound designed by Fred Gabrsek

2001 September 21

ANATOL by Arthur Schnitzler

Anatol	Blair Williams
Franz	Joe Wynne
Hilda	Severn Thompson
Lona	Helen Taylor
Max	Robert Benson
Opera Dame	Jane Johanson

Directed by Eda Holmes

Stage Manager   Dana Pew

Designed by Deeter Schurig
Lighting designed by Melinda Sutton
Sound designed by Angela da Rocha
Choreographed by Jane Johanson

BLACK 'ELL by Miles Malleson

Mrs Gould	Donna Belleville
Mr Gould	Terrence Bryant
Ethel	Susie Burnett
Colonel Fane	Christopher Blake
Jean	Caroline Cave
Margery Willis	Katherine Slater
Harold	Mike Wasko

Directed by James MacDonald

Stage Manager   Lisa Whittaker

Designed by Deeter Schurig
Lighting designed by Melinda Sutton
Sound designed by Angela da Rocha

2002 September 13

THE TENOR by Frank Wedekind

Valet	David Leyshon
Bell Boy	Jamie Burnett
Gerardo	Kevin Bundy
Isabel Coeurne	Lisa Norton
Professor Duhring	William Vickers
Unknown Woman	Fiona Reid
Helen Marova	Fiona Byrne
Muller	Micheal Querin

Directed by Heather Inglis

Stage Manager	Heather Lewis

Designed by Michael Greves
Lighting designed by Peter Gracie
Sound designed by Fred Gabrsek
Music composed by Alan Moon

THE ROPE by Eugene O'Neill

A Drifter	Peter Krantz
Mary	Stephanie Tope
Abraham Bentley	Peter Millard
Annie	Catherine McGregor
Pat Sweeney	Jeffrey Renn
Luke Bentley	Andrew Bunker

Directed by Richard Beaune

Stage Manager	Stéfanie Séguin

Designed by Michael Greves
Lighting designed by Peter Gracie
Sound designed by Fred Gabrsek

Appendix II: The Directors Project

2003 September 19

WAYS AND MEANS by Noel Coward

Stella	Glynis Ranney
Toby	David Leyshon
Olive	Severn Thompson
Chaps	Andrew Bunker
Nanny	Jillian Cook
Muriel	Diana Donnelly
Stevens	Ric Reid
Princess Elena	Caroline Cave

Directed by Glenda Stirling

Stage Manager	Jaime De Pippo
Sound Operator	Peter Gracie

Designed by Michael Greves
Lighting designed by Mark Callan

THE LONG CHRISTMAS DINNER by Thornton Wilder

Mother Bayard / Genevieve	Susie Burnett
Leonora	Trish Lindström
Ermengarde / Nurse	Catherine O'Brien
Lucia I and Lucie II	Blythe Wilson
Brandon	Neil Barclay
Roderick I and Roderick II	Patrick Galligan
Charles	Graeme Somerville
Samuel	Sam Strasfeld

Directed by Paul Rivers

Stage Manager	Kate Brown
Sound Operator	Mark Callan

Designed by Michael Greves
Lighting designed by Peter Gracie
Music composed by Jason Jestadt

2004 September 17

MOUTHING OFF by George Feydeau
or *Hortense said: "I Don't Give a Damn!"*

Follbraguet	Peter Millard
Vildamour	Anthony Bekenn
Adrien	Jeff Meadows

Marcelle	Patty Jamieson
Hortense	Glynis Ranney
M. Jean	Andrew Kushnir
Mme Dingue	Donna Belleville
Yvette	Lisa Horner
Leboucq	Michael Ball

Adapted and directed by Kelly Daniels

Stage Manager	Patti Neice
Sound Operator	Mark Callan

Designed by Lindsay Walker
Lighting designed by Peter Debreceni

VOTE BY BALLET by Harley Granville Barker

Parlourmaid	Ashley Taylor
Lord Silverwell	Micheal Querin
Mary Torpenhouse	Darcy Dunlop
Honourable Noel Wychway	Andrew Bunker
Lewis Torpenhouse	George Dawson

Directed by Andrew Freund

Stage Manager	Kinnon Elliott
Sound Operator	Mark Callan

Designed by Lindsay Walker
Lighting designed by Peter Debreceni

2005 August 18 to 20

PASQUE FLOWER by Gwen Pharis Ringwood

Jake Hansen	Jeff Meadows
Lisa Hansen	Nicole Underhay
David Hansen	Graeme Somerville

Directed by Ruth Madoc-Jones

Stage Manager	Michael Haltrecht

Designed by William Schmuck
Lighting designed by Julia Vandergraaf
Original music composed by Alexander Cann

Appendix II: The Directors Project

IN THE SHADOW OF THE GLEN by J.M. Synge

Tramp	Andrew Bunker
Nora Burke	Catherine McGregor
Daniel Burke	Benedict Campbell
Micheal Dara	Martin Happer

Directed by Katrina Dunn

Stage Manager	Eamonn Reil
Dialect Coach	Sarah Shippobotham

Designed by William Schmuck
Lighting designed by Julia Vandergraaf
Original score composed by Alexander Cann
    and recorded by Richard Thomson (clarinet)
    and Alexander Cann (piano)

2006 August 24 to 26

HALF AN HOUR by J.M. Barrie

Withers	Jeff Madden
Lilian Garson	Catherine McGregor
Richard Garson	Jim Mezon
Hugh	Patrick Galligan
Susie	Taylor Trowbridge
Dr Brodie	Benedict Campbell
Mrs Redding	Kelli Fox
Mr Redding	Norman Browning

Directed by Liza Balkan

Stage Manager	Rachael King

Designed by Tyler Sainsbury
Lighting designed by Julia Vandergraaf
Original music composed and recorded by
    Ryan deSouza (keyboards), with Alex Grant (cello),
    Karen Graves (violin) and Kathryn Sugden (violin)

THE VALIANT by Holworthy Hall and Robert Middlemass

Warden Holt	Douglas E. Hughes
Father Daly	Cameron MacDuffee
Wilson	Michael Strathmore
James Dyke	Jeff Meadows
Josephine Paris	Marla McLean

Adapted and directed by Lee Wilson

Stage Manager   Eamonn Reil

Designed by Tyler Sainsbury
Lighting designed by Julia Vandergraaf
Sound designed by Greg Gibson

2007 September 6 to 8

HANDS ACROSS THE SEA by Noel Coward

Walters	Charlotte Gowdy
Lady Maureen Gilpirn	Deborah Hay
Peter Gilpirn	David Jansen
Alastair Corbett	Blair Williams
Mrs Wadhurst	Trish Lindström
Mr Wadhurst	Jay Turvey
Mr Burnham	Ken James Stewart
Clare Wedderburn	Gabrielle Jones
Bogey Gosling	Gray Powell

Directed by Kate Lynch

Stage Manager   Marisa Vest

Designed by Tyler Sainsbury
Lighting designed by Jennifer Jimenez
"World Weary" written by Noel Coward and arranged
    by Greg Gibson. All other music written and arranged
    by Greg Gibson

THE YALTA GAME (*after Chekhov*) by Brian Friel

Dmitry Dmitrich Gurov	Mike Nadajewski
Anna Sergeyevna	Krista Colosimo

Directed by Lezlie Wade

Stage Manager   Rachael King

Designed by Tyler Sainsbury
Lighting designed by Jennifer Jimenez

APPENDIX III
PRODUCTION SUMMARY
PLAYS PRODUCED

1962

COURT HOUSE THEATRE

Don Juan in Hell (from *Man and Superman*, Act 3) by Bernard Shaw
Candida by Bernard Shaw

1963

COURT HOUSE THEATRE

You Never Can Tell by Bernard Shaw
How He Lied to Her Husband by Bernard Shaw
The Man of Destiny by Bernard Shaw
Androcles and the Lion by Bernard Shaw

1964

COURT HOUSE THEATRE

Heartbreak House by Bernard Shaw
Village Wooing by Bernard Shaw
The Dark Lady of the Sonnets by Bernard Shaw
John Bull's Other Island by Bernard Shaw

1965

COURT HOUSE THEATRE

Pygmalion by Bernard Shaw
The Millionairess by Bernard Shaw
The Shadow of a Gunman by Seán O'Casey

1966

COURT HOUSE THEATRE

Man and Superman by Bernard Shaw
Misalliance by Bernard Shaw
The Apple Cart by Bernard Shaw

1967

COURT HOUSE THEATRE

Arms and The Man by Bernard Shaw
Major Barbara by Bernard Shaw
The Circle by Somerset Maugham

1968

COURT HOUSE THEATRE

Heartbreak House by Bernard Shaw
The Importance of Being Oscar based on the life and works of Oscar Wilde, by Micheál MacLiammóir
The Chemmy Circle by Georges Feydeau, translated by Suzanne Grossmann

1969

COURT HOUSE THEATRE

The Doctor's Dilemma by Bernard Shaw
Back to Methuselah (Part I) by Bernard Shaw
Five Variations of Corno di Bassetto from the music criticism of Bernard Shaw, arranged by Louis Applebaum and Ronald Hambleton
The Guardsman by Ferenc Molnár, English version by Frank Marcus

Appendix III: Production Summary

1970

COURT HOUSE THEATRE

Candida by Bernard Shaw
Forty Years On by Alan Bennett

1971

COURT HOUSE THEATRE

The Philanderer by Bernard Shaw
O'Flaherty, V.C. by Bernard Shaw
Press Cuttings by Bernard Shaw
Summer Days by Romain Weingarten,
  translated by Suzanne Grossmann
Tonight at 8:30 by Noel Coward
A Social Success by Max Beerbohm

1972

COURT HOUSE THEATRE

Getting Married by Bernard Shaw
Misalliance by Bernard Shaw
The Royal Family by George S. Kaufman
  and Edna Ferber

1973

FESTIVAL THEATRE

You Never Can Tell by Bernard Shaw
Fanny's First Play by Bernard Shaw
The Brass Butterfly by William Golding

COURT HOUSE THEATRE

*Sisters of Mercy: A Musical Journey
  into the Words of Leonard Cohen*
  conceived by Gene Lesser

1974

FESTIVAL THEATRE

The Devil's Disciple by Bernard Shaw
Too True To Be Good by Bernard Shaw
Charley's Aunt by Brandon Thomas

COURT HOUSE THEATRE

The Admirable Bashville by
  Bernard Shaw
Rosmersholm by Henrik Ibsen

1975

FESTIVAL THEATRE

Pygmalion by Bernard Shaw
Caesar and Cleopatra by Bernard Shaw
Leaven of Malice by Robertson Davies

COURT HOUSE THEATRE

The First Night of Pygmalion by
  Richard Huggett
*G.K.C.: The Wit and Wisdom of Gilbert
  Keith Chesterton* devised, arranged, and
  performed by Tony van Bridge

1976

FESTIVAL THEATRE

Mrs Warren's Profession by Bernard Shaw
Arms and The Man by Bernard Shaw
The Apple Cart by Bernard Shaw
The Admirable Crichton by J.M. Barrie

COURT HOUSE THEATRE

Arms and The Man by Bernard Shaw

1977

FESTIVAL THEATRE

Man and Superman by Bernard Shaw
The Millionairess by Bernard Shaw
Thark by Ben Travers

COURT HOUSE THEATRE

Great Catherine by Bernard Shaw
Widowers' Houses by Bernard Shaw

1978

FESTIVAL THEATRE

Major Barbara by Bernard Shaw
Heartbreak House by Bernard Shaw
John Gabriel Borkman by Henrik Ibsen

COURT HOUSE THEATRE

*Lady Audley's Secret: A Musical
  Melodrama* by Mary Elizabeth
  Braddon, adapted by Douglas Seale,
  music by George Goehring,
  lyrics by John Kuntz

311

Appendix III: Production Summary

1979

FESTIVAL THEATRE

You Never Can Tell by Bernard Shaw

Captain Brassbound's Conversion by
  Bernard Shaw

The Corn is Green by Emlyn Williams

Dear Liar by Jerome Kilty

COURT HOUSE THEATRE

Village Wooing by Bernard Shaw

Blithe Spirit by Noel Coward

My Astonishing Self from the writings of
  Bernard Shaw, by Michael Voysey

1980

FESTIVAL THEATRE

Misalliance by Bernard Shaw

The Cherry Orchard by Anton Chekhov

A Flea in Her Ear by Georges Feydeau

The Grand Hunt by Gyula Hernády

COURT HOUSE THEATRE

The Philanderer by Bernard Shaw

Overruled by Bernard Shaw

A Respectable Wedding by Bertolt Brecht,
  translated by Jean Benedetti

Canuck by John Bruce Cowan

ROYAL GEORGE THEATRE

Puttin' on the Ritz the music and lyrics
  of Irving Berlin

Gunga Heath compiled and performed
  by Heath Lamberts

1981

FESTIVAL THEATRE

Saint Joan by Bernard Shaw

Tons of Money by Will Evans and
  Valentine

The Suicide by Nikolai Erdman

Camille by Robert David MacDonald

COURT HOUSE THEATRE

In Good King Charles's Golden Days
  by Bernard Shaw

The Magistrate by Arthur W. Pinero

ROYAL GEORGE THEATRE

The Man of Destiny by Bernard Shaw

Rose Marie music by Rudolf Friml
  and Herbert Stothart, book and
  lyrics by Otto Harbach and
  Oscar Hammerstein II,
  adapted by Paula Sperdakos

1982

FESTIVAL THEATRE

Pygmalion by Bernard Shaw

See How They Run by Philip King

Camille by Robert David MacDonald

Cyrano de Bergerac by Edmond Rostand,
  translated and adapted by Anthony
  Burgess

COURT HOUSE THEATRE

Too True To Be Good by Bernard Shaw

The Singular Life of Albert Nobbs adapted
  by Simone Benmussa from *Albert Nobbs*
  by George Moore

ROYAL GEORGE THEATRE

The Music-Cure by Bernard Shaw

The Desert Song music by Sigmund
  Romberg, book and lyrics by Otto
  Harbach, Oscar Hammerstein II,
  and Frank Mandel, adapted by
  Christopher Newton

1983

FESTIVAL THEATRE

Caesar and Cleopatra by Bernard Shaw

Cyrano de Bergerac by Edmond Rostand,
  translated and adapted by Anthony
  Burgess

Rookery Nook by Ben Travers

Private Lives by Noel Coward

COURT HOUSE THEATRE

The Simpleton of the Unexpected Isles
by Bernard Shaw

Candida by Bernard Shaw

The Vortex by Noel Coward

ROYAL GEORGE THEATRE

O'Flaherty, V.C. by Bernard Shaw

Tom Jones an operetta by Sir Edward
German, libretto by Robert
Courtneidge and A.M. Thompson,
from the novel by Henry Fielding,
lyrics by Charles H. Taylor and Basil
Hood, libretto and lyrics adapted by
Christopher Newton and Sky Gilbert

1984

FESTIVAL THEATRE

The Devil's Disciple by Bernard Shaw

Private Lives by Noel Coward

The Skin of Our Teeth by
Thornton Wilder

Célimare by Eugène Labiche, adapted
by Allan Stratton

COURT HOUSE THEATRE

Androcles and the Lion by Bernard Shaw

The Vortex by Noel Coward

The Lost Letter by Ion Caragiale,
adapted by Christopher Newton
and Sky Gilbert

ROYAL GEORGE THEATRE

The Fascinating Foundling by
Bernard Shaw

How He Lied to Her Husband by
Bernard Shaw

Roberta music by Jerome Kern,
book and lyrics by Otto Harbach,
adapted by Duncan McIntosh
and Christopher Newton

COURT HOUSE THEATRE, ROYAL
GEORGE THEATRE, FESTIVAL
THEATRE, ACADEMY WAREHOUSE,

AND THE STREETS AND PARKS
OF NIAGARA-ON-THE-LAKE

1984 by George Orwell, adapted by
Denise Coffey

1985

FESTIVAL THEATRE

Heartbreak House by Bernard Shaw

The Madwoman of Chaillot by Jean
Giraudoux, adapted by Maurice
Valency

One for the Pot by Ray Cooney and
Tony Hilton

Cavalcade by Noel Coward

COURT HOUSE THEATRE

John Bull's Other Island by Bernard Shaw

The Women by Clare Boothe Luce

*Tropical Madness No. 2: Metaphysics of
a Two-Headed Calf* by Stanislaw
Witkiewicz, translated by Daniel
and Eleanor Gerould

ROYAL GEORGE THEATRE

The Inca of Perusalem by Bernard Shaw

Murder on the Nile by Agatha Christie

Naughty Marietta music by Victor
Herbert, book and lyrics by Rida
Johnson Young, adapted by
Christopher Newton

1986

FESTIVAL THEATRE

Arms and The Man by Bernard Shaw

Back to Methuselah by Bernard Shaw

Banana Ridge by Ben Travers

Cavalcade by Noel Coward

COURT HOUSE THEATRE

On the Rocks by Bernard Shaw

Holiday by Philip Barry

Tonight We Improvise by Luigi Pirandello

313

Appendix III: Production Summary

Passion, Poison, and Petrifaction
  by Bernard Shaw
Black Coffee by Agatha Christie
Girl Crazy words and music by George
  and Ira Gershwin, libretto by John
  McGowan and Guy Bolton

1987

FESTIVAL THEATRE
Major Barbara by Bernard Shaw
Hay Fever by Noel Coward
Marathon 33 by June Havoc
Peter Pan by J.M. Barrie

COURT HOUSE THEATRE
Fanny's First Play by Bernard Shaw
Night of January 16th by Ayn Rand
Playing with Fire by August Strindberg
Salomé by Oscar Wilde

ROYAL GEORGE THEATRE
Augustus Does His Bit by Bernard Shaw
Not in the Book by Arthur Watkyn
Anything Goes music and lyrics by Cole
  Porter, book by Guy Bolton and P.G.
  Wodehouse, revised by Howard
  Lindsay and Russell Crouse

1988

FESTIVAL THEATRE
You Never Can Tell by Bernard Shaw
Peter Pan by J.M. Barrie
War and Peace by Leo Tolstoy, adapted
  by Alfred Neumann, Erwin Piscator,
  and Guntram Pruefer, translated by
  Robert David MacDonald
Once in a Lifetime by Moss Hart and
  George S. Kaufman

COURT HOUSE THEATRE
Geneva by Bernard Shaw

The Voysey Inheritance
by Harley Granville Barker
He Who Gets Slapped
by Leonid Andreyev

ROYAL GEORGE THEATRE
The Dark Lady of the Sonnets
  by Bernard Shaw
Hit the Deck music by Vincent Youmans,
  book by Herbert Fields, lyrics by Leo
  Robin, Clifford Grey, and Irving Caesar
Dangerous Corner by J.B. Priestley

1989

FESTIVAL THEATRE
Man and Superman by Bernard Shaw
Berkeley Square by John L. Balderston
Once in a Lifetime by Moss Hart and
  George S. Kaufman
Trelawny of the 'Wells' by Arthur W. Pinero

COURT HOUSE THEATRE
Getting Married by Bernard Shaw
Peer Gynt by Henrik Ibsen, translated
  by John Lingard
Nymph Errant music and lyrics by Cole
  Porter, libretto by Romney Brent,
  from the novel by James Laver

ROYAL GEORGE THEATRE
Shakes versus Shav by Bernard Shaw
The Glimpse of Reality by Bernard Shaw
An Inspector Calls by J.B. Priestley
Good News music by Ray Henderson,
  book by Laurence Schwab and B.G.
  DeSylva, lyrics by B.G. DeSylva and
  Lew Brown

1990

FESTIVAL THEATRE
Misalliance by Bernard Shaw
Trelawny of the 'Wells' by Arthur W. Pinero
The Waltz of the Toreadors by Jean Anouilh,
  translated by Lucienne Hill
Present Laughter by Noel Coward

20000

Appendix III: Production Summary

COURT HOUSE THEATRE

Mrs Warren's Profession by Bernard Shaw

Nymph Errant music and lyrics by
Cole Porter, book by Romney Brent,
from a novel by James Laver

Ubu Rex by Alfred Jarry, translated by
David Copelin

ROYAL GEORGE THEATRE

Village Wooing by Bernard Shaw

Night Must Fall by Emlyn Williams

When We Are Married by J.B. Priestley

1991

FESTIVAL THEATRE

The Doctor's Dilemma by Bernard Shaw

A Cuckoo in the Nest by Ben Travers

Lulu by Frank Wedekind, adapted by
Peter Barnes

COURT HOUSE THEATRE

The Millionairess by Bernard Shaw

Henry IV by Luigi Pirandello, translated
by Robert Rietty and John Wardle

Hedda Gabler by Henrik Ibsen, adapted
by Judith Thompson

ROYAL GEORGE THEATRE

Press Cuttings by Bernard Shaw

A Connecticut Yankee music by Richard
Rodgers, lyrics by Lorenz Hart,
book by Herbert Fields

This Happy Breed by Noel Coward

1992

FESTIVAL THEATRE

Pygmalion by Bernard Shaw

Counsellor-at-Law by Elmer Rice

Charley's Aunt by Brandon Thomas

COURT HOUSE THEATRE

Widowers' Houses by Bernard Shaw

Drums in the Night by Bertolt Brecht

Point Valaine by Noel Coward

ROYAL GEORGE THEATRE

Overruled by Bernard Shaw

On the Town music by Leonard
Bernstein, book and lyrics by Betty
Comden and Adolph Green, based on
an idea by Jerome Robbins

Ten Minute Alibi by Anthony
Armstrong

1993

FESTIVAL THEATRE

Saint Joan by Bernard Shaw

The Silver King by Henry Arthur Jones

Blithe Spirit by Noel Coward

COURT HOUSE THEATRE

Candida by Bernard Shaw

The Unmentionables by Carl Sternheim,
translated and adapted by Paul
Lampert and Kate Sullivan

The Marrying of Ann Leete by Harley
Granville Barker

ROYAL GEORGE THEATRE

The Man of Destiny by Bernard Shaw

Gentlemen Prefer Blondes music by Jule
Styne, lyrics by Leo Robin, book by
Anita Loos and Joseph Fields, adapted
from the novel by Anita Loos

And Then There Were None by
Agatha Christie

1994

FESTIVAL THEATRE

Arms and The Man by Bernard Shaw

The Front Page by Ben Hecht and
Charles MacArthur

Sherlock Holmes by William Gillette

COURT HOUSE THEATRE

Too True To Be Good by Bernard Shaw

Eden End by J.B. Priestley

Ivona, Princess of Burgundia by
Witold Gombrowicz

Appendix III: Production Summary

ROYAL GEORGE THEATRE

Annajanska, the Bolshevik Empress by
Bernard Shaw

Lady, Be Good! words and music by
George and Ira Gershwin, book by
Guy Bolton and Fred Thompson

Busman's Honeymoon by Dorothy L.
Sayers and M. St Clare Byrne

Rococo by Harley Granville Barker

1995

FESTIVAL THEATRE

You Never Can Tell by Bernard Shaw

The Petrified Forest by Robert Sherwood

Cavalcade by Noel Coward

COURT HOUSE THEATRE

The Philanderer by Bernard Shaw

An Ideal Husband by Oscar Wilde

Waste by Harley Granville Barker

ROYAL GEORGE THEATRE

The Six of Calais by Bernard Shaw

The Voice of the Turtle by John van
Druten

Ladies in Retirement by Edward Percy
and Reginald Denham

The Zoo by Arthur Sullivan and
Bolton Rowe

1996

FESTIVAL THEATRE

The Devil's Disciple by Bernard Shaw

Rashomon by Fay and Michael Kanin

Hobson's Choice by Harold Brighouse

COURT HOUSE THEATRE

The Simpleton of the Unexpected Isles by
Bernard Shaw

An Ideal Husband by Oscar Wilde

The Playboy of the Western World by
J.M. Synge

Marsh Hay by Merrill Denison

ROYAL GEORGE THEATRE

Mr Cinders music by Vivan Ellis and
Richard Myers, libretto and lyrics by
Clifford Grey and Greatrex Newman,
additional lyrics by Leo Robin and
Vivian Ellis

The Hollow by Agatha Christie

Shall We Join the Ladies? by J.M. Barrie

The Conjuror by David Ben and
Patrick Watson

1997

FESTIVAL THEATRE

Mrs Warren's Profession by Bernard Shaw

Hobson's Choice by Harold Brighouse

Will Any Gentleman? by Vernon Sylvaine

The Seagull by Anton Chekhov,
translated by David French

COURT HOUSE THEATRE

In Good King Charles's Golden Days by
Bernard Shaw

The Playboy of the Western World by
J.M. Synge

The Children's Hour by Lillian Hellman

The Secret Life by Harley Granville Barker

ROYAL GEORGE THEATRE

The Chocolate Soldier music by Oscar
Straus, adapted and arranged by
Ronald Hanmer, original book and
lyrics by Rudolph Bernauer and
Leopold Jacobson, new English
book by Agnes Bernelle, new
English lyrics by Adam Carstairs

The Two Mrs Carrolls by Martin Vale

The Conjuror, Part 2 by David Ben and
Patrick Watson

Sorry, Wrong Number by Lucille Fletcher

1998

FESTIVAL THEATRE

Major Barbara by Bernard Shaw

You Can't Take It With You by George
 S. Kaufman and Moss Hart
Lady Windermere's Fan by Oscar Wilde

COURT HOUSE THEATRE
John Bull's Other Island by Bernard Shaw
The Lady's Not for Burning by
 Christopher Fry
Joy by John Galsworthy

ROYAL GEORGE THEATRE
Passion, Poison, and Petrifaction
 by Bernard Shaw
A Foggy Day words and music by
 George and Ira Gershwin, book by
 Norm Foster and John Mueller
The Shop at Sly Corner by Edward Percy
Brothers in Arms by Merrill Denison
Waterloo by Arthur Conan Doyle

1999

FESTIVAL THEATRE
Heartbreak House by Bernard Shaw
You Can't Take It With You by George
 S. Kaufman and Moss Hart
Easy Virtue by Noel Coward
All My Sons by Arthur Miller

COURT HOUSE THEATRE
Getting Married by Bernard Shaw
The Madras House by Harley Granville
 Barker
S.S. Tenacity by Charles Vildrac
Uncle Vanya by Anton Chekhov,
 translated by John Murrell

ROYAL GEORGE THEATRE
Village Wooing by Bernard Shaw
Rebecca by Daphne du Maurier
A Foggy Day words and music by
 George and Ira Gershwin, book by
 Norm Foster and John Mueller
Waterloo by Arthur Conan Doyle

2000

FESTIVAL THEATRE
The Doctor's Dilemma by Bernard Shaw
Easy Virtue by Noel Coward
Lord of the Flies adapted for the stage
 by Nigel Williams from the novel
 by William Golding
The Matchmaker by Thornton Wilder

COURT HOUSE THEATRE
The Apple Cart by Bernard Shaw
A Woman of No Importance by
 Oscar Wilde
A Room of One's Own adapted for the
 stage by Patrick Garland from the essay
 by Virginia Woolf
Six Characters in Search of an Author by
 Luigi Pirandello, in a new translation
 by Domenico Pietropaolo

ROYAL GEORGE THEATRE
Time and the Conways by J.B. Priestley
She Loves Me book by Joe Masteroff,
 music by Jerry Bock, lyrics by
 Sheldon Harnick
Still Life by Noel Coward

2001

FESTIVAL THEATRE
The Millionairess by Bernard Shaw
Peter Pan by J.M. Barrie
The Man Who Came to Dinner by
 Moss Hart and George S. Kaufman

COURT HOUSE THEATRE
Fanny's First Play by Bernard Shaw
Picnic by William Inge
Six Characters in Search of an Author
 by Luigi Pirandello
The Return of the Prodigal by
 St John Hankin

Appendix III: Production Summary

ROYAL GEORGE THEATRE

The Mystery of Edwin Drood a musical
  by Rupert Holmes, based on the
  unfinished novel by Charles Dickens
Laura by Vera Caspary and George Sklar
Love from a Stranger by Frank Vosper,
  based on a story by Agatha Christie
Shadow Play by Noel Coward

2002

FESTIVAL THEATRE

Caesar and Cleopatra by Bernard Shaw
Candida by Bernard Shaw
Detective Story by Sidney Kingsley
Hay Fever by Noel Coward

COURT HOUSE THEATRE

The Return of the Prodigal by
  St John Hankin
The House of Bernarda Alba by Federico
  García Lorca, in a new translation
  by Richard Sanger
His Majesty by Harley Granville Barker
Chaplin by Simon Bradbury

ROYAL GEORGE THEATRE

The Old Ladies by Rodney Ackland
Merrily We Roll Along music and
  lyrics by Stephen Sondheim, book
  by George Furth
The Old Lady Shows Her Medals by
  J.M. Barrie

2003

FESTIVAL THEATRE

Misalliance by Bernard Shaw
Three Sisters by Anton Chekhov, a new
  version by Susan Coyne
The Coronation Voyage by
  Michel Marc Bouchard, translated by
  Linda Gaboriau
The Royal Family by George S. Kaufman
  and Edna Ferber

COURT HOUSE THEATRE

Widowers' Houses by Bernard Shaw
Diana of Dobson's by Cicely Hamilton
The Plough and the Stars by Seán O'Casey
Afterplay by Brian Friel

ROYAL GEORGE THEATRE

On the Twentieth Century book and lyrics
  by Betty Comden and Adolph Green,
  music by Cy Coleman
Blood Relations by Sharon Pollock
Happy End lyrics by Bertolt Brecht, music
  by Kurt Weill, original German play by
  Dorothy Lane, books and lyrics adapted
  by Michael Feingold

2004

FESTIVAL THEATRE

Pygmalion by Bernard Shaw
Man and Superman by Bernard Shaw
Three Men on a Horse by John Cecil
  Holm and George Abbott
Nothing Sacred by George F. Walker

COURT HOUSE THEATRE

Ah, Wilderness! by Eugene O'Neill
Rutherford and Son by Githa Sowerby
The Tinker's Wedding by J.M. Synge
Floyd Collins music and lyrics by
  Adam Guettel, book by Tina Landau,
  additional lyrics by Tina Landau

ROYAL GEORGE THEATRE

The Importance of Being Earnest by
  Oscar Wilde
Pal Joey music by Richard Rodgers,
  lyrics by Lorenz Hart, book by
  John O'Hara
Waiting for the Parade by John Murrell
Harlequinade by Terence Rattigan

2005

FESTIVAL THEATRE

You Never Can Tell by Bernard Shaw

Major Barbara by Bernard Shaw

Gypsy book by Arthur Laurents, music by Jule Styne, lyrics by Stephen Sondheim

COURT HOUSE THEATRE

Belle Moral: A Natural History by Ann-Marie MacDonald

Journey's End by R.C. Sherriff

The Autumn Garden by Lillian Hellman

ROYAL GEORGE THEATRE

The Constant Wife by Somerset Maugham

Happy End lyrics by Bertolt Brecht, music by Kurt Weill, original German play by Dorothy Lane, books and lyrics adapted by Michael Feingold

Something on the Side by Georges Feydeau and Maurice Desvallières, adapted by Neil Munro, based on a new translation by Maureen LaBonté

Bus Stop by William Inge

2006

FESTIVAL THEATRE

Arms and The Man by Bernard Shaw

The Crucible by Arthur Miller

High Society music and lyrics by Cole Porter, book by Arthur Kopit, additional lyrics by Susan Birkenhead

COURT HOUSE THEATRE

Too True To Be Good by Bernard Shaw

Rosmersholm by Henrik Ibsen, adapted by Neil Munro

Love Among the Russians [*The Bear* and *The Proposal*] by Anton Chekhov, adapted by Morwyn Brebner

The Magic Fire by Lillian Groag

ROYAL GEORGE THEATRE

The Invisible Man by Michael O'Brien, adapted from the novel by H.G. Wells

The Heiress by Ruth Goetz and Augustus Goetz

Design for Living by Noel Coward

2007

FESTIVAL THEATRE

Saint Joan by Bernard Shaw

Mack and Mabel book by Michael Stewart, music and lyrics by Jerry Herman, revised by Francine Pascal

Hotel Peccadillo based on the play *L'Hôtel du Libre-Echange* by Georges Feydeau and Maurice Desvallières, adapted by Morris Panych

COURT HOUSE THEATRE

The Cassilis Engagement by St John Hankin

Tristan book, music, and lyrics by Paul Sportelli and Jay Turvey, adapted from the story 'Tristan' by Thomas Mann

The Kiltartan Comedies [*The Rising of the Moon* and *Spreading the News*] by Lady Augusta Gregory

A Month in the Country (after Turgenev) by Brian Friel

ROYAL GEORGE THEATRE

The Philanderer by Bernard Shaw

The Circle by Somerset Maugham

Summer and Smoke by Tennessee Williams

INDEXES

ABBREVIATIONS USED IN THE INDEXES

A	actor
adapt.	adaptation *or* adapted by
CH	choreographer
D	director
DS	designer
F	fight director
I	instrumentalist
MD	musical director
SM	stage management
TP	Toronto Project
tr.	translator

Note: Appendix I is indexed
Appendices II and III are not indexed

WORKS PRODUCED
(plays by Bernard Shaw are *italicized*)

Admirable Bashville, The 1974
Admirable Crichton, The 1976
Afterplay 2003
Ah, Wilderness! 2004
All My Sons 1999
And Then There Were None 1993
Androcles and the Lion 1963, 1984
Annajanska, the Bolshevik Empress 1994
Anything Goes 1987
Apollo of Bellac, The 1999
Apple Cart, The 1966, 1976, 2000
archy and mehitabel 2001, 2002
Arms and The Man 1967, 1976, 1986, 1994, 2006
As Is TP/1986
Augustus Does His Bit 1987
Autumn Garden, The 2005
Back to Methuselah 1969 (Part I), 1986 (full work)
Ballad of Oscar Wilde, The 1998
Banana Ridge 1986
Bear, The 2002, 2006
Belle Moral 2005
Berkeley Square 1989
Big Blonde 2005
Billy Bishop Goes to War 1981
Birds, The 1999
Black Coffee 1986
Black Girl in Search of God, The (adapt.) 1986, 1999
Bliss 2004
Blithe Spirit 1979, 1993
Blood Relations 2003

Bloomer Girl 2004
B-Movie the Play TP/1987
Brass Butterfly, The 1973
Breaking the Silence TP/1986
Brothers in Arms 1998
Busman's Honeymoon 1994
Bus Stop 2005
Caesar and Cleopatra 1975, 1983, 2002
Camille 1981-2
Candida 1962, 1970, 1983, 1993, 2002
Canuck 1980
Captain Brassbound's Conversion 1979
Cassilis Engagement, The 2007
Cavalcade 1985-6, 1995
Cecè 2001
Célimare 1984
Chaplin 2002
Charley's Aunt 1974, 1992
Chat with Mrs Chicky 2004
Chemmy Circle, The 1968
Cherry Orchard, The 1980
Children's Hour, The 1997
Chocolate Soldier, The 1997
Circle, The 1967, 2007
Conjuror, The 1996
Conjuror Part 2, The 1997
Connecticut Yankee, A 1991
Constant Wife, The 2005
Corn Is Green, The 1979
Coronation Voyage, The 2003
Counsellor-at-Law 1992
Crucible, The 2006

Works Produced

Cuckoo in the Nest, A 1991
Cyrano de Bergerac 1982-3
Dangerous Corner 1988
Dark Lady of the Sonnets, The 1964, 1988, 2005
Dear Liar 1979
Dear Sir 2000
Delicatessen TP/1984
Desert Song, The 1982
Design for Living 2006
Detective Story 2002
Devil's Disciple, The 1974, 1984, 1996
Diana of Dobson's 2003
Diary of Samuel Marchbanks, The 2000
Digestible and Interactive Shaw, The 2006
Doctor's Dilemma, The 1969, 1991, 2000
Doll's House, A 2006
Don Juan in Hell: *see* Man and Superman
Dreaming and Duelling TP/1982
Drums in the Night 1992
Dunwich Horror, The 2004
Easy Virtue 1999-2000
Eden End 1994
Emma, Queen of Song 1984
Experiment with an Air Pump, An 2007
Family Album: *see* Tonight at 8:30
Fanny's First Play 1973, 1987, 2001
Farfetched Fables 1996
Fascinating Foundling, The 1984
Feuille d'Album 2004
Fire TP/1988
First Night of Pygmalion, The 1975
Five Good Reasons to Laugh 1986
Five Variations from Corno di Bassetto 1969
Flea in Her Ear, A 1980
Floyd Collins 2004
Foggy Day, A 1998-9
Forty Years On 1970

Front Page, The 1994
GBS in Love 1973, 1983, 1988
GBS versus GKC 2001
Geneva 1988
Gentlemen Prefer Blondes 1993
Getting Married 1972, 1989, 1999
Ghosts 2006
Girl Crazy 1986
G.K.C.: The Wit and Wisdom of G.K. Chesterton 1970, 1975, 1979, 2002
Glimpse of Reality, The 1989
Golden Apple, The 2006
Good News 1989
Goodnight Disgrace TP/1985
Grand Hunt, The 1980
Great Catherine 1977
Guardsman, The 1969
Gunga Heath 1980
Gypsy 2005
Happy End 2003, 2005
Harlequinade 2004
Hay Fever 1987, 2002
He Who Gets Slapped 1988
Heartbreak House 1964, 1968, 1978, 1985, 1999
Heart of Darkness 2000
Hedda Gabler 1991, 2006
Heiress, The 2006
Hello Again 2002
Henry IV 1991
Here We Are 2005
High Society 2006
His Majesty 2002
Hit the Deck 1988
Hobson's Choice 1996-7
Holiday 1986
Hollow, The 1996
Homebody / Kabul 2007
Hot House Plays from the 1890s: *see* Salomé *and* Playing with Fire
Hotel Peccadillo 2007
House of Bernarda Alba, The 2002
How He Lied to Her Husband 1963, 1984

How the Vote Was Won 2004
Ideal Husband, An 1995, 1996
Importance of Being Earnest, The 2004
Importance of Being Oscar, The 1968
In Good King Charles's Golden Days
  1981, 1997
Inca of Perusalem, The 1985
Inspector Calls, An 1989
Intruder, The 1997
Invisible Man, The 2006
Ivona, Princess of Burgundia 1994
John Bull's Other Island 1964, 1985,
  1998
John Gabriel Borkman 1978
Journey's End 2005
Joy 1998
Jubilee 2003
Kiltartan Comedies, The 2007
Klee Wyck 2001
Ladies in Retirement 1995
Lady Audley's Secret 1978
Lady, Be Good! 1994
Lady Windermere's Fan 1998
Lady's Not for Burning, The 1998
Laura 2001
Leaven of Malice 1975
Le Grand Meaulnes (The Wanderer)
  2001
Lessons from Leacock 1999
Lilies 2007
Little Eyolf 2006
Lord of the Flies 2000
Lost Letter, The 1984
Love Among the Russians 2006
Love and How to Cure It 2002
Love from a Stranger 2001
Loved One, The 2005
Lulu 1991
Mack and Mabel 2007
Madras House, The 1999
Madwoman of Chaillot, The 1985
Magic Fire, The 2006
Magistrate, The 1981
Major Barbara 1967, 1978, 1987,
  1998, 2005

Man and Superman 1966
  with Act III (Don Juan in Hell) 1977,
  1989, 2004
  Don Juan in Hell (separately
  presented) 1962
Man of Destiny, The 1963, 1981, 1993
Man Who Came to Dinner, The 2001
Man with the Flower in His Mouth
  2001
Marathon 33 1987
Marrying of Ann Leete, The 1993
Marsh Hay 1996
Master Builder, The 2006
Matchmaker, The 2000
Merrily We Roll Along 2002
Metaphysics of a Two-Headed Calf 1985
Millionairess, The 1965, 1977, 1991,
  2001
Mirrors, Masques and Transformations
  1980
Misalliance 1966, 1972, 1980, 1990,
  2003
Month in the Country, A 2007
Mr Cinders 1996
Mr Shaw 1997
Mr Shaw Interviews Himself 1998
Mrs Bach 1985
Mrs Warren's Profession 1976, 1990,
  1997
Murder on the Nile 1985
Murder Pattern 1996
Music-Cure, The 1982
My Astonishing Self 1979
Mystery of Edwin Drood, The 2001
Naughty Marietta 1985
Night Must Fall 1990
Night of January 16th 1984, 1987
1984 1984
Nona, La 2006
Not in the Book 1987
Nothing Sacred 2004
Nymph Errant 1989-90
O'Flaherty, V.C. 1971, 1983
Old Ladies, The 2002

Works Produced

Old Lady Shows Her Medals, The 2002
On the Rocks 1986
On the Town 1992
On the Twentieth Century 2003
Once in a Lifetime 1988-9
One for the Pot 1985, 1987, 1996
Over the Rainbow 2001
Overruled 1980, 1992
Pal Joey 2004
Panama Hattie 2002
Passion, Poison, and Petrifaction 1986, 1998
Patria I: The Characteristics Man TP/1987
Peer Gynt 1989
Peter Pan 1987-8, 2001
Petrified Forest, The 1995
Philanderer, The 1971, 1973, 1980, 1995, 2007
Picnic 2001
Place of the Lion, The 2002
Playboy of the Western World, The 1996-7
Playing with Fire 1987
Plough and the Stars, The 2003
Point Valaine 1992
Potato People, The 1986
Present Laughter 1990
Press Cuttings 1971, 1991, 2006
Private Lives 1983-4
Proposal, The 2002, 2006
Purgatory 2003
Puttin' on the Ritz 1980
Pygmalion 1965, 1975, 1982, 1992, 2004
Queens of France 2002
Rally, The 2004
Rashomon 1996
Rebecca 1999
Respectable Wedding, A 1980
Return of the Prodigal, The 2001-2
Rising of the Moon, The 2007
Roberta 1984

Rococo 1994
Ronde, La 2002
Rookery Nook 1983
Room of One's Own, A 2000
Rose Marie 1981
Rosmersholm 1974, 2006
Royal Family, The 1972, 2003
Rutherford and Son 2004
S.S. Tenacity 1999
Sadie Thompson 2000
Saint Joan 1981, 1993, 2007
Salomé 1987
Seagull, The 1997
Secret Life, The 1997
See How They Run 1982
Shadow of a Gunman, The 1965
Shadow Play 2001: *see also* Tonight at 8:30
Shakes versus Shav 1989
Shall We Join the Ladies? 1996
She Loves Me 2000
Sherlock Holmes 1994
Shewing-up of Blanco Posnet, The 2003
Shop at Sly Corner, The 1998
Silver King, The 1993
Simpleton of the Unexpected Isles, The 1983, 1996
Singular Life of Albert Nobbs, The 1982
Sisters of Mercy 1973
Six Characters in Search of an Author 2000-1
Six of Calais, The 1995
Skin of Our Teeth, The 1984
Social Success, A 1971
Something on the Side 2005
Sorry Wrong Number 1997
Souvenirs TP/1985
Spreading the News 2007
Starting Here, Starting Now 1986
Still Life 2000
Still Stands the House 1997
Stories by Ethel Wilson 1998
Suicide, The 1981
Summer and Smoke 2007

Summer Days 1971
Sun Never Sets, The 1983-4
Ten Minute Alibi 1992
Thark 1977
Theatrical Trip for a Wager, A 2003
This Happy Breed 1991
Three Men on a Horse 2004
Three Sisters 2003
Time and the Conways 2000
Tinker's Wedding, The 2004
Titanic, The 1997
To Have and To Hold 1996
To the Lighthouse 2000
Tom Jones 1983
Tonight at 8:30 1971
Tonight We Improvise 1986
Tons of Money 1981
Too True To Be Good 1974, 1982,
    1994, 2006
Trelawny of the 'Wells' 1989-90
Trifles 1998
Tristan 2005, 2007
Tropical Madness No. 2: *see* Metaphysics
    of a Two-Headed Calf
Two Brothers 2007
Two Mrs Carrolls, The 1997
Ubu Rex 1990
Uncle Vanya 1999
Unmentionables, The 1993
Village Wooing 1964, 1979, 1990,
    1999
Voice of the Turtle, The 1995
Vortex, The 1983-4
Voyage in the Dark 2003
Voysey Inheritance, The 1988
Waiting for the Parade 2004
Waltz of the Toreadors, The 1990
War of the Worlds 1996
War, Women and Other Trivia: *see* A
    Social Success, O'Flaherty, V.C., *and*
    Press Cuttings
Waste 1995
Waterloo 1998-9
We Were Dancing: *see* Tonight at 8:30

Weather Breeder, The 2004
What a Swell Party 2000
When We Are Married 1990
Why She Would Not 1997
Widowers' Houses 1977, 1992, 2003
Will Any Gentleman? 1997
Wind Blows, The 2004
Woman of No Importance, A 2000
Women, The 1985, 1987
Words upon the Window-Pane, The
    2003
You Can't Take It With You 1998-9
You Never Can Tell 1963, 1973, 1979,
    1988, 1995, 2005
Zoo, The 1995

RICHARD FARRELL, NICOLA CAVENDISH, AND BARRY MACGREGOR IN *PYGMALION*, 1982 (PHOTO BY DAVID COOPER).

ELIZABETH SHEPHERD
AND TONY VAN BRIDGE
IN *PYGMALION*, 1975
(PHOTO BY ROBERT C.
RAGSDALE).

AUTHORS, COMPOSERS, LYRICISTS
**(Composers resident with the Shaw Festival are included
as "Musical Directors" in the next index)**

Abbott, George 2004
Ackland, Rodney 2002
Andrews, Alan (adapt.) 2000
Andreyev, Leonid 1988
Anouilh, Jean 1990
Applebaum, Louis 1969
Arlen, Harold 2001, 2004
Armstrong, Anthony 1992
Balderston, John L. 1989
Barker, Harley Granville 1988, 1993-5,
  1997, 1999, 2002
Barnes, Peter (adapt.) 1991
Barrie, J.M. 1976, 1987-8, 1996,
  2001-2
Barry, Philip 1986
Beerbohm, Max 1971
Bell, Lindsay (adapt.) 2000-1
Ben, David 1996-7
Benedetti, Jean (tr.) 1980
Benmussa, Simone (adapt.) 1982
Bennett, Alan 1970
Berlin, Irving 1980
Bernauer, Rudolph 1997
Bernelle, Agnes 1997
Bernstein, Leonard 1992
Birkenhead, Susan 2006
Bock, Jerry 2000
Bolton, Guy 1986-7, 1994
Bouchard, Michel Marc 2003, 2007
Bradbury, Simon 2002
Braddon, Mary Elizabeth 1978
Brebner, Morwyn (adapt.) 2002, 2004,
  2006
Brecht, Bertolt 1980, 1992, 2003, 2005
Brent, Romney 1989-90

Brighouse, Harold 1996-7
Brooks, Mel 2001-2
Brown, Lew 1989
Burgess, Anthony (tr./adapt.) 1982-3
Burns, Robert 1979
Byrne, M. St Clare 1994
Caesar, Irving 1988
Caragiale, Ion 1984
Carr, Emily 2001
Carstairs, Adam 1997
Caspary, Vera 2001
Chekhov, Anton 1980, 1997, 1999,
  2002-3, 2006
Chesterton, G.K. 1970, 1975, 2002
Christie, Agatha 1985-6, 1993, 1996,
  2001
Coffey, Denis (adapt.) 1984
Cohen, Leonard 1973
Cole, Allen 2003-4, 2006
Coleman, Cy 2003
Comden, Betty 1992, 2003
Conrad, Joseph 2000
Cooney, Ray 1985, 1996
Copelin, David (tr.) 1990
Cossa, Roberto M. 2006
Courtneidge, Robert 1983
Cowan, John Bruce 1980
Coward, Noel 1971, 1979, 1983-7,
  1990-3, 1995, 1999-2002, 2006
Coyne, Susan (adapt.) 2003
Crouse, Russell 1987
Darion, Joe 2001-2
Davies, Robertson 1975, 2000
Denham, Reginald 1995
Denison, Merrill 1996, 1998, 2004

327

Authors, Composers, Lyricists

A SCENE FROM *HAPPY END*, 2003 (PHOTO BY DAVID COOPER).

Authors, Composers, Lyricists

McIntosh, Duncan (adapt.) 1984
McKenzie, Jonathan (tr.) 1988
Mercer, Michael TP/1985
Miller, Arthur 1999, 2006
Molnár, Ferenc 1969
Moncada, Raul (tr.) 2006
Moon, Alan 2003
Moore, George 1982
Moross, Jerome 2006
Morpurgo, Jean 2001; (adapt.) 2001
Mueller, John 1998-9
Munro, Neil (adapt.) 2004-6
Murray, William (tr.) 2001
Murrell, John (tr.) 1999; 2004
Myers, Richard 1996
Neumann, Alfred (adapt.) 1988
Newman, Greatrex 1996
Newton, Christopher (adapt.) 1982-5,
   2002
O'Brien, Michael 2006
O'Casey, Sean 1965, 2003
O'Hara, John 2004
O'Neill, Eugene 2004
Orwell, George 1984
Panych, Morris (adapt.) 2007
Parker, Dorothy 2005
Pascal, Francine 2007
Percy, Edward 1995, 1998
Peterson, Eric 1981
Pietropaolo, Domenico (tr.) 2000-1
Pinero, Arthur W. 1981, 1989-90
Pirandello, Luigi 1986, 1991, 2000-1
Piscator, Erwin (adapt.) 1988
Poliakoff, Stephen TP/1986
Pollock, Sharon 2003
Porter, Cole 1987, 1989-90, 2000,
   2002-3, 2006
Pratt, E.J. 1997
Priestley, J.B. 1988-90, 1994, 2000
Pruefer, Guntram (adapt.) 1988
Rand, Ayn 1987
Rattigan, Terence 2004
Rayson, Hannie 2007
Renard, Jules 1996
Rhys, Captain Horton 2003

Rhys, Jean 2003
Rice, Elmer 1992
Rietty, Robert (tr.) 1991
Ringwood, Gwen Pharis 1997
Robbins, Jerome 1992
Robin, Leo 1988, 1993, 1996
Robins, Elizabeth 2004
Rodgers, Richard 1991, 2004
Romberg, Sigmund 1982
Rosen, Sheldon TP/1985
Rostand, Edmond 1982-83
Rowe, Bolton 1995
Saidy, Fred 2004
Sanger, Richard (tr.) 2002
Sayers, Dorothy L. 1994
Schafer, R. Murray TP/1987
Schnitzler, Arthur 2002
Schwab, Laurence 1989
Seale, Douglas 1978
Sherriff, R.C. 2005
Sherwood, Robert 1995
Sklar, George 2001
Sondheim, Stephen 2002, 2005
Sowerby, Githa 2004
Sperdakos, Paula (adapt.) 1981
Sportelli, Paul 2006-7
St John, Christopher 2004
Stephenson, Shelagh 2007
Sternheim, Carl 1993
Stewart, Michael 2007
Stothart, Herbert 1981
Stratton, Allan 1984
Straus, Oscar 1997
Strindberg, August 1987
Styne, Jule 1993, 2005
Sullivan, Arthur 1995
Sullivan, Kate (tr./adapt.) 1993
Sylvaine, Vernon 1997
Synge, J.M. 1996-7, 2004
Taylor, Charles H. 1983
Thomas, Brandon 1974, 1992
Thompson, A.M. 1983
Thompson, Fred 1994
Thompson, Judith (adapt.) 1991
Tilly, François Louis TP/1984
Tolstoy, Leo 1988

KELLI FOX AND MARY HANEY IN *SIX CHARACTERS IN SEARCH OF AN AUTHOR*, 2000 (PHOTO BY DAVID COOPER).

ACTORS, DESIGNERS, DIRECTORS
(includes Stage Management, Choreographers, Fight Directors, Musical Directors)

Acaster, Donald (DS) 1964-6,
1968-9, 1971-6
Ada, Kawa (A) 2007
Adams, Chris (A) 1998
Adams, David (A) 1991-3
Adams, Steve (A) 1984
Adler, Doug (A) 1988-9
Adriaans, Mark (A) 2003-5
Ainslie, Robert (Bob) (CH) 1981-3;
(D) 1982-3; (A) 1988-90
Aitken, Robert (MD) TP/1987
Akin, Kathryn (A) 1991
Akin, Philip (A) 1975; TP/1986
Allan, Andrew (A) 1963; (D) 1963-5
Allison, Don (A) 1975
Allman, Daniel (A) TP/1984
Amos, Janet (A) 1978
Anderson, Al (DS) 1972, 1974-5
Anderson, Bart (A) 1990
Anderson, Carol (CH) 1994
Anderson, Evelyne (A) 1995
Anderson, Keith (A) 1975
Anderson, Susan (A) 1978
André, Susan (A) 1978
Ardal, Maja (D) 1987
Armstrong, Malcolm (A) 1969, 1972
Armstrong, Pat (A) 1991
Arthur, William (A) 2001
Asherson, Renée (A) 1967
Askey, Maggie (A) 1977
Asselstine, Elizabeth (DS) 1992-7,
1999-2000

Atherton, Leonard (MD) 1978
Atienza, Edward (A) 1975
Atkins, Damien (A) 1997
Aubrey, Larry (A) 1981
Austin, Karen (A) 1974
Austin-Olsen, Shaun (A) 1984
Avaria, Carolina (SM) 1989-92
Avery, Robin (A) 1991
Baggley, Ann (A) 1990, 1992-5, 1998
Bailey, Lorretta (A) 1991
Baillargeon, Denise Alaine (A) 1977
Bain, Michael (A) 1966
Baker, Bob (D) 1990; TP/1987
Baker, Peggy Smith (A) 1980
Baldaro, Barrie (A) 1978
Baldwin, Jenna (A) 1995
Ball, Michael (A) 1976-7, 1981-4,
1986-2007
Bannerman, Guy (A) 1986-8, 1991-2007
Barclay, Neil (A) 1990-2007
Bard, Margaret (A) 1985; (D) 1985;
TP/1986
Barkhouse, Janet (A) 1978
Barlow, David (SM) 1970
Baron, Marie (A) 1978
Barrington, Diana (A) 1971, 1978
Barry, Christopher (A) 1979
Barsanti, Kim (SM) 1989
Barsky, Barbara (A) 1980
Barton, Mary (A) 1963, 1965
Barton, Rodger (A) 1983-5, 1999
Bastedo, Alexandra (A) 1976
Bata-Walsh, Lila (A) 2006

Baugh, Hume (A) 1984-5
Bawtree, Michael (D) 1971
Beales, L. James (A) 1985
Beattie, Lawrence (A) 1964-5
Beatty, Jill (SM) 1997-9
Beatty, Nancy (A) 1971
Becker, Michael (MD) TP/1987
Becker, Oliver (A) 1995-6
Beckow, Joan (MD) 1980
Beecher, Bonnie (DS) 1992,
    1997-8, 2000
Beecroft, Eleanor (A) 1968, 1974
Beeler, Elizabeth (A) 1987
Beggs, James (A) 1963
Behavy, Karel (A) 1980
Behrens, Bernard (A) 1999-2006
Bekenn, Anthony (A) 1993-2007
Belding, Stephanie (A) 1995-7
Bélin, Sacha (A) 1980
Bell, Tracy (A) 1983
Belleville (Quenan), Donna (A)
    1975, 1999, 2001-7
Ben, David (A) 1996-7
Benjamin, Debra (A) 1989
Bennett, Christine (A) 1975
Bennett, Peter (A) 1970
Benning, Mary (A) 1964
Benson, Robert (A) 1981-97, 2001-4
Berg, Brad (A) 1981
Berai, Louis G. (DS) 1962
Bergeron, Jennifer (DS) 1987
Bergmann, Jean (SM) 1967
Bernstein, Karen (A) 1988
Berry, Lisa (A) 2006
Berthelsen, Detlef (A) 1967
Bertrand, Henry (SM) 1996
Besworth, Michael (A) 1985-6
Bettis, Paul (D) 1981-2
Bindiger, Emily (A) 1973
Binsley, Richard (A) 1987-9, 1994-8
Bisch, Ann (A) 1997

Bishop, Ronald (A) 1977
Black, Shauna (A) 1995-9
Black, Stephen (A) 1984
Blacker, David (A) 1984
Blackmore, Hilary (SM) TP/1988
Blais, Peter (A) 1973
Blake, Christopher (A) 2001-2
Blake, Maggie (A) 1995-7, 2004
Bloom, David (A) 1988
Blue, W.W. (A) 1963-5
Blunt, Charlotte (A) 1973
Blythe, Domini (A) 1973-5
Boake, Nancy (SM) 1973-4
Boal, Stephen (A) 1966
Boechler, David (DS) 1997-2004
Böggild, Hans (A) 1984
Boland, Jane (DS) 1970
Boult, Debbie (SM) 1990-2
Bowden, Judith (DS) 2000-7
Bowering, Bonnie (A) 1963
Bowes, Geoffrey (A) 1982-3
Boxill, Patrick (A) 1966-9, 1971,
    1973-7; (D) 1969, 1971
Boyd, Joan (A) 1975
Boyes, Derek (A) 1991
Boyle, Valerie (A) 1984
Bradbury, Simon (A) 1989-2005
Bradecki, Tadeusz (D) 1994, 1997,
    1999-2003, 2005-7
Bradley, Gertrude (A) 1969
Bradshaw, Michael (A) 1966
Branton, Milton (A) 1973
Braund, Catherine (A) 2007
Braunstein, Inga (A) TP/1987
Brazier, Adam (A) 2004
Breaugh, Sean (DS) 1991-2
Brennan, Roderick (A) 1963
Briand, Simon (A) 1973
Bricker, Todd (SM) 1993-5
Brine, Adrian (D) 1982
Britton, Christopher (A) 1974, 1976

Actors, Designers, Directors

Brockenshire, Brian (A) 1995

Broczkowski, Tamara (A) 1997

Brodie, Alan (DS) 1999-2000, 2002-4, 2006-7

Brokenshire, Judie M. (SM) 1997

Brook, Pamela (A) 1967, 1976

Brooks, Dana (A) TP/1987

Brown, Blair (A) 1973

Brown, Christopher (SM) 1983

Brown, David (A) 1980

Brown, Elizabeth (A) 1991-4

Brown, Jared (A) 1996, 2003-4

Brown, Norman (A) 1978

Brown, Patrick R. (A) 1997-2003

Browning, Norman (A) 1984-7, 1993-2007

Bruce, Corinna (A) 1963

Bruhier, Catherine (A) 1992

Brunton, Jennifer (A) 1963

Bryan, Robert (DS) 1976

Bryant, Nancy (DS) 2005, 2007

Bryant, Terrence (A) 2001-2

Bryden, Jon (A) 1987-8

Buckingham, Joan (A) 1974

Buliung, Evan (A) 2003-5

Bundy, Kevin (A) 1999-2004

Bunker, Andrew (A) 2002-7

Bunyan, David (SM) 1973-5

Burgess, Mark (A) 1988-90

Burgess, Maynard (A) 1962-3, 1973-5; (D) 1962

Burkett, Ronnie (A) 1989; (DS-puppets) 1989

Burley, Candace (SM) TP/1987

Burnett, Jamie (A) 2001-2

Burnett, Susie (A) 2000-3

Burns, Barry (SM) 2005-7

Burns, Martha (A) 1980, 1985, 1987

Burrafato, Gabriel (A) 2001

Burroughs, Jackie (A) 1974, 1979

Burt, Vincent (A) 1963

Butler, Anne (A) 1965

Bye, Bill (A) 1966

Byrne, Fiona (A) 1998-2005, 2007

Cadeau, Amy (A) 1997

Cadeau, Lally (A) 1987

Cahill, Terry (A) 1962

Cairney, John (A) 1979

Caldwell, Zoe (A) 1966

Calkins, Michael (A) 1973

Callan, Meghan (SM) 1997, 1999

Cambone-Mannell, Katie (A) 2006

Campbell, Beatrice (SM) 2005-7

Campbell, Benedict (A) 2003-7

Campbell, Douglas (A) 1978; (D) 1979

Campbell, Graeme (A) 1975

Campbell, Martha (SM) 1981-2, 1984-5, 1989-90

Campbell, Rod (A) 1981-8

Campbell, Stancil (DS) TP/1987

Campion, Joyce (A) 1964-5, 1983-7, 1989-90, 1994; TP/1984, TP/1986

Caplette, Pattie (A) 1980

Carlson, Ben (A) 1995-2005, 2007

Carlson, Leslie (A) 1970

Carmichael, Grant (A) 1987; TP/1987

Carrier, Donald (A) 1993-4

Casson, Ann (A) 1977

Casson, Jane (A) 1981

Cave, Caroline (A) 2001-3

Cavendish, Nicola (A) 1982-3, 1990-1

Celli, Tom (A) 1974

Cernovitch, Nick (DS) 1977, 1979, 1981

Chamberlain, Douglas (A) 1986

Chameroy, Dan (A) 2006

Champagne, Laurie (SM) 1986-2002

Chapple, Susan (A) 1972

Charlesworth, Marigold (D) 1969

Chesworth, Jason (A) 1997-2001

Chevrier, Micheline (D) 2000-1, 2004, 2007

Chiappetta, Frances (A) 1992, 1994

Chilcott, Barbara (A) 1969

Chow, Leonard (Siew Hung Chow) (A) 1983-4, 1986

Christmas, Elizabeth (A) 1981

Christoffel, David (A) 1991-2

Christopher, Patrick (A) 1978

Clair, Sandy (A) 1963

Clark, Adele (A) 1992

Clark, Ian D. (A) 1988-90

Clark, Jo-Anne Kirwan (A) 1982-6, 1990, 1997; TP/1987

Clark, Patrick (DS) 1988, 1991, 2000

Clark, Susan (A) 1966

Clark, Thomas (A) 1967

Clarke, Robert (A) 1994-6

Clarkson, Phillip (DS) 1989-91

Clayton, Bruce (A) 1983

Cleland, John (A) 1998, 2000-1

Clemo, Simon (DS) 2006

Cloran, Daryl (D) 2003-4

Coderre-Williams, Margaret (DS) 1986

Coffey, Denise (D) 1982-7

Coffey, Peggy (A) 1979

Cohen, Faye (A) 1985

Cohen, Miles (A) 1975

Cole, Allen (MD) 2004

Cole, Beth Anne (A) 1978, 1981-2, 1988

Cole, Bill (A) 1978

Cole, Vincent (A) 1974

Coles, Stanley (A) 1982

Colicos, Nicolas (A) 1984

Collins, David (A) 1983

Collins, Martha (A) TP/1987

Collins, Patricia (A) 1971

Collins, Paul (A) 1967

Collins, Sean (A) 1984

Colosimo, Krista (A) 2006-7

Comerford, Jon (A) 1979

Cook, Jillian (A) 1985-7, 1994-2004

Cooney, Dean (A) 1988-9

Cooper, Maury (A) 1973

Cooper, Roy (A) 1967

Copeland, Bill (A) 1982

Corbett, Hilary (DS) 1967-77, 1979

Cormack, Lynne (A) 1999-2002

Correia-Damude, Nicolá (A) 2007

Corser, Mavis (A) 1962

Cotroneo, James (A) 1977

Cowan, Grant (A) 1991

Cox, Susan (A) 1980, 1982, 1984, 1987, 1992; (D) 1991-4

Coyne, Susan (A) 1992

Craig, Paul (A) 1964-6

Craig, Robin (A) 1981-2, 1985, 1987-9

Craik, Allan (A) 1999-2000

Crawford, Carol (A) 1973

Crawley, Alice (A) 1974; (DS) 1962

Crean, Patrick (A) 1983-4; (F) 1982-4

Creley, Jack (A) 1968, 1971

Cressman, Michael Todd (A) 1997

Cross, Gregory (A) 1985

Crowley, June (A) 1988

Crumb, Christopher (A) 1979

Cselenyi, Joseph (DS) 1968

Cull, James (A) 1966-8

Cullen, Kate (A) 1985

Cumyn, Steve (A) 1987; TP/1987

Cunningham, Jocelyn (A) 1981

Current, Cathy (A) 2005

Cutts, John (A) 1976

Cygan, Philip (DS) 1997

Dague, David R. (DS) 1975

Daigle, Jean (A) 1982

Dalcourt, Brad (A) 1985

Dallas, Jeffrey (DS) 1980-7; TP/1985, TP/1988

Dann, Hugo (A) 1983-5, 1990

Dann, Larry (D) 1991

D'Aquila, Diane (A) 1993-4

Dauphin, Roger (A) 1965

Actors, Designers, Directors

Davidson, C. Holte (Craig) (A)
 1987-8, 1992
Davies, Bruce (A) 1994-5, 2000
Davies, Geraint Wyn:
 see Wyn Davies, Geraint
Davis, Donald (D) 1972
Davis, Eric (A) 1962
Davis, Faye (A) 1974-6
Dawson, George (A) 1986-2004;
 TP/1987
Dawson, Tracy (A) 2000
Day, Marie (DS) 1977
Dean, Charlotte (DS) 1984,
 1986, 1991, 1997-9, 2006
Debreceni, Peter (DS) 2004-5
de Carteret, Laura (A) 1999
DeGruijter, Deann (A) 1987-90
De Jonge, Levi (A) 1979
Delaney, Kenneth (A) 1996-7
Demers, Colombe (A) 1998
Denman, Jeffry (A) 1998
Dennis, Christopher (DS) 1995
Dennis, Kevin (A) 2003-5
Dennison, Holly (A) 1992
Denomme, Kelly (A) 1986
Deschambeault, Mike (SM) 2000
Desormeaux, Marc (MD) 2000;
 (DS) 2004
Devlin, Tim (A) 1962
Diamond, Tom (D) 1991
Dietrich, Jason (A) 1997-9
Dight, Kenneth (A) 1968-9, 1974-5
Di Iorio, Mario (A) 1984
Dillman, Peter (DS) 1992
Dinning, John (DS) 1990
Doane, Melanie (A) TP/1988
Dodimead, David (A) 1980
Doherty, Denny (A) TP/1988
Doherty, Janet (A) 1973-4
Doherty, Tom (DS) 1972
Dolgoy, Sholem (DS) 1985, 1987-9

Domville, Philippa (A) 1997, 1999
Don, Carl (A) 1969
Donaldson, Peter (A) 1981
Donison, Christopher (A) 1985-6,
 1995; (MD) 1980, 1982-98
Donnelly, Diana (A) 2003-6
Donnelly, Donal (A) 1979
Doremus, Allen (A) 1981
Dorey, Kerry (A) 1987; TP/1987
Douglas, Ross (A) 1981
Douglass, Diane (A) 1980, 1983
Downie, Ian (A) 1967
Doyle, Robert (DS) 1974
Doyle, Rosemary (A) 1993
Drake, Ronald (A) 1972
Driedger, Ross (A) 1987; TP/1987
Dufault, Monica (A) 1989, 1991
Dunlop, Darcy (A) 2004
Dunn, Juliet (A) 2002-3
Dunn, Kim (A) 1984
Dvorsky, Peter (A) 1981
Dykens, Hollis (DS) 1987
Dykstra, Ted (A) 1986-9; TP/1985-6,
 TP/1988
Eagan, Michael (DS) 1979; TP/1986
Eden, David (A) 1970, 1979
Edison, Matthew (A) 2001
Edmond, James (A) 1963,
 1969, 1974, 1986
Edwards, Hilton (D) 1968
Eldred, Gerry (SM) 1967
Elliott, Brian (A) 1997-2001
Elliott, David (A) TP/1987
Emelle, Michelyn (A) 1984, 1986
Erickson, Craig (A) 1999-2000
Etienne, Tania (DS) 1994
Evans, Dillon (D) 1969
Evans, Judy (A) 1977
Evans, Laird (A) 1974
Eves, Paul (A) 1981
Ewer, Donald (A) 1964
Eyman-Johnson, Linda (A) 1983

Fallis, Alex (A) 1989
Fallis, Mary Lou (A) 1984-5
Farrell, Richard (A) 1973, 1981-7,
  1990-1, 1993-2004; TP/1985
Farthing, Judy (SM) 1995-2007
Fattah, Suleyman (A) 1996-7
Fawkes, Michael (A) 1980-2, 1984
Fehereghazi, Tibor (A) 1969
Feigel, Sylvia (A) 1969
Fellbaum, Richard (A) 1984
Fenney, John (DS) 1973
Fenwick, Gillie (A) 1974-5, 1977-80
Fenwick, Moya (A) 1964, 1972, 1975
Ferencz, Keri (A) 1997-8
Ferencz, Tracey (A) 1985-90, 1992-6
Ferguson, John (DS) 1988; TP/1988
Ferguson, Mark Cassius (A) 1991
Fergusson, Denise (A) 1963
Ferley, Susan (D) 2000
Fermanian, Leon (A) 1974-5
Ferrall, Glenda (SM) 1971
Fiddick, Kelly (A) 1979
Finlayson, Donald (DS) 1981;
  TP/1984-5
Finn, Helen (A) 1969
Fisk, Michelle (A) 1985
FitzGerald, Nuala (A) 1965, 1995
Flawn, Matthew (DS) 1991
Flemyng, Robert (A) 1969
Flett, Sharry (A) 1988-91, 1993-2007
Flett, Stephen (A) 1991
Fleury, David (MD) 1982
Flowers, Ellen (SM) 1993-6
Flynn, Marilyn (A) 1974
Foran, Owen (A) 1972, 1977
Fordham, Joan (SM) 1962
Foreman, Lorraine (A) 1974
Forham, Edward (A) 1962
Forte, Carol (A) 1981
Foster, Herb(ert) (A) 1981-3,
  1985-9, 1991
Foster, Neil (A) 1998

Fox, Colin (A) 1979
Fox, Kelli (A) 1995-2004, 2006
Francis, Ron (SM) 1973, 1975
Frankish, Leslie (DS) 1989-99;
  TP/1987
Franks, Michael (A) 1977, 1979
Frappier, Jill (A) 1979, 1987
Frappier, Paul-Emile (A) 1974, 1976
Fraser, Bill (A) 1968
Fraser, Kevin (DS) 1987
Frederick, Ray (SM) 1973
Freedman, Ginny (SM) 1973
Freeman, Elaine (A) 1965
Freeman, Laurie (A) 1973;
  (SM) 1974-7
Freeman, Robert (A) 1971
Frehner, Harry (DS) 2003; TP/1982
French, Timothy (CH) 2001
Freund, Peter (SM) TP/1985
Fry, Aaron (A) 1999
Fusco, Angela (A) 1978
Fyfe, Heather (A) 1963
Fyfe, Margo (A) 1963
Gable, Betty (A) 1976, 1979
Gage, Patricia (A) 1968, 1971-3
Gale, Lorena (A) 1984
Gallagher, Alfred (A) 1963-6
Galligan, Patrick (A) 2003-7
Galloway, Carole (A) TP/1985
Galloway, Pat (A) 1966, 1978-9
Galvin, Valerie (A) 1983
Gambell, Linda (A) 1984
Gann, Merrilyn (A) 1979
Ganne, Randy (A) 1998-2000
Gardiner, John (A) 1980
Gardner, Craig (A) 1999-2000
Garnett, Gale (A) 1973, 1979
Garnhum, Dennis (D) 1997-2001
Gatchell, Paul (A) 1982, 1985-6, 1994
Gates, Larry (A) 1967
Gaze, Christopher (A) 1976-7, 1979

Actors, Designers, Directors

MICHAEL BALL AND KATE TROTTER IN *MAN AND SUPERMAN*, 1989 (PHOTO BY DAVID COOPER).

Grant, Thomas (A) 1999-2000
Gray, Allan (A) 1984-6, 1990,
    1994-6; TP/1986
Gray, John (D) 1981
Green, Charlotte (SM) 1988-97
Greenblatt, Richard (D) 2000
Griffin, Adrian (A) 1988-9
Griffin, Dwight (SM) 1969
Griffin, Lynne (A) 1976-8
Griffin, Margaret (A) 1963
Griffith, Kristin (A) 1977
Gropman, David (DS) 1981
Grossman, Danny (A) 1985
Grossmann, Suzanne (A) 1967
Grove, Paula (A) 1989
Gudgeon, Susan (A) 1985
Guenther, John (A) 1984
Guinand, Louise (DS) 1988,
    1990, 2004-7
Guinn, Alana (DS) 1984
Gunvordahl, Terry (DS) TP/1984
Gurney, Christian (SM) 1964
Gzowski, John (DS) 2006
Hair, Stephen (A) 1986
Hakala, Gail (A) 1985-9, 1994-7
Haley, Robert (A) 1988-90
Hall, Amelia (A) 1970, 1978
Hallett, Wendi (A) 1975-6
Haltrecht, Michael (SM) 2005
Hamilton, Barbara (A) 1971
Hamilton, Patricia (A) 1997-2007;
    (D) 2003; TP/1982, TP/1985
Hammond, Mark (SM) 1980
Hammond, Todd (D) 2001-2
Han, Sally (D) 1994
Hancock, Molly (A) 1966
Handy, Matt (A) 1994-6
Haney, Mary (A) 1978-80, 1986,
    1988-2002, 2004-7
Haney, Sheila (A) 1966, 1973, 1975
Hannant, Gillian (A) 1974
Hanson, Debra (DS) 1985, 1987

Hanson, Tim (A) 1966
Happer, Martin (A) 2004-7
Harapiak, Mark (A) 2004
Hardacre, Richard (A) 1985
Harding, D. Garnet (A) 1998-9
Harding, Norman (A) 1965-8
Harding, Paul (A) 1978
Harford, Terry (A) 1980, 1982, 1993-7
Harley, Graham (A) 1989-90
Harlond, Alistair James (A) 1999-2000
Harris, Robert (A) 1970
Harrison, Barbara (A) 1963
Hartmann, Ron (A) TP/1985
Hartwell, Peter (DS) 1992,
    1994-2001, 2003-7
Harvard, Bernard (SM) 1970
Harvey, Robin (A) 1980
Hassell, Ereca (DS) 1989-91,
    1993, 1996-2002
Haug, Dorothy-Ann (A) 1974
Hawes, Grant (A) 1966
Hawkins, Steven (DS) 1986
Hay, Deborah (A) 2007
Hayward, Joyce (A) 1974-5
Hecht, Paul (A) 1975
Hechter, Joel (A) 1998, 2000
Hemblen, David (A) 1981-4;
    (D) 1983-4; TP/1984
Henderson, Scott (DS) 1994, 1996
Heney, Matthew (A) 1991
Hennessy, Ellen-Ray (A) 1987
Hennig, Kate (A) 2005
Henry, Edward (A) 1975
Henry, Martha (A) 1967;
    (D) 2003, 2005
Henson, Jeremy (A) 1980
Herbert, Larry (A) 1998-9
Heredi, Monika (DS) 1992
Herzog, Jean (A) 1963
Hewgill, Roland (A) 1969, 1978, 1980
Hewitt, Robert (A) 1964

Actors, Designers, Directors

Hill, Brian (A) 1989-91
Hill, Declan (A) 1988
Hillier, Emma (A) 1997
Hirsch, John (D) 1980
Hiscott, Pam (A) 1963
Hodges, Ann (D) 2000
Hodgman, Roger (D) 2000
Hogan, David (A) 1989-91,
  1994, 1997
Hogan, Irene (A) 1974-5, 1980-9,
  1991-2, 1994-5
Hogan, Michael (A) 1971-2
Hogan, Susan (A) 1971-2, 1976
Holloway, Ann (A) 1991
Holloway, Stanley (A) 1970, 1973
Holmes, Eda (D) 2003-4, 2006-7;
  (CH) 2004
Holmes, Judy (A) 1966
Honeywell, Roger (A) 1992-6
Hopper, Roy (A) 1970
Horbulyk, Melody (A) 1973
Horner, Lisa (A) 2003-6
Horsburgh, Don (MD) TP/1988
Horton, John (A) 1968-9, 1974
House, Eric (A) 1967, 1971,
  1978-9; (D) 1971
Houston, Evert (A) 2004-6
Hovan, Nadia (A) 2002-3
Howell, Michael (A) 1986-7
Howlett, Noel (A) 1972
Huculak, Maggie (A) 1991
Huggins, Joan (A) 1965
Hughes, Colin (DS) 1988
Hughes, Douglas E. (A) 1995-2007
Hughes, Evan (A) 1974-5
Hughes, Howard (A) 1973
Hughes, Sheila (A) 1997
Hughes, Stuart (A) 1982-5, 1993-4
Hughes, Trevor (DS) 2002
Humphries, James (A) 1982
Hunt, Garry (A) 1979

Hurry, Leslie (DS) 1975
Hustleby, Ann (A) 1963
Hutcheson, David (A) 1969
Hutt, Peter (A) 1979-80, 1985, 1987-98,
  2003-7; TP/1985, TP/1987
Hutt, William (A) 1989-90
Hutton, Robin (A) 1998-9
Hyde, Lynne (DS) 1972, 1974
Hyland, Frances (A) 1968-70, 1978,
  1982-8; (D) 1970, 1986-7
Ingram, Terry (SM) 1981-4
Inksetter, Elizabeth (A) 1996-7
Irving, Jeff (A) 2003-7
Isaac, Gerald (A) 1982
Ishmael, Marvin (A) 1977
Ivanans, Henriette (A) 1992
Ivey, Dana (A) 1977, 1980
Ivey, Roger (A) 1966
Jackson, Andrew (A) TP/1986
Jackson, Brian H. (DS) 1971,
  1973, 1977
Jacobs, Tanja (A) 1987
James, Camille (A) 1998-2000
James, Keith (A) 1981
James, Michael (A) 1981
Jamieson, Bill (SM) 2006-7
Jamieson, Patty (A) 1994, 1998-2007
Jansen, David (A) 2006-7
Janson, Astrid (DS) 1979-80, 1983
Janzen, Melanie (A) 2006-7
Jazrawy, Jason (A) 2001
Jeffery, Alicia (A) 1982
Jenson, John (DS) 1977
Jessop, Carol O. (SM) 1965
Jewell, Amy (SM) 1998-9, 2001, 2005-7
Jobin, Peter (A) 1979
Johanson, Jane (A) 1991-7, 2001-2,
  2006-7; (CH) 1995, 1998-2001,
  2003, 2005
Johnson, Geordie (A) 1986
Johnson, Pam (DS) 1986-7
Johnston, Chris (D) 1985

Johnston, Denis (D) 1996-2003
Johnston, Jennifer (White) (SM)
    1986-91, TP/1986
Johnston, Susan (A) 1988-90
Jones, Gabrielle (A) 1987-8, 1990, 1993,
    1998-9, 2005, 2007; TP/1987
Jones, Jim (A) 1984-6; TP/1987
Jotkus, Peter (SM) 1996-7
Journard, S. Tigger (SM) 1984
Judd, Terry (A) 1975
Judge, Harry (A) 2005-7
Judge, Ian (D) 1986-8
Jurychuk, Joanna (SM) 1999-2005
Kainth, Dil (A) 1995-6
Kamino, Brenda (A) 1996
Kaminski, John (A) 1980
Karch, Jerrold (A) 1971
Katz, Stephen (D) 1974, 1981
Katzman, Jack (A) 1975-6
Kaut-Howson, Helena (D) 1998
Kedrova, Lila (A) 1969
Keene, Rosalind (A) 1990
Keens-Douglas, Ricardo (A) TP/1985
Keleghan, Peter (A) 1983
Kelk, Chris (A) 1973
Kelly, Terence (A) 1974, 1980
Kennedy, Chilina (A) 2005, 2007
Kennedy, Janet (SM) 1983-9
Kennedy, Lorne (A) 2000-4, 2006-7
Kent, Stuart (A) 1974-5
Kenyon, Richard (A) 1992
Keppy, Chris (A) 1976
Keppy, Don (A) 1979
Keppy, Robert (A) 1977
Kerr, Charles (A) 1982
Kerr, Matt (A) 1982
Kerr, Mary (DS) 1974, 1982-4,
    1988-9; TP/1982
Kerr, Nancy (A) 1982-91
Kerr, Stephanie (A) 1988
King, Charmion (A) 1972
King, Rachael (SM) 2006-7

King, Susan (A) 1969
Kinsman, Pamela (A) 1982
Kipp, Deborah (A) 1967, 1980
Kirwan Clark, Jo-Anne:
    see Clark, Jo-Anne Kirwan
Klanfer, François-Régis (A) 1975
Klassen, Evan (SM) 2006-7
Kligman, Paul (A) 1972
Kneebone, Tom (A) 1966, 1972, 1978
Knight, Keith (A) 1982-4, 1986, 1988
Kochergin, Eduard (DS) 1989, 1994
Koslo, Corrine (A) 1986, 1996-7,
    2000-1; TP/1987
Koss, Dwight (A) 1987
Kottke, Ingrid (SM) 2000
Kotyk, Glen (A) 1970-1
Kozak, Sid (SM) 1979
Kozlik, Al (A) 1980-9, 1993-2007;
    TP/1984, TP/1986, TP/1987
Krantz, Peter (A) 1981-5, 1987-92,
    1999-2007; TP/1982
Krawford, Gary (A) 2002-3
Kruse, Michael (DS) 1999-2001
Kudelka, James (A) 1980
Kufluk, Peter (A) 1972-3
Kushnir, Andrew (A) 2004
Kuzma, Paul (DS) TP/1985
Kyle, Bruce (A) 1977
Lagassé, Michelle (SM) 1990-2001
Laing, Alan (MD) 1998
Lake, Billy (A) 2007
Lamb, Margaret (A) 1973
Lamberts, Heath (A) 1967,
    1972, 1974-5, 1977-8,
    1980-5, 1996; (D) 1977
Lambie, Deborah (A) 1990-3, 1997
Lamotte, Kevin (DS) 1988-2007
Lampert, Paul (A) 1992,
    1994-5; (D) 1990-6
Lane, Cyrus (A) 1999-2000
Lane, Stephen (A) 1970

Actors, Designers, Directors

Lang, Patsy (DS) 1985-7; TP/1985-6
Larocque, Paul (A) 1987; TP/1987
Latham, David (D) 1997
Laufer, Murray (DS) 1977
Laurence, Dan H. (A) 1973,
 1983, 1986, 1988, 1990
Lawrence, Alison (A) 1984
Lawrence, Les (DS) 1969
Lawrence, Richard (A) 1970
Lawrence, Walter (DS) 1987-90;
 TP/1986
Layton, Irving (A) 1979
Leacock, Christine (SM) TP/1985-6
Leblanc, Diana (A) 1968, 1990
Lee, Baayork (CH) 2007
Lee, Cosette (A) 1972
Lefebvre, John (A) 1981
Legg, Tom (SM) 1966
Le Gros, Don (A) 1974
Leicester, Wendy Thatcher:
 see Thatcher, Wendy
Leigh-Johnson, Judy (A) 1977, 1979
Leighton, Betty (A) 1964-7, 1972,
 1974, 1976, 1978-9
LePage, Sue (DS) 1985, 1998-2007
Lesk, Stan (A) 1986
Lesser, Gene (D) 1973
Le Strange, Marjorie (A) 1973
Lett, Dan (A) 1981-5, 1987-9;
 TP/1982, TP/1984
Leung, Ian (A) 1998-9
Lever, Howard (A) 1965-66
Levert, Patricia (SM) 2000
Levine, Michael (DS) 1984-7
Lewarne, Andrew (A) 1981-4; TP/1982
Lewis, Heather (SM) 2007
Lewis, Roy (A) 1987
Leyden, Leo (A) 1964
Leyshon, David (A) 2001-7
Leyshon, Glynis (D) 1990-1, 1994-7
Lillico, Jeff (A) 2001-5

Lillo, Larry (D) 1984
Lindström, Trish (A) 2003-7
Lipp, Tiina (DS) 1969-71, 1974
Liszak, Robin (A) 1997
Livingston, Linda (A) 1964
Lo, Janet (A) 1996
Lockhart, Araby (A) 1981
Logue, Jeff (DS) 2000-1, 2003-5, 2007
Long, Mary (A) 1974
Lopez, David (A) 2006
Lorimer, Lois (A) 1982-7
Lott, John (DS) 2007
Loveless, David (A) 1962
Lowry, Jessica (A) 2004-6
Lubeck, John (A) 1966
Lundmark, Nikki (D) 1999
Lundy, Andrea (DS) 2002-5
Mabee, Elizabeth (A) 1979
MacDonagh, Richard (A) 2003
MacDonald, Ann-Marie (A) TP/1982
MacDonald, Bruce (SM) 1995-2001
MacDonald, James (D) 2002
Macdonald, Jay (A) 1981
MacDonald, Ken (DS) 2003-7
Macdonald, Meredith (SM) 1992-6,
 1999, 2001-7
MacDonald, Trevor (A) 1985-6
MacDonell, Arwen (SM) 1997-8, 2000
MacDougall, Lee (A) 1991-3
MacDuffee, Cameron (A) 2000-1,
 2004, 2006
MacFadzean, Matthew (A) 1999-2000
MacGregor, Barry (A) 1981-2, 1984-7,
 1989-93, 1997-2000
MacGregor, Fiona (SM) TP/1987
MacInnis, Allen (D) 1987-90,
 1997, 2001
MacInnis, John (CH) 2006
Mackenzie, Carolyn (SM) 1980-3,
 1985-98
MacKenzie, John (A) 1984
Mackie, Chris (A) 1993

MacLaren, Ian (A) 1970
MacLeod, Margaret (A) 1966-7
Macliammóir, Micheál (A) 1968
MacMaster, John (A) 1983
Macomber, Carole (SM) 1982-8
Macpherson, Rafe (A) 1974-5
Madden, Jeff (A) 2001-7
Maertz, Randy (D) 1990
Magner, Colm (A) 1998
Magoon, Marshall (DS) 2006
Maguire, Mary Ellen (A) 1983
Mahon, Jackie (A) 1987
Mainprize, James (A) 1999
Major, Leon (D) 1986
Malloy, Jean (A) 1962
Malmo, Merton (A) 1975
Mancuso, Sam (A) 1994
Mann, Martha (DS) 1963
Mannell, Larry (A) 1979
Maraden, Marti (A) 1982-9; (D) 1986,
    1988-9; TP/1986
March, Richard (A) 1989-90
Marchuk, Adrian (A) 2001-2
Marcil, Mario (A) 1992
Marcroft, Sandra (DS) 2004
Marcuse, Judith (A) 1980; (CH)
    1980; (DS) 1980
Marian, Erin (A) 1987-8
Markle, Stephen (A) 1973
Marleau, Louise (A) 1971
Marler, Brian (A) 1995-7
Marotte, Carl (A) 1983
Marrella, Joanne (A) 1999-2000
Marriott, Thom (A) 2007
Marsh, Diz (DS) 1983-5, 1988; TP/1985
Marshall, Robin (A) 1972, 1975, 1977
Martell, Julie (A) 2005-6
Martin, Janet (A) 1992
Martin, Michelle Cecile (A) 1990
Martyn, Jesse (A) 2007
Martynec, Eugene 1969
Maskow, Harro (D-mime) 1983

Masurkevitch, Patric (A) 1987-9,
    1994; TP/1987
Matheson, David (A) 1986
Matheson, W.J. (A) 1992
Mathiesen, Paul (DS) 2005
Mawson, Howard (A) 1974
Maxwell, Jackie (D) 2001-7
Maxwell, Roberta (A) 1976
Mayeska, Irena (A) 1967
McAsh, F. Braun (F) 1987-8; TP/1982
McAuliffe, Ken (A) 1982-5
McBoyle, Peter (DS) 2005-6
McCaig, Shannon (A) 2004
McCamus, Tom (A) 1981-8
McCarthy, Sheila (A) 1980; (CH) 1978
McCowan, Evan (A) 1970
McDayter, Lance (A) 1987-8; TP/1987
McDonald, Kate (A) 1978
McDonald, Ken (DS) 1980
McEwan, Susan (A) 1965
McEwing, Sandra (SM) TP/1987
McFarlane, Sherri (A) 1992-7
McGeough, Joe (D-flying) 1987-8
McGrath, Derek (A) 1971; (SM) 1971
McGregor, Catherine (A) 1997-2000,
    2002, 2004-6
McGrinder, Mark (A) 1998-2002
McIntosh, Duncan (A) 1981-7; (CH)
    1983-5; (D) 1983-9, 1995-6; TP/1985
McIntyre, Melissa (A) 1997
McKay, Debra (SM) 1986-7, 1994,
    TP/1986
McKeehan, Cathy (SM) 1968-9, 1972
McKeehan, Gary (A) 1968
McKendrick, Kevin (A) 1975
McKenna, Jennifer (SM) 1996
McKenna, Seana (A) 1992-3
McLaren, Hollis (A) 1973-4
McLean, Marla (A) 2006-7
McLellan, Nora (A) 1980-9, 1995-2006
McLeod, Gary (A) 1979

Actors, Designers, Directors

McMahon, Kirk (A) 1979
McManus, Patrick (A) 2007
McMeekin, Ellen R. (A) 1982
McMillan, Richard (A) 1991
McMillan, Weston (A) 1994
McMullan, John W. (A) 1964-5
McMurran, Fiona (A) 1981
McNamara, Stephanie (A) 1997-8
McNeil, Jean (A) 1980-2
McQueen, Jim (A) 1972
McQuigge, Stephen (A) 2001-2
McQuillan, Paul (A) 1993
McRae, Calvin (A) 1980
Meacham, Michael (D) 1977-8
Meadows, Jeff (A) 2000-7
Medland, Logan (MD) 1997-8
Medley, Jack (A) 1964, 1979-81,
    1983-7, 1989-96
Meister, Brian (SM) 1988
Mellor, Kenneth (DS) 1990
Mendes, Tanit (DS) 1987-9
Mendioro, Joanne (A) 2004
Mercer, Johanna (D) 1984
Mercier, Yves (A) 1977
Merrithew, Lindsay (A) 1986
Messaline, Peter (A) 1978
Meunier, Shawn (A) 2003
Meuse, Allan (SM) 1980
Mews, Peter (A) 1976-7
Meyers, John (A) 1974
Mezon, Jim (A) 1980, 1983-9,
    1992-2006; TP/1985-6;
    (D) 1992-9, 2005-6
Michailidis, Tracy (A) 2001
Michener, David (A) 1962
Middleditch, Gary (A) 1963
Miles, Cassel (A) 1992-3
Millan, James (A) 1983
Millard, John (MD) 2000
Millard, Peter (A) 1987-2007;
    TP/1987, TP/1988

Miller, Colin (A) 1987
Miller, Jeff (A) 1988
Miller, M. Rebecca (SM) 1998-2000
Millerd, Bill (SM) 1971
Mitchell, Camille (A) 1981-4, 1987-8
Moffat, John (A) 1986; TP/1986
Monis, Susan (SM) 1980-1
Moore, Charlotte (A) 1989-90, 2002
Moore, Claudia (A) 1980; (CH) 1992-3
Moore, Linda (D) 2004
Moore, Valerie (CH) 1987, 2002-3,
    2005; (D) 2003-5
Morgan, Karim (A) 2002
Morgan, Lorelyn (A) 1986
Morgan, Winston (SM) 1980-1,
    TP/1985
Morley, Greg (A) 1976-7
Morpurgo, Jean (D) 2001
Morris, Greg (A) 1991
Morrison, Murray (A) 1984
Morse, Barry (A) 1966, 1976;
    (D) 1966, 1976
Morse, Hayward (A) 1978, 1980
Moses, Sam (A) 1969, 1976
Moyer, William (A) 1978
Mucci, David (A) 1984
Mueller, Zizi (MD) 1973
Muir, Kiri-Lyn (A) 1994
Mulcahy, Seán (A) 1963-5; (D) 1963-5
Mulloy, Paul (A) 1986-8; TP/1987
Munch, Tony (A) 1991-2
Munro, Jock (DS) 2007
Munro, Neil (A) 1977; (D) 1988-9,
    1992-2007
Munroe, Lyn (A) 1963
Murdoch, Richard (A) 1973
Murphy, Dick (A) 1993-5
Murray, Brian (D) 1973-4
Muszynski, Jan (A) 1975
Nadajewski, Mike (A) 2003, 2007
Nairn, David (A) 1979
Nance, Marcus (A) 2004

Nelles, John (F) 1996
Nelson, Ruth (A) 1972
Newhouse, Miriam (A) 1978
Newton, Christopher (A) 1964,
    1980-4, 1987-8, 1990, 1992-3,
    1996-7, 2003; TP/1986; (D)
    1980-2005, 2007; TP/1982, TP/1987
Nicholl, John (A) 1970
Nicholls, Sandy (A) 1968
Nicholls, Terry (DS) 1986-7
Nipper, Ron (SM) 1971-4, 1978-2000
Noel, Wendy (A) 1988
Noell, Andrew (A) 1976
Norman, Marek (A) 1980
Norton, Lisa (A) 2000-4
Nunn, Alan (A) 1973
Oakey, Christine (SM) 2001, 2005-6
O'Brien, Catherine (A) 2003
O'Connell, Moya (A) 2007
O'Connor, Candace (A) 1976
Odele, Charlotte (A) 1975
O'Hearn, Patrick (A) 1999
Oiye, David (D) 1995
O'Krancy, John (A) 1986
Olafson, Roddy (A) 1971
Oliver, Murray (A) 1990
Oliver, Pierre (A) 1979
Ollerenshaw, Duncan (A) 1987-90, 1993
Olsson, Ty (A) 1997
O Neill, Isolde (A) 1996
Orenstein, Joan (A) 1974, 1989-92
Orenstein, Sarah (A) 1988, 1991-7,
    1999, 2001-2
Orion, Elisabeth (A) 1974
Orlowski, William (A) 1994, 1996;
    (CH) 1994, 1996-2001
Orme, Peter (A) 1970; (MD) 1970-1
Ormerod, John (A) 1991, 1993
Osborn, Jane Vanstone (SM) 1998,
    2000-1
Osborne, Deborah (SM) 1979

Osborne, Season (SM) 1992-4
Oster, Leah (A) 2001
O'Sullivan, Barney (A) 1980
O'Sullivan, Bridget (A) 1992
Ouimette, Stephen (A) 1981; TP/1987
Palk, Nancy (A) 1997
Palmer, Alisa (D) 2003-5, 2007
Palmer, Charles (A) 1981
Paluzzi, Pamela (A) 1973
Panych, Morris (D) 2004-7
Pardy, Lorne (A) 1995
Parkes, Gerard (A) 1963-5, 1973, 1975
Partington, Richard (A) 1988
Paton, Laurie (A) 1996-7,
    1999-2005, 2007
Patrick, Dennis (MD) 1977
Patterson, Lowell (A) 1963
Payne, Maggi (A) 1974, 1976
Payne, Thom (SM) 2000-4
Peacock, Russell (SM) 1972
Pearce, Chris (SM) 1978
Peddie, Alison (SM) 2003-7
Penciulescu, Radu (D) 1980
Pennoyer, John (DS) 1986-7
Perchaluk, Brian (DS) 2000-1
Perera, Imali (A) 2000
Perez, Pat (MD) TP/1988
Perkins, Roger (A) 1985-7, 1995;
    (MD) 1982-8
Perry, Jane (A) 1999-2003
Persichini, Robert (A) 1991-2
Petchey, Briain (A) 1978
Peters, Melissa (A) 2006
Pew, Dana (SM) 2001
Peyton-Ward, Judy (DS) 1972
Phillips, Lawrence (A) 1981
Phillips, Leo (A) 1964
Phillips, Shaun (A) 1995-6; (CH) 1996
Phillipson, Melanie (A) 2007
Phipps, Jennifer (A) 1967, 1970,
    1982-2004, 2006

Actors, Designers, Directors

Phythian, Ted (A) 1976
Picken, Roger (A) 1963-5
Pierce, Ellen (A) 1966
Pilgrim, Peter (A) 1970
Pilgrim, Tim (A) 1970
Pithey, Wensley (A) 1976
Plaxton, Jim (DS) 1982, 1984
Playfair, David (A) 1985
Pleasants-Faulkner, Isolde (SM) TP/1987
Plunkett, Christine (DS) 1988-90
Poddubiuk, Christina (DS) 1986-7,
    1989, 1995, 1997-9, 2001-7
Polischuk, Caesar (A) 1983
Pollard, Frank (A) 1974
Pope, Carole (A) TP/1987
Pope, Nicholas (A) 1970
Porteous, Cameron (DS) 1980-98,
    2000, 2002-5; TP/1986
Porter, Sean (A) 1999
Porter, Stephen (D) 1969
Potter, Miles (D) 1993
Powell, Brenda (DS) 1984-5
Powell, Gray (A) 2007
Pownall, Leon (A) 1980-1; (D) TP/1985
Prentice, Jeffrey (A) 1992-3
Press, Maureen (A) 1977
Price, Ted (A) 1991
Pringle, Marie (A) 1965
Prinsloo, Ian (A) 1986-7; TP/1987;
    (D) 1998-9
Przybylski, Teresa (DS) 2001-3, 2005-6
Quenan, Donna (A) 1975.
    See also Belleville, Donna
Querin, Micheal (A) 2001-7
Rabe, Pamela (A) 2000
Raby, Gyllian (D) 1998
Radcliffe, Rosemary (A) 1973
Rae, Allan (MD) 1981
Raiman, Stephen (MD) 1985
Rain, Douglas (A) 1967, 1983,
    1985, 1987-9, 1999

Ralph, Janine (SM) TP/1982
Ramer, Henry (A) 1966
Rand, Calvin (SM) 1962
Rand, Gordon (A) 1993-9
Rand, Robin (A) 1963
Rankin, James (A) 1978, 1980-1
Ranney, Glynis (A) 1999-2000,
    2002-5, 2007
Ransom, Barbara (A) 1962
Raven, Bing (A) 1974
Rebiere, Richard (A) 1983
Reh, Virginia (A) 1976
Reid, Chick (A) 1985-8
Reid, Fiona (A) 1983-5, 1990-2,
    1995, 1997-8, 2002; TP/1986
Reid, Kate (A) 1967, 1976, 1978
Reid, Ric (A) 2003, 2005-7
Reil, Eamonn (SM) 2005-6
Renés, Trudi (A) 1969
Renn, Jeffrey (A) 2002
Rennie, Callum (A) 1989
Renton, David (A) 1980
Reynolds, Katrina (A) 2007
Reynolds, Lani (SM) 1972
Reynolds, Larry (A) 1972
Reynolds, Paul (D) 1980-9
Rhodes, Randolph (A) 1965
Richardson, Elizabeth (A) 1989
Richardson, Ian (A) 1977
Richmond, Brian (D) TP/1988
Riley, Michael (A) TP/1988
Ringwood, Susan (A) 1967
Robbins, Carrie F. (DS) 1973
Roberto, Pat (A) 1972
Roberts, Jack (A) 1979
Roberts, Peter (SM) 1975
Roberts, Scott (A) 2000
Robertson, Betty (A) 1963
Robertson, Katherine (SM) 1975, 1978
Robins, Brenda (A) 1984
Robinson, Brigitte (A) 1987, 1995-2004,
    2007; TP/1987

GOLDIE SEMPLE, JENNIFER PHIPPS, ROBERT BENSON, AND ALLAN GRAY IN *HEARTBREAK HOUSE*, 1985
(PHOTO BY DAVID COOPER).

Robinson, Kelly (D) 1998-9, 2006
Robinson, Sandra (SM) 1977-80
Robson, Wayne (A) 1974
Rodriguez, Percy (A) 1963, 1966
Rogers, Clarke (SM) 1967-8
Rogers, Pam (A) 1975
Roll, Grant (A) 1977
Romeril, Jeanette (A) 1974
Root, Christopher (DS) 1967
Rose, Gabrielle (A) 1989
Rosling, Tara (A) 2003-4, 2006-7
Ross, Stephen (DS) TP/1987
Ross, Tyley (A) 2002
Rosser, Tom (A) 1966
Rowat, Graham (A) 1996
Rowland, Roger (A) 1991-2002
Royal, Christopher (A) 1994-5
Royston, Jonah (A) 1972
Rozen, Robert (A) 1978
Russell, Catherine (SM) 1976-8, 1980
Russell, Drew (A) 1974
Russell, Franz (A) 1966
Rutledge, Molly (A) 1969
Ryan, Maralyn (A) 1998

Salbaing, Geneviève (CH) 1981
Saltzman, Avery (A) 1978
Samples, William (A) 1975
Sampson, Aisling (DS) 1993
Samuda, Jackie (A) 1984
Samuel, Reg (DS) 1970
Sanders, Amy (A) 1992
Sandor, Anna (A) 1975
Sangster, Kiera (A) 2004-5, 2007
Sanvido, Guy (A) 1963
Sarabia, Ric (A) 1984-6
Sarandon, Chris (A) 1970
Sarosiak, Ronn (A) 1980
Sarvasova, Hanna (A) 1969
Saunders, Donald (A) 1978
Sauriol, Yvonne (DS) 1990,
    1992-4, 2001, 2003
Savidge, Mary (A) 1973, 1975, 1979
Savoy, David (D) 2001
Saxton, Juliana (A) 1963, 1965
Scarfe, Alan (A) 1970, 1974
Schafer, Lawrence (DS) 1964-6
Schellenberg, August (A) 1973

Actors, Designers, Directors

Schipper, Steven (D) 1985

Schmuck, William (DS) 1993-2007

Schota, Ilona (A) 1980

Schouten, Renée (SM) 1975

Schurig, Deeter (DS) 2002, 2004, 2007

Schurmann, David (A) 1981-5,
1987-8, 1990-2007; TP/1985

Scott, Camilla (A) 2006

Scott, Malcolm (A) 1996-8

Scott, Nelly (A) 2006

Scott, Robert (A) 1982

Seale, Douglas (D) 1974-5, 1978

Semple, Goldie (A) 1981-5,
1994, 1999-2007

Severin, Jessica (A) 1984-6

Severin, Matthew (A) 1984

Shaetzman, Poldi (MD) 1971

Shamata, Michael (SM) 1976-8

Shara, Mike (A) 1985-6, 1995-8, 2000-6

Shaw, Joe-Norman (A) 1985; TP/1986

Shaw, Joseph (A) 1979; (D) 1973

Shaw, Kenneth (DS) 1993

Shaw, 'Wenna (A) 1972-3

Sheffner, Nancy (SM) 1968

Shelley, Carole (A) 1971, 1977, 1980

Shepherd, Elizabeth (A) 1974-5

Sherman, Hiram (A) 1967, 1971

Shipley, Don (D) 1980

Siegel, Laurence (A) 1965; (SM) 1965

Silver, Phillip (DS) 1979

Simmons, Mary (A) 1969

Simms, Stephen (A) 1982-6, 1990-1,
1995, 1997

Simpson, Ian (A) 1988, 1993-4

Simpson, Sandi (A) 1977

Sinclair, Jenny (SM) 1998

Sinclair, Patrick (A) 1975

Sinkins, Morag (A) 1984

Skelly, Andy (A) 1993

Skidmore, Karen (A) 1991-6

Skog, Troy (A) 1993

Skolnik, William (MD) 1978

Slater, Katherine (A) 2001, 2003

Smith, Amanda (A) 1998-2000

Smith, Caroline (CH) 1991

Smith, Carolyn (DS) 1990

Smith, Cedric (A) 1981

Smith, Jan Alexandra (A) 1993-7, 2000

Smith, Jerrard and Diana (DS) TP/1987

Smith, Kathleen P. (SM) 1988

Smith, Ken A. (SM) 1978, 1981-4

Smith, Linda (SM) 1970

Smith, Maggie (A) 1963; (SM) 1963

Smith, Molly (D) 2007

Smith, Sherry (A) 1988-91, 1993, 2001

Snetsinger, Janet (A) 1990

Snow, Michael (A) 1964-5

Snow, Victoria (A) 1985

Sokoluk, Dianne (A) 1981

Somerville, Graeme (A) 2003-7

Souchotte, Mary (A) 1977

Southam, Bradley (A) 1972

Sperdakos, Paula (D) 1981

Spigel, Margaret (A) 1963

Sportelli, Paul (MD) 1999-2007

Spottiswood, Greg (A) 1994-6

Stackhouse, Susan (A) 1983-9, 1992-3

Stainer, Jean (A) 1965

Staines, Kent (A) 1986

Stammers, John (DS) 1977

Stanford, Gully (SM) 1974

Stead, John (F) 2000-1

Stevens, Harry (A) 1986

Stewart, Duncan (A) 1999-2002

Stewart, Jennifer (SM) 1966

Stewart, Julie (A) 1989-90

Stewart, Ken James (A) 2007

Stewart, Todd (A) 1988

Stewart-Coates, Allen (A) 1983

Stichbury, Allan (DS) 1986,
2001; TP/1986

Stilwell, Barry (A) 1981

Actors, Designers, Directors

Tullock, Devon (A) 2000-1, 2005, 2007

Turnbull, Ann (A) 1982, 1985-7; TP/1986

Turner, Corey (A) 2002

Turvey, Jay (A) 2000, 2002-7; (MD) 2001

Tute, John (MD) 2004

Tweed, Terry (A) 1964; (SM) 1964

Twiby, David M. (SM) 1963

Uhre, Mark (A) 2007

Underhay, Nicole (A) 2004-7

Usher, Jane (A) 1975

Vacratsis, Maria (A) 2002

Valentine, James (A) 1968, 1971-5, 1979

van Bridge, Tony (A) 1968, 1970, 1974-5, 1977-9, 1988-2001; (D) 1970-1, 1974-5, 1977, 1979, 1988-90, 2002

Vanderburgt, Ian (A) 1993-4

Vandergraaf, Julia (DS) 2006-7

van de Ven, Sven (A) 1988-90, 1993, 1997

Vanstone, Patricia (A) 2005

Vartanian, Vikén (A) 1979

Vasileski, Victoria (SM) 1986-9

Veal, Melissa (SM) TP/1986

Veeneman, Jonathan (A) 1992

Vernik, Leo (A) 2001-2

Vest, Marisa (SM) 2007

Vickers, William L. (A) 1987-91, 1993-6, 1998-9, 2002-7

Villafana, Martin (A) 1995

Vingoe, Mary (A) 1982

Vipond, Neil (A) 1974-5

Volker, Francine (A) 1980

Voros, Darren (A) 2005

Voyatzis, Athena (A) 1984

Waibel, Noreen (MD) 1981, 2004

Waines, Lisa (A) 1995-8

Waite, Todd (A) 1994-6, 1998-9

Waldman, Risa (A) 1998-2000

Walker, Craig (A) 1983-4

Walker, Matthew (A) TP/1985

Wallace, Ted (A) 1986

Wallis, Alan (A) 1986; (SM) 1982-7

Wardle, Paul (A) 1975

Warfield, Donald (A) 1970

Warne, Larry (SM) 1966

Warnke, William (SM) 1970

Wasko, Mike (A) 2000-2

Watson, Patrick (D) 1996-7

Watton, Jonathan (A) 1998

Waugh, Richard (A) 1986-91; TP/1986, TP/1987

Weaver, Cloyce (A) 1975-6

Weber, Scott (A) 1985

Webster, Hugh (A) 1966

Webster, Sandy (A) 1966-7, 1973, 1979-80, 1982-3, 1985-90, 1993-8, 2000

Webster, William (A) 1981, 1994-6

Wechsler, Gil (DS) 1970

Weld, Thomas (A) 1970

Welsh, David (A) 1995

Welsh, Norman (A) 1964, 1966, 1971, 1973-4, 1977

Welsman, Mary (A) 1964

West, Emily (A) 1985-6

West, Lockwood (A) 1973

Wheeler, Jane (A) 1988-9

White, Jennifer *see* Johnston, Jennifer White

White, Jonathan (A) 1969, 1972

White, Ron (A) 1984

Whitehead, Paxton (A) 1966-71, 1973-7; (D) 1967-8, 1970-2, 1974-7

Whitfield, Michael J. (DS) 2000

Whitham, Scot (A) 1977

Whittaker, Lisa (SM) 2001

Whynot, Geoffrey (A) 1993

Wickens, Leslie-Anne (A) 2003

Wickes, Kenneth (A) 1968, 1974-5, 1978

Wiedman, Mark (A) 2000
Wiens, Karen (A) 1975
Wilds, Peter (A) 1991-3
Wilhite, Steve (A) 1986
Wilkinson, Leslie (DS) 1988-9
Willes, Christine (A) 1986
Williams, Bill (DS) 1981, 1983
Williams, Blair (A) 1988-92,
    1997-2002, 2005-7
Williams, Nigel Shawn (A) 1995-6, 2001
Willis, Reid (A) 1970
Willman, Noel (D) 1976
Willows, Alec (A) TP/1988
Willows, Alexander W. (A) 1970, 1972
Wilson, Blythe (A) 2000-1, 2003
Wilson, Brigit (A) 1983
Wilson, Lorna (A) 1988, 1990
Windrem, Peter (A) 1987-9
Wingate, Peter (DS) 1981-6, 1988
Winkler, Robert (DS) 1976
Winsby, Sandy (A) 1983, 1997, 1999
Winter, Angela (A) 1976
Winton, Colleen (A) 1984
Witham, Todd (A) 1996, 2001-2
Wolf, Kelly (DS) 1995-2001, 2006
Wood, Angela (A) 1972
Wood, Karen (A) 1988-90, 1995-9, 2001
Wood, Tom (A) 1983-6, 1989; TP/1987
Woodrow, Diane (SM) 1978-81, 1983-7
Woodyard, Luke (A) 1995
Woolridge, Alison (A) 1994-8
Wordsworth, Roy (A) 1963
Worthy, Barbara (A) 1985-90;
    (D) 2004-5
Wright, Amy (CH) 2004
Wright, Jenny L. (A) 1996-2006
Wright, Katey (A) 2001
Wright, Shawn (A) 1988-9
Wright, Susan (A) 1980, 1985, 1989
Wylie, Moira (A) 1979
Wyn Davies, Geraint (A) 1979-80,
    1982-4; TP/1985

Wynne, Joe (A) 2001
Yanik, Brian (A) 1963
Yates, Eddie (A) 1963
Yeager, Caroline (A) TP/1985
Yeo, Leslie (A) 1966-7, 1976,
    1978-9; (D) 1976, 1979
Young, Cavan (A) 1993
Yulin, Harris (D) 1970
Zarrillo, Viviana (A) 1991, 1993
Zednik, Peter (A) 1981
Ziegler, Joseph (A) 1980-2, 1988;
    (D) 1997-8, 2003-6

Marquis Book Printing Inc.

Québec, Canada
2008